LIBERATION

Mrs. DeBell,

I enjoyed Pre-AP Bio in your class!

R.M.

(Oct 10, 2013)

LIBERATION

A Novel

REBEKAH MICHAEL

TATE PUBLISHING
AND ENTERPRISES, LLC

Published by Tate Publishing & Enterprises, LLC
127 E. Trade Center Terrace | Mustang, Oklahoma 73064 USA
1.888.361.9473 | www.tatepublishing.com

Tate Publishing is committed to excellence in the publishing industry. The company reflects the philosophy established by the founders, based on Psalm 68:11,
"The Lord gave the word and great was the company of those who published it."

Book design copyright © 2013 by Tate Publishing, LLC. All rights reserved.
Cover design by Junriel Boquecosa
Interior design by Mary Jean Archival

Published in the United States of America
ISBN: 978-1-62746-671-4
1. Fiction / Christian / Fantasy
2. Fiction / Action & Adventure
13.08.12

DEDICATION

To my dad, for without him, this book would never be.

ACKNOWLEDGMENT

I would like to acknowledge all of the people who have planted into me the seeds that have bloomed so this book would become possible. First, I must thank my parents, who are willing to give up their own time to pursue my interests, and they have taught me to be a devout disciple of Christ.

Without all of the English teachers who have taught me grammar, punctuation, and interesting vocabulary, I would be lost in an ocean of daydreams, unable to share them with anyone. Of these I most definitely must make note of Mr. Maus, who was one of the key contributors who got me started in this whole writing gig.

I also owe some of my friends a part for making me who I am. Erica stuck with me when I felt lonely and hated, and it was with her that the stories started to take shape in my mind. Cassie prompted me to write down my daydream for her to read, and she is a loyal friend I love having by my side. Of course, I must thank those crazy two friends of mine, Megan and KatyAnn, who have bragged about me almost too much to bear.

Ms. Gloria is my role model, and I will forever be in her debt for helping me with getting a hold of this idea that my writing could turn into a book. I love Mrs. White with as much love as a bookworm can love a librarian, and she has been a constant friend throughout my middle school career and so far in my high school career.

I must thank the entire Church on the Move staff for shepherding me since my young age.

Last, I need to acknowledge all of the people who picked up a book written by a teenager and are about to read it. Oh, and the publishers who are taking a risk with my work.

CONTENTS

PROLOGUE

Matty held her husband's hand as he breathed his last breath. She collapsed at his side and sobbed. She had done all that she could do. She had tried everything she knew on him and the others who had gotten the plague; nevertheless, she watched as each one died. Even her fellow nurses and the town's only doctor fell to the curse on Ranly, their town. All in all, 132 died, leaving 290 to mourn.

A few days after her husband, Aylik, died, Matty noticed the first symptoms of pregnancy, in herself. When she told Lena, her best friend, they rejoiced. It was a ray of sunshine that no one had expected. For seven months, Matty worked as the only nurse for Ranly. She survived the colds, fevers, birthing babies, and flues. Her patients did too. Dr. Ravishee arrived from Orvinta, the capital of their country, right when she needed him. With him around, she had more time to rest and let the baby grow.

Matty's son, Fly, and Lena took care of her as she went through her last month of pregnancy. Her water broke in the middle of the night. Lena rushed to get the doctor as fast as she could. Fly was going to have a sibling soon! The baby came at eleven thirty. They all loved the little girl. She had strawberry-blonde hair, which covered her tiny head. She didn't open her eyes as if she knew that they all wanted to know what color they were. The doctor had to leave to treat a fever in another home, but Lena stayed to watch over her friend. Fly sat watching his mom hold the baby.

"What are you going to name her?" asked Lena.

"I don't know yet. She hasn't opened her eyes."

"You Raggies and your silly traditions!"

"You think ours are weird! What about the Orv tradition where you don't name your kids until they are five?"

"I happen to like it. You all end up with odd names."

"My name is *not* odd!"

"Mom," said Fly, "her eyes are open!"

Matty looked down at her beautiful baby girl—with red eyes. She was speechless. Lena saw them too; therefore, she was just as lost for words. Fly wasn't fazed because he didn't know the prophecy; he was still too young. Matty and Lena remembered the legends from their grandparents' time about the last red-eyed Raggy.

The prophecy was this: "When the war drums beat against all the Raggies, a liberator will be born from the womb of a widowed mother." There, looking right back at them, was a red-eyed baby; her red eyes indicated that she could fight, unlike most anyone else of her race.

Fly broke the silence by asking, "Isn't she so very cute, Mom?"

Matty looked up at her son, her green eyes scared.

She answered, "Yes, hon. Can you make dinner, dear?"

"Yes, ma'am." He kissed her and the baby. They could hear him whistling down the hallway to the kitchen.

"Well, there is only one name for you, little one," said Matty. "Your name is Red."

"The prophecy is real then?" asked Lena.

"I'm guessing so. She won't be able to stay here long."

"Why?"

"In the past, the liberators didn't have to solve problems until they were older, but I have a feeling that the problems might start arising soon."

Matty held little Red close to her chest. Tears slipped down her cheeks. She kissed the top of her baby's head. Lena left to go tend to her own family and to leave Matty alone with Red.

———◦◦◦———

The sun rose the next morning to find Matty's family gone. Lena searched every road, yet could not find her or her children. The town gossips discussed her sudden disappearance for weeks, wondering what the cause had been, for Lena had decided not to tell anyone else about Red. Three weeks passed before her house was occupied again. They appeared just as suddenly as they had gone. Lena came to see her and to have a talk with her.

As soon as Matty opened the door, Lena came in.

"What were you doing for these past three weeks? Were you anywhere near the capital?"

"No. Why?"

Lena, who, being an Orv, was easily two times the height of Matty, grabbed her by the collar of her shirt, saying, "Where did you put your baby, Matty?"

"I put her up for adoption. What has gotten into you?"

Lena let go of her.

"The queen was killed by a mob of Raggies. I repeat: were you anywhere near the capital?"

"Queen Ruth! Why would anyone kill *her*? Everyone loves her."

"I don't know. You tell me."

"Why are you even suggesting that I helped kill the queen? You know me."

"You need to leave. Most of the other Raggies have left. I'm being civil compared to my neighbors." With a slam of the door, Lena was gone.

"Fly," Matty tiredly called, "don't unpack. We're going on the road again."

They left with another Raggy family, joining the mass exodus from Rov.

—ᴓᴓᴓ—

Mrs. Dell carried their new baby home, and her husband looked at his little family with pride. They knew that the girl was a Raggy because of the brown paste on her skin, but they didn't care. They didn't want to take off her brown permanent contacts that hid her eye color because they wanted to convince themselves and the child that she was *their* baby. They wouldn't tell the girl she was adopted, and everything would be fine. Right?

LIFE AND DEATH

She sidestepped a downward head swipe and thrust her right blade into the attacker's chest. She jumped as a pike came sailing for her feet. It was utter chaos on that battlefield. She had been fighting with her friends, but the tide of the battle separated her from the others. She fought her way back to her best friend, but it was too late. She lay dead with a dagger in her heart, breathing her last breath.

Red's eyes popped open, and she found herself breathing hard. She looked at the ceiling and realized that it was just a dream. A very vivid dream, but still a dream. She quickly forgot about it as she realized that she had awoken to her birthday.

She quickly hopped out of bed and started her morning routine. She changed into her day clothes and glanced in the mirror. She sighed and picked up her hairbrush. Usually, she just let her wild hair do whatever it wanted, but her mom had threatened to not hold any party if Red came downstairs looking like a hooligan. Red's hair was red; thus, her parents gave her the nickname Red, but it was also an abbreviation of her full name, Redache. If she didn't do anything to her hair after she cleaned herself up, it dried into dreadlocks.

As she took the time to brush her hair, she let her mind wander, and she started to wonder why her hair looked so different from everyone else's. Everyone else in her village had dark skin, like her; they all had brown eyes, like her; and they were all humans, also like her. Why then did she not have brown or black hair like everyone else in her village? These thoughts had never occurred to her before.

Oh well, she thought as she put the brush down and raced to the kitchen.

Her mom was busy in the kitchen making something that smelled delicious.

"Hi, Mom!"

Her mom turned around and smiled at her. "Hello, birthday girl! How was your sleep?"

"Pretty good, until the end, where I dreamed I was in a battle!"

At that, her mom's usually happy visage darkened. "A battle, sweetheart? Where have you heard about battles?"

"The other kids."

Her talkative mom was quiet for an uncharacteristically long period of time, so long that the usually quiet Red felt like saying something to dispel the silence.

"Why is my hair so different from everybody else's?"

That wrenched her mom out of her stupor. "You are not different from anybody else, honey!"

Red's confused look told her mom that that was not what she was asking.

"I mean, your hair is really special, because you are a special girl."

Red's confusion cleared up, and she smiled.

"Okay, thanks."

Her mom sighed and thought, *That was close.*

She then started talking about how everybody in the village was coming to the party and barely gave her daughter room to talk. That was the mom Red was used to. A few minutes later, Red's mom served her breakfast; then Red's dad came in through the door, announcing that today's party was going to be outdoors. Red hopped out of her chair and ran to hug him.

"Hi, Daddy!"

He picked her up and twirled her around. "There's my little girl! Are you enjoying being ten?"

She giggled. "Oh yah!"

They sat down at the table and enjoyed a family breakfast, blissfully ignorant of where they would be by the end of that day.

—⁓⁓⁓—

It was a week after Princess Alexandra's birthday, but it was the only day her aunt could find the time to celebrate with her. Her aunt was Kim, the queen of the country of Rov.

Alexa, as Alexandra liked to call herself, sat at the table in her minicastle, waiting for Kim. It was almost lunchtime, and Kim had said they would have breakfast together. This tardiness wasn't unusual, Kim was always late for personal matters, but Alexa was quite annoyed this time. She had *specifically* told her aunt that this was an important birthday for her; she was a whole decade old.

After an hour of waiting, Alexa was extremely ticked off. She put her feet up on the table and leaned her chair back, knowing that Kim didn't like that. She wasn't there, so why did it matter?

Around eleven, the queen finally decided to make an appearance. She came through the doors to the ballroom in Alexa's minicastle with much pomp, but Alexa did not acknowledge her; she just looked at her fingernails.

"Hello, niece."

Alexa didn't respond, but Kim didn't get the message. She sat down heavily across from Alexa and said, "Get your feet off of the table, darling."

Alexa did not comply; she just looked up at Kim from over her fingernails. The girl was only ten, but she already had the gaze that could scold anyone who got in her way. She also had the royal attitude. Her clear-blue eyes drilled into Kim's skull just like her mother's had.

"That is no way for the future queen of Rov to hold herself, young lady."

Alexa dragged her feet off of the table and slammed her chair on the ground.

"You're late. If my mom was alive—"

"But she isn't. How many times do I have to tell you not to bring your mother into recollection?"

"Until you drive it into my thick skull, I suppose."

That took Kim's words right from the tip of her tongue.

"Seven years and three hundred and fifty-three days until I replace you on the throne, *Auntie*."

"You've started a countdown now? You know it's not my fault your mother died!"

"Right, it's the Raggies' fault. They killed her after I was born. That still doesn't give you the right to treat me as if I mean less to you than the kingdom that is *mine* by right of inheritance!"

Kim stood forcefully enough to scoot her chair back five feet. "Don't you dare put the blame on me! I'm doing what I can so that you have a kingdom when you come of age!"

Alexa stood with equal force and yelled back, "Well, maybe you should just forget about me until then!"

"Maybe I will!"

Kim stormed out of the ballroom and out of the castle. Alexa's staff didn't want to interrupt the royal discussion, so they hadn't come out to serve brunch. After Kim stormed out, the only one with any guts to come out was Alexa's teacher. When any Orv, let alone a royal Orv, was angry, it was not pretty.

Orvs were a race of pitch-black–skinned giants, all of whom were muscular. They usually had square ears, their eyes looked large for their faces in comparison to humans, and they were all around more blocky than humans. The shortest an Orv could get was ten feet tall; thus, they dwarfed humans and Raggies, who were about the same size as humans.

Ms. Writ, Alexa's teacher, approached her pupil carefully. They were about the same height, because Alexa wasn't anywhere near full grown, but Alexa had muscle and a temper, both of which she had displayed on occasion when her aunt had done similar things.

"Alexandra?"

The answer was taut. "Yes?"

"Would you like your breakfast?"

"No. I'm not hungry."

With that, Alexa, the crown princess, went to her room and cried.

———✑✑✑———

The party was quite fun. The whole village came to Red's family's front yard and ate a potluck lunch on a few picnic tables and then gave Red presents. There were only four families in the village, and the entire population was eighteen humans. After Red had received the few homemade presents, she and all the other kids played as the adults sat at the tables and talked. All was peaceful in the little village.

During a momentary lull in the adult conversation, Red's dad listened to the happy sounds of the kids playing. He heard something beyond that, though. He faced the sound to try to identify it and realized what it was. It was the creak of wagons and the stomping of feet in unison. Small talk ceased when he said, "Soldiers are coming."

Almost as one, all the adults stood up and went to go gather in their kids. They all directly went inside their houses. Red went to her parents when they called her, but they seemed much more on edge than the other parents. They ushered her inside.

Her dad stopped her inside and talked to her with his serious voice, eye to eye, "Red, honey, I need you to hide and don't come out until I call you."

"Hide? Why?"

"I'll tell you after everyone is safe, just hide where no one can find you."

Red was scared by the urgency in his voice, so she nodded and quickly went to her favorite hiding place, a secret cubby hole her dad had made for her, just inside her bedroom. From there, she could hear whatever was going on outside the house.

After a few minutes of silence, she heard a trumpet and an announcement for every person to come out of their homes and into the street. Red didn't because her dad told her not to leave unless *he* called her out.

After everyone was out, the mysterious announcer said, "By order of the queen, every household in this country is to be inspected for runaway Raggies. If any family is found to be hiding one, the penalty is death, so if you are hiding one, give it up now, and we shall enslave you instead."

No answer was given, as Red expected. There were no Raggies in their small village. Why did her dad tell her to hide?

Raggies were a paste-white-skinned race, and they all had twice as many joints as humans, so they looked like human rag dolls, which was why they were called Raggies. Though those were odd traits, the oddest trait all Raggies shared was the fact that their eye color told others what talent they had. If a Raggy had blue eyes, then his or her talent was in the mathematics; green was the sciences, and yellow was anything athletic. Black symbolized talents in the arts, and silver indicated that the Raggy had an amount of all of them.

A thought that maybe she was different from everybody else crossed her mind but was gone in a moment.

The villagers watched the queen's soldiers ransack their houses, unable to do anything about it. Red's house was at the end of the row of five houses, and it was the last one the soldiers searched. Red's parents were panicking as the soldiers searched their house, but they were trying to hide it.

The soldiers all came out, and the captain made a beeline for the owners of the house.

"There was an extra bedroom in your house that seemed to have been inhabited recently. Care to explain?"

All of the soldiers were Orvs, and the captain was the largest of them; therefore, his presence was quite formidable.

"Our daughter died, and we haven't had the courage to go in her room yet."

"Then why was the door to her room open?"

"That's how she left it."

The captain did not look convinced. "Show me her grave."

Red's dad nodded and silently led the captain to the grave of a neighbor's dog, who had died a year before. The captain squatted down and touched it. There was grass growing thick on the mound of dirt that was the dog's grave. He stood up and took out his dagger, which was as long as Red's dad's forearm, and showed it to him.

"This grave is not fresh enough for your story. You better hope we don't find anything in your house. Get back with your wife."

With a sense of dread, Red's dad complied. The captain called for his men to check Red's house one more time, especially in the "deceased" girl's room.

———

Red had heard people come stomping all the way through the house and even in her room, but no one had come in her cubbyhole. She was curious about what was going on, but she stayed in it like a good girl. She heard the stomping come back into the house and into her room. Then she heard a loud crash and a bunch of thumping. She heard her closet door open and someone rifling through her clothes. The thumping moved out of her closet and to right in front of her.

Right before the hidden door was opened, Red knew she had been found.

The door to her cubbyhole flew open, and a hand with a palm as big as her head came in. She was roughly grabbed, and she barely had time to notice that her room was torn apart before she was carried, not gently, outside.

Red was dropped on the ground in front of a *huge* pitch-black, blocky giant and her parents. She quickly stood up and went to hug her mom, who was crying, but the black giant stopped her by grabbing her hair.

"She's dead, is she? I hate it when people lie to me."

Before Red knew what was happening, the giant had used the hand that was not holding her to plunge a dagger into her father's gut. Time seemed to slow down for her as her dad doubled over and the dagger came back into view, stained red. The time it took for her dad's body to reach the floor seemed like a millennium; it haunted her for the rest of her life.

Red didn't know how it happened; in one moment she was being held three feet from the ground, and the next she was at her dad's side. She looked at her mom, her eyes pleading for an answer, but none came.

She heard her whisper, "Don't kill anyone."

Three seconds later, her mom's head was rolling on the ground, and the sword that cut it off was under Red's chin, forcing her to stand. She felt it trembling under her chin, and she looked up to see who was holding it. It was the same giant who had held her by the hair ten and a half seconds ago. He was holding his left hand to his chest; it looked like his elbow had moved to his wrist. He was about to say something, but Red didn't hear it.

Again, Red found herself in one position one moment and another the next; she went from being held at sword point to holding the giant at sword point. He was flat on his back, and she was holding his sword to his neck. He looked as shocked about it as she was. She remembered what her mom had said, so she plunged the sword into the ground right next to his neck and stood up. She then walked to her parents' bodies and fell to her knees, sobbing. No one was there to comfort her; all the villagers had disappeared into their houses.

Red was alone.

——◦◦◦——

The captain sat up and looked at the girl whose parents he had just killed. He was dumbfounded; no Raggy was able to break his arm, let alone take his sword and almost kill him with it. If there was one thing everyone knew about Raggies, it was the fact that if told or inclined to violent acts, they were incapable. Even if every one a Raggy cared for was tortured and killed in front of him or her, he or she would never even think of hurting their tormentors, let alone be able to. It was a well-known fact that Raggies were weak, so he summarized that he had been mistaken and the girl was a human.

If the girl wasn't a Raggy, then he had killed innocent people. If he had killed innocent people, then the general would kill him; thus, if she turned out to be human, he'd have to run for his life, literally.

He ordered the Orv closest to him, "Get a barrel and dump it on her."

"But, sir, I thought you said not to waste good whiskey on Raggies."

"Did she just *act* like a Raggy?"

"No…"

"Then we better make sure she is one!"

His subordinate nodded and went to fetch a barrel of whiskey from the wagon that was set aside for its transportation. The soldiers were carrying a wagonload of whiskey for two reasons: they liked drinking it, and any Raggy with dark skin, like Red, only had it because of a lotion applied to the skin. This lotion only came off when exposed to alcohol.

The soldier went back to Red and threw the contents of a whole barrel on her, but she barely seemed to notice. As the whiskey made contact with her skin, the brown color washed off. Her paste-white skin was exposed. She was soaked thoroughly, but she just kept crying.

She continued crying and didn't respond a bit when an Orv grabbed her arms and tied them behind her back. She didn't struggle as she was led to the line of slaves, and a rope was tied around her neck. There was not a hint of her earlier fire as she was tied in the middle of the line of slaves between a Raggy and a human.

Red just cried her heart out.

After about three hours of walking in the slave lines, Red stopped crying, but she still walked with her head down and her feet dragging. At one point in the past three hours, a soldier had whipped her around the ankles to try to make her go faster, but she noticed it as much as she would notice a mosquito on her leg. When he noticed that she had stopped crying, he tried again. She had to notice that time, because he tripped her. She quickly regained her feet and picked up her pace.

They traveled for another five hours before they came to a stop to make camp. Red and all the other prisoners were forced to sit down, and the soldiers set up their tents around them. After it was all ready and the night watches were set, the soldiers broke out a barrel of whiskey. In a little more than an hour, all of them except for those on watch and the captain were drunk.

The prisoners knew it was useless to try to sleep before the soldiers did, because some of them had tried it before, and the results were not pretty. After a while, the Raggy next to her struck up a conversation.

"Hi, my name is Pholip. What's yours?"

"Redache."

"How did you overpower the captain?"

Red shrugged. "I don't know, I didn't really do it."

"You didn't do it? What do you mean?"

"One second he was holding a pointy thing at my neck, and the next thing I know, I'm holding the pointy thing to his neck."

"So, you don't remember jumping, kicking his chest, or grabbing the sword?"

Red shook her head.

"That there is stuff of legend."

"Legend?"

"Yah, no Raggy but the liberators could ever have even thought to do that."

"What?"

"No Raggy is ever inclined to violence, which means that we, as a race, just can't fight. We are not only not inclined to it, we also don't even see it as an option. It is the rare Raggy that can push someone in defense or even *consider* carrying a weapon around. That's how God made us."

"Would Raggies wrestle with friends?"

"Nope. I've seen humans and Orvs do it, but I find it frightening and useless."

Red looked confused.

"Am I a Raggy?"

"Are you kidding me? Just look at your skin! Of course, you are." He took a sniff and added, "Speaking of your skin, you smell *horrible*!"

She sniffed and agreed. After a few minutes of silence, she asked, "What did you mean by 'liberators'?"

"Child, you know nothing about Raggies!"

Red didn't respond to that.

"Do you know how our eye color tells the world what our talent area is?"

"Kind of…"

He didn't feel like explaining it, so he just said, "That's good enough. Liberators have red eyes, which means that they are able to fight."

"But my eyes are brown."

"There's this thing called contacts that change a person's eye color. You might have some on."

"Does that mean that you think my eyes are red?"

He looked at her for a few minutes, and she was afraid that he was not going to answer her.

"I don't know. None of the liberators in the past were girls."

Their conversation lapsed into silence for a while as Red thought about these nuggets of information.

"Why are they called liberators?"

"Because they are only ever born before a time of crisis for the Raggy race, and their sole purpose is to free us from that crisis."

"Are we in a crisis right now?"

"Yes!"

"Okay."

Silence came upon them again, and they did not talk again until the next morning.

The soldiers and their prisoners traveled for another three days and arrived at another village. This one was a village of Orvs, and the soldiers followed the same routine that they always had; they called all the inhabitants out and told them to give up any hidden Raggies.

No one said anything, so all the houses were searched. As soon as the soldiers went into the house in the middle, the back door burst open, and a Raggy ran out. She was *fast.*

The captain yelled, "We have a runner!" And a soldier that had been waiting near the wagon took off after the Raggy. That soldier had no weapon on him, and his clothes were rather tight fitting, enabling him to run faster.

The Raggy was fast too, and it was a long chase, but the Orv eventually came back with the Raggy knocked out and flung over his shoulder. He gave the Raggy to the captain and got himself a drink of whiskey.

The captain looked at the owners of the house, a married couple and their two children, and told them, "You knew the rules, no Raggies. But, for once, I'm willing to compromise. If you kill this Raggy, I *won't* enslave your children, but I'll kill you and your wife no matter what."

He shoved the unconscious Raggy at the father with his good hand, and he caught the Raggy. He looked from her to his kids and back at her. Red could see the conflict going on within his mind.

"You've got five seconds, and she better be dead," the captain said, referring to the Raggy.

The father looked up and happened to see the prisoners in line. Most of them were dejected and looked at the ground, but a few people were looking at him with many differing emotions. One human was looking at him with pity; another was glaring at him. Several Raggies were looking at him with hope in their eyes.

Finally, he answered the captain, "It's better to have three alive than three dead. Besides, since when do the queen's men keep their word?"

"When there's whiskey involved," the captain answered as he chopped off the poor man's head.

He heard several "Ow, stop it!" lines from the line of prisoners and figured that the Raggy who had broken his arm was trying to break free of the line. That's why he had put her in the middle. He finished off the mother and told his men to tie the children and the Raggy in line. The soldiers had searched the other houses during the chase and found no one, so they promptly headed out on their way.

That night, the captain saw that his men were riled up and bloodthirsty. If he didn't do something to appease them, a fight would take place between two of them and he'd be less one soldier. He banged his sword against the side of the wagon, and the soldiers and prisoners alike shut up.

"We had a runaway today, didn't we?"

The soldiers nodded and grinned, seeing what he was thinking. He nodded at one of his men and told him, "Untie her and show her what we do to runaways."

The soldier took out his dagger, cut her bonds, and dragged her by the hair to the middle of the other soldiers. They formed an impenetrable circle that none of the other prisoners could see through, but they heard what was happening. The soldier who was told to "show her what we do to runaways" took a whip that he usually used to drive the prisoners faster and started hitting her. She tried to run away, but she couldn't get away from it without running into a soldier. She started crying and begging him to stop.

At the first sound of the whip, Red got angry. She strained against her restraints and only succeeded in giving herself rope burn. Then the Raggy started begging. Red snapped the rope around her wrists and reached up and snapped the rope around her neck in two seconds. Red broke through the ring of soldiers and grabbed the tip of the whip just as it was about to hit the runaway, and then she jerked the whip out from the surprised soldier's hand.

Of course, Red really wasn't aware of what she was doing. At one moment, she was tied next to Pholip, and at the next she was standing in the circle of soldiers holding a whip. She was still outraged, so she took it in stride. She only noticed the dumbfounded silence when she replayed the scene in her head later.

"What did she do to you to cause this cruelty? What did any Raggy do to provoke this hatred of our race? You are all monsters!"

Red helped the runaway stand up, and together they walked back to the line of prisoners.

The captain was seething. He told his men to get some sleep but pulled the only archer under his command to the side, behind the wagon.

"Do you have any knockout arrows?"

"Yah, three. Why?"

"I want you to knock out that Raggy, the one who broke my arm. She's too much trouble."

"Why don't we just kill her?"

"Because I think that at Alebu we can get a bunch of money from her."

"How?"

"Is it any of your business? Go do your job."

The captain left, and the archer went around behind the prisoners. He took out one of his knockout arrows and loaded the arrow with a wooden block at the tip instead of an arrowhead into his bow. He aimed at the specified Raggy's head and pulled back only halfway. If he had pulled back all the way, he would have caved in her skull.

Red didn't sense it coming at all.

———⟨◈⟩———

Red awoke rolled up in a ball, four hours after she was knocked out. She couldn't get up, and wherever she was at smelled like moldy bread. She was so tightly rolled into a ball that she was no bigger than the ball she had kicked around with her friends back at her village. She tried to wiggle out, but a large object hit her, and she stopped. It was dark, so she suspected that it was still night.

After a while, she got cramped, so she tried to wiggle into a different position, but the large object hit her again; she stopped. After what seemed like—and what was—hours, she was able to see a faint outline of the edge of her stomach, the thing right in front of her face. After another few minutes, she could see enough to realize that she was in a bag that the soldiers used to carry the bread they gave their prisoners. She tried to reposition again and was hit again.

Red realized that she was going to have to get used to being uncomfortable, at least until they reached their destination. Wherever that was.

INITIATION

The assassin landed and tucked in his wings. For a brief second, he thought about the fact that he was the only person in the world with wings, which led to another brief second of thought about how maybe he *wasn't* alone and that there might be others like him out there somewhere. He had never, to his knowledge, met another of his race, but they could still be out there.

The assassin was a Rept, and his name was Ricky. He didn't quite know what a Rept was; he just knew that he was one. Of course, he knew what he looked like, a cross somewhere between a human and a dragon, but closer to the dragon than the human. He had the stature of a normal human, and his body parts were of the same proportion as a human, but that was pretty much where the humanity ended.

Instead of a mouth, Ricky had a kind of snout that stuck out from his face; he didn't have hair but had scales, and he had wings and a tail. He couldn't breathe fire; he had tried, but all that happened was that smoke came out of his nostrils when he was agitated. The one thing that he could not attribute to either humans or dragons was the fact that his scales were pointy. Normal dragons' scales were rounded at the end, but his were like arrowheads and looked to be made of solid gold. A good thing they weren't, because then he would have several more enemies, all of whom would be prospectors.

He pondered what it would be like to have prospector enemies as he walked the remaining mile to Alebu. Fort Alebu was the place he liked to go after a job, and he had just knocked off a sheriff that was causing trouble for General I. The sheriff had refused to enlist any of the young men in his town into the Rovian army, and the general could not punish him for that within the law.

That's what assassins were useful for, outside the law. They didn't have to have any other reason than payment to knock off somebody. The sheriff had an unfortunate and untimely death from food poisoning. A pity too, he had just accepted that office. Usually, Ricky would take a more direct and intimate approach, such as removing his targets' heads from their shoulders, but the general didn't want it to seem like an execution. That's why the assassin was delighted to go to Alebu.

Alebu was where all the Raggies were taken to be tortured for information about an "underground resistance" that everybody knew didn't exist. Raggies had too much trouble evading search parties, angry mobs, and loner bounty hunters who scoured other countries to even consider a resistance. After a while, the soldiers who ran Alebu started to realize that, so they stopped interrogating them and just started torturing them for fun. Then they realized that since they were having so much fun with it, other Orvs would too and pay money for it. Sooner rather than later, they developed shows of strength that others could pay to see or pay to participate in. One such show was picking a Raggy from a line of them and facing another person who did the same to see who could keep his Raggy alive the longest while torturing it.

Ricky—a trained assassin, torture expert, and mind reader— found these contests a good way to blow off steam after an easy job that did not satisfy his need for violence—thus, his trip to Alebu after poisoning a sheriff in a small town on the border of Rov.

He saw the northwest tower of Alebu and picked up his pace. He arrived there a few minutes after he landed. At the gate, the guards let him in without paying. The last time they had tried to extract a toll from the assassin, they were less three guards the next day, so they always left him alone. He strolled contentedly through corridors and slipped quietly into the auditorium that used to be the soldiers' bunks. In the name of money and greed, they had sacrificed their bunks and built this amphitheater that seated two thousand on a good day, just like that day.

Ricky stayed at the top and looked down on the arena floor, wondering what had drawn such a crowd. In the arena was a solitary Raggy who looked tiny next to the Orv that was charging at her. The whole amphitheater was ringing with the sound of onlookers cheering on the Orv and booing the Raggy; the deluge hurt the assassin's sensitive ears, but that was part of the appeal of this place. As the Orv came within arm's length of the Raggy at a full on charge that was sure to flatten her, she jumped and roundhouse-kicked him in the chin. The Orv's momentum carried him straight up into the air and over her head; he landed on his head and was knocked out cold.

The Raggy stayed right where she was in the middle of the arena as soldiers removed the Orv who had rushed her. The crowd went nuts and almost as one cursed at her, but she was unfazed.

Ricky went up to a spectator and asked him what was going on.

The response was too coated with curse words for him to understand. Ricky was about to ask him to explain without cussing when an Orv with the markings of a captain stepped onto the arena.

The captain spoke loud enough for most of the back row to hear, "That was the fifth challenger to try taking this Raggy's contacts off, and she doesn't even have a scratch! Isn't there someone who can prove that this is, in fact, a red-eyed Raggy? Remember, there is a fifty *dahl* entrance fee and the prize is one-hundred dahls!"

No one stepped forward.

"Oh, come on! Are you all afraid of a *Raggy*?"

A shout came from the audience, "A Raggy that broke your arm!"

Now this was getting interesting, a Raggy who had broken an Orv's arm and knocked out five others. The assassin wondered if she would be fun to fight but didn't give in to the idea of trying. He usually cased his opponents in a full battle before batting an eye and fighting them.

Finally, a soldier accepted the challenge. He paid the entrance fee and faced the Raggy, assessing his options. He couldn't charge her, head-on approach her, or try to provoke her into the first move because none of those tactics worked. He tried something new; he drew his sword.

Now that caused a reaction. She started to glare at him, but no one but the opponent and the assassin noticed. He pointed it at her and approached cautiously. She backed away from the sword tip. It was the first time she had moved from the middle of the arena, or so that's what the assassin concluded from the audience's reaction.

The opponent pushed the Raggy all the way to the wall of the arena. There she stopped, and he reached for her face. It happened so fast that very few people saw it, and absolutely no one expected it. The Raggy grabbed the sword by the blade and jerked it across to the soldier's hand. He screamed as the blade he always meticulously sharpened sliced through his hand like a hot knife through butter. Blood squirted all over the Raggy, and she stepped away from the soldier. Everyone was stunned. Those who had not seen the Raggy grab the sword thought that the soldier had cut off his own hand.

His comrades rushed to his aid but stayed away from the Raggy. The assassin smiled and gave in to the idea. He made his way down to the arena as the soldier was led away to where he could receive medical treatment. The Raggy was not acting like a victor but more like the victim. Tears were streaming out from her eyes, and from what Ricky could tell, she was trying her best to keep her composure, and she wanted to run away from it all.

The captain sounded shaken as he asked the audience, "Anybody else feels like facing this Raggy, or is it time for her to face the firing squad?"

The crowd yelled loudly for the firing squad, which was composed of ten soldiers, all with bows, who surrounded a prisoner and shot him or her until he or she died. It was an extreme rarity for the firing squad to be called out, but before they were, the captain heard, "I'll face her."

He turned and saw that the assassin was standing next to him. The Orv was twice the assassin's size, but his reputation demanded a stature twice the Orv's size. The audience started to notice him standing next to the captain, and the booming roar for the firing squad was dimmed to whispers about the assassin.

The captain sounded terrified as he said, "*You* want to face *her*!"

"All I have to do is take her contacts off, right?"

The captain nodded.

Ricky responded, "Then I'll double the wager. I'll give you one hundred dahls, and you'll give me two hundred if I win and take her contacts off."

The captain almost had a heart attack.

"And if that's not enough, I'll do it with one hand tied behind my back. You can tie the knot."

The captain held out his hand. "If you want to, I'm not going to stop you."

The assassin handed him one hundred dahls and took off his sword belt and quiver. As the captain tied his hand behind his back, the assassin said, "If anyone touches my weapons, he'll pay with his life."

Then he jumped over the side of the arena and faced the Raggy. She was scared; he could tell it in her eyes and in her mind. She had been scared that whole time and had barely wrapped her mind around the fact that she was fighting. He would use that to his advantage.

Ricky walked toward her, and she looked at him the same way she had looked at everybody else who had approached her, with fear. Ricky didn't let that fool him. He started with a test punch straight at her face just to see her reaction. She grabbed his fist out of midair and twisted his arm behind his back; thus, she twisted his whole body. She kicked his back and let go of his arm, which sent him sprawling. He checked his momentum and faced her again.

He projected his thoughts so that she could hear him, *This is going to be fun.*

He grinned at the fear that it produced in her. He approached her again, faked a punch at her face, and dropped to the ground where he swiped his legs through hers, making her fall. He repositioned himself back on his legs and aimed a downward punch at her face, but she was gone before his fist connected with the floor. He stood and found her foot right in front of him; in other words, she kicked him in the face. He fell back and immediately bounced back up. He spit a crimson wad out of his mouth, and his tongue felt the hole that the tooth should've been in.

That's when it got personal for Ricky.

He recalled that whenever she went on either offense or defense, her mind had become blank; therefore, she was operating on an autopilot. That meant that she would do the same thing every single time, and that meant that she would be predictable. With this, the assassin concluded that he would have to be unpredictable.

He started it just as he had the last time; he approached her, faked a punch at her face, and swiped her feet out from underneath her, but instead of standing up, he flipped sideways and landed on her as she started to stand. He wrapped his legs around her chest and his tail around her legs, and they landed heavily with the Raggy on the bottom.

She tried to struggle free, but the assassin's weight was too much for her to overcome. She saw his hand coming toward her face, so she closed her eyes tight. She felt pressure on a spot on her skull next to her face, and her eyes popped open without her consent. Before she could shut her eyes, she felt something come off her right eye. When she shut them again, the assassin repeated the process of pressing the pressure point on her skull, and he took off her left contact.

He looked at her eyes for a moment. They were startlingly bright red, and the mixture of fear and confusion in them appealed to him in some way he didn't understand.

He stood up and yanked his hand out of the rope, holding it behind his back before he walked calmly to the captain. He held the contacts in his hand, palm up for him to see, and said, "My money, please."

〜

Red sucked air, grateful that the lizard-man's weight was off of her. She heard the crowd going crazy, but it seemed distant. She was trying to tell herself that it was all a dream. The Orvs had not killed her parents. An outlandish person did not just pinch her eyes. She wasn't constantly having blackouts where she was in a different position than she had been the second before. Above all, she was not in an arena in front of a bunch of Orvs screaming at her. She was in her bed. She was dreaming.

No matter how much she told herself these things, the opposite was true. She didn't want to acknowledge the truth, so she curled up in a ball and blocked out the world. She felt someone grab her and toss her around, but she refused the blackout to come. She just kept refusing it until a few minutes later when she heard screaming, Raggies screaming.

Red uncurled and saw that she was being tossed past several people beating on Raggies. She felt the blackout coming and heard one word in her mind. *Liberator, liberator, liberator.*

She gave in to the blackout.

—⦿⦿⦿—

After Ricky picked up his weapons and the tooth the Raggy had knocked out, he went to his usual haunt, the Raggy torture area. What he found there was mass chaos. The Raggy had broken free of her captors and was in the process of trying to free the Raggies being tortured. The soldiers were trying to catch her and having zero success.

Ricky usually carried a knockout arrow in his quiver just in case he was hired for a kidnap-and-ransom job, so he took it and his bow out. The Raggy was knocked out on the floor before she realized he was in the room. The soldiers looked at him with a mixture of fear, awe, and gratefulness as they picked her up.

The assassin watched them take her down to the dungeon level, and an idea came to mind. He dismissed it as ludicrous at first, but he soon realized that it was a great idea. He went to go talk to the colonel in charge of Alebu.

—⦿⦿⦿—

Red awoke in a bag, again. She was getting annoyed at being bagged. She moved a little to get comfortable, and a voice that was not her own entered her head.

Don't move.

Red stopped moving but started to panic at the weird voice in her head.

The voice told her, *If you don't stop hyperventilating, you will suffocate in the bag.*

Who is this?

I'm the assassin that took your contacts off.

It took Red a few minutes to fully digest that information.

Wait, you're an assassin!

Not just an *assassin,* the best *assassin.*

Still, assassin!

Stop thinking it; it's getting annoying!

Red was still freaking out about the voice in her head and that she was being carried by an assassin, so he left her mind for a little bit. When he went back in, she had calmed down.

As I was trying to say, don't move!

What's the deal with moving? The other guy who bagged me didn't like it either.

I don't know why he didn't like it, but when you move, you set off my balance, and if you do it enough, you'll knock me out of rhythm, and I might fall out of the sky.

You're flying?

Yes.

And carrying me?

Yes!

That's interesting.

He was incredibly annoyed at her persistent questions, so he retreated from her mind. He could still hear a constant itching of her thoughts because she was so close to him. After another hour, he went back in because he was that bored.

He asked her, *What is your name, Raggy?*

Redache, but everyone has always called me Red. What's yours?

Ricky.

After that, he decided not to go into her mind until they arrived at their destination.

Ricky softly landed on the roof of the castle and looked into the skylight without letting his shadow fall on the floor far below his feet. He was looking to see if the court was in session. If it was and the nobles were there, then Ricky couldn't drop in uninvited, but if the nobles weren't there, he could. He had done it once, and he had loved the way he had startled Queen Kim. She had almost called her guards on him.

There was no one in the throne room, not even the queen, which made sense because it was getting dark. He knew where else she would be, eating in the dining hall. Her dinners were usually extravagant events with an honored guest, so he really didn't want to crash that party; besides, he had a much more fun way to surprise her. He had found the window to her room in the past—just in case he ever decided to go traitor or she was outbided for his services— so he went to it and climbed in.

Her room was dark and getting darker; shadows were an assassin's best friend. He checked the whole room for foes out of habit and sat on the end of her bed, waiting. He waited for hours, and soon enough, it was pitch-dark.

—◦⁄◦⁄◦—

Kim led her lover through the hallways and toward her room. He held the torch and every now and then on the way there, they would kiss each other in a fit of passion. They were deeply in love and had been for years.

The queen's lover was also her general; his full name was General I. No one quite understood why his name was I, but if anyone had dared to ask him to his face, his or her head was promptly removed from his or her shoulders. He ruled by fear, which was why Kim was attracted to him.

They had talked about getting married, but Kim wanted to wait until her throne was fully established; in other words, they'd marry when Alexandra was dead. Since she was too young for most "accidents" devised to work on her, Kim had not yet ordered an assassination for her, but she, Ricky, and General I all knew that the time was coming closer.

Of course, Ricky didn't cross either noble's mind until Kim opened the door to her room. The light from the torch I was carrying illuminated Ricky's scales, and she wasn't expecting anyone to be in her room, let alone her assassin, so she jumped back in fear and screamed.

General I thought that someone was there to accost her, so he jumped between her and the door. Seeing Ricky did not in any way help his image of someone trying to hurt her.

He yelled at Ricky, "What are you doing here, assassin!"

"I want an apprentice."

His answer apparently just made the general even angrier, "Then pick one from my men for all I care! What in the blazes are you doing in the queen's room talking about an apprentice when you know full well it is not her concern?"

"I picked one already, and she is most definitely the queen's concern."

Kim pushed past her lover. "Why is your apprentice my concern?"

"If you'll come inside and shut the door, I'll show you."

They begrudgingly obliged and sat on the bed. Ricky took a bag off his back, opened it, and spilt the contents onto the floor. Red came tumbling out, and as soon as she hit the floor, she rolled into a squat close to the ground. Her hair was in her face, so the nobles didn't see her eyes.

General I looked confused. "A Raggy?" But Ricky read his thoughts and got the real meaning behind that comment, *This guy has gone insane.*

Ricky told Red, "Move your hair."

She hesitantly reached up and parted the hair on her face. As soon as he saw the color of her eyes, I stood up and partly drew his sword while eyeing her warily. Kim gasped and then sighed in dismay.

"I thought that keeping one alive meant that another would not be born," she said.

"Well, you were wrong. Does this mean I can kill Tor now?" the general replied.

"No, he is still too important."

He looked disappointed but said nothing as Kim stood and approached Red. Red stood up and started to back away from her. The queen ordered her to stop, so she did. Kim towered over her, and Red tried to shrink as much as possible.

"You're right, your pick is my concern. Why her?"

"She knocked one of my teeth out."

General I was bewildered. He had once sparred hand-to-hand with the assassin for fun, and all of his hits had been blocked. How could a Raggy hit him?

Red wanted to melt into the floor, but she doubted that would solve her problems. She had heard stories about the queen, stories that could make a grown man shudder. One such story was about how she had killed her first Raggy at age eleven and how that was supposedly the reason her twin sister became heir to the throne over her. As the queen inspected her, she felt that all those stories were entirely correct.

After a few more minutes of consideration, the queen directly asked Red, "How old are you, Raggy?"

Red was almost scared speechless, "T-t-ten, Your Maj-j-jesty."

"How long ago was your birthday?"

"A few w-weeks ago?"

Kim nodded to herself and turned to Ricky.

"Come to my throne room with the Raggy at four tomorrow; I'll give my answer then."

The assassin, who never bowed, dipped his head in acknowledgment of her command and grabbed the Raggy by the back of her neck; she let out a yelp. He proceeded to drag her out but stopped a few steps into it when he felt sharp, sudden pain flair up in the forearm that was holding her. He kept holding her and used his other fist to knock her out. He threw her over his shoulder and walked out of the queen's bedroom, closing the door on his way out.

———⟨ɷⱱɷ⟩———

Red awoke in a bag, again, for the third time. She was beginning to hate bags in general.

A voice that was not her own spoke in her head, *You're awake.* And it took her a moment to figure out that it was Ricky.

He asked her, *Are you hungry?*

Yes, sir.

Then if you can get out of the bag. I'll feed you.

41

How am I supposed to do that?

I don't know, because I've never been in a bag before. Figure it out.

Red realized that she had a headache. It was extremely rare for her to get sick, let alone a headache, but she just thought it was a symptom of hunger. She started to think of a way out of the bag by considering the facts. She was curled into a ball with her head in her belly, and her feet tucked over her head and behind her back. The mouth of the bag was next to her feet. She thought it would be easiest to just uncurl, but when she started, it just made the space seem tighter, so she relaxed.

She was unfamiliar with half of her joints, the half that humans didn't have and Raggies did, so she was unable to see that all she needed to do was pull her legs out of the bag one joint at a time. Instead, she worked on a slow process of trying to uncurl and relaxing, over and over. Every time she uncurled and recurled, she would reposition her head slightly closer to the mouth of the bag.

It took her twenty minutes, but she eventually got out of the bag and jumped to the ground from where it was hanging.

"Took you long enough," Ricky said.

He was sitting on a narrow bed in a crappy-looking, little room. The bag she had been in was hanging on the doorknob, and she was standing next to it only a foot away from him.

Red didn't know how to respond to his statement, so she just said, "Do you have any food?"

Ricky held up a lump of moldy bread. "This is what a Raggy gets."

He threw it at her, and she caught it. Before she started to eat it, he held up another piece of bread. That piece was warm, and Red thought it smelled like her mother's fresh-baked bread. Thinking about her mother brought back that horrible memory of how she died.

Ricky continued his minilesson, "And this is what *I* eat. Remember your place."

That was the end of what he had meant to be a humiliating ordeal, but Red didn't get it. She hurriedly gulped down the moldy bread and sank down to the ground, thinking about her parents. She was still hungry, but it barely registered in her mind.

All she could think about was that she was alone, her parents were dead, and she didn't understand anything going on around her. The fact that she was starving beyond any measure she had felt before just added to her confusion.

Ricky, who was reading her mind, ordered her, "Stop moping and moaning! They knew that harboring a Raggy, especially one of your caliber, would result in death, and they deserved it. You should've been handed over to officials years ago."

Red was on the verge of tears, "Is this supposed to make me feel better?"

"Feel better? No! I don't care how you feel; you just need to stop thinking about it, because parental thoughts are weak thoughts. You need to be strong."

Red didn't understand, so she kept silent and put her head in her hands. As she sat there, Ricky stared at her. She was a child; what should he care about a Raggy child? What was he thinking, sticking his neck out for a Raggy? If Kim didn't take to his idea, then his reputation would be stained with something he couldn't clean it of, kindness to a Raggy. He had saved her from Alebu for goodness' sake!

Neither talked for quite a long time until Ricky stood up and told her to move. When she did, he walked out the door and told her not to leave the room, or he'd kill her. She took the threat at face level, and he reveled in the fear that it produced.

Ricky didn't come back until three thirty, and Red stayed in the room.

———⟞⟋⟍⟞———

When Ricky slammed through the side door to the throne room, Kim jumped in her seat on her throne. I, who was standing right next to her, slightly unsheathed his sword. Red was slightly behind Ricky because he had been unable to convince her to get in the bag, so he told her to follow him closely. They passed a few people in the hallway, and all of them looked at both Ricky and Red like they were contaminated.

"What is it with you and dramatic entrances?" Kim asked Ricky.

"I don't know, something about knowing that no one in the room poses a threat to my well-being."

Ricky's arrogance was one of his constant characteristics. The queen snorted— not in laughter, more like annoyance—and got right to the point.

"If you want the one Raggy that poses any sort of threat to my kingdom as your apprentice, then she is going to have to be worth the effort it would require to turn her."

"Turn her?" Ricky asked.

"I can't have you training her to be a killer if all she is going to do is use that training to *help* the Raggies. Do you catch my drift?"

"I'm going to have to teach her to hate Raggies."

"No, you're going to give her to I for the first month; he has… talents that will make sure that she never likes her own race again."

Ricky wasn't so sure he liked that idea, but he didn't say anything yet.

Kim continued, "So we want to see if she's worth the effort, by testing her worth. If she can survive ten minutes in combat with you, then she's worth it."

Ricky noticed Red scoot away from him.

"So, I attack her for ten minutes, and if she survives, she's worth it."

"Yes. Show no mercy."

Ricky smiled at those three words, his three favorite words in succession. They meant go fast, go hard, don't hesitate, don't forewarn, and, of course, show no mercy all rolled into one phrase.

Ricky quickly turned and threw a dart that he kept in his belt at all times straight at Red. She was only two yards away, so it should have hit her before she even noticed that he had thrown it. Instead, Red's arm snapped up, and she caught it. She looked just as startled as anyone else in the room.

Before she had completely recovered from the shock of catching a dart, Ricky drew his sword and closed the distance between Red and himself. He lunged at her stomach, and she clapped and caught the blade between her hands. His momentum kept the sword moving after she stopped it, so it continued for an inch, cutting her hands. Ricky hadn't expected that, nor did he expect her next move of rotating around the sword and kicking it out of his hand. She flipped it so that she was holding the handle and then stared at the sword, not knowing what to do with it.

Ricky had another sword drawn and was attacking her in the time it took for Red to flip the sword. He went straight down at her from her head, to her waist, but she sidestepped and chopped at his arm. He twisted his wrist to block it. As time passed, Ricky found that fighting fair wasn't going to help him at all, so he started resulting to trickery that Red's autopilot couldn't block. One trick—entering a power struggle and kicking her shin— made her fall, and he ended up cutting her shoulder. He was aiming for her head, but she had moved enough for him to miss.

Every time he used a trick, he would cut Red, or worse, so he started doing them frequently. While she was blocking a one-handed hip-to-jaw fake, he took out a dagger with his other hand and cut her hands holding the sword. She dropped it, and he kicked it out of her reach. He was about to end her when the queen said, "Stop."

He redirected the backhand slash aimed at Red and turned to face the queen.

She said, "That was twenty minutes."

No one said anything. When I had sparred with Ricky, he had only lasted seven minutes before the assassin had neutralized him, and he was the best dueler in the army. It should have been impossible for Red to survive two, let alone twenty.

"Okay, Ricky, you've got yourself a Raggy apprentice."

I added, "Which is either insane or genius, that has yet to be decided."

Ricky was breathing too hard to say anything.

"I will send someone to check on your progress with her in two years. If anyone other than royalty gets within a mile of her, kill them."

"Since when did you get to tell me what to do with my apprentice?"

The giantess stood up, and the assassin realized that she was twice his size. "Since the one you picked was the only one in Rov that could pose a threat to my rule!"

She heard a growl coming from her assassin; it was a growl that would have scared a full-grown, confident lion. She didn't know he could growl, and apparently neither did he, because it stopped, and he swallowed as if he hadn't meant for that to come out.

"Fine, but if I see even *royalty* within your parameters of a mile in those two years, I don't care if it is you, I'll kill them."

With that, he slammed the sword he was holding into its sheath and went to retrieve the other one. He glared at I and said, "You have a month. If she is not in the same condition she is in now, then I will kill her *and you*."

He left with that threat hanging in the air.

I looked at Red with disgust.

"I have to get a liberating Raggy to hate other Raggies. Great. Follow me."

He walked out a side door, and Red followed after bowing to the queen.

This left Kim all alone in her humongous throne room.

She rubbed her temples and told herself, "We are all going to regret this."

—◦◦◦—

When I told Red to get in a sack later that night, she flatly refused. He tried to force her in but ended up with a bloody nose and a bruised shin. He then waited until she was asleep, which took quite awhile, and then he got her into a sack. He traveled the two-day walking distance in a day and a night and arrived at Alebu at the same time as captured Raggies from the other side of Rov.

The soldiers didn't dare question their superior officer when he asked for the closest room to the Raggy torture area, even though they knew that everyone who slept in that room had nightmares for a month afterward. The only thing separating the room from that area was a wall of brick with just enough mortar to keep the wall up. This easily let the inhabitants of the room hear the tormented screams of the Raggies who were usually tortured only during daylight hours. General I put his package in the room and shut and locked the door. Then he went to the torture area and told the current torturers that he would pay them to do it throughout the night for a week.

—⟨ω/ω⟩—

Red heard the screams as soon as they entered Alebu. She tried to get out of the sack, but she was hit by what seemed like a ton of bricks, so she stopped. She felt herself dropped on the ground, and within seconds, she was out of the bag.

She looked around and saw a room with nothing but a bed in it and a plain, wooden door. She heard screams that seemed to emanate from everywhere. She felt a blackout coming, so she gave in to it. When she came back to herself, the screams were still just as loud as ever, and her knuckles were bloody. She looked at the door she had been beating on and saw that it looked just as it had before. The screams died off for a moment, and then a high-pitched scream seemed to vibrate throughout Red's being and reverberate throughout the room she was in. She faced the wall it was coming from and balled her hands into fists. The scream stopped, but only a moment later it rang forth again, and this time it was louder.

Red's entire body started to shake, and she had to fight hard to keep the blackout from taking over. It did not stop for a long time, and when it did, she could hear someone sobbing, "Please stop! Please…please…"

Then it grew weaker and weaker until the voice stopped. Red couldn't hold it back any longer. She let her instincts take over.

—◦◦◦—

The Raggies in the holding pen and torture area were all huddled next to the wall farthest from the torturers and their victims. Those who were there on their first day looked stronger than those who had been there for several days, but all were haggard and looked underfed. While the current torture session of who could make their victim scream the loudest went on, they had heard thumping from the other side of the wall but had thought nothing of it. It stopped for a minute, but when one of the victims died, the wall behind them seemed to be hit with a battering ram.

They all scooted away from that wall and stared at it as it shook, and dust shot from between the bricks, especially at the middle around Raggy height. Their captors noticed their shift of position and started to stare at it too. In a few minutes, the whole room, including the torturers, was staring at the wall. As soon as the torturers stopped, the wall stopped moving.

Right about that time, General I came in.

"What in the blazes do you think you are doing? Keep going, or else she'll have time to think!"

They continued their jobs with renewed vigor, and the screams and wall thumps continued. The lieutenant in charge of the captives came up to the general and asked, "What's happening, sir?"

"We're teaching a Raggy a lesson."

"That's a *Raggy* doing that to the wall?"

"Yes, it is, and if I don't hear torture for any more than a few seconds, I will have the heads of those on duty, whether soldier or civilian."

With that, the general walked away.

—◈◈◈—

Red came back to herself when her left pinky finger broke. Her autopilot had been slamming her against the wall, but the only progress that had made was the appearance of a bunch of dust in the room. She sat down and held her hand to her stomach, staring at the wall. Pain throbbed in her hand, and tremors shook her body as each tormented scream burst forth.

For a brief minute, she let the blackout take over again, but she soon took back over when the pain in her hand wouldn't let her continue. As she came back to herself, she noticed a hole in the wall where a brick had fallen out. She scooted to that hole and looked through it. What she saw made her cry because she knew that she could do nothing about it.

—◈◈◈—

Ricky went to the castle exactly a month after he had left it. He had avoided Alebu because he assumed that was where I would be "turning" Red, so he spent the month preparing what he called the valley of training. It was a valley in the Dead Mountains that no one traveled to, for in that mountain range, there was only one mountain covered with trees; all the rest were as dry and bare as a desert. It was said that this was caused by a war between Sunny and her brother Droydox, but very few people believed that because those mountains had never been part of Syn-Cynthia, their country.

When Ricky had trained under Chafgee in that same valley, there had been two huts, one for sleeping in and another for holding weapons; the second had been locked for the longest of times. Since then, the huts had fallen apart, and the walls could be seen on the bare, hard ground, totally undisturbed. Otherwise, the valley looked exactly as Ricky remembered it. He repaired the huts and started to think about *how* he would go about training someone who couldn't control when she fought.

At the castle, he went to General I's quarters and found him there with Red huddled against a wall. Her hands were bandaged, and Ricky could tell that one of her fingers was broken. She looked just as underfed as any other time he had seen her, but she looked weaker due to the lack of something, he couldn't tell what.

"She is no longer a threat to the queen, so she is all yours," I said.

"Thanks, that's exactly what I want in an apprentice," Ricky answered sarcastically. "Come with me, Raggy."

Red stood up and followed him out of I's room. I left right after they did and disappeared down the hallway. Ricky told Red to curl into a ball so that he could put her in a bag, and she did so without hesitation or complaint, which Ricky did not see as a good sign. He found a window and flew out of the castle toward the training valley.

Ricky's first course of action upon arriving at the training valley was to dump Red out onto the ground. He had noticed that she had not squirmed at all on the way there, which was, from what he knew, uncharacteristic of her. He had looked into her thoughts and found only sorrow and an overwhelming sense of failure. He hadn't been able to pinpoint why she felt like a failure, because she hadn't been thinking clearly, so he decided to straight up ask her after he dumped her out.

"What did he do to you?"

Red had not risen from the ground and was content to stay there, curled into a ball. She did not answer.

"Stand up," he snapped at her.

She slowly uncurled and rose to her feet, but she looked at the ground, ashamed.

"Answer me! What did he do to you?"

She mumbled, "He tried to make me kill Raggies, and when I didn't, he tortured them in front of me."

"And you couldn't stop him?"

Red nodded.

"Why?"

"I just can't save them."

Ricky looked in her mind and saw that she saw a brick wall between her and any other Raggy. It was a wall that she couldn't pass or knock down, because it would hurt her if she tried. The full weight of what General I did to his apprentice struck Ricky at that moment. He had shaped her mind so that she believed that she was entirely unable to save Raggies, and if she did try, then she would hurt herself. Since she was a Raggy, this meant that she was unable to save herself as well.

Ricky unsheathed a sword and used the tip to push Red's chin up, making her look at him. He then noticed what was missing that made her look weaker, her defiance.

"Get this sword off of your neck," he told her.

She stepped back, and he matched her pace, keeping it on her chin.

"That's not going to work."

Red trembled for a second and said, "Do you want me to black out?"

"Yes."

"It doesn't work."

"I'll be the judge of that."

So Red let the autopilot take over, and next thing she knew, she had a sword in her hands. By then Ricky had taken out another one and slashed at her cheek. She refused the autopilot control, and pain spread from just below the right side of her lip to just under her earlobe. She still refused the autopilot control. Ricky put his other sword at her neck and growled, "Defend yourself!"

Red still refused the autopilot, but she lifted the sword, not knowing what to do with it. She brought it up and hit his sword aside but had no idea what to do after that. He down-slashed straight at her head, and she had no clue that the sword she held was for blocking it, so she dropped it and stepped back, all the while fighting the blackout.

When Ricky saw what she had done, he slammed the sword he was holding into a sheath and walked toward her. Another tremor shook her as she fought for complete control of her body. Before she even realized that he was attacking her, his arm was around her neck, choking her.

He softly said, "I should kill you right now." He squeezed a little tighter, getting a tremor from her. "And I will unless you get out of my grip."

Red started to see spots, and the next thing she knew, she was standing over Ricky with her foot on his back between his wings. Her neck flared with pain, and when she reached up to touch it, her fingers returned to her sight covered in blood. As she got her foot off Ricky, she coughed, and the pain worsened. She doubled over and held the flaps of skin on her neck, where his sharp scales had dug into her.

"That is why I don't want to attack."

Ricky stood up slowly, his anger building. He wasn't angry with her, really. More likely he was angry at General I for making his apprentice as dangerous as a normal Raggy unless her life was definitely threatened, and he was angry at Kim for making him agree to that. He would just have to scare Red into listening to him, and the only way he knew how to scare a Raggy was to beat it.

Red felt him grab her hair and drag her. She did not resist but just held her neck and started to cry. She didn't sob; tears just leaked from the corners of her eyes. He threw her into the second shack and slammed the door behind him. She felt him tie ropes around her wrists, but she was unable to see due to the dark.

He spoke in clear, loud syllables, "If you don't do what I tell you, I will hurt you much worse than you can hurt yourself, and you are about to find out just *how* bad."

TRAINING

After he was done teaching Red the lesson that he was sure she would never forget Ricky bandaged her wounds. It was about midnight when they went to the first hut to sleep on mats that were a good five feet apart. Red didn't sleep.

The next day, Ricky started a routine that they adhered to for the entire first year. He and Red woke up an hour before sunrise, and they would run for hours. He expected Red to keep up with him, but she was unable to, for her sprint was only as fast as his jog. He was annoyed at this for a few days, but then he realized that there was no way either he or Red could change it; she was just slow. He solved the dilemma of not being able to run his pace and having to watch her by telling her to run up a mountain, and doing it himself. When he got at the top, he would sit down and watch her on the bare surface of the mountain. When she got close enough for him to see her from the other side of the mountain, he would run down and she would have to follow him. It was helpful that they were relatively low mountains.

Then he would teach her about edible plants and insects by using the only mountain covered with trees in the Dead Mountains range. If she didn't learn, then she didn't eat lunch. After lunch, he would explain to her the various uses of each type of weapon and how to make and identify poisons.

He didn't use any time at all within the day to focus on actually fighting, because as long as her autopilot took over, he couldn't teach her about it. He was hoping that on her eleventh birthday, she would be able to at least be aware of how she was fighting. If not, she was a blind robot that would be of no use as an assassin; thus, she would not live out the day.

———⟨∞⟩———

Red's eleventh birthday went just like any other day had before, until after lunch. Instead of going to the forest, Ricky threw a sword at Red. She had become used to him throwing things at her by then, so she easily dodged it. He told her to pick it up, and she complied.

"Now, attack me."

Red knew not to argue, but she asked, "How?"

"Figure it out."

She looked at the sword and back up at him several times. Finally, she said, "If you don't at least give me *a* tip, I have no idea how to start."

He thought about that for a second and conceded.

"First of all, you need to hold your sword properly. Hold the handle with both hands and put the tip about two feet away from your face."

Red did as instructed. "Like this?"

"Yes. Now swing it at me."

She swung the sword, but he was a good eight feet away, so she didn't come anywhere near close to him. He mentally sighed; it seemed like a lost cause.

"You're supposed to come close enough to actually *hit* me."

"Oh."

So Red walked forward and swung her sword at his head. As soon as it came within a foot of him, she felt the autopilot take over, but this time was different. She didn't lose complete control of herself, and she was aware of what she was doing. In the past, she had no clue what her autopilot was doing, but now she could feel her muscles moving as she faked at his head and jabbed at his knees. She could see her sword's intended target and his sword's retaliation.

After a short bout, she saw a moment where his chest was unprotected, and her autopilot made her body kick him, making him fly back five feet. After he was no longer in front of her, she regained complete control of her body. She smiled and laughed at the sword.

"What's so funny?" Ricky asked as he picked himself up off the ground.

She was delighted. "*I* did that, not some person that took over my body. I actually know what I am doing!"

"Well, then do it again."

She did so by walking up to him and swinging her sword at his belly. This time, Ricky looked into her mind while she was fighting and saw that she was indeed aware of what was happening. He didn't have to kill her.

He disengaged contact by stepping out of her swinging range; thus, she regained control of her body.

"I just noticed something," she said. "Whenever you are reading my mind, I have a headache. Why's that?"

"Why does that interest you?"

Red shrugged.

"You don't need to know."

"Does that mean that you don't know?"

"No. It means that I don't want to tell you."

"Then you *don't* know."

He growled, ending the conversation, but she was right. He sheathed his sword and told her to give him hers; after that was done, they went to the forest to work on walking quietly in the woods.

A week later, he was thinking about how his mind-reading caused headaches when the answer seemed to show itself to his brain for no reason. His brain pushed upon anyone else's, wanting to meld and join together. Once his brain was melded with another's, then he would be able to use his power.

The next year proceeded much like the previous year, with one exception. Instead of explaining weapons to Red, Ricky would make her use them. If she had paid attention to his explanations the year before, then she understood the basic principles of each weapon, but some of them were just odd. She had no idea how to use a mace, but when she did, she handled it like an expert. Ricky found that to be a quite annoying characteristic of hers; she was a pro with any weapon she touched.

Every night for at least an hour after dinner, Ricky and Red would sword fight. It was a rare thing for him to point out a flaw in her form or any other novice problems. In fact, without trying to be, she was better than him. Of course, he never told her this.

———

The morning of Red's twelfth birthday, they did not go running as usual. Ricky handed Red a sword and told her to attack him, something that had become a routine that they both followed strictly after dinner. It was odd for him to start it in the morning. By then, Red had perfected several leading moves that would trigger her autopilot, so as soon as he handed her a sword, she swung at his left hip.

He blocked it, but her autopilot did not take control when he retaliated by parrying her swing and lunging at her belly. She dodged to the side and stared at him as he seemed to bring his sword back slowly. In reality, he was moving as fast as usual, but Red was moving so fast he seemed slow. He swung sideways at her, and he seemed to be swinging through jam. She moved her sword between his and her body, effectively blocking him.

He took so long to move his sword that she noticed something she had never noticed before: his wings were slightly unfurled. She had a headache, so she assumed that he had noticed her observation; this was emphasized by the fact that they tightened on his back. They fought for a few minutes with Red trying to get used to controlling her body when fighting; then she saw his wings unfurled again. Before he could fix that, she swatted an attack of his away and twirled to his right, toward the wing that was unfurled. He would have to turn to block any attack of hers, but with his wing unfurled it was just a little too much time. Red had her sword on the front of his neck, holding him in a headlock, before he could have turned around.

Red smiled because it was the first time that she had bested Ricky that fast.

"Let go."

Red held on a few seconds longer, then obeyed. Ricky stood back all the way up and looked at her in a way he had never looked at her before, with respect.

"Over the past year, your body has been teaching you how to fight. I guess you were listening."

That was the closest thing Red had gotten to a compliment from him.

A few weeks later, some guests arrived. There were two to be exact, the queen's younger brother, Prince Kardum, and his niece, the queen-to-be Alexandra.

As they got out of the carriage, Ricky and Red stood at attention.

He looked at her and asked, "This is the Raggy?"

"Do I disappoint you?" Red asked.

Ricky shot her a glance, but she didn't see it.

"You're young," he answered. "You two show me what you got. Save the pleasantries for later. I'm bored, so go ahead and attack each other."

Red was waiting for this and had her sword drawn before Ricky so much as blinked. He had his own out before she could do anything. They entered a place that they had gone hundreds of times before: combat mode. Red aimed a downward swipe at Ricky's knees, but he parried and swiped at her neck. As they continued, each blow got more and more deadly; if one of them had relaxed for a split second, he or she would have died.

"Stop," said the prince.

Red and Ricky stood motionless, Red with her sword held in the air and Ricky with his sword right on top of that. They were in what was called a power lock. The prince peered at them from every angle and then declared that they were both very precise swordsmen.

"How?" asked Alexandra.

Kardum looked askance at her and said, "I thought you were not interested in combat."

"I am. It's just that Kim won't let me learn. She says that a queen has no need of combat training, but she herself practices with her bow every day."

"Your mom wasn't able to fight."

"And that's how a mob of her kind," the princess started sarcastically, pointing at Red, "a peaceful race, overcame her. I think it's important!"

The prince's answer to that was a tight-lipped, "Go do twelve-year-old stuff and leave the fighting to those who know how to do it."

"The Raggy is twelve."

"Go!"

With a glare at her uncle, the giantess stomped into the surrounding forest. Kardum looked down at the two still assassins and told them to continue. They did so, if a little less vigorously. An hour later, he had them stop and get washed up. Then they went to a place in the woods where there had been three chairs set up. The prince started the following conversation.

"Well, Red, what are your thoughts about Raggies?"

Red's left eye twitched, but otherwise she did not respond. The prince gave her a few minutes, but it soon became clear that she wasn't going to answer him.

"If you don't answer, the queen will take it that you still think that you can rescue them, and then she may force Ricky to give you over to I again."

"I cannot rescue them."

"And if I told you that I have a Raggy in my carriage that I am going to bring to Alebu?"

No emotion showed on Red's face. "Then I would say, I hope you run into thieves on the road."

He thought about her answer for a minute.

"Ricky, what is she best at?"

"Fighting, no doubt about it."

"And her weakest skill?"

"Running and making poisons."

Kardum nodded. "Well she is a Raggy; they're known to only be good at one thing per person."

Red's anger flared, but it didn't show on her face. "And I'm proud to be a Raggy."

The prince's lip twitched as he sat there staring at Red. "You do have guts."

Red just looked at him.

That was not well thought out, Ricky told Red in her mind.

Actually it was. I'm trying to get someone mad at me.

You accomplished that, at least in my regard.

Red smiled at both men.

"Leave, Red. Go do something," said Kardum.

Red nodded and left.

After a minute, the prince asked, "What was that about? What was she trying to do?"

"She was trying to annoy you."

"Does she have a death wish or something?"

"I have no idea; not even her thoughts explained it."

Red sat at the base of a tree a ways away but still in sight and stared at a dagger in her hand.

"So what do you think of my apprentice?" asked Ricky.

"I'm not sure yet. Does she ever talk like that to you?"

"She did at first, but then I beat the meaning of servitude into her."

"So she is probably going to have to stay with you or die."

"I'd prefer if she stays with me."

"Getting attached?"

"No, she is a great asset if she is under control. If she is not, I agree with you: she needs to be extinguished."

"Does she talk much to you?"

"We normally converse mentally."

"Then you should contact her right now and let her hear this next stage of her testing." The prince paused for a second. "She is to kill my niece, the Orvian girl I brought with me."

"Isn't she the future queen?" asked Ricky.

"Yes. That is why the queen, my sister, wishes her dead so that only she may have the throne."

At the fact that the prince had just implied his authority over the assassin, Ricky nodded and answered, "Yes, sir."

Ricky told Red what to do then went out of her mind.

Red took off toward the hill where she noticed the princess disappear over earlier. At the other side, Red stood in the shadows and watched the Orvian girl who was her age making a dirt replica of some valley or another. Red picked up a dart she was carrying on her belt and tried to throw it, but it wouldn't get away from her hand. She couldn't kill this girl.

Red unsheathed her sword and stepped into the light. The princess looked at her and stood up.

"Let me guess, you were told to kill me."

Red's raised eyebrow answered her question.

"And I'm not dead. Why?"

Red looked as confused as Alexandra. "I have no idea." Red shrugged. "I can't kill you."

"That's good, I guess."

"The only problem is that if you do not die, I will."

"Yes, that is a problem."

There was silence as both girls scrutinized the other. Red tried to lift her hand, but it wouldn't move. She had been trained to keep her emotions off her face, so the princess didn't see the war going on in Red's head.

"I am going to need proof that I have killed you, even though I won't."

"You can cut me with your sword and spread the blood all over it as proof that I am 'dead.'"

"Good idea, but you are going to have to do it. I physically can't hurt you. I have been trying to."

The queen-to-be raised her pitch-black eyebrow and took the hilt of the sword Red offered. She took it and cut a gash in her hand; she then spread her blood all over the sword. She handed the sword back to Red.

"Thank you," said the princess.

"You are welcome. The prince would probably kill you, so you have to walk back to wherever you live."

"I will. I won't forget you, Red. I promise that if we meet again, I will not forget this act of kindness."

"What kindness?"

Red turned on her heel and walked back to Ricky and the prince. Once she was in his sight, Ricky went in to Red's mind to see how she had done. He made no outward sign, but Red knew that he knew she had cheated.

Ricky said, "Wow, impressive."

"What?" asked the prince.

Act like you did kill her. I won't kill you this time. *You better not do this again. Ever!*

"The princess is dead, and she will never be seen again," said Red.

I'm going to pay for this, aren't I? Red asked Ricky in his mind.

Yep, you're also going to have to explain to me exactly why you did this.

"Good, I thought you wouldn't do it. Your first assignment is to infiltrate a Raggy group that gets caught, but then escapes within one day. I want to know their secrets, and I want them executed. They are being held right now in Alebu."

"Yes, sir," said Ricky. "We will leave as soon as we are ready."

The guest left at noontime. Ricky and Red left at the same time as their guest, but they traveled in separate directions. After they had stopped for the night, Ricky asked the question Red had been dreading.

"So, why didn't you kill her?"

"I just couldn't. I tried, but it didn't work. My body wouldn't do it, and I had no inclination to do so."

"Did you go soft because she was your age?"

"No! I'm telling you I just was not physically able to kill her!"

Red recalled the memory, and Ricky pondered the information he had just received.

Red asked, "Do you know what it means?"

"Yes, but I'm not telling you. All that you need to know is that you're going to be punished for it."

After a few minutes with nothing happening, Red asked, "We're going to rescue Raggies?"

"No. We are getting them out of Alebu, finding their secret, and then killing them."

This saddened Red, but she said nothing. Ricky stomped out the fire and told Red to go to sleep. They both fell asleep with troubled minds.

TREASON

In the morning, Ricky punished Red. She felt the beating, but she tried to disconnect herself from the pain like she tried to do the five other times he had beat her.

Ricky was operating from a state of anger. If she had so much as cried out, he might have actually killed her; he was that mad. He stopped as he heard a snapping sound. Red was on the ground, and tears were coming out of her eyes. He stepped back in horror, for her right ankle was at a very unnatural angle, even for a Raggy.

"Okay we're done," Ricky said.

They then packed up camp. Ricky still expected Red to keep up with his jog. He was upset at seeing her hurt; he had never broken any of her bones before. They came within sight of the fort called Alebu at dusk the next day. Red wasn't speaking at all, but she was wearing her only shirt that wasn't red. That indicated that she thought being around him didn't deserve her favorite color.

"You're probably wondering what your backup story is. You run away from your foster parents in Syn-Cynthia, and you heard about them so you have come to free them. That's all they need to know. You have to actually spring them and KO the guards; otherwise, they will know something is up. I'll be in your mind, and I'll be following you around."

Red sighed, unsheathed her sword, and walked toward the gate of Alebu. When the two Orvian guards saw her, they took their battle-axes from their belts and yelled at her to stop. She did not take their warning and kept coming. She blocked the pain in her ankle out of her mind and ignored it until later, when she would deal with it. As she came within the range of the guards, one swept with his ax high while the other swept low. She jumped over both and chopped off the hands holding the ax that was swung high. The handless Orv ran away from the fort and into the surrounding countryside.

His comrade yelled, "To arms men!"

The whole fort came alive with that call. Red's brow creased as she hit the remaining guard over the head with the handle of her sword.

Multiple people combat. It seems as if I forgot to go over that, Ricky joked to Red, but as soon as he saw what her mind looked like, he left—fast.

Her mind was full of anger and hate. They burned so hotly against him, if she were a volcano, everyone within a hundred miles would die.

Red walked into the gate and drew a second sword with her left hand. Five Orvs came running at her. She had them all either dead or knocked out in less than a minute. Another Orv came running, and before he knew what was happening, Red had a sword pointed at his throat.

"Where are the Raggies?" Red asked sternly.

Recognizing her from two years earlier, he answered, "In the dungeon. Find the stairs leading down somewhere to the right."

"Thank you," said Red as she knocked him out.

She found the dungeon but had to fight through at least ten Orvs to get there; it was definitely in a different place two years ago. She took the keys from one of them and went to the cell that the Raggies were in. As she tried to find the correct one, she heard people coming.

Red threw the keys at them and told them, "Try to get out. Don't take too long."

Orvs came down, and Red kept them busy as the Raggies tried to unlock the cell. About the time that they had finished,

Red finished as well. There were four yellow-eyed Raggies, two blue-eyed Raggies, one silver-eyed Raggy, and one green-eyed Raggy in the group. They looked at the people on the floor and then at Red with awe.

At this Red said, "Stop staring, it is kind of rude."

"Thank you," said a blue-eyed Raggy.

"Don't thank me until we're home free," Red answered.

Red led the way out of the fort; on the way, they ran into ten Orvs. At the gate, thirty came out on their tales.

"Keep running," Red yelled. "I'll catch up."

She then ran back to dispatch the people following them. As soon as the Raggies found a suitable resting place, they stopped and had a conference.

"Is this really happening?" asked a blue-eyed Raggy.

"As far as I can tell," answered the green-eyed Raggy. "All I know is that the guards knew nothing about it."

"What about the fighting Raggy?" asked a yellow-eyed Raggy.

"There was something in her mind that was not supposed to be there, but I don't know what; that is why I didn't mind speak to her."

"I thought you wouldn't do that until you know if someone is for real anyway."

"Okay, anyway no one mention it."

Red appeared out of nowhere and said, "Mention what?"

Improvising, the green-eyed Raggy said, "That we are kind of freaked out about you, we didn't want to offend you."

"Oh, okay," said Red, only a little upset. "I'm Red."

The green-eyed Raggy introduced the group starting with himself. He was Jach, the blue-eyed Raggies were Fern and Thrive, the silver-eyed Raggy was Rattio, and the yellow-eyed Raggies were Acrito, Deran, Falloo, and Fico.

"Let's get out of here then," Red said. She squinted at Jach and asked, "Do you guys know where to go? I have no idea."

"Yes, let's head west," said Jach.

That is toward Syn-Cynthia, but not by the most direct route, Ricky told Red in a brief mind-speaking second.

Jach gasped, and Red asked why.

"Oh, I'm just not used to seeing red eyes."

Red shrugged it off, and they headed out. While they ran, Ricky followed and tried to do so without having to look in Red's mind or being seen.

She is not for us. Someone mention Red's limp, I want to make sure she is not hurt, Jach told all the Raggies. They agreed.

"You seem to be having trouble keeping up, Red. Are you all right?" Acrito asked between breaths.

Red spoke through gritted teeth, "Yah, just a minor wound."

"Let me look at it," said Jach. "My specialty is the body. Everyone, stop."

Red stopped, shrugged, and pulled up her pant leg. Once she saw it, she sat down on the ground. It was purple and puffy; you could even see a bump on her leg that was a part of her bone. Jach got on his knees and poked it.

When Red winced, he said, "How in the world are you even using that leg?"

"Sheer determination, and it doesn't hurt as bad as it looks."

It was a total accident, Ricky told Red.

Oh, be quiet! You kind of have been leading up to it, don't you think? Yah.

Jach frowned and asked, "How did you break it?"

"I tripped or something." The excuse sounded lame to just about everyone.

"Please sit. I'll put a splint on it. Under normal conditions, I would ask you to not move it for days, but these aren't normal."

"That's the understatement of the century," muttered Thrive.

Jach continued, "One of us could carry you, if you'd like. Falloo can make a backpack out of leaves and bark in four minutes flat."

"No, thank you! I'd rather run with two broken legs than be carried around in a bag."

"You may change your mind after this," Jach said as he put his hands on Red's ankle. He pushed them both together, forcing the bone back into place. Red was taken by surprise and yelped quite loudly.

"You could have warned me a little."

"And then you might have tried to stop me. Doesn't it feel all better now?"

She nodded and pulled her pant leg down, saying that he need do no more even though he still wanted to put a splint on it and wrap it.

As they got ready to head out again, one of the other Raggies whispered to Jach, "Sir, I think we are being followed."

Ricky, having heard this, went on the alert, wondering how he might have given himself away.

Jach frowned and whispered back, "Why do you say that?"

"If no one is following us, then most animals would be happy to come up to us, knowing we Raggies are incapable of killing them, but I have not seen one creature this whole time."

"Maybe they know that Red here can and are trying to keep away from being dinner."

"I doubt they would know the difference between her and any of us, and the only other explanation is that someone is following us."

"Then we might as well camp here and try to lose them tomorrow," Jach said quietly to Rattio. He then said this to everybody else, "The sun is going down, and this looks like a good place to rest for the night. Let's make camp, no fire though."

As the group swept the ground for rocks and sticks, Jach's mind spoke to Rattio, telling him that he did a great job acting that part out. Jach had been analyzing Red's memories of Ricky and had found that he had great hearing and was trying to find a reason their groups of Raggies always evaded capture. The animal thing was something they used, but it wasn't the main reason. Obviously the main thing they used was Jach's mind-speaking ability.

Simultaneously to Jach's congratulations to Rattio, Ricky told Red the following, *I am going to report. I think the catchers would like to know the fact about animals so that they can better catch runaway Raggies. Can you cope by yourself for the night?*

I can definitely handle myself with eight peaceful Raggies. You know the next time we fight, it will be the fight to the death.

I know it will probably happen eventually; I am sorry.

Only because I can beat you in a fight.

I'll be back around dawn. So saying, Ricky left Red's mind and walked to a spot where he could fly off without being seen.

Red had cleared off her own little space to sleep in and had gathered some grubs to eat. As she ate, she watched the other Raggies acting like normal Raggies—flopping, poking, laughing, and just having a merry time. It was obvious that she had spent little to no time with her own people.

Needing something to do, Red walked twenty yards away and took out her sword. She flipped it into the air and caught it by the blade, not cutting herself. She started rotating it as fast as she could; her hands only touched the blade for milliseconds at a time. She just stood there flipping and spinning the sword because it relaxed her. Not once did she cut herself.

Jach voice came from behind her, saying, "It feels good not having Ricky around, doesn't it?"

Red's hand slipped, and she cut her finger on the sharp edge of her sword. She put the finger in her mouth and asked, "What did you just say?"

Jach repeated himself.

Red took her finger out of her mouth and held her sword with both hands. "How do you know about him?"

"I mind speak. I know you are not really trying to rescue us, and I know that you were ordered to kill us once you learned our secret, which, by the way, is me. But I also know that you couldn't kill the princess. I am betting that you couldn't kill us."

Red was uncertain, and her stance proved it; she was squatting in the normal fighting stance, but her sword tip was lowered to the ground.

"We are leaving now, while he is gone. If you want to come with us and be free of him, be my guest."

"I thought that Raggies don't have powers."

"That's what we tell people, but we are just as likely as humans or Orvs. My power is reading the mind, and I can look back into memories as well."

"And if I don't want to go with you?"

"Then we will be forced to bring you along somehow."

"And how do you plan on doing that? I will not go with you. If I did, Ricky would *kill* me."

"Literally?"

"I have no idea what that word means."

Red had relaxed a bit from her defensive stance and was now barely crouching. From behind her, she heard the hiss of air going past a flying object and turned around just in time to see a rock one inch from her head, and then she was knocked out. Deran stood over her with the rock in both hands.

"How did you do that?" asked Fico, coming out from behind the bushes.

"I have no idea. The thought came to me to do it, and I replied as if on instinct."

"Can you do it again?" asked Falloo.

"No, the feeling is gone now." Fico looked down at Red and thought aloud, "I wonder if it had to do with her?"

"It doesn't matter right now," Jach said. "We have to be away from here before either she wakes up or the dragon comes back."

The Raggies went to work getting a bag made to carry Red in and climbing trees in order to look out for Ricky. They left within six minutes with an unconscious Red. They sped along the countryside.

Four hours later, Red awoke. One of the other Raggies was carrying her sword, so she had to use her metal to get out of the bag. Her metal were knives that were naturally sheathed inside a special hollow somewhere in her body. Every fighting Raggy had had such metal, some in the form of one knife, others in the form of two smaller ones. Red had two smaller ones sheathed in the gums of her teeth.

She took one of these tooth-knives and cut a line in the bag and sprang out. Rattio, who was carrying her, felt her weight disappear and called for a halt. Red was running away in the opposite direction.

Surround her, Jach told everybody else.

They were faster than her, so this was easily accomplished. Red stopped when she ran into Fico. She was in a circle of Raggies. She did not have a weapon, so she got in a hand-to-hand stance instead.

"Red, we are miles from where we last knocked you out, and you have no idea which direction we have been taking. I will not force you to come with us any longer, but if you leave us, there is no guarantee you will find Ricky, or even that you're in Rov any longer."

"And how do I know that you're not lying?"

Jach ignored her accusation and told the others to get going again. They left a bewildered Red staring at their receding backs. She had no idea what to do, so she followed them at a distance. There was a full moon that night, so Red was able to follow from fifty feet pretty easily. They stopped at dawn the next morning. A curious Thrive asked Jach the question they were all wondering.

"What did she do?"

"She is following us. You guys get some sleep; I'll take first watch and wake someone up in an hour. After four such watches, we will get going again."

There was a sigh of relief throughout the group at the news of Red. After the others had fallen into an exhausted sleep,

Jach looked with his mind to see what Red was up to. She was watching his group sleep.

Why don't you join us? There is room.

You are annoying.

Me? I'm not the one in a group but not in the group. If you don't think that is annoying, you probably don't think anything is annoying.

If Ricky finds us, I can say that I was keeping tabs on you by staying far away. If I'm in the group, he'll think I'm running away with you.

If you come down here, I'll make a splint for your ankle.

I'm fine, thanks.

Get some sleep, kid. How old are you anyway?

Twelve.

Okay. Go to sleep.

Jach then left her mind and continued his watch, not telling Red that he had spotted a gold glint on the horizon. Ricky was on the hunt.

———❦❦❦———

Ricky was not thrilled about the Raggies' disappearance, but he wasn't surprised either. They had a reputation of disappearing, and the fact that they did it to him was no surprise. The surprise was that Red was gone too and that she had left no message, like an arrow. He had to find and punish her before his next scheduled report in a week, or he would be ordered to kill her. He didn't want to kill Red because he had used two years of his life on her, and he was actually starting to care about her. Not like a lover, but more like a father. It was weird really. If she had run away with them, she would probably fight him when he caught up to her, and if she did, one of them would probably die. The key word here was *probably*. It was possible that Red was taken against her will, however improbable. All these thoughts ran through Ricky's head as he looked for the runaway Raggies.

He searched for a whole week, but all that he found was a scrap of cloth from a blue shirt that didn't help anything. It was a week from his last report, and if he didn't report then the queen might send someone to find him, and put a blemish on his near perfect record.

"That's it!" Ricky said aloud. He then flew straight northeast, toward the capital, Orvinta.

———⟡———

Red, it has been a week. I don't think he is going to show up. Why don't you join us?

I am beginning to have my doubts too, but you never know. He is an expert. Since it has been a week, when he does find me, he may have orders to kill me.

Then join us!

I could still talk my way out of it.

If you aren't part of our group, I'll start our evasion tactics, and you won't be able to follow us anymore.

But won't the others be uncomfortable around me?

Why do you say that?

I'm just so different…

You haven't been around your own race long enough. Come join us.

With that, Jach left her to her own thoughts. Red thought for a moment, and finally came to a conclusion. She walked toward the Raggies. A call came up as Fern saw Red coming. Everybody tackled Red and they rolled around in an undignified, giggling heap. Red was taken by surprise, but found the exchange thrilling.

"Okay now," said Jach from the bottom of the pile. "Let's get a lunch and start off again. Everybody, off."

One by one each of them peeled themselves out from the pile. They got their own lunch and started running again. This time, she felt freer than the last time Red had run with them. They were more open and more conversational now that she had decided to try to be one of them.

Red had more fun that day than she had had since before her tenth birthday.

———⟡———

Ricky saw the castle in the distance, and the scales on the back of his neck prickled. He was about to risk his life on a little girl he had beat up! What was he thinking? It was the last moment to go back, and he decided his final course of action. Ricky landed near a sunroof, where he had landed so many times before, but not nearly as quietly as he did in the past. He looked in the throne room of the queen's castle. She was occupied with an officer in the army. As he waited until she was alone in the room, he played in his head what he was about to do. He heard a call from inside. He jumped in.

When Ricky landed in front of the queen, she could tell by the look in his eyes—the fact that he had landed loudly—and his posture that something fatal had happened. She waited for him to speak.

"I am as of this moment a rouge."

Queen Kim sighed, put her head on a hand, and asked, "Why in the world would you do something like that? It's not that I'm surprised, all the non-Orvian assassins always do, but why?"

Ricky's response was not one that she expected. "Red ran away."

"And I would have ordered you to kill her and those with her, and you could get on with your life. You're going to kill her anyway, right?"

"Yes." Ricky lied, not wanting to expose that weird feeling in him. "But it is as good an excuse as any."

"I'd understand if I wasn't paying you enough, but because your apprentice ran away!"

"Good-bye, Your Majesty."

Queen Kim stood, towering over the assassin. She yelled, "Guards!"

Ricky ran in order to gain momentum so that he could launch into the air better, but he ran out of floor. Instead, he ran up the wall. He was flying out of the skylight before any of the guards could so much as draw his bow.

Now to go get that Raggy, he thought to himself.

BLINDSIDED

It was another week before the Raggies reached their destination. By then Red had warmed up to the others. They walked up to a town Deran said was called Fith. They were in the country to the west of Rov that was known as Syn-Cynthia. As they passed happy farms, with kids playing around their houses, Red couldn't help but miss her village. It seemed as if it had been forever since she had played ball with the other kids. They passed all of the farms and went into the market.

As they passed through the market at Fith, a girl appeared out of nowhere right next to Jach. She had short, red hair and wore a dress with a sword belt around her waist and a shield strapped to her back; she appeared to be about twelve or thirteen. The oddest thing about her was that during the following events, her eyes changed color from a dark green to an orange and then to a brown-and-black mix.

"Hi, Jach! Are you all safe?"

"Whoa! Where did you come from? Yes, we are safe."

She pointed in a direction and said, "Over there. Good, and is Ricky following you?"

"No."

Red looked at the girl like she was crazy. "How do you know about Ricky?"

"I'll explain everything later. I just need you all to get in the closest building and stay in it. *Now!*"

All of the Raggies hurriedly ran into a store to their left—that is, all of them except Red. She stayed behind the crazy girl, who didn't seem to notice her. She walked past all of the happy homes and told those outside to go in. As soon as any one saw her, they would immediately drop everything and do what she said. Red thought about what this girl must have done to garner so much respect.

The girl, with Red following, stopped at the edge of the town on the road, just past the last house and stared at the road. They were now in the plains of Liebochney and were able to see for miles; thus, it was not an astonishing fact that Red saw a large group of Orvs about five miles away. Neither girl said a thing as the Orvs got closer, but the odd human did glance at Red. As they got closer, Red also noticed a few humans among the group, but they were a minority.

When they were about one hundred yards away, the girl yelled, "Stop right there!"

The large company did not stop, but kept coming. A few of them even drew their weapons. When they were fifty yards away, she yelled again, but still, they did not stop. Finally the girl had had enough, so her whole body burst aflame. That made them stop in their tracks.

She looked directly at their commander and asked him, "What is a whole platoon of Rovian soldiers doing heading toward a Syn-Cynthian border town?"

Red could tell he was annoyed as he replied, "Nothing that concerns you."

"Everything concerns me. You are coming to this peaceful village to pillage it and take its Raggies, yes?"

He looked at her slack-jawed. "How do you know that?"

"I just do. If you or your men come even one step closer, I will retaliate."

He looked perplexed. "But then we have to go back."

"Then go back!"

As she spoke, the girl had increased the amount of flame coming off her body so that there was an inferno between the soldiers and the town. Some of the soldiers broke out into a run back to Rov, and pretty soon they all were running away. Red, who was only a foot away from the girl, felt a wave of heat wash over her, but it was gone in a moment.

The girl yelled after them, "And don't come back!"

The flame on her body was then gone, and she turned to Red and smiled. She said almost jokingly, "Didn't I tell you to go inside?"

Red was confused, so she just said, "Yes."

The girl sighed, "You're no fun."

She walked back to the middle of town calling the all clear and ignoring Red again. She made a beeline for Jach and told him, "I'm taking Red."

Jach squinted at her. "Why?"

"She might end up hurting you if she stays."

"But—"

The girl cut him off, "Red, come with me."

The girl walked off, and Red looked back and forth between her back and Jach. He rolled his eyes and motioned for her to follow the girl. She led her the other way outside of the town, and no one followed them.

A few hundred yards away from the town, the girl turned and faced Red.

"I'm Tess, you're Red, and there are our introductions. I know things I shouldn't know because I am a prophetess, and you are a liberating Raggy who thinks that she can't save Raggies. Am I right?"

Red hesitantly nodded, still confused.

"So you would have chickened out at an importune time—thus, strengthening your idea. Do you understand?"

"No"

"Well, you don't need to. I'm going to prove your idea wrong."

Red just stared at her.

"You've had a tough few years, haven't you?"

Red kept staring at her.

"You are going to The Fort with me."

"Which fort?"

"It's technically not a fort; it is the capital of Syn-Cynthia. People named it The Fort because it moves around so much that everyone who lives there lives in tents."

Red shrugged.

"You need to learn to talk. Follow me."

The girl called Tess walked away from Fith and Red, expecting her to follow. Red longingly looked back past Fith to what she knew to be the Rovian border. She sighed and followed Tess.

About the time the sun went down, Tess stopped and pointed to a spot just off the road.

"We'll camp there. Could you collect some grass for fuel for a fire? Whenever I do, it bursts aflame before I get it to the spot I designate it for."

Red nodded and used her sword to chop some long grass and brought it to Tess. She took it from Red, and as soon as she touched it, it caught on fire. She hurriedly put it in a bunch on the ground. Red stood about five feet away from her, watching her as she seemed to become mesmerized by the crackling fire. She passed her hand through it, and it came out holding a small ball of fire. She shook herself and looked at Red.

"You should get some sleep. I'll keep watch."

Red lay down on the opposite side of the fire and closed her eyes, wondering if Tess was only going to watch the fire.

——⟨ΘΛΘ⟩——

As they walked down a country road the next day, Red took in the sights of peace and prosperity. She felt strangely at ease with Tess, who was easily hyper and very talkative. Red was definitely not either of those; she was more standoffish and quiet, which was accentuated by what Ricky did to her for training. She had always been more of a loner, but she did enjoy watching other people instead of conversing.

Tess noticed this in Red, so she just really talked about nothing in particular. Eventually both of them were quiet and enjoying the fall afternoon. Around noon they stopped, and Red gathered bugs and other things that she preferred to eat, but Tess did not eat anything. Tess said the first thing either of them had said for a while.

"What do you believe about God, Red?"

"What do you mean?"

"Like, do you believe that there is a God, and if so, what do you think is his purpose for all of this?" Tess said, waving her hand around and indicating their surroundings.

Red thought for a minute as she ate her bugs. Finally, she answered, "Yes, I do believe that there is a God. I also think that he puts random people together just to see what happens and is happy about any outcome. He has fun watching us go to the top of a mountain and then plummet down in a ball of flame."

"That is a gloomy outlook. How did you figure that?"

"That is how it seems in my life."

"So you think that an unknown God randomly threw you and I together?"

Red shrugged.

Tess stood up as she said, "Well, I think that he brought you to me with a purpose."

"Why is that?"

"He wants you to know the real him." Tess swung a backpack around her back and put her hand out to help Red stand up.

"What if I don't want to know him?"

"He is God, and he wants you to know him."

They walked in silence for a while before Red said, "What do you believe about God's character then?"

"He loves everybody—"

"That's impossible!"

Tess acted shocked at that statement.

"Why in the world would you say such a thing?"

"A loving God would not let Ricky do what he did to me! A loving God would stop the Raggy persecution!"

"But he has! He put you here with your power, and Ricky did what he did by himself. God wouldn't stop his free will."

"What power do I have? All I can do is hold my own in a fight."

"And how long did you have to train before you were able to do that?"

"Almost two years."

"Exactly, that's power. It took Ricky eight years."

"Then I have no choice but to save my race?"

"Exactly, he is going to use you to save the Raggies one way or another." She pointed to their right and said, "Let's camp on that clover patch. I know it is really early, but the sooner you hear this, the better."

Red shrugged, a popular movement for her, and set her blanket down on the clover. Tess put her blanket next to Red's and looked at the ground in front of them. A sapling grew from the ground. In less than a minute, it was a full-grown tree. In another thirty seconds, it was a tree older than any on earth or anywhere else. It seemed to shine with a green, healthy radiance.

"Now, Red, I want you to close your eyes and imagine what God looks like, how powerful he is."

Red did so with some reluctance. "Please try to describe what you are seeing."

"I see a being made of power. He can do anything he wants to. If he so much as blinks, the whole world is gone. He is perfect, ultimate, and ultrapowerful." Red grinned. "I didn't even know I knew all of those words."

"Open your eyes and imagine that this tree is God. Of course, it is not, but for the sake of my example, it is."

At Red's timid nod, Tess continued, "God, in his ultimate power, wanted someone to socialize with, so he created people."

Out of the ground came a sapling. It grew until it was half the size of the big tree and radiated life. "The people and God lived in harmony for a while. He gave them a garden of such beauty that it beat all imaginable gardens by leaps and bounds. He only gave them one rule: 'Don't eat the fruit of the tree in the middle of the garden.' An evil angel had rebelled against God, and he wanted to destroy God's perfect creation. Look behind us."

Red looked behind her and saw a black tree that was very depressing. That tree seemed to suck the light and life from its surroundings. The ground around it was black and desolate.

"He told one of God's people that God didn't want them to eat of the tree because it would make them more powerful. She ate the fruit and gave some to her husband, who also ate it. This, the first sin, made them join the evil angel. It made them submit to him and gave him all of their real power."

Red watched the smaller tree get up and walk toward the black tree. As it moved, it grew darker and darker. It stopped next to the evil tree, and it looked totally devoid of life, yet it was alive.

"Since they were the parents of all the people, their seeds all fell into the evil ground. They all were born in a world of sin. There was no way out."

Tess was silent as seeds dropped from the dead tree next to the black tree. These seeds grew and multiplied, all on the evil ground.

"God knew this was coming, but he had to give them the choice of doing wrong; otherwise they would have no choices and no real feelings. Love cannot be understood by people without the ability to choose it. It would have been forced servitude. He gave them rules to live by, but they sinned and broke them. He gave them sacrifices to redeem themselves, but that only did so for a very short period."

The whole time that Tess talked, the forest of living trees that looked mostly dead grew.

"Again, God knew this would happen. He did all of this to prove to them that they could not save themselves."

"But," Red interrupted, "they have no choice to join God."

"Which was exactly what God took care of. He loved them so much that he decided to go down and teach them himself. God, the creator of everything, the all powerful, humbled himself by becoming a man. Not just any man, a baby. The Lord of all made himself dependent on the people he created."

The great tree shrunk back to the size of a seed. It rolled into the black forest.

"You would expect God to have himself born to royalty; he did deserve it. Instead, he was born to a lowly teenage virgin. God himself was born in a stable. A stable!"

Red saw a little green sapling shaking in the wind.

"He grew up, not entirely knowing exactly who he was. He experienced the life of a normal person, a carpenter to be exact. Really, the only difference between him and the rest of the world was the fact that he never sinned, not even once."

The sapling grew to the size of the trees around it. It looked like a normal tree, not dead, but not as awesome as it had been before it turned into a seed.

"At the age of thirty, God, named Jesus, was baptized by his cousin, John the Baptist. He was filled with the parts that he had given up so that he could teach what the people needed to learn. He called twelve men to follow him, and each man dropped what he was doing and followed him. Everywhere he went, he attracted a crowd. He taught those who followed him the ways to live a perfect life."

The trees around the regular tree showed signs of becoming renewed. They weren't as dead as they had been, but they still looked really bad.

"He taught for three years. This still wasn't enough. In order for their sins to be totally forgiven, he had to give the ultimate sacrifice. What greater sacrifice was there than the life of God? Red, this next part is impossible for me to show with trees, so please close your eyes."

Red willingly obliged. She now understood that this small choice she couldn't make was not the biggest ever, but she was unsure about Tess's last few sentences.

"People who heard of Jesus either loved him or hated him; there was no middle ground. He was betrayed by one of his followers. Those who hated him had him arrested and put in a trial. The judge found him innocent, but he was so influenced by those who hated Jesus that he had Jesus beaten. Jesus could have stopped this at any time, but he didn't. He took that beating for the healing of those who believe in him.

"Still those who hated him wanted him to die. The judge, who was also a ruler, gave the choice to the people, either set Jesus free or set free an outlaw. Guided by the evil angel, the crowd wanted the outlaw set free instead. The angel wanted God to die. So, the judge was convinced by the people to kill him. Jesus was forced to carry a heavy cross up and down the hills. He was so weak, they had to make someone help him carry it."

Red could hear a sob in Tess's voice.

"He was God, and they treated him as if he were garbage. They hung him on the cross he had carried on a hill outside of a city. The soldiers in charge of him took his clothes, spat on him, and made fun of him for being God. His followers and his mom cried as he hung there, dying. He could have stopped it, but he didn't. It had to happen so that we could join him in heaven. He died with a cry, thunder, and an earthquake."

Red opened her eyes and looked at Tess, who had tears leaking out from both eyes. She looked at Red beseechingly. Red looked at the black forest and saw that the green tree was dead, really dead, in the branches of the black, evil tree. It had seemed to grow.

"God died so that you don't have to live in your sins. All you have to do is believe it happened and tell him that you accept his free gift. In fact, he made it easier by defeating the devil, the fallen angel, and reclaiming man's place as the king of the world. The way he did that was that three days after he died, he raised himself from the grave."

Red watched as the dead tree in the black tree's branches became greener and took the appearance of life. The black tree recoiled and shrunk to a size smaller than the size of the other trees. The green tree moved to an outer portion of the dead forest, and some others followed. The ones following it turned green and lively.

"Jesus defeated death so that those who believe in and follow him may have eternal life with him. Anyone who accepts his gift will find a new life in him. Plus he promises to never leave you nor forsake you. That, Red, is love."

"It is all nice in theory, but how could that really happen?"

"Red! For you to say that, it is spitting in God's face! Imagine for a second a man so badly beaten you can't even recognize him as human. Now imagine this man hanging on a cross. I want you to try and spit in his face. Just try it!"

Red shook her head and pursed her lips.

"Of course, you can't even imagine that! It would be the rudest thing to do ever! That is what your words do. Saying that there is no love is to spit on God's face."

Thoughts raced through Red's head; it was a jumble of confusion in there.

"How do I except this gift?"

"You believe me now? If you don't and you just want to get on my good side, forget it. You'd be degrading yourself. Also, before you answer, you must know that we Christians are heavily persecuted on this world."

Red wasted no time in saying, "If God will die for me, I can give my life to him."

Tess was ecstatic. "Then please bow your head, close your eyes, and repeat after me. Dear Heavenly Father, I know I am a sinner and that I have done wrong, and I know that you sent your one and only son to die on the cross for my sins. I believe that you raised him from the grave. I now receive eternal life with you. I confess that Jesus is my lord, and I give my life to him. In Jesus's name. Amen."

Red prayed it with Tess, and after she was done, she felt her heart filled. She felt God's love for her, and she felt complete. Nothing in her life had felt better than this.

Tess handed Red a book. "This is the Bible. It is God's word. It is what all Christians should live by. It explains God better than I ever could."

"Do you have one?"

"Yep, but I always carry extras just in case I run into somebody who needs one. It's getting late; we should retire for the night."

Red looked around; it was definitely late. A fire was three feet away from her blanket, and she had no idea how it had gotten there. Probably Tess. Red shrugged and went to sleep.

While walking the next day, Red and Tess talked as Red had never talked before. They talked of God and of the best places to read in the Bible, which excited Red about being able to read it that night. She did so and quenched a thirst she didn't even know she had. It was as if she had been a desert, and God had flooded her life with his word. She was now a tropical oasis.

I get it! It is all about love. How did I ever miss it? Red thought to herself. Abruptly, her thoughts turned to Ricky and how she should tell him about God.

"No," she said aloud. "He doesn't deserve it."

"Neither do you," Tess answered.

Red shrugged and wondered at Tess's quick thinking.

"And, no, I don't read minds."

"You said it, I didn't."

"It's called a calling."

"What is?"

"What you are supposed to do. The fact that no matter what you do, you will free the Raggy race. And what you are thinking right now, about sharing with Ricky, it is what God wants you to do."

"And how do you know this?"

"I just have this weird insight. You wouldn't believe me if I told you, so don't ask."

Red thought about that for a moment but decided to let the subject go.

"Are callings something you have to do?"

"Nope. Do you want to go on a mission trip with me in four months?"

"What?"

"Never mind, I'll ask you in three months."

So Red spent three months in the Fort learning about God.

A CALLING

About a month after Red's disappearance, Ricky gave up looking for her. He knew that she was now gone for good. Since he had broken his commitment to Kim, he had nowhere to work; thus, he became a mercenary for hire. He didn't know exactly where to go or who would want a mercenary, so he just wandered around Rov and Slythia hoping someone important would note his presence and run for his or her life.

Ricky ran into Red on December 20. He was in Robber's Forest, so named because it was impossible to go in for ten minutes without losing something to any one of the gangs or highwaymen. It was so densely populated with robbers because you had to go through it to get to Rov's main trade city, Orvto. The weird thing was, he had been in it for an hour, but he hadn't met a single robber or traveler. He heard talking, so he crept silently toward the sound. He stopped outside a large clearing and stared at what he immediately dubbed a convert rally.

A tall, redheaded human girl was standing on a tree limb, looking grown Orvs in the eye. There were all types of Orvs there, from vagabonds to peasants, to lords. It was happening at a crossroad, so it not only attracted highwaymen, but also the travelers. She was obviously the legendary Tess he had heard about. He could see her eyes that change colors from where he was. She was talking.

"Which is why I came, because you are being controlled by a selfish ruler. I want to show you the other side of the coin—love. God's love to be precise."

Ricky tuned her out; he had heard this crap before. He was about to interrupt when he saw a Raggy sitting at the base of a tree surrounded by a red cloak. He did a double take and saw the tip of a sword poking out from the Raggy's left side. Definitely Red. Thinking for a second, he tried to find a way to make Red join him.

When Ricky looked up again, Tess was staring right at him, still delivering her speech. She looked at Red. Ricky also looked that way and saw a flash of fire. Red turned around and saw Ricky. She ran away to his right.

Is she really running away? he asked himself, but he didn't try to look in her mind for an answer.

He followed her to a clearing; little did he know that this was what she wanted.

As he entered the clearing, Red said, "Your fight is with me, not them."

"Is that supposed to mean that you are trying to keep me away from the convert rally?" he asked.

"If I were doing anything else, you wouldn't be here."

"How do you plan on doing that? With a fight?"

"However you want to solve this. Our conflict ends today."

Ricky was confused by her allusion to what he wanted. "Then let's do it. The only way I know of to decide dominance is a fight to the death."

Red looked at him as he drew his sword. Neither of them moved. Ricky took his stored anger toward the world and compacted it into one thought: this was his fight, and she would die. Her death would be the end of his dealings with her, and Kim would have no liberator to deal with. He took all his anger in his heart and transferred it to his hands. It started to control him, and he attacked Red.

Red unsheathed her sword and easily swatted his attack away but didn't attack herself. She went into defense mode, making no offense. This just angered him further; he would give her a parry and an intentional opening; however, she wouldn't take it.

As they circled each other, Ricky asked, "Why are you not attacking, Raggy?"

Red shrugged. "If you want me to fight, I will."

Again, Ricky was momentarily confused at her reference to what *he* wanted. She charged at Ricky, feigning a head swipe and tried for his feet. He blocked that and stabbed at her chest. She hit his sword with hers and held it down while kicking at his head; he ducked and swiped at her feet.

He did a move that worked most of the time with her, a combo that normally made her dizzy because it forced her to spin to block a jab at her head with his tail and then to spin away from his tail to block a swipe at her feet. Sometimes she would try to step back from that, and then he would jab at her belly, making her go back farther. That happened this time as Red wanted it to. They circled each other.

"You know, Tess was right: you need God's love."

"You are caught up in that junk?"

"It's not junk! I can prove it too!"

"Yah right!" said Ricky as he ran at Red.

Red then did a move that he had never seen before, let alone taught her. She did this weird twirling with her sword around his, and it flew between two trees, out of sight. She held it at his chest on the left side, and they maneuvered around each other.

Red said, "Would someone sacrifice themselves for junk?"

Ricky looked confused. "No?"

"Then…" Red said as she put her sword behind her head as if she was going to throw it. Instead, she plunged it down and bent to her knee.

"I sacrifice my will to you, Ricky."

Ricky was baffled. "What in the world are you talking about?"

"I will do whatever you say."

"Whatever I say?"

Ricky was so baffled that he actually looked in her mind, something he had sworn to himself that he wouldn't do again if he caught up with her. Instead of the hatred of him that had saturated her mind before, there was love. The fire was gone and was replaced by a cool, clear, peaceful lake. He also saw that she didn't quite understand what she was doing.

"As long as it's not to kill somebody."

Ricky took time to process this. Not only was she kneeling in front of him, but she was also submitting to him, something he had never even thought her capable of without some type of persuasion. She had done what he told her to do before, but out of fear, not loyalty.

"I don't believe that you will ever be a servant; you're tricking me somehow."

"You see my mind. How am I trying to trick you?"

Ricky scowled; this plan of hers was crazy. Did she know that he would make her his slave? And she was going into this willingly? He kept the scowl on the outside, but on the inside, he was grinning wickedly. She knew he would, so he might as well take as much advantage of it as he could. He knew that she would follow her word no matter what.

"If you are so devoted to show me your loyalty—"

"No! I'm showing you God's love, not my loyalty."

"*Complete* sacrifice?"

"Complete."

"Then repeat after me: I swear to obey Ricky fully and completely, even if he tells me to do something that I don't wish to do, and I won't argue with him. I will respond to all of Ricky's questions, and I will not give him any back talk. This vow will last all of my life, even if for some insane reason he should release me."

Ricky was done, but Red added, "And I won't ever obey an order to kill a person."

"Then what use are you as an assassin?"

"I guess you'll figure it out."

Red started laughing. When Ricky asked why, she said that she had no idea. He looked in her mind, and sure enough, it was true. She barely noticed when he left; she was laughing so hard.

When Ricky came back, Red had calmed down.

"They are gone, aren't they?"

"I have no idea what you are talking about."

"You tried to stop the 'convert rally.'"

"Yes, I did, but they were gone."

"What did you expect? Tess is smart enough to go away from a potentially dangerous situation."

"Where do you think she would go?"

"Home to Syn-Cynthia."

"With or without her new converts?"

"Without. She probably gave them each a Bible and told them to tell their friends and family."

"So let's head west."

"Why do you want to follow her?"

"It's better than meandering nowhere in particular."

Red shrugged because she knew that they could never catch up with her. Of course, she didn't want Ricky to know this.

They promptly set off east. They traveled for a day, and two things became apparent to Ricky over that day: they weren't going to catch up with Tess, and Red wasn't going to stop doing whatever he told her to do. Even so, they pressed on.

While Ricky was searching for an edible plant for lunch, Red searched for a few insects. While Red searched, a thorn cut her arm. As she watched, it healed back.

Hmm, I think that will be of some use.

She did not tell Ricky about it when he came back, and she fell asleep overly happy.

Ricky awoke grabbing his sword hilt. He sat up and looked around to find what had made him wake up. The only strange thing was Red looking out into the trees and giggling.

"Red, what's so funny right before sunrise?" Ricky asked.

She shook her head and laughed at him. She managed a "nothing" before she broke out into a fit of laughter that had her rolling on the ground. He looked in her mind, and it was true, for the second time within twenty-four hours.

He scowled. "Stop laughing."

She tried to stop by holding her breath but started giggling when she let it out.

"I'm sorry…I am not really…controlling…it!"

"Then get control! Do I need to repeat the no-emotions lesson?"

Red automatically stopped and flinched.

"That's better. Since we are awake, we might as well start heading out."

"Okay."

They quickly packed up their small camp and had been traveling for a while before the sun came up over the plains.

They caught up with Tess around one. She was sitting on a low branch and playing with a fireball. She noticed them a little late, but that seemed to be fine with her.

"Finally! You travel really slowly, V-scale."

Ricky frowned at her and tried to take out his dagger from his belt without her seeing. It was no use; she noticed.

"Unless you want to have the scales on your left hand burned off, don't even *try* to attack."

"Then why did you wait for us if you aren't wanting to fight?"

"I knew that you wanted to get rid of me in order to appease Kim. I knew you were coming too. So why did I wait? You tell me."

"I have no idea!"

"Aren't you wondering why Red doesn't hate you anymore?"

Ricky looked at Red, who was trying really hard not to laugh.

Ricky was silent for a moment. "Kind of, but can't she tell me?"

"She's not going to be able to talk for the next week, because she is in her giggle week."

"Giggle week?"

"Every Raggy goes through it once in his or her life, and if you make them stop, they'll be extremely moody for the rest of their life. You only kind of want to know why she doesn't hate you?"

"Okay, not just kind of, but what has this got to do with anything?"

"She was going to try to tell you herself, but like I said, she won't be able to in time."

"In time?"

"If someone doesn't try to explain this to you within the week, then something terrible will happen, but it will be very hard for her to carry on a conversation in just a few hours."

"I'm confused."

"Can you please stop trying to take that dagger out"

Tess's hair had caught fire, so Ricky stopped. Red started laughing, and she walked away so that she wouldn't interrupt this important moment.

"Red doesn't hate you because she was shown love beyond comprehension."

"If it's beyond comprehension, then how can you be shown it?" Ricky argued.

"Because every Christian has seen it and wants to show it to everybody. We show it by acting like Christ, and he doesn't hate."

"So she traded her hate for love, and she wanted to show me that? I still don't understand why she can't tell me this."

"Well, get over it. The only way she could think of was to pledge herself to you. She thought that you wouldn't notice her change unless she forced you to."

"This is all intriguing, but I really don't see—"

"You have a one-track mind, sir. Maybe you should think about what I'm saying for a second. God changed her; it wouldn't be any harder to change you if you asked him to."

"What makes you think that I want to change?" Ricky said as he unsheathed his sword.

"You are tired of killing. You stopped being Queen Kim's assassin because you care about Red. She opened that part of you, the love. Now, you just need to widen it."

How in the world does she know this? he thought.

"So, how does he love anyway?"

"Sit down, this could take awhile."

Ricky sat down hesitantly, with his sword in front of him. Tess told him the same true story that she had told Red about Jesus. She used the same tree illustration as well. At the end, Ricky said nothing. He had his chin in his hand while he stared at his sword.

Finally, after a few minutes, he said, "He died to forgive *me*? Do you even know what I've done?"

"He knows every sin that you have committed."

"Then he definitely won't forgive me. I'm a piece of trash that's not worth saving."

Tess smiled inwardly. *The Holy Spirit is convicting him!*

"God sees you as a priceless piece of jewelry worth his own life. God thought that your life is worth his! All you need to do is accept his gift and live for him."

"Live for him? Does that mean to give up my life?"

"No, God makes you the best you, better than you are now and better than you can imagine. He'll bless your life beyond your own hopes and dreams."

"What would I do besides being an assassin? You're asking me to give up the only lifestyle I've ever known for a bag of riddles."

"Not a bag of riddles, a book of wisdom." while saying that, Tess took out a Bible.

She held it out to Ricky, and he just looked at it for a few minutes. Then he took it.

"It'd be best if you started by reading in Matthew. The rest is additional stuff for us Christians."

Ricky growled a bit in frustration and tucked the book behind his belt. He still wasn't sure about this Christian stuff. He looked up; he saw that Tess had already stood up.

"When you accept God's gift, tell him by using Romans 10:9. Build a relationship with him. I need to be off. Trouble at home, you know. Oh yah, and always pray in Jesus's name."

Ricky watched in bewilderment as she flew off while engulfed in a ball of flame. He had no idea what to do. It was obvious that she didn't want him to be able to follow her, so he just sat down and read the book she had given him. Red came back a few minutes after Tess left, and she was only giggling a bit. When Ricky looked up at her, she started full-out laughing again.

It was annoying him, but he realized for pretty much the first time that Red was a Raggy, and that was usually how Raggies acted. He laughed a bit and kept reading. Red eventually giggled herself to sleep.

The next day he set off in a random direction and traveled for all of five minutes because he was having a war within himself. He had just started feeling as if his life was missing something.

Red managed to get a word out in between bouts of laughter, *love.*

Just that one word was enough to convict him. He had never shown love, and there was no one in his memory but Red, who had recently shown it to him. If Tess was right then, there was someone else who genuinely loved him: God.

Ricky looked at the sky. He said, "Okay, God, I believe."

Then he remembered what Tess had said, so he looked up Romans 10:9 in the Bible she had given him. He then finished what he had been saying.

"You are Lord, Jesus. I believe that you died for my sins and rose from the grave. Thank you for loving me and saving me. In Jesus's name, I pray."

He really didn't feel all that different. He still felt dirty.

"I wonder how I could become a better me."

Red started laughing harder even though she had kept it at a giggle for the last few hours.

"What's so funny?"

He looked in her mind, and she had a response.

Just hearing you say those words is such a relief.

"Well, I guess I need to learn how to be a good guy."

He spent the rest of that day reading the Bible. He went hunting and cooked his kill that night. The next few days passed by similarly. He found whole new meanings in each sentence that he read. He analyzed and cross-analyzed the meaning of many verses. He actually found it refreshing to think for a long time on how to act instead of how to kill a dignitary.

Three days after Tess left, Ricky asked Red while she was just waking up and barely giggling, "Will you please forgive me for how I have treated you?"

Red cocked her head to the side and nodded without laughing. For the first time, Red wished that she could look into his mind to see if he was being truthful.

Red managed to say, "How about we go to Syn-Cynthia?"

"What's there?"

"Tess."

That was when Red started laughing, so Ricky started to read her mind so that they could converse.

And other scholars that could help us with our brand-new faith.

"We have Bibles."

But we cannot do this by ourselves. We'll go back to being assassins.

Ricky had to think about that for a minute. "You're probably right. Let's go there."

She nodded, laughed, and doubled over. Ricky wondered if her laughing week was ever going to end.

SELLING OUT

Red stood on an auction platform in chains listening to rich lords and ladies determine the fate of a pretty human female. She noticed Ricky in a dark robe standing out like a sore thumb in the corner of the outdoor market. It was impossible to tell who he was, but it was easy to see that he was different from the frilly ladies and the ornate lords. He had only agreed to this crazy plan as long as he was allowed to make sure she wasn't sold to a torturous soul.

Tess inspired the plan, and Red had grabbed it up. She was taking a step of faith and trusting God to put her where he wanted her to be. Tess had asked one of the powered people named Niki to change Red's eyes and skin brown, and she made Red's hair black and straight. If Red massaged her temples, something she never did out of habit, all of her color would go back to normal. She looked 100 percent human, and the only thing she had to do was not use her nonhuman joints.

Red had gotten caught by slave catchers on the Syn-Cynthian and Rovian border, and they had rubbed whiskey on her arm to make sure that she was not a Raggy. Red had smiled inwardly when her skin stayed brown.

Two slave guards grabbed Red's chains and dragged her to the front of the platform. The auctioneer yelled out, "This is a strong little twelve-year-old female human. She'd make a nice breeder. Starting bid one hundred dahls."

A flag was raised, and the auctioneer said, "One hundred going–"

Another flag was raised with a shout, "Hundred fifty!"

The first flag popped up with a, "Two hundred!"

The price went back and forth between the two increasing by fifty each time. The second voice let the other win at four hundred.

"Four hundred going once, going twice, sold to the count!"

The man walked up to the platform, and Red was led to him.

Ricky entered her mind, *He's buying a welcome-home gift for the princess. Are you okay?*

Red looked at the sharp-nosed count in front of her. His beady eyes bored into her and inspected her whole body. He indicated for one of his assistants to hold her chain.

I'm fine with it. My only problem is this weird headache.

Haha, Red, very funny.

He left her mind and walked away, not letting any part of him be seen. He disappeared into the crowd. After that, the count bought another twelve-year-old human with white skin, blond hair, and blue eyes; and his party left. His assistants put Red and the other new slave on the top of the count's carriage. Red fidgeted as the carriage rolled to its destination.

The other girl decided to try to converse. "Hi, I'm Zera." She held out a hand for Red to shake. Red preferred not to shake hands because her own hand was more floppy than a human's hand, and she didn't want anyone to notice that.

"I'm Ache," she said, ignoring the outstretched hand.

Zera carefully put her hand down and watched the passing buildings. Red was afraid that she had seemed rude, so she asked Zera where she was from.

Zera answered, "Ki-Vee in Slythia. I was headed to Syn-Cynthia when some slave catchers took me captive. Where are you from?"

"Hume, here in Rov."

"How'd you get caught?"

"I was coming back from a trip to Syn-Cynthia when I ran into a band of slave catchers."

There was silence as they pulled into a gate in front of a sizable mansion. The count got out right in front of the doors leading in, but no one else did. The servants got out at the stable and took Redache and Zera into the house through the back. Some of the household slaves gathered around the two new slaves. They took off the chains and led the girls to an unoccupied room. In that room, they were pampered to an extreme for five hours, while being taught the fundamentals of being a slave to royalty. As they had pedicures, manicures, haircuts, and facials, they were supposed to sit straight and not move to practice being around royalty. The servants put make up and new dresses on the two "lucky young ladies."

Red hated the entire process; her body yelled at her to *move,* but she didn't. Instead, she quoted second Timothy 1:7 in her mind. Zera loved the process of being pampered and dolled up. Red thought that Zera looked amazing in her dark-blue dress with gold lining and silver embroidered stars, but she hated the feel of the silk of her own dress. It was bright yellow on her right shoulder with light blue beneath it and then a field of wildflowers beneath it.

At four o'clock, it was finally over, and Red thought that she could slouch. Nope. An older lady told them the basic rules of being a slave:

1. Answer only direct questions with "Yes, ma'am" and "No, ma'am."
2. Do everything that is demanded.
3. Sit and stand straight and never look anyone in the eye.

After that crash course, they were put into the carriage. After ten stuffy minutes, the count climbed in and sat across from them. Neither girl looked him in the eye, as instructed. They didn't fidget and sat up straight, also as instructed. This was *incredibly* hard for Red to do, but she kept saying second Timothy 1:7 in her head and managed to do it.

The carriage lurched forward, and the following ride seemed endless to Red; eventually, the carriage stopped, and the count got out. Neither Red nor Zera moved until the carriage moved and stopped again. A page opened the door and peered in.

"Where are the presents?" he asked.

"We are they," Zera responded.

The boy nodded and told them to follow him. He led them into a castle. There were two castles; one was in the center of the capital and was Queen Kim's home, and another was a mile away from the capital, much smaller, and had been built by Kim when Alexandra was two to get her away from the capital. The page led them through a side door into a grand ballroom and to a stack of things. He told them to get on their knees behind the things, and they complied.

That night there was a party being held for Alexa's homecoming. After Red didn't kill Alexandra, Alexandra slowly made her way back to the capital over the time period of a few months. She had thought that her uncle was the one who ordered her assassination, so she went to Kim and told her what happened. The temporary queen faked surprise and had an execution date set for her "traitorous" brother. He told whoever would listen that it was Kim's order, but no one listened. That night was the execution with the homecoming party afterward, which every noble was required to attend with a homecoming present by Kim's order.

The ballroom with the enormous gift pile containing Red and Zera had two incredibly large doors that none of the servants who were serving food on the tables around the dance floor or bringing in presents used. As soon as those doors cracked open, an hour after Red and Zera arrived, the servants fled through numerous concealed doors. The huge doors opened, and Orvian nobles entered. There were ladies with frilly dresses and their escorts with medals and important-looking clothes. After they were all there, the doors closed. Once the hidden orchestra started playing, the nobles quieted and looked at the doors. The doors opened in agonizing slowness, and the royal entourage entered. All those gathered bowed.

First came two criers followed by a slave-carried litter with Queen Kim sitting on a throne in the center. Then a smaller figure came in with eyes flashing, Princess Alexandra. Both of them wore crowns, with Kim's bigger; wore jewelry, with Kim more; and wore splendid dresses that put the nobles to shame. Kim's throne was put on a raised dais, and the princess stood to her right. Alexandra bore an untrusting look, and anyone who dared look at her was met with a scowl.

An army of pages formed a line next to the presents. A noble would tell a page which present was his or hers, and the page would carry it behind him or her in the line of waiting nobles. Once a noble got to the throne, the page would hand him or her the gift, and he or she would present it to the princess. The nobles who had finished the ceremony or were waiting for the line to get shorter mingled and ate the treats on the tables.

The girls' master beckoned them to join him in the line, and they followed on his heels. Waiting in line was never enjoyable to a Raggy, so Red was having trouble staying still *and* waiting in line. She managed to pull it off by imagining a battle that she had just read about in her Bible. Finally, they were first in line.

Alexandra was both happy and sad at being back into the politics. She had been avoiding civilization on her way back to her aunt to stay hidden; therefore, she was accustomed to quiet. She had to get used to all these people and the noise for the first time in her life. She was also wary of the many nobles who might want to kill her. She had just watched her uncle's head chopped off, so she thought that if she couldn't trust him, she couldn't trust anyone. She didn't touch any of the paintings, tapestries, or other gifts presented, but just nodded in thanks and told the pages to put them in a new pile.

Then Count Blerg came with his present: two female humans. Alexa was immediately suspicious. Were they trained to kill her?

"Your Majesty," said the count, bowing to the princess. "I give you two of the finest slaves I could find on the market. For the queen, I bring my loyalty as a humble servant."

He backed away, and the girls went to the pile of presents. Alexandra was going to have to deal with those two that night.

⋘ ❧ ⋙

Red and Zera watched nobles slowly leave the ball, unable to stay awake any longer, but unwilling to leave. Once they were all gone, Alexandra sent her aunt's servants back to the capital, for only five of them served her. Among those were two cooks, two maids, and a librarian/tutor. The princess stretched her cramped limbs, and Red saw a new scar on her palm. Alexandra looked at her new slaves as if they were a threat. She walked up to them with short, slow steps. When she was five paces away, she told them to stand up. She looked them up and down, inspecting the folds in their cloth for sharp points.

She asked a question that Red was kind of expecting, "Are either of you trained assassins?"

Zera said a surprised, "No, ma'am!" But all Red could do was shift her feet in uneasiness.

"Well? Answer me!"

Red couldn't lie, so she said nothing. The princess stepped right in front of Red. She put her finger under her chin and forced her to look her in the eyes. Red knew what she had to do, but she thought it might be humiliating. She swallowed loudly, made her eyes go as wide as possible, and started to hyperventilate. The princess glared down at her.

"Are you dumb, human? Answer me!"

Come on, self! Do it!

Red's vision minimized, and all she could see was the princess's eyes filled with fear and hate. Her blood rushed in her ears, and she felt a tingling in her whole body. She was trying to make herself pass out because no assassin could pass out in front of his or her target. The problem was, Red was an assassin, and she couldn't pass out. Her senses returned to normal, and she was still standing.

"If you don't answer me right this second, I will have you executed for treason," Alexandra said through gritted teeth.

Red took a hint from a roundabout answer Tess had once given her and said, "If I were an assassin sent to kill you, then you would be dead right now."

"So are you saying that you are an assassin but not sent to kill me?"

Red could find no way to get out of this without lying. She prayed a silent prayer and said, "Yes."

The princess backed up and said, "Then what is your name, and why are you here?"

"Ache and because I ran away from my master and was caught by your authorities."

Alexandra smiled. "How long have you trained?"

"Two years."

Alexandra's smile fell a little but remained in place. Red thought that it might've hit a familiar chord.

"What was your master's name, and why did you run away?"

Red knew that she knew who Ricky was. These questions were getting harder and harder to answer. Just then Ricky entered her mind.

Red quickly asked, *Do I tell her about you?*

Ricky assessed the situation. *No. The less she knows at this time, the better.*

Red had an idea.

"I ran away to become a Christian."

"You are a Christian!?" Alexandra said appalled. "You believe in a god? That is illegal here."

"And in Slythia."

The princess nodded.

"You are going to teach me how to fight, and in return, I won't have you killed for not being atheist. Deal?"

I really need you to tell me the basics about sword-fighting that we skipped, Red told Ricky.

"Deal."

Ricky told Red the basics as the following conversation passed.

The princess then turned her gaze to Zera, who had listened to that conversation with awe. She was still looking at the ground when the princess looked at her.

"And you said that you are not an assassin?"

"No, but I am a Christian."

Alexandra looked at the bold girl. "Of course you are, Count Blerg is, so he got me two Christian slaves. I won't have you killed unless you try to sell me your mumbo jumbo. I've heard it before, so I know what it sounds like. Understood?"

"Yes, ma'am."

"You both will sleep in here tonight, or this morning, whichever it is, and I'll find you both more appropriate clothing."

Both slaves said, "Yes, ma'am." And the stately princess left.

Alexandra had an established schedule that she had to get back to the next day. Breakfast was at seven thirty, lessons started at eight and ended at three with a thirty-minute lunch break at noon, and finally dinner was served at six thirty. The rest of the day was hers to do with as she wished.

The slaves were not allowed anywhere near the library by the princess's orders, so during that time, the two girls chatted. They told each other how they had been led to Christ and of ideas of how to bring the princess to him. All of their ideas ended in Zera dieing, so they eventually stopped that line of conversation. At three, Alexandra told the girls to follow her to her chariot. That day, they went to the market and bought three wooden swords and two sets of leggings and shirts for the slaves. The last thing that was bought was a small mattress for both Ache and Zera. They were expected to share.

They got back at the castle at sunset, and the slave bed was put outside the door of Alexandra's room. Once the princess had retired to her room, the girls had to decide who would get the mattress.

"Do you want it tonight, and then I'll have it tomorrow?" Zera asked.

Red shook her head. "You can have it all the time. I'm used to sleeping in random places."

"Oh, are you sure?"

"Positive."

So Zera got the mattress in front of the door, and Red slept on the floor.

TRAINING OTHERS

After the princess's lessons, the three girls went to one of the three unoccupied rooms. There Red taught them some basics. They did push-ups and sit-ups and other exercises until Alexandra's muscles were quaking, which was thirty minutes after Zera had to stop. Orvs were naturally stronger than humans, so it confused Alexandra when Red could keep going. She didn't show off much, but she hadn't even begun to break a sweat.

"Right, now time for the fun part."

Red stood and stretched. It was four o'clock; thus, they had only worked out for an hour.

"How in the world are you standing?" Alexandra managed to puff out.

"I've done it for years. You haven't."

The princess managed to struggle to her feet. "I will not sit where a *human* can stand. What's next?"

Red smiled and thought to herself that the princess would be more outraged if she knew that it was a *Raggy* standing where she had to sit.

"Now, we run outside."

Zera struggled to stand and asked the princess if she could skip the rest of the exercise that day. Alexandra flatly denied that request, so they all filed out into the snowstorm. It was January, and the weather did not want people outside.

Red yelled at her trainees through the gale, "Take as many laps around the castle as you can, but don't die of overconfidence."

Red set off at a jog, and the other two followed. Red was not and never will be fast by any standard except that of slugs and turtles. Within five yards, the princess had passed her, and within another forty, so had Zera. Zera stopped halfway around the castle and went in the back door. That was all she could handle.

Alexandra didn't understand the running in the snowstorm, but she put as much energy as she could into it. She had done two laps and stopped at the front gate. She had her hands on her knees and felt like if she took one more step, she would collapse. Then Ache's voice came from behind her.

"Get your hands off your knees and put them on your head! If you stay like that, you are going to throw up!"

The princess muttered something very inappropriate about the bossy human that Ache did not catch. She came up beside the Orv and asked, "Are you done?"

Alexandra nodded, and they went in. Ache was breathing evenly, and the princess sounded like a horse that had pulled a wagon a few miles in a canter, what with her puffing in and out.

"That was supposed to be fun?" Alexandra gasped.

"Oh yah! It's way better than other things I went through."

"What things?"

"Running in one hundred and five degrees and when you pass out finding your master with his sword at your neck telling you never to do that again or he will kill you."

The princess was shocked at that. Then a thought hit her.

"You know, I've only ever heard of one female assassin, and she was a Raggy."

"A Raggy would make a terrible assassin."

"No! She was better than anyone! Don't you ever insult that Raggy."

Ache held up her hands in submission, but Red's inner thoughts were glad that the princess's reaction was so strong. She almost revealed her secret right then but restrained herself. It wasn't time yet.

"Sorry!"

"Now can we do some actual sword work?"

"What do you think we were doing, lollygagging? First, we worked on strength, then stamina, and now we work on finesse."

Alexandra was too tired to ask what that meant, and she was a little scared when Ache took a torch from its place on the wall. Red was tempted to start twirling the torch, but she concluded that that would be beyond the skill level of an average two-year-trained assassin. At the spare room, they found Zera sitting in a corner with a towel around her shoulder and shivering as if she were still outside. Red couldn't help but think that if Ricky had found her like that, he would've beaten the living daylights out of her.

"Come on, Zera, you need to toughen up," said the princess.

Red didn't think that was nice, but she stilled her tongue. Ache gave her torch to Alexandra and took another one off the wall for Zera.

"What are we doing with these?"

Zera was too exhausted to say anything. Red got herself a torch and told them to try to do what she was doing. She moved the torch so fast that it seemed like she wrote an *A* in the air with fire. The princess tried but was too slow; Zera tried, but her arm gave out too soon.

Alexandra was frustrated. "How is this supposed to help anything?"

Ache didn't say anything but picked up one of the wooden swords. She drew an *A* in the air with the sword and then said, "The first up of the *A* is a diagonal upward swipe, the down is a diagonal downward swipe, and the bridge is a quick feint. All of which are quite important moves."

Alexandra tried again and failed again. She tried until her right arm was too tired to continue, and then she switched to her left arm. At five o'clock she was too tired to continue. She slumped against the wall and joined Zera, who had stopped shivering. The princess was no longer drenched with melted snow, but with sweat.

"Princess, you should take a shower."

Alexandra stood up slowly and said with anger, "If you ever, *ever*, call me princess again, you will not only be executed but also tortured beyond recognition. Understand, human?"

Ache nodded at the figure looming over her.

"I don't want to be called Alexandra, either; it's way too formal. You are both to call me Alexa. Got it?"

"Yes, ma'am," they said.

"And if I hear another *ma'am* from either of you, I'll send you, Ache"—Alexa pointed at Red—"back to your assassin master."

Zera nodded in fear, but Red was about to burst into laughter. Alexa went out of the room and slammed the door behind her. The two other girls stared at the door. Ache giggled a bit, but Zera took it as nervous giggling.

What they didn't know was that Alexa was starting to warm up to them. The only people she ever wanted to call her Alexa were people whom she was around a bunch or trusted. Since she had only known them for two days, it was probably because she trusted them. Another sign that she was warming up to them was that she got angry with Redache. She had been trained since she was three not to show emotion in court and to have a perpetual poker face, so if her concentration shifted, it was around someone she was sure could handle it.

After Alexa took a shower, Zera then Ache did as well. At six thirty, they went to the small dining room next to the kitchen. There was a table that seated six in there, and all those six spots were claimed, so the slaves had to eat on the floor. Red didn't see why they all didn't want to eat on the floor with their stew in their laps, because that was how most Raggies preferred to eat. They usually hated stiffed-backed chairs.

After dinner, the girls went to Alexa's room and sat on her bed.

Alexa declared, "I want to know how both of you came to be my slaves. Zera, start from the beginning of your life, please."

Zera had to take a minute to put it together in her head.

"I was born and lived in Ki-Vee in Slythia until I turned eleven. When I was ten, a traveling missionary converted me to Christianity. Because Christianity is prohibited in Slythia, my own family persecuted me. I ran away a week after my eleventh birthday because instead of showing love and companionship, my family burned my Bible. I went through Slythia like a refugee. At the border of Rov and Slythia, some slave catchers took me captive. I was sold to an unrighteous man who did many bad things to me. Two weeks ago, he sold me to the market, saying I was not worth keeping anymore. I was then sold to Count Blerg, and you know the rest."

"What sort of bad things did your former master do?"

As Zera explained the horrors she had gone through, Red scrambled for true bits and pieces that would tie the parts of the parts of the story she had already told Alexa.

When Zera finished, Alexa looked at Ache and said, "Your turn."

"I am from Hume, but then I was taken by some of Kim's soldiers when I was ten. I ran into the assassin who eventually became my master while in the middle of a humiliating ordeal. I was with him for two years before I got the nerve to run away, and that was with help from someone who had a power."

Red paused to think, and Alexa urged her to keep going.

"A few weird things led me to being converted to Christianity by Tess of Syn-Cynthia, and eventually I came back to Rov where I ran into slave catchers. I was sold to Count Blerg for four hundred dahls."

Alexa looked Ache up and down, but said nothing.

She started her own life story. "After I was born, a group of racist Raggies killed my mom, Queen Ruth, but my dad ran into the basement with my aunt and I before they could kill us. He was too late to save Mom. He abdicated the throne and let Kim step in. Since then I have been taught how to rule my country, which I will inherit when I turn eighteen."

"A few months ago when I was going with my uncle on a diplomatic mission, he tried to kill me. I got away and walked back here. He was executed, and you know the rest."

Red narrowed her eyes because she knew more than one part of Alexa's story was a lie; therefore, she wondered if Alexa knew that the beginning was a lie. They talked a little more but stopped once they were tired, which wasn't that long in coming.

The next year or so was really no different in any way except the conversations, weather conditions, exercises, and the meals. Red used the same training techniques until both of the other girls could write the whole alphabet in the air one at a time with a torch; then they switched to using the wooden swords. She taught them the basic moves: slash, parry, lunge, etc. Once they could do what she called out automatically without a pause for consideration, she taught them harder moves. A year after their first exercise session, Alexa could do ten laps around her castle without stopping and lapped Ache three times in the process. Ache would do those extra three while Alexa recovered. Zera could do five laps nonstop and keeping up with Alexa, but she had to stop after that. Only once they were both as tired as possible would Ache let them start sword practice.

At a year and a half from the beginning, they actually started sparring. The problem with that for Red was that she had to pretend that she was an average two-year trained assassin. The only physical thing Red was average at was running. It did help a little that her body would not allow her to hit Alexa. She tried to extend that cone of protection to Zera as well, but that barely worked. Luckily, they didn't comment on her skill. She guessed that they thought she had more practice; thus, she was better.

Around their second year of being together, Alexa didn't show up to the spare room on time. In fact, she was thirty minutes late. Ache and Zera went looking for her and found her sitting on her bed surrounded by her pillows and sobbing her heart out. Ache was about to scold her, but she softened. She and Zera quietly and slowly got onto their places on the bed. Alexa didn't notice them until her heart-wrenching sobs died to quiet bursts.

"What's wrong?" Red asked.

Alexa looked up at her two slaves. In answer, she said, "Ms. Writ, my tutor, told me the truth of my mom's death. She died because I was born!"

She looked back down at her hands and cried silently.

"It would've been better if I had never been born," she said.

"You shouldn't question God's decisions, Alexa," said Ache.

Zera took up Ache's idea. They were sticking their necks out. "He made you the way he wants you."

"Why did he make a meaningless life like mine?"

"You are to be queen of Rov!" Zera answered. "Is that meaningless? The creator made you and loves everything about you. Why would he make something that is meaningless?"

Alexa stopped crying and looked at Zera with hope in her eyes.

"And if you feel meaningless," said Ache, "then serving God sends a whole new meaning to life."

"He loves you so much that he died for you, giving you something to live for. All you have to do is accept his gift and serve him."

"How do I do that?"

"Repeat after me," Zera started. "Dear Heavenly Father, I admit that I am a sinner, and I am sorry that I have not believed in you. I now believe that Jesus, your Son, died on the cross for my sins, and I believe that you raised him from the grave. Jesus is Lord, and I allow him into my heart to change me and give me meaning. Thank you for saving me. In the name of Jesus Christ I pray. Amen."

Alexa prayed it with Zera and felt satisfied and complete. She didn't understand it, but she felt peace.

"Now you need to build a relationship with him, but for that, we need a Bible," said Ache.

So they went to Ms. Writ. When they were at the library, Alexa said, "I know that this will sound very, unusual, but I need you to get me three Bibles."

Ms. Writ's left eyebrow went up in surprise, and she smiled. "What would you need a Bible for?"

Alexa answered strongly, "Building a relationship with God."

She was surprised when her sixty-year-old teacher clapped and jumped up and down like a schoolgirl.

"You're all Christians? Oh! What a relief!"

"You are a Christian?"

Ms. Writ wore a bold smile. "And I am proud of it! I have a stash of Bibles that I would be happy to share. Follow me."

They followed her to the very middle of the library. She unhooked a small door to a hidden compartment. In there were at least ten Bibles that the girls could see.

Ms. Writ explained, "Once Bibles became illegal, I bought and gathered as many as I could. Whenever I encounter another Christian in need of one, I give them one. Before you left with your uncle, I was beginning to run low, so while you were gone, I went to Syn-Cynthia and replenished my stock. I got back about the same time you did."

Each girl picked up a Bible from the hidden compartment. Instead of doing physical exercises that day, they did some mental exercises. With Ms. Writ, they started at Matthew and analyzed every verse, gaining wisdom and satisfying thirsts that had grown in the two years without God's word.

After that day, from two to three o'clock, Alexa's lessons were dedicated to Bible study, and Zera and Red were allowed to participate. The rest of the day went on as normal. Red finally got used to sparring at Alexa's and Zera's level a month after the anniversary of their second year being together.

FOUND OUT

The rest of that year was spent with pleasant company and no changes. One cool May night, the girls started an interesting conversation after dinner on Alexa's bed.

They had just got done with dinner and were in silence.

"So, what should we talk about?" Zera asked no one in particular.

With a thought, Alexa said, "I want to know your opinions about Raggies."

Red's face remained impassive, but her muscles tensed.

Zera asked, "What exactly are you wanting us to state an opinion on?"

"Whether or not they deserve the persecution we are putting them under."

Red was thinking that right then would be a great time to tell Alexa her secret, but she couldn't do so without Ricky's permission, unless Alexa figured it out herself.

"What do you think, Ache?"

"Well, Queen Kim's whole basis on persecuting them was the lie that she made about them killing your mom. She doesn't like them and uses that to make the rest of her country exterminate them."

"I agree with Ache," Zera said

"The common thoughts are that Raggies are the scum of the earth and that Rov should invade other countries and demand that they kill their Raggy population. Since Kim is not allowed to declare war because she is not the rightful queen, she can't wage such a war," said Alexa.

"All you have stated are other people's thoughts, not your own," Zera pointed out.

"That is all Ache said as well."

Redache then said, "I think that the best thing for Rov would be to reintroduce the companionship that Orvs and Raggies had years ago, before we were born. More was accomplished then, and more people were happy."

"There was also freedom of religion at that time," Zera said.

This type of exercise was definitely best for Red. When they did a debate, one person would take a side, another person would take the opposite side, and the last person would point out flaws with both sides. This helped Red's communication skills a great deal.

Alexa added, "And the bond between a Raggy and an Orv was sometimes a cumbersome ordeal that didn't let either partner relate to another of their race, and it was hard to get either partner married."

Ache argued, "Those instances were few and far between, and usually both were content to be loners and didn't want a spouse."

"Even today there are people who God made that prefer to be alone," Zera said.

Alexa retorted, "And most of those people end up being homosexual."

"But when Orvs and Raggies were together, they didn't let each other become homosexual and would pressure them onto a different course."

"It was also possible for one to pressure the other into *being* homosexual," Zera said.

"When one of them was a Christian and the other wasn't, then the non-Christian could pull the other down," Alexa argued.

"But that bond was never nearly as strong as marriage and was much easier to break if the Christian saw it coming," Ache stated.

As soon as Red said, "Saw it coming," she had a very strange feeling. She turned and saw that the window was open. A dart suddenly appeared out of nowhere. The world slowed, and the dart seemed to be flying through water. Red lunged forward and grabbed it, rolling as she hit the floor. She hurried and shut the window. She looked and saw a figure climbing down a tree. It was not big enough for an Orv, and Orvs hated trees. When the moonlight shone on the figure, Red didn't see a golden twinkle, so she knew it wasn't Ricky.

There was a new assassin serving Kim.

Red's senses went back to normal, and she looked at the dart in her right hand. She pivoted to face the bed. Zera's mouth was agape, and she was staring at the dart, but Alexa was looking at Ache's eyes. Her mouth was in a straight line.

"Only one assassin can train for only two years and be able to do that," Alexa said. "Isn't that right, Red?"

"Red?" Zera asked.

Alexa answered, "That is her real name."

Red didn't move as Princess Alexandra stood and walked directly in front of her. This reminded her of that first night when Alexa interrogated her about being an assassin. Alexa looked the girl she knew as Ache in the eyes. Neither pair of eyes flinched.

"Are you going to say anything for yourself?" Alexa asked.

Red slowly put the dart filled with an orange liquid on a nightstand. She said nothing as she closed her eyes and started to massage her temples.

Alexa watched Ache's skin fade from a human black to a tan to a pink, and lastly to the normal Raggy paste white. After that, her straight, black hair frizzed and popped into a strawberry blonde. When Red stopped massaging her temples, she opened her eyes. Zera gasped as Red expected from knowing her so long. All Alexa did was take a deep breath.

Alexa held out her scarred palm and told the Raggy in front of her, "Tell me how I got this scar."

Red didn't flinch or pause. "I was told to kill you, and I found you in a clearing making something in the dirt. I tried to throw a dart at you, but I couldn't. I stepped out, and you knew what I had been told to do. I convinced you to cut yourself and spread the blood on my blade as proof. You did and ran away."

"What was your consequence?"

"Ricky beat me and broke my ankle."

"At least he didn't kill you."

Red said nothing. Alexa went back to her place on the bed and sat down.

"Tell me everything that happened since then."

Red did as she was told, and Alexa didn't interrupt. Zera sat quietly, knowing she was not needed right that second. Once Red was finished, Alexa took a minute to digest the new information.

"So you never lied." It was more of a question.

"I never lied to you; I just didn't tell you things like who my master was."

"I did notice that you avoided mentioning his name. You said that you will always do whatever he tells you to do. Does that mean that his word would supersede mine?"

Red nodded.

"When was the last time he came to check on you?"

"Six months ago."

"Then I want you to wait in one of my castle towers until he comes back. I will have Zera bring you food. You are not to leave that tower at all until Ricky returns to check on you, then I want you to interrupt anything I am doing and have him talk to me. Am I clear?"

"Yes, Alexa."

"Then go pick a tower."

"If I may, I suggest that you keep the windows of whatever room you are in closed at all times."

"Good idea. Now, go."

Red went out the door and was gone. Alexa sighed, closed her eyes, and leaned on her headboard.

"I guess that explains why I found her sleeping in a chandelier once," Zera commented.

Alexa opened an eye. "Which one?"

"The one in the ballroom."

The ballroom chandelier hung twice as tall as an average Orv in the air, and there was no ladder leading to it.

"And you never told me about that?"

Zera shrugged. "She asked me not to."

"Before or after jumping down and surviving that?"

"After."

There was silence for a few minutes.

"Get some sleep, Zera."

Zera went to her mattress, but both girls had trouble sleeping that night.

Red watched the sun rise from the roof of the northeast tower. She could see for miles in all directions, and that way she could see anyone coming, assassin or former assassin alike. It had been a month since Alexa had exiled her up here with only Zera's brief company, which was just barely enough to satisfy her Raggy needs. Red sighed at the sun that was bringing another hot day.

She had seen Alexa and Zera run at least fifteen laps each every day, and she was proud of them. She did her own exercises until she was dripping sweat from head to toe. At noon that day, she heard Zera ascending the ladder up to the roof.

Red looked eagerly at her visitor and saw that she carried a plate with two sandwiches. Usually she just got one for lunch.

At Red's quizzical look, Zera said, "I asked Alexa if I could eat with you."

Red nodded. It was a great improvement from the beginning. Then Zera wouldn't even look at her. She sat next to Red and placed the plate between them. Red reached for her sandwich and took a bite. She was watching the western horizon.

After a few minutes, Zera said, "I'm sorry how I reacted those first few days. I grew up being told that red eyes only belonged to demons. Now, I think yours are like two rubies."

"Thank you," Red mumbled.

This was the first time that Zera had said more than just a salutation, and Red was kind of used to silence.

"So what is it like living up here?"

"Hot."

"You're going back to when we first met! You couldn't form a complete sentence to me then either."

"Sorry, it's just that I have never been that great of a speaker."

"Except around Alexa. What's up with that?"

Red shrugged as she consumed the last bite of her sandwich. Zera was only halfway done with her own. Red scanned the ground and noticed a lone figure approaching the back door of the castle. She stood and looked over the edge of the tower. The skinny human had an array of weapons that identified him as some type of a military official, most likely an assassin.

Red turned to Zera and said, "I need you to go to Alexa as fast as you can and tell her that there is an assassin knocked out by her back door. Oh, and I need the plate."

Zera quickly handed her the plate and stuffed the remainder of her sandwich in her pocket. She went down the ladder as fast as possible and ran to Alexa, who was just finishing lunch. She told her what Red had said, and they hurried to the back door. There they found a white human dressed all in black with too many weapons to count in a minute lying on his face with broken shards of plate lying on him. Alexa looked up at Red on the tower, put the assassin over her shoulder, and carried him to one of the rooms that they never used. She took all fifty of his weapons and tied him to a chair that she took from the dining hall. She left the room and locked the door.

Alexa sent Zera to ask Red what happened, and she came back with an incredible answer.

"Red saw him approaching and asked me to give her the plate. She waited until he was close to the back door and threw the plate like a discus. It hit the back of his head, and he fell to the ground. Red also said that she thought she might charge a fee of another sandwich, but decided not to."

"She threw a plate from the tower to the back door and hit the back of a man's head! That is definitely worth another sandwich. Go get one from the cook and go give it to her."

Zera said, "Yes, Alexa!" and left to go do so.

Alexa returned to her new interrogation room. The assassin was awake.

———◦◦◦———

Red returned to watching the horizon. In a few minutes, Zera came up with a second sandwich.

"I was just kidding, Zera! You didn't have to get me another one!" Red exclaimed.

"But I told Alexa about your comment, and she insisted that you needed at least another sandwich."

Red rolled her eyes and gratefully accepted the sandwich.

Zera started to say, "Well, see you—" when Red interrupted her. "There's a dot on the horizon!"

Zera went to the edge of the tower to look and beheld a dot on the horizon that was *way* too small to be the sun but glowed almost as brightly from reflecting it.

"Is that Ricky?" Zera asked.

"It might be Tess, but I doubt it."

"Want me to tell Alexa?"

"No, I'll tell her myself if it is him. You go watch that assassin like an eagle watches prey."

Zera nodded and left.

———◦◦◦———

Alexa and the assassin eyed each other.

"How was I caught?" he asked, breaking the silence.

Alexa answered with a voice as sweet as honey, "My Raggy threw a plate at you from a tower."

"You lie!"

"Nope. I want you to tell me who hired you."

The door behind her opened, but Alexa did not bother to look at Zera come in and stand to her right.

"Why would I tell you anything? Who said you are my target?"

"So you were coming to my castle to kill someone."

"I didn't say that!"

"But you implied it."

Alexa saw the anger in his face. Obviously he had need of better emotions training.

"I am not talking any more to you!"

"But you just did, and that means that you need to hide something from me."

He said nothing.

"Am I your target?"

The assassin just looked at her with hate.

"I'll take that as a yes. On just that, I could have you executed, Mr...."

His look became one of fear as he said his name, "Jontosh."

"Who is your master, Jontosh?"

All he did was glare at her.

"Glaring at the future queen of Rov is a ground for torture."

"You wouldn't be here to be the queen if I had not been caught!"

"So I was your target. Who sent you?"

"Someone who wants you dead."

"I get that, but I need a name."

Suddenly he sprung up from the chair, his bonds cut. He held a dagger in his hand and stabbed at Alexa's chest. A white blur came from her left and knocked him over. Red had him on the ground sitting on his chest and was holding the hilt of his dagger. Red forced his arm to the ground, and he tried to get up, but she squeezed her knees until he couldn't breathe. Red wrenched the dagger out of his hand and held it at his throat.

"Luckily for you, Alexa, Ricky is here."

"Where?"

Ricky's deep voice said, "Behind you."

Alexa twirled to see Kim's former assassin looking the part, but he didn't have nearly as many weapons as the human had.

"You really need some other defense besides Red," he said.

"No kidding." Alexa's heart was still beating a mile a minute from the close call.

"What do you want me to do with him?" Red asked.

"Make him tell who sent him and kill him if he doesn't cooperate," Alexa said.

Red winced a little but said that she would. She heard the door close behind her, and she knew that she was alone with Jontosh.

"You know," she said to the captured man, "from one assassin to another, it would be easy for me to kill you, but I don't want to. I repeat. I will kill you if need be, but I don't want to."

Jontosh nodded.

"Who sent you to kill the princess? Tell me true or don't say a word."

He tried to buck her off, but all it made her do was push a little harder on the dagger at his neck. She was looking into his eyes, and he couldn't hold her gaze.

"Who?" Red pushed a little harder.

The man gulped. "Just kill me now. I'll die if I tell you, and I'll die if I don't."

"No. Not yet."

The assassin plunged a dart that he had hidden behind his belt into Red's shoulder. She fell limp. Jontosh grabbed the dagger she dropped and snuck out the door and went to go find Alexa. He was sure that Red was going to die because that dart contained venom from a hundred daddy long legs, which was said to be the deadliest venom of all.

———ᴕᴥᴕ———

Alexa was trying to figure out the dilemma that was now standing before her; his name was Ricky.

"I do not like that idea in the slightest," said Alexa.

"But it is her decision, not yours," Ricky argued.

"It has nothing to do with her. I trust her with my life, but I *don't* trust you in the slightest."

"Why not?"

Alexa put venom in her answer, "Your reputation precedes you, *assassin!*"

Ricky breathed hard and fought to control his temper, which was starting to rise up. He had refused it room enough times that it disappeared in a few seconds.

"I gave up that title when I accepted Jesus Christ as my Lord and Savior."

Alexa mumbled something that she didn't mean for him to hear.

"Just because I told Red to kill you doesn't mean that I was the one who initiated the order. Is that why you don't trust me, a grudge? While I'm thinking about it, I must say that it wasn't your uncle who initiated it either. It was your aunt."

"You know this for sure?"

"Yes, you don't seem surprised."

"I'm not in the least surprised. I would bet that she was the one who sent Jontosh to kill me."

"Wait a second, did you say that the assassin's name is Jontosh?"

"Yah, why?"

Ricky started running back to where they had left Red.

He yelled at Alexa as he left, "He is the only other person I can see succeeding at hurting Red!"

On the way there, he saw Jontosh and stopped in front of him. He was leaning against a wall, fiddling with the dagger.

"Hello, Ricky. So I heard that you quit."

"You heard right."

"Then I must thank you. The king of Slythia had run out of jobs for me. I have this gig for the queen of Rov. Pays one hundred thousand dahls, if you're interested."

That was a bunch of money, but Ricky didn't even have to think about it.

"Nah, I like being the good guy."

Alexa appeared around a corner, and Jontosh gripped the dagger harder.

"If you just step to the right about a foot, I'll give you half."

Ricky looked back, saw Alexa, and drew a dagger of his own. He advanced upon the assassin.

"You're not going to touch her."

He grinned and threw his dagger over Ricky's shoulder. In the split second he had, Ricky deduced that he did not have enough time to catch it with his hands, so he crashed open his wings. The dagger hit the upper left-hand corner of his right wing, and its momentum snapped Ricky's wing backward at an odd angle. Ricky walked over to Jontosh and had knocked him out before he was able to discern his intent.

A small growl escaped from Ricky's throat as he pulled the dagger out of his wing and folded it back onto his back.

"Are you okay?" Alexa asked.

"I'm fine." But he didn't sound fine, what with the half growl that came out with.

———❦❦❦———

Red felt numb. She fell over, and the dagger dropped from her hands. She had the weirdest sensation of not being able to move any part of her own body. She couldn't breathe, her heart wasn't beating, and she couldn't move her eyes. Luckily, that only lasted for a heartbeat. She would've died had it been longer. She still couldn't move anything, but her bodily functions were working.

Red said a silent prayer, and a few minutes later, Ricky came rushing in. He looked at Red in dismay and bent down to check her pulse. He sighed with relief when he saw that it was there.

He was still thinking about the thing that he and Alexa couldn't agree about, so he couldn't look in her mind and let her know about it before they agreed.

Alexa came running in, and she stopped when she saw Ricky stooping by Red.

"It's okay. She's alive."

"Good, but are you sure that you are okay?"

"Yes."

"What did he do to her?"

"He hit her with a poison dart." He held up the dart for her to see. "This dart has purple venom in it. Purple is only used for one type of spider venom, daddy long legs. It instantly paralyzes the victim and shuts down his or her internal organs for one to five heartbeats. If it is more than two, the victim dies, and if the victim can't move after that within ten minutes, it happens again, but longer. The problem is that no one has ever been able to move."

"No one has ever survived?"

"No one."

There was a dead silence for a few seconds.

"I think I forgot to tell you something," Red said as she sat up.

Ricky stared at her.

"I heal fast."

There was quiet for a minute.

"You've changed, Ricky," Red said.

"Why do you say that?" asked Alexa.

"He knows."

Ricky nodded because he did know. It was because he would have never come running to her aid before, let alone protect the princess.

Red leaned on the wall and declared that she was going to take a nap. She was asleep in three minutes, but by that time, everyone was gone.

—⟨◈⟩—

After they left the room, Alexa said to Ricky, "You really do care for her."

Ricky breathed in and slowly let it out. "Yes. Yes, I do. You know at one point in time I would have thought that caring for a Raggy meant certain death."

"Me too."

Alexa looked at him for a moment or two before she said, "All right, if she is okay with it, I'll be okay with it, but if she refuses, then I want you gone, and don't you ever come back."

"That's a little harsh."

"If she trusts you, I will; if she doesn't, I won't. And if that's the case, I don't want you around telling her what to do."

Ricky nodded. "I understand."

"Do you want a bandage for your wing?"

"No, thank you, I can take care of myself."

Ricky left to attend to his wing and take care of Jontosh.

———

Red awoke in the chandelier again. The only difference was that she didn't remember getting up there herself. She stayed up there and soaked in the peace of nothing to do.

Are you okay with being up there? Ricky asked.

How did you know that I like heights?

I was in your mind for two years with the only rests once a week at the very most. It's hard not to learn your likes and dislikes.

Oh.

I was wondering if you would like to meld with me.

Meld! When did that idea cross your mind?

A month ago. Does that mean that you don't want to?

No, it means that I am surprised. I am going to need to think about that by myself for a few minutes.

I'd understand if you said no.

I haven't said anything yet!

Ricky left her mind with a, *Okay, I'll give you five minutes.*

Red thought about it. First, she would need to know if he had indeed changed. She had learned what he had been doing when he checked up on her, so she used what she knew to inspect his fruits. He had repented, and she had forgiven him. From his actions, she could tell that he meant it. He had been living a solitary life and was content with it, and he was not envious of those better off than him. She wondered if he had developed a selfless attitude.

She also had to know if she wanted to do it. If she said yes, then she would have his voice in her head 24-7, and whatever he told her to do, she had to do. If she said no, then she would have to wait for months to get permission for something important. She prayed about it and then looked at what her heart wanted. For some reason, she did not object to it. When he came back into her mind, she checked him for a selfless attitude. She saw that he, indeed, had it since he had protected the princess.

Yes, I'll not object melding with you, Ricky.

But do you want to?

For some crazy reason, I do.

Okay then, come outside the back door.

Red jumped down and landed with no pain because she flexed all of her leg joints. She landed in front of Alexa. Red hadn't noticed that she was there.

"So what did you decide?" Alexa asked.

Red knew that Alexa knew, but she didn't know how. "I decided that I will."

Alexa nodded but said nothing. Red wondered if she was disappointed.

She walked to the back door and each step had a thought of turning back. Red was not a quitter. She walked out the door and met Ricky there.

"Thank you," he said.

"Thank you?" Red echoed.

"Once I meld, I can use my power."

Red raised an eyebrow. "Is that your only reason?"

"Nope. You are the only person that I trust enough to be in my mind, Red."

"Then let's get it over with."

Ricky extended his mind to Red's, and she grabbed his wrist. Ricky's mind locked into Red's with no headache caused. Red let go of his wrist, and their minds were intertwined until they died. They couldn't separate no matter how hard they might try later.

Ricky lifted his wings and flew off, and Red noticed a bandage on his right wing. She watched him disappear with her eyes, but he didn't fade in her mind. Ricky tried to remember what he didn't want her to know, but she heard him remembering.

Well that's weird, because I don't have an alive biological or adopted dad. I'm glad I have a mental one now.

Ricky blushed mentally. *I really didn't want you to know that.*

We can't exactly have secrets, you know.

Yep.

Red walked inside and went to see Alexa. She found her still in the ballroom with Zera sitting on the floor in front of her.

"Glad you can join us, Red. Please sit with Zera."

Red eased down next to Zera and looked up at Alexa.

"As of this moment, you both are no longer slaves. I will give you both a choice whether to stay with me or go to Syn-Cynthia. I have enjoyed your company, even if it has been a little less honest than I would've wished."

Alexa shot a look at Red, and her gaze did not waver.

"It is your decision to make individually. Stay or go."

This was not a hard decision for Red to make. She had just spent the best three years of her life with Alexa and Zera, even if she had to hide most of the time.

Red stood and declared, "I want to stay with you, Alexa, and I promise that I won't hide a thing from you anymore."

"Good. That's what I expected from you, but I have no idea what Zera will say."

Alexa looked at Zera, and Red fidgeted back and forth on her feet. The decision was much harder for Zera to make. She stood.

"I have liked being with you two...and I really don't know what I'd do in Syn-Cynthia, so I'd really like to stay."

Alexa smiled and wrapped them both in a big hug. "I was hoping that you would stay."

She let go of them and said, "Now we need to confront Kim."

"About what?" Zera asked.

"It wasn't my uncle that tried to kill me; it was my aunt." Alexa looked at Red. "Did you know that from the beginning?"

Red nodded. Alexa didn't say anything, but it was obvious that she was more than a little mad at her aunt.

General I and Queen Kim were beginning to make wedding plans when they heard the guards start to open the doors. Only one person ever walked into Kim's presence unannounced: Alexa.

"Go out the servant door, now," she told I.

He hurriedly ran out the servant's door, and just as that door closed, the main doors opened, and in walked Alexa with two other girls flanking her. One of those girls was obviously a Raggy, but Kim didn't even bother looking at her eyes.

"How dare you bring that abomination in here!" Kim said.

Alexa responded coolly, "For my own protection."

Kim was about to ask what kind of protection a Raggy could give when she realized that the Raggy was Red.

Alexa said casually, "If I were you, I wouldn't want anyone in here to hear what I have to say."

Kim understood the wisdom in that right away, so she told the guards who had followed Alexa in to the throne room to return to their posts outside.

Kim looked at Red and said, "You." She said it so fiercely that Red raised her eyebrows.

Alexa accused her aunt, "You, not Kardum, ordered my assassination when I went with him to check on *your* assassin's progress."

Kim tried to formulate an answer to Alexa's accusation, but she couldn't think of anything, so she said something to Red instead.

"You are the reason my most loyal assassin quit on me, Raggy."

"You only ever had one until recently."

Kim glared at Red.

Alexa stated, "The very fact that you are ignoring me tells me that what I said is true. Trying to have me killed so that you may keep the throne is not only illegal, but also not acting like a family."

Kim didn't look her niece in the eye as she said, "You are the heir to the throne. Why would I want you dead, my dear?"

"Because you are next in line, which is made obvious by the fact that you have it while I am coming of age. Because you tried to have me killed, I could lawfully force you to abdicate the throne and put whomever I chose on it."

"But you won't do that."

"Why not?"

"I am the only one, besides yourself, with the skills to govern Rov, and the people love me. Do you want to start your rule with the impression that you don't like who the people like?"

"I will not dethrone you now because of your first reason, but if there is another attempt on my life, I will put Ms. Writ in your place until I am eighteen."

Kim sighed. "I understand."

"Good."

Alexa pivoted and walked out of the throne room, opening the doors for herself. Her two friends followed.

Kim called for I to come back in.

"It looks as if we still have to postpone the wedding."

———◈◈◈———

The next day was the first day that Zera and Alexa sparred with Red as Red, not Ache.

"I don't want you to go easy on me," Alexa declared.

"But I can't hit you, and if I were to go even my normal, it would bruise you a bunch!"

Why can't I hit her anyway? Red asked Ricky, who had hinted that he knew why before.

*Every fighting Raggy has had one Orv whom they can't hurt;
yours is Alexa.*

Oh.

They were still working on getting used to conversing in their heads again.

"But it might be possible," Red continued, "that I could just touch you where I would normally hit you, will you stay still please?"

Alexa obliged, and Red lightly tapped her on the shoulder. The fact that she was able to do it meant that she could do it subconsciously when fighting.

"So you can go hard on me?" Alexa asked.

"Yep. Zera, do you want me to go hard on you?"

Zera shook her head. "I'll just watch right now, thank you."

Alexa understood that idea, but someone had to fight Red first. They spread out, and neither girl made a move. Red didn't want to make the first move because her normal first moves against Ricky had been *crazy*. Alexa stepped forward and did a hard lunge at Red's belly. Red easily stepped to the side and tapped Alexa's head.

"Dead," Red said.

Alexa swiped sideways at Red's new position. She jumped over that and tapped Alexa's chest. Alexa then tried to "cut" Red's feet off. Red blocked that with one hand and then faked a knee jab only to tap Alexa's shoulder.

Alexa was getting annoyed at the tapping. She faked at Red's head and went for her waist. She saw Red disappear and felt a small tap on the top of her head. She whirled and saw Red leaning idly on her swordstick.

"It seems to me that you are just playing with me," Alexa said.

"That's why I prefer to go on your level; it is harder for me and easier at the same time. Your decision."

Alexa thought for a minute. "Your playing will make me faster. Are you going to join us, Zera?"

"Will you only tap me too, Red?"

Red shrugged. "I don't know."

Zera sighed. "I'll join, just try not to kill me."

She stood and picked up her sword.

"Team up on Red?" Alexa asked Zera.

"Sure."

They both attacked Red, Alexa with a powerful head swipe, and Zera with a fast diagonal upward strike starting at Red's left hip. She ducked Alexa's and blocked Zera's, and she kicked Zera in the stomach. She had barely kicked her, so all Zera did was double over and try to regain her breath. Red was watching Zera, but she instinctively jumped back from a hard downward strike from Alexa.

Red advanced on Alexa, touching her rapidly in many different places while blocking Alexa's attacks. Red twirled and blocked an attack from Zera and touched her multiple times before turning to block Alexa's next attack. This cycle continued until someone became tired.

The sparring session seemed to go on for hours to Red. She had noticed that whenever she wasn't going easy or playing, time seemed to slow down for everyone but her. Alexa would put full force into a swing, and it would take two seconds to hit Red. Those same fast two seconds would seem like two minutes to Red, and she would tap Alexa at least twice before needing to block that swing. Red would then automatically turn to block Zera's next strike and tap her a few times before needing to block something.

Red might have had a harder time doing this if they had timed their attacks at the same time. She would have to tell them that when they had time to listen.

Alexa and Zera had pretty much the same perspective about that fight. They would try the most clever or strongest attack that they could, but then they would feel a few taps before their weapon came to a halt, and they would have to start all over again.

Zera was the first one to tire. She stopped attacking Red and backed away. Red turned to block an attack that she expected from Zera, but then turned quickly again, when she noticed that she wasn't there. Alexa noticed Zera's absence by the fact that Red no longer gave her time to think in between taps; it was now steady tap, tap, tap, block, tap, tap, tap instead of tap, tap, block, momentary silence, block, tap, tap.

Zera decided to use her mind to figure out Red's fighting style. She watched her tapping away at Alexa, and the only pattern that she saw was three taps and a block. She wasn't strategically placing the taps, just tapping random spots. Zera noticed that Red really wasn't putting much effort into it at all, but Alexa was being jarred by her own powerful swings being blocked.

Alexa decided that the best course of action would be to change her course of action; so, instead of attacking Red, she started to try to block Red's taps. Red noticed the change of tactic and changed hers along with it. Her taps ceased to be random and started being in strategic places that would have horridly hurt Alexa had she been swinging harder.

Finally, Alexa had had enough.

"Okay time to stop," she puffed out.

Red's stick stopped tapping her, and she leaned on it. Alexa had not yet seen Red in need of a rest, not while they were running, nor right now when they had been sparring heavily for an hour.

After Alexa had regained her breath, she asked Red, "How was assassin training any different than what we have done every day?"

Red didn't answer for a few seconds. She really didn't want to remember that time, but Alexa asked.

"I had to wake up before sunrise and run until noon, and I wasn't allowed to stop. The whole rest of the day was physical exercises of other sorts."

"Oh." Alexa knew that Red was purposefully leaving a bunch out, but she thought that it might be better not to know.

About two weeks after the confrontation with Kim, Alexa decided that she, Zera, and Red were in need of proper sparring and defensive equipment. In other words, she wanted to go buy swords. Red said that it would be best for the wielder to pick out her own sword, which would be based on the wielder's fighting style, so she dragged Red and Zera to the market instead of exercising and sparring. They traveled in Alexa's carriage.

They were in a crowd in the capital headed toward the market when Red saw a flash of paste white among the black and tan people in the crowd. At first, it did not alarm her, but then she saw what was happening. A Raggy and the Orvian family that had hidden him were being dragged out of a house and beaten. Red's blood boiled, and she jumped out of the carriage and ran to the house. She stepped right in front of the soldier dragging out the first prisoner, the Raggy.

He didn't seem to notice her as he raised his whip to strike the Raggy. As the whip came down, time slowed again. She grabbed the end of the whip and wrapped it around her palm. She yanked it out of the soldier's hand, and he yelped in shock. Before he could do much else, Red had grabbed the whip's handle and flicked it at his wrist. He let go of the Raggy as a reflex and drew his sword. The other soldiers noticed his predicament and let go of their captives as well. Now Red was faced with five soldiers and had to move them so that those who had helped the Raggy could get out. As a rule, every house in the capital was back-to-back with another house, and the two houses never had a door between them, so there was no back door that they could escape from.

The first soldier slashed down at Red, and the only weapon she had was the whip. She backed up and narrowly avoided being hit. Another soldier swung his axe at Red, and she sidestepped that and the rest of the attacks. The soldiers didn't notice that she was leading them away from the door until they were five feet away from it, but by then, it was too late. As soon as they noticed, the last of their prisoners had run away, and when they looked back at whom they were attacking, Red was gone. The soldiers were left with no prisoners and no one to attack.

Red followed the last of the escaped prisoners to where they had established a meeting point. She saw them meet up in a nearly abandoned street of the capital. Only the scum of the earth and those looking for a place of temporary refuge ever came to this street. Red watched the family and the Raggy that they had kept safe, from a distance. They conversed quietly. One of the kids noticed Red and pointed her out to his dad.

They walked up to Red, who was leaning on the wall of a broken-down building.

The dad stepped up to her and said, "Thank you for saving us. If you require some type of payment—"

"That's not why I followed you. I came to tell you that if you want to stay free, then you have to get out of here. Once Kim's soldiers get wind of a Raggy in the capital and a sympathetic family, they will hunt you down like prey."

The wife seemed skeptical. "Thank you for the warning, but wouldn't they be hunting you down too?"

"I am Princess Alexandra's vassal and the fighting Raggy. It would take a virtual army to capture me."

The father nodded. "Then we will leave right away. God will provide a way."

"It might be best if you go to Syn-Cynthia," Red added.

The father nodded and turned to leave. The adult Raggy stayed as the others left.

"Aren't you coming?" the Orv father asked.

"No, I think I need to stay here."

The children went up to the silver-eyed Raggy and hugged him. They cried and asked him to come with them. He was firm in his resolve to stay. Eventually, the Orvian family left, and the Raggy looked at Red.

Adult Raggies looked like human teenagers. At fifteen, Red was fully grown by Raggy standards. The silver-eyed man before her was a few inches shorter than her.

"I want to stay with you," he told her.

"And if I say no?"

"You won't."

"Why do you say that?"

"You are the Raggy liberator. You innately want to help and gather our people."

"We'll have to ask Alexa—"

Red was cut off when he hugged her exuberantly. All Raggies were the polar opposite of touchy feely and didn't know the meaning of the word *awkward*. Red hugged him back. Once they were done, Red led the way to the blacksmith. Halfway there, they ran into Alexa, who was looking for Red on foot, with the carriage driver following her, nervous about her being out in the open.

"Where have you been?" she demanded as soon as she saw Red.

"I had to solve an issue."

Alexa saw the Raggy and shook her head. "There will be no more going into public with you after this."

Red shrugged.

Alexa sighed and looked at the Raggy. "What is your name?"

"Narlin."

"Red, take him home, and we'll meet you there later. You can pick your sword some other day."

Red nodded and started toward the minicastle with Narlin in tow. Alexa and Zera went to the blacksmith.

Red and Narlin talked while they walked to the minicastle. They were about one-fourth of the way there when Red sensed someone behind them. She turned and saw no one. She knew that someone was there, so she stopped. Narlin turned and stopped too.

"What is it?" he asked.

"Someone is following us."

Red was silent for a minute and then yelled, "Whoever you are, get out where I can see you."

Whoever it was choose to remain silent.

"I don't think that there is anyone there," Narlin said.

"There is."

A bush rattled, and a few birds flew off. Red headed to that bush and parted the leaves. There was no one there. Red shrugged and walked away. After walking and talking for several minutes, she suddenly turned and said, "Aha!"

There behind them was a Raggy with one blue eye and one green eye. He was trying to follow the Red and Narlin without getting caught, but Red had other plans.

Red asked him, "Why are you sneakily following us when you could join us freely?"

He scraped the ground with his toe.

"I, uh, just wanted to watch you."

"Are you not a people person?" Narlin asked.

He nodded.

"What's your name?" Red asked.

"Vic."

"Come on, Vic. You can join us if you wish."

He did, and they walked in silence the rest of the way to the minicastle.

———❦———

Alexa came back to find three Raggies on her chandelier.

"Okay at least one of you needs to come down from there before you break it."

Red jumped down and landed in front of Alexa.

"You are not going to the capital anymore, Red."

Red shrugged, again.

"So how'd you get the new one?"

"He saw my fight in the street from his hiding place and followed me and Narlin."

"Narlin and me."

"Huh?"

"You need to work on your grammar."

Red rolled her eyes.

From that day on, Red started attracting Raggies. Alexa set up a Raggy haven in one of her towers and hired another cook to keep up with the seven Raggies who eventually came out of the capital.

UM...

Red's eyes were closed, but she was not asleep. Ricky was reading a book, and she didn't feel like sleeping, so she tried to fall asleep by boring herself with his geology book. It was almost working when she heard a slight jingle that she had only ever heard Ricky make. A floorboard creaked. Red dropped silently to the floor from her bed in the chandelier. She always ended up sleeping there for some reason.

Red followed the jingle and some very faint footsteps. She knew the castle so well that she closed her eyes and steered herself by ear alone in order to better hear those faint noises. When she was sure that she was close to the source of the noises, she opened her eyes.

There in front of Alexa's bedroom door was a shadow that reflected light. It was vaguely shaped like Ricky, but she could tell his scales were black. Ricky started to become interested. The shadow's hand rested on the door handle. Red knew that it did not have good intentions, so she pounced on it. She had him belly down on the floor with an arm twisted behind his back in the blink of an eye.

"Why are you sneaking around Princess Alexandra's castle?" Red asked the intruder.

He said nothing but had Red pinned belly up on the floor with her arms pinned to her sides before she realized he was moving.

"Who are you?" he asked. Red noticed that he wasn't looking at her.

Ricky didn't know how, but he recognized the voice.

"My name is Red, if that's what you mean."

Red suddenly bucked and knocked him over her head. He landed and stood next to a torch. Ricky gasped at the face Red was seeing. He urged Red to ask, "Is your name Justin, and are you a Rept?"

He frowned at her.

"Only my family and the council know that name. How do you?"

Red was confused. "Who is the council?"

Then it hit Ricky exactly who this person was. He told Red to ask another question.

"Are you Ricky's older brother?"

He tensed, but he still didn't look at her. "He is dead."

"No, he isn't."

"I stabbed him through the heart; he can't be alive."

"Well, I know he's not dead."

He finally looked at her. "You have some explaining to do, Raggy, but not here."

Red tried to say, "Why do people always downgrade me with Raggy?" But her muscles wouldn't move. She noticed that she wasn't controlling her breathing or her swallowing or any other normally controlled bodily function; it felt like she had been hit with daddy long legs venom again but somehow different.

He got behind her and said, "Walk."

Red's body walked even though she wasn't telling it to. He told her body what to do all the way outside the castle and past the spot where he couldn't see it any longer. He looked away from her after making her face him.

"How do you know about my deceased brother?"

What does deceased *mean?*

Dead.

Oh. Should I tell him?

Yah.

"He's definitely not dead because I had to ask him what *deceased* means."

He had to think about that for a minute.

"So you are not only telling me that my brother is alive, but that he also melded minds with you."

"Yes. Your name *is* Justin."

"Yes. You are coming with me."

He looked at her, and she froze, unable to move.

"My original mandate was to spy on the future queen of Rov, and on Rov itself, but that can wait. I need to show you and Ricky something. Turn southeast and start running."

Red's body ran without her telling it to. She thanked God that she wasn't a natural klutz.

Now what? Red asked Ricky.

I'm coming. I don't remember enough about him to trust him.

What do you want me to do?

Try to escape, find his weakness.

Okay.

At that time, Ricky started packing his normal taking-everywhere stuff. He had a bag mostly full of weapons but had a pocket full of clothes. He was currently in a hotel, and it was around eleven o'clock at night. The only other people up were teenagers and partygoers. Ricky packed all his things and was about to jump out a window when a memory hit him.

———◦∕∿∕◦———

The trees were a blur in his peripheral vision. He parried, swung, and was rewarded with the metallic clang of sword meeting sword. His brother had a five-year advantage on him, but Ricky was confident that he could beat him.

You can't win. You're drunk, Justin thought.

Ricky's only response was to push his mind harder into Justin's. He grinned, and Ricky's strength dropped dramatically.

A little trick Dad taught me, Justin thought.

Ricky fell to his knees. He no longer had the strength to push his mind into Justin's.

"You are a disgrace to our family and our race. Dad taught us to never kill in cold blood, but he was the one who told me to do this. Good-bye, brother."

Justin plunged his sword into the left side of Ricky's chest, where most Repts' hearts were. Ricky fainted.

Ricky! Ricky, wake up! he heard Red say.

He mumbled, "What happened?"

You fainted, and I couldn't hear you.

The memory came back but not as strongly this time. Red didn't see it the first time, so it shocked her.

I guess that that was the moment that I got amnesia. The beginning of my life before this was when I woke up in a doctor's office as an unknown person. The only thing I could remember was my name and my race.

Red mentally nodded. She knew that; he was just reviewing his facts.

The only things that I remember before that are about Justin. I guess that seeing him through you triggered my memories.

Ricky stood up from where he had fallen to the floor. He grabbed his bag and jumped out the window, snapping open his wings. He was going to confront his brother.

It was a month before Alexa's eighteenth birthday. Alexa and Zera had fallen into exhausted sleep and awoke the next morning to find Red gone. They searched the whole castle and asked the Raggies if they knew what happened to her. No one knew where she was, so they packed some bags and left in a hurry. If Red was gone, then something bad was about to happen.

That afternoon, the minicastle was burned and pillaged.

None of that had to do with Red's disappearance.

Kim had found Jontosh in her dungeon, where Ricky had put him, and then told one of her nobles to hire him to kill her. The noble gladly obeyed his queen. A week later, the assassin was caught; and Kim told the country that it was Alexa who hired him in order to get the throne earlier. They believed her and insisted that the assassin and Alexa be executed.

They went in force to apprehend Alexa, but she wasn't there. They took this to mean that she was guilty, and the queen was right. In the confusion, they forgot about the assassin's execution. She now permanently held control of Rov.

Alexa found a few Christians who were leaving the country. They had stayed while the atheist Kim was on the throne temporarily but unable to enforce her laws, but now she had complete control and could enforce her anti-God laws. These Christians knew that Alexa was innocent, so they found her and joined her, but there were only one hundred of them.

Red's disappearance had nothing to do with that. It was caused by the demons wanting her to get away from Alexa so that they could better attack them individually, but God was also using it to set up something greater.

RESTORATION

It was about noon. Red noticed a new horizon of trees. They had been running in the plains of Liebochney for a week, so she was used to a grassy horizon occasionally dotted with towns or cities. Justin always avoided those. Red hadn't controlled her own body in a whole week, especially because Justin slept with his eyes open.

Red had figured out that whatever living thing he looked at was either frozen or controlled by his voice. She also figured that they were going to the Uncivilized Woods. Ricky agreed, so he was waiting there, at the edge. He had calculated that Red and Justin would be there at sunset that day.

Justin noticed how slow of a runner Red was. It took her fifteen minutes to do a mile where it only took him ten. It made what was a three-day journey for him a week's journey. He wished that he could fly and get at his destination before sunset. At this rate, it would take another week and a half. He wondered if Ricky was following him.

Ricky watched the two blotches against the green grass. He knew that one of those was Red. He was up in a tree, waiting. He would follow them after they got in the woods.

The rest of the day was monotonous running until right before sunset. That was when they first stepped into the fringes of the Uncivilized Woods. They traveled for another hour after they got there; then Justin decided that it was time to rest for the night.

He made a fire and situated Red on one side and himself on another. Ricky and Red decided to wait until they got to Justin's destination to decide whether or not she needed to be rescued. They all had uneasy sleep that night.

After a week of following Justin and Red deeper and deeper into uncharted territory, Ricky was starting to think of a way to rescue Red.

He used his new power over earth and rocks to put a wall up between Justin and his captive. Red used her momentary freedom to dash out of sight. Justin saw the bushes to his left moving, so he went that direction. It wasn't that hard to find her because she stood out like a sore thumb in the leafless, winter forest.

Red heard Justin coming, so she started to climb a tree. He caught her in his gaze before she could get on the first branch. Justin saw a gold flash to his left but kept his gaze on Red.

"Where are you, Ricky?"

There was no answer, so Justin took out a dagger and said, "If you don't come out, I will kill her."

To reinforce his threat, he stepped up to her and held the dagger to her neck after telling her to stand straight.

"If you kill her, you kill me." Ricky's voice came from his left.

"I've done it once; I can do it again."

Ricky stepped out into the wan sunlight.

"What do you want?" Ricky asked.

Before Justin could answer, a voice he recognized said, "Aren't you supposed to be in Rov, Freeze Gaze?"

Ricky turned to see the owner of this new voice. It was a dark-green Rept with five other Repts behind him.

"Bug off, Far Shot," said Justin.

Far Shot then noticed Ricky. His eyes grew wide, and he asked, "Is that the V-scale?"

"Yes, now go patrol somewhere."

"But as far as I know, you can only freeze one person at a time. You need help."

Justin growled, a sound that Red had only ever heard Ricky do when he was extremely annoyed, angry, or in pain.

"I can handle it."

As they continued to argue, Red tried to convince Ricky to leave.

I still don't know enough to leave you alone with them.

I can protect myself; we don't both need to get captured. Go hide somewhere until we know for sure about what's going on.

Okay, in a second.

Ricky then used his power over earth to make a room of dirt around Justin. As soon as he was done, Red leaped on top of it and dropped down on Far Shot and his patrol. She landed on the shoulders of an aqua Rept. She managed to tip him over and grab his quiver with a bow and some arrows in it. She rolled into a ball upon impact with the ground and used her momentum to knock a few Rept over.

Red then ran to a tree and climbed to a place that she hoped they could not fly to. From there she used her newly acquired weapon to wreak havoc on those below. She aimed for the back of joints, where she had learned years ago that Ricky had smaller, less-protective scales. Within a minute, almost all the Rept had left in a panic after seeing one of their comrades shot behind his knee from fifty feet away. The only ones who were left were Far Shot and a yellow Rept.

Red dropped from the tree holding the bow and a notched arrow. During the confusion, no one had noticed Ricky's departure until then.

Red had intended to meet up with Ricky, but stopped when she heard, "Freeze. If you move or turn around, I'll shoot your thigh."

Red's answer to that was, "You, sir, have no idea who you are messing with."

"Yes, I do, a want-to-be archer of some weird race."

"You try hitting the back of joints from a tree, it's harder than it looks."

"Where is the V-scale?"

"Ricky? He left."

Red flexed her arms and pulled back on the bow's string. Far Shot noticed the movement.

"If you turn around, I'll shoot you."

Red drew it even harder.

"Drop the bow."

"No."

Red pivoted on her left foot and saw Far Shot shoot at her. It would take the arrow three seconds to reach her, but before it did, Red had fired her own arrow. Red's arrow hit half a second after Far Shot's. She watched Far Shot's bow shatter from the impact of her arrow, even as pain raced up her thigh, then was gone. She started to feel a little sleepy.

As these things happened, Justin dug his way out of the earthen room. He watched the arrow duel with mild interest and then froze Red. Far Shot was taken aback at his bow being destroyed, but Justin calmed him down and tried to convince him to stay with the wounded. He also told Red to pull the arrow out of her leg.

Far Shot told Inept Nurse, the yellow Rept, to take care of the injured instead, and he helped Justin escort Red to a cave that had many well-worn trails leading into it. They turned so many times in the caverns inside that cave that Red lost count, but Ricky didn't.

Soon, they walked into a cavern bigger than any of the others. It was open to the sky, but it looked like dark volcanic glass covered the hole to the outside world. This provided more light in this room than all the others.

It was mostly empty except for a half-circle table on top of a stagelike rock. There were five Rept debating something sitting at the table. Their scale colors were gray, maroon, brown, teal, and medium orange. They stopped debating and stared as the unannounced escorts came in.

The teal dragon stood and said coldly, "Freeze Gaze, you were sent to spy on Rov, finding their weaknesses so that we could attack them. So, why are you here with that whatever it is?"

Justin gulped. "This Raggy attacked me as I was spying on Rov's queen-to-be and revealed to me that not only is my brother alive, but she is also his meld."

The Rept on the stagelike rock exchanged surprised looks.

"And what do you have to do with this, Far Shot?"

"Nothing but helping escort."

"Then please leave us."

Far Shot complied unwillingly.

"Leave us for a moment, Freeze Gaze."

Justin left the cavern and waited just outside. In a few moments, Justin and his frozen prisoner were called back in.

The teal Rept dragon stepped down from the rock that acted like a stage. He went to stand in front of Red and told Justin to look away from her. As soon as she was released, she straightened a little but still had to look up to look him in the eyes.

"Who are you, and what do you want?" she asked.

"I am the head council member, Commander, and we want to conquer the other inept races. Is it true that you are the V-scale's meld?"

It took Red a second and Ricky's help to figure out what he said.

"You just called me stupid, and I am definitely not stupid enough to want to kill other races."

"Did you even hear my second sentence?"

"You have the same plan as Kim. You should ally, kill the rest of us, and then turn on each other. Who knows? You might kill each other before you hurt anyone else."

He was getting annoyed at her. "Where is the V-scale?"

"Okay, I think it's time to go," Red said.

She turned suddenly and kicked high at Justin's head. He fell to the ground, and she jumped over him. She ran out of the huge chamber and followed Ricky's instructions out. She was out in the sunshine when everything changed. The trees and bushes were replaced by walls, and the maroon Rept from the chamber was behind her, closing a door before she knew exactly what was happening. There was no knob on her side of that door.

What in the world happened? Ricky asked.

I don't know! I did what you told me to do, and I was outside, but I was brought here!

The room was entirely enclosed with the one door as entrance and exit. The walls were made of an igneous rock; that much Ricky knew. He didn't know how she had gotten in there.

Red tried to open the door with no success. She looked all over the room and even started to call for help but thought better of it.

In the boredom that followed, Red and Ricky recapped her brief conversation with the guy that Justin called Commander. After that, Ricky started on an escape plan, just in case it was needed. They still weren't quite sure why Justin brought Red there.

———⟡———

Justin stood in front of the stagelike rock facing the five Rept of the council.

"I thought that you said that you had killed your brother, Freeze Gaze. Explain," said the gray dragon.

"As you know, you had sent me to get valuable information on the first country that you plan to take, Rov. I was seeing the aptitude of the future queen, when that Raggy attacked me. She asked me if my name was Justin, which I know only you of the council and my family knew. I was confused until she asked me if I was Ricky's brother."

He then told them almost every detail of his conversations with Red.

After he had concluded, the teal Commander said, "And you did not leave anything out of what you told us?"

Justin shook his head.

"Look me in the eyes and say it out loud," said the gray Rept.

Justin looked him in the eye and said, "I have not left anything out, General."

General nodded as Justin was still looking at him. "He's not lying."

Justin wondered why General, the second in command, was helping him. He could have said that Justin was lying, and then Justin would reap terrible consequences.

"I want you to tell me what he was like when you knew him," Commander said.

Justin sighed. This wasn't going to be good.

———

Two days later, Red was staring at the wall. She was wishing for a sword, and Ricky was wishing that something interesting would happen. They were both itching for a fight.

Red looked at the door when it opened. The maroon council member entered. He was the one who had put her in here, however he did it. Red stood up.

"Someone is finally here. Can you please explain how I got in here?" she asked.

"I have the power to bend reality, so as you thought that you were leaving, you were actually coming here. Now you answer one of my questions: Where is the V-scale?"

"His name is Ricky. And mine is Red."

"That doesn't answer my question."

"I'm not going to tell you unless you clarify exactly why you want to know."

"We are going to eradicate all the other races, and we are sure that the V-scale would like to join us from what his brother told us about him."

Eradicate?

Extinguish.

You lost me again.

Get rid of.

You would want to do that? I'm confused.

Justin probably told them what I was like when we knew each other.

Oh, but you weren't an assassin then.

I was pretty bad.

"Are you going to say anything?" demanded the maroon Rept.

"Sorry, I was talking with Ricky. What is your name?"

"Power Master."

"You Rept seem to have the weirdest names, but then I can't say much in that area."

"I'll ask one more time before things start getting unpleasant." He was definitely agitated. "Where is the V-scale?"

Do you want me to tell him or not?

Don't. I really don't like their agenda.

Agenda?

Plans.

"He told me not to tell you."

"If that is how it is to be, then fine."

Red felt at least a dozen places on her body start to hurt like crazy. She looked at her left arm and saw a long, deep gash gushing blood on her upper forearm. It didn't heal. All of the other spots looked similar and didn't heal.

Power Master said, "Things will just get worse as you don't answer."

Tell him, Ricky ordered.

"Okay then, he is right below you."

Red saw Power Master's look of confusion right before she fell into a hole in the ground. As soon as the hole sealed, the pain left.

"Let's leave this place."

"I couldn't agree more."

They were in an underground maze that Ricky had made using his power over earth while waiting for someone to go see Red. There was one entrance deep in the woods that let in air. They headed toward that entrance, discussing where to go after this in their minds. Red knew that Alexa's birthday was in ten days and that she needed to be there for when things got unpleasant.

Ricky was the first one to turn the corner leading to the entrance. He instinctively reached for his sword. Red turned the corner one second later and saw Justin leaning on a wall with his hands in front of him in a "I'm harmless" gesture.

"So you are an assassin," Justin said.

Red wasn't sure how he saw all of Ricky's weapons without looking at him.

"*Was* an assassin. We are going to leave, brother, and I don't feel like fighting in order to do so."

Ricky started walking past Justin. His next words stopped him cold.

"Mom and Dad are in a prison in that cave."

Red felt that Ricky was trying to remember his parents. He failed on that account.

"Well, at least that thought made you stop. It wouldn't have eighteen years ago."

"I don't remember eighteen years ago. I got amnesia after our fight."

"I guess that makes sense. You don't remember our parents?"

Ricky shook his head.

Red went down to one of the passages. She was curious and wanted to explore the maze. She was not needed with Ricky unless it turned hostile, but she seriously doubted it would. Besides, Ricky could handle himself, but she stayed close enough to come if Justin froze him.

"What do you remember?"

"A few things about you, but nothing else."

"Do you remember what you were like?"

"Sort of. What happened to you? I remember that you were always the good guy, but you are a spy now?"

Justin sighed. "Mom and Dad kept us away from the rest of our race because of your...uniqueness. When the old V-scale died, when you were born, all the families separated and decided not to have anything to do with each other until a new king arose.

When I was about ten and you were five, our parents caught wind of five individuals calling themselves the council that were out to unite all of our race under a single banner.

"At first that seemed like a good idea, but then Dad learned what they did to those who wished to remain alone. They tortured and blackmailed every Rept that they encountered into serving them, willingly or unwillingly. They did it one family at a time, so they only grew stronger. Mom and Dad took us to a place far away so that we would not fall into the council's grasp.

"We were safe until a month after our fight to the death. I was in the library reading a book when the front door slammed open. I stood to see what the problem was, and a slate-blue Rept that I had never seen before came into the library. I looked him in the eyes, and he seemed to stop moving. Dad came rushing in with a sword, and I looked at him. I didn't know that I had a power because that was the first day it had manifested.

"Before I knew what was going on, I was blindfolded, and I heard a sword fight going on. I was hit over the head, and the next thing I remember was hearing Mom scream. My wings and tail were pinned to my back, and my wrists and ankles were chained to a chair. They noticed I was awake and made me swear allegiance to them so that they wouldn't hurt Mom. Over the years, all they have gotten out from me and our parents was that you were dead, but they searched high and low for a baby V-scale and didn't find one.

"We were the last family captured. The council has had full control of our entire race, except you, for eighteen years. We need your help."

"Why are you so sure that I can or want to help?"

"You can because our people will follow you. Whether or not you do is totally up to you."

Ricky thought about it for a minute, and wondered at what he said.

"Why would they follow me?"

Justin tried to avoid the question. "Well, anyone who tries to lead is usually followed, right? And that's what helping might require, leadership."

He inwardly sighed when Ricky seemed to accept that answer. He couldn't tell Ricky the truth, which was that the V-scale was traditionally the monarch, because he didn't know if that would drive Ricky away or if the rest of their race would *want* a king.

"Well, I haven't done anything interesting in a long time. This sounds interesting."

"I just have one question: Do you drink anymore?"

"I used to drink?"

"Good."

Justin was about to say something else when Ricky said, "That's weird."

"What?"

"Red normally is only absent from my mind when she is asleep, but then there are always these weird images in her head. She isn't there at all right now."

"That isn't good."

"Nope."

Ricky turned and went to the last place he remembered her being.

While Ricky and Justin were talking, Red was exploring the maze that Ricky had made. She was at an intersection when she heard a voice that did not belong to either Ricky or Justin.

"What are you doing?"

"Who are you?"

"A friend. Why are you wandering around?"

"I don't consider somebody a friend who won't show his or herself."

An angel appeared in front of her.

"Happy?" he asked.

Red was stunned at this angel's beauty. He was the most handsome man she had ever seen; yet he also radiated strength. He looked like a man any teenager would dream of as prince charming.

"Red, why are you wandering aimlessly when you could be at your queen's side, fighting for her?"

Red was entranced by his beautiful voice but managed to say, "Alexa won't be queen for ten more days."

"I'm not talking about Alexandra. She doesn't serve me, but Kim does. Alexandra is a deluded, self-righteous girl who will never make an adequate queen."

Red was about to ask Ricky what those words meant when she noticed that he was not in her head. Then Red understood. This wasn't an angel; it was a demon. She shook the cobwebs that had collected in her head out of her mind. She was about to call on her recollection of a verse to get rid of him, when he waved his hand in the air. She was unable to speak; her vocal chords wouldn't work.

"I will make it even easier for you to understand. You can bow down to me and live for a much longer time, or I will kill you here and now. I promise that if you reject my power, you will die a most unpleasant death. Did you not know that I am the king of the worlds? If you just bow to me, I will make you the ruler of this world."

"In the name of—" she started to say, but the demon paralyzed her vocal chords again.

"You dare to defy me? Me, Lucifer! For this crime you will die."

Red felt her strength not just fail, but also downright leave. She fell to the floor and felt her life start to drain away.

So this is how it ends, she thought as the beautiful man disappeared.

She used some of her remaining strength to thank God for her life and for his love.

—◦◦◦—

Ricky heard Red's prayer. He started to run. He almost hit several walls before he got to Red. He did what he had done the last time he thought she might die; he checked her pulse. This time it was as wild as a wild mustang.

"Red! Talk to me!"

Red barely managed, *Demon.*

Ricky watched, unable to do anything. Her skin did something that was unnatural for a Raggy; it turned pink. It turned into a darker pink as Ricky watched. It turned peach, then faded into a red, as red as Red's eyes. As more color came into her skin, more pain rushed through her body.

Justin arrived to find Ricky frantic.

"What's happening?"

"I don't know! She's not thinking clearly enough!"

Ricky stood and paced. Then he felt his health being sucked into Red.

"We're dying," Ricky said.

"No! We can't afford to give the council a baby to influence."

"What?"

"Whenever one person of our race dies, another of that same scale shape and color is born. When you die, a baby V-scale will be born. You can't die."

"Well, too late," Ricky said as he sank to the ground, and his voice became weaker. "Tell Mom and Dad that I wish I could've met them again, and I'm sorry that I couldn't help."

He closed his eyes.

—◦◦◦—

Red watched the intersection fade. With her last ounce of strength, she closed her eyes, and the pain left. She reopened her eyes and saw a totally different scene. She was at the top of a grassy hill with beautiful flowers. She sat up and saw a magnificent city on the hill next to her own. Really, all she could see of it was a gate, but that was the most amazing thing that she had ever seen. It was pure white but seemed to shine with colors she didn't know existed. It opened, and a being stepped through. Red stood and ran to him. He was an average-looking human, but she knew right away that this was her Savior. Once she was in his arms, she kissed his cheek. He laughed and spun her in a circle.

Red was elated. He put her down, but she was not sad about this new change.

"Well done, Red."

"Does this mean that I get to stay here with you?"

"It would normally, but not this time. Satan killed you directly, something he is not allowed to do because you prayed for my Father to keep destruction from you. He told me to send you back. You must finish your task."

Red nodded; she knew what he meant.

She hugged him hard and said, "I love you, Jesus."

He smiled, and if she had seen it, she would've wanted to never let go of him.

"I love you too, Red. When you get back, help Ricky and then find Alexa. I promise that no Raggies will be harmed because of this wait."

Red let go of him, relieved, and said, "Yes, sir."

He still smiled. "That's my girl. I'll be with you, and I will never leave you or forsake you."

<hr />

Justin had checked all the vitals of the two bodies in front of him. They were obviously dead, but he stayed because Ricky's body hadn't disintegrated yet. After he could bear it no longer, he turned to leave, expecting to hear flames behind him.

Instead, he heard a rustle, and then Ricky said, "Where are you going?"

Justin turned and saw them both sitting up, looking at him. He gaped at them.

"You were dead. I checked ten times."

Ricky smiled. "But we aren't now."

"How?"

"God raised himself from the dead; I don't think we are that hard to do as well."

"What are you talking about?"

Ricky stood and looked at his brother.

"You know that God is real, yes?"

Justin nodded, dumfounded. His brother was dead two minutes ago but was now talking about God!

"Did you know that he became a man?"

Justin blinked. "What?"

Ricky explained the whole story of how God was born and died on the cross. Justin listened attentively, not interrupting. When Ricky told him that he had done it all for him, Justin was ecstatic. He eagerly accepted Jesus into his heart to be his savior.

After that, they went into the woods to make a camp for Ricky and Red for the night. As they did, Ricky asked, "What do most Rept believe?"

Justin laughed. "We have an oral tradition that the first Rept were created by a benevolent being, the one and only God, who gave them a set of rules to follow, called the ten things God hates. What I, along with everyone else, believed before you told me about Jesus was that when the first Rept transgressed God forgot about us and left us to fend for ourselves in a world with races older than our own."

He didn't mention that most believed the only way God interacted with the Rept was to provide them with a ruler, the V-scale of their generation. Ricky nodded, thinking about this. Justin took his leave to go sleep in his assigned room. The three spent the night thinking about the best way to overthrow the wicked council.

—◦◦◦—

Ricky was awoken by the continuous sound of arrows hitting wood. It would stop for a few blissful seconds; then something else would hit the wood. He cracked open an eye and went automatically on alert. There was a red person shooting his arrows at a tree. He slowly stood up.

The red person noticed Ricky and turned. Ricky let out his held breath. It was just Red. Then it hit him what she was thinking, and he heard it and vice versa.

I'm just making sure everything works, Red explained.

I know, it's just that you look so much like your name, it scared me.

"I scared you?" Red asked out loud.

"Yes."

Red shrugged and turned to retrieve the weapons lodged in the tree. The sun was just sending its wan light among the trees when Justin burst into their camp.

"I have a plan!" he declared.

Red came back from the tree at that time.

"What is it?" she asked.

Justin jumped away from her. "Oh, it's you, Red. You look *very* much like your name, what I can see out of my peripheral vision at least."

Red frowned. "So I've been told."

Justin shook his head to clear his thoughts. "In an hour, there is a mandatory population check in the council hall. Everyone that is not on a mission far away needs to attend."

"So you are suggesting?"

"That we confront the council."

"How?"

Justin shrugged. "I don't know. I came up with the idea; you provide the means."

Ricky closed his eyes and recalled Red's memory of the council hall.

He asked Justin, "Is there normally anyone right in front of them?"

"No."

Red provided another idea to Ricky's original. He nodded and spoke out loud.

"That would help too."

"What are you thinking?" Justin asked.

"Are you okay if I show you?"

Justin nodded an affirmative, and Ricky showed him his plan in his mind. After a few minutes, Justin said, "I have to do what?"

Ricky explained. The scales on his face stood on end, which was the way the Rept turned pale.

"It's just talking."

"In front of a crowd!"

Red agreed with Justin. Ricky rolled his eyes.

"Is my part at least possible? Would they take it?"

Justin breathed in and closed his eyes. "Yes, they would."

"Then we should get to work."

———

Justin walked in with the other unwilling. That was how the population was supposed to come in. The unwilling servants would come in first and go to the left; then the loyalists would come in to separate the unwilling from the next people to come in, the prisoners. Any kid would sit in a ring in the middle surrounded by loyalists. The last to come in would be the prison guards, who were all loyal. This way, the unwilling could see what condition their families were in.

Any baby that was born would be presented and named at these monthly population checks. Also, any unwilling who had gone near the dungeons or had rebelled would have to watch one of their family members beheaded. However, both of those occasions were rare, but if one happened, the other usually followed.

Justin was nervous as he sat down among his comrades. He was about to rebel. He went over the plan in his mind, and it did nothing to calm his nerves. He would give Ricky the cue to come down by saying that he had had enough of the council's leadership and would tell everyone his real name; then Ricky would come down in the uproar or stone silence that followed, before their dad could be executed. Of course, that was only the beginning.

The council stood, and everyone was silent, either out of respect or fear.

Commander said, "Big Mother, please bring the child."

A chubby olive Rept stepped forward with a bundle of cloth against her chest. She went to the stage and handed it to Commander. He pulled the cloth off the infant and everyone saw a silver, V-scale baby girl in his arms.

Commander spoke into the relative silence, "God has finally decided to end his wrath on us, and he has sent a leader. We of the council have decided that we will raise her to be an admirable leader. I am sad to say that most of you will not see her turn two days old, for she should lead an army of willing, strong individuals, whom we will also raise, not a multi-generational rabble of rebels."

Power Master then said, "Those of you who are under my direct command, please come to the front."

In the confusion of moving to the front with the others with power, Justin barely heard Ricky tell him, *Change of plan. You don't need to do your part.*

Ricky didn't stay long enough to explain why.

"In case you are confused as to why we told you not to bring your weapons, it is because you are no longer needed," stated General. He seemed to take as much pleasure in that as declaring his own death sentence. A mere four thousand took out their weapons, while the rest started to protest and back up in fear.

"In twenty years, this baby will lead an army of twenty-year-olds to war against the other races."

At that, those Rept with weapons turned on those without. However, before anyone died, there was a thud and a growl that made everyone look behind the council.

"Stop!" Ricky yelled.

Every eye turned to him, including the council's. Many gaped at the fact that there were two V-scales alive at once and that they were different colors.

Commander was so stunned that Big Mother was able to take the crying infant from his arms without a problem. She went into a corner, muttering that anyone who could be so mean as to expose a baby in public was unfit to rule.

"That's right, I'm alive and kicking. I challenge the council to a battle for leadership. If I lose, I will submit to you; however, if I win, the people may decide what they want to do."

The Rept who had weapons drawn put them back. There was an adult V-scale on the stage; they needed to listen to him. The rest of the crowd was ecstatic. They were about to be mass executed just so the council could raise a bunch of kids that would adore and fully obey them, but now there was at least a little time for them to prepare themselves. Sure they knew what an adult V-scale meant, but could he really beat the whole council?

No one noticed the red Raggy leaning on a side of the doorway. No one even thought to look there. Her job was boring and uneventful; she just had to make sure no one left the chamber.

General was the first to find his voice. "A battle? You versus us? All five?"

Ricky nodded.

Commander found his voice next. "Where in the world did you come from?"

"The ceiling," Ricky said. He was implying that he wasn't in the mood for pleasantries. "I challenged you, so it is your turn to pick the details."

Commander thought about using Justin and the V-scale's dad to make him listen to him, but he thought about what Justin had told him. The V-scale wouldn't care.

"Now, and with a sword," General said.

"Meeting," Commander said.

The councilmen huddled together to confer.

"What are we supposed to do?" asked the medium-orange Craft Master.

"We have to answer him!" General said.

"Yes, we answer him," Commander said.

The brown Fighting Master asked, "Is it to the death?"

"No, we don't want him dead. We'll make it a knockout of the ring or kill fight," Commander said.

"Can I use my power?" Power Master asked.

"Yes."

"But that would mean that the V-scale could too." interjected Craft Master.

"We'll have to take that risk," General explained.

"There we go then," Commander said.

He turned to Ricky and explained the terms. He then turned and ordered the ring that was usually used for holding the kids cleared. That was done in less than a minute.

"All, I can use is a sword?" Ricky asked.

Until he had called attention to the fact that he had more than one weapon, no one had noticed his array of them.

"Yes," Commander said.

Ricky shrugged off his pack and his quiver. He then removed the many hidden daggers and darts on his person.

"Is that all?" Fighting Master asked sarcastically.

Ricky held up a finger. "I always forget about this one."

He took his shoe off and took a tiny dagger out of the top of his sole.

"Now all I have is my sword," Ricky said as the tiny dagger fell on to the pile of weapons.

Some of the unwilling decided that it was possible for Ricky to win. How could someone who had that many weapons not be a master with a sword?

Ricky moved to the ring, and the people parted to let him through. They stayed where they were to let the council pass but closed in behind them. No one wanted to miss this.

Ricky stood on one side of the circle, and the council spread out on the other half.

He posed a question, "Does the ring go straight up, or is the air free?"

"The air is free," Commander said.

Ricky nodded to say that he understood. "When do we start?"

"In five, four, three, two, one. Now!" Commander said.

Upon Commander saying *now*, the whole council seemed to charge at Ricky. He made a hole in the ground that dropped four of the council into an underground cavern in the maze. They found a glowing rock marking the exact perimeters of the ring and a small hole out of their reach a few feet from the edge of the circle. They looked up to see the hole that they had fallen through seal before they could stand and fly out.

The second thing that Ricky did was block an invisible head swing that would've done its job and chopped his head off. Power Master was keeping an image of himself at the spot he was supposed to have started at, but in reality, he had been in front of Ricky. Ricky knew what he was doing because he had listened to all of the council's thoughts in the beginning.

Power Master kept up the pretense that he was at his original spot while making Ricky feel as if he was fighting nothing. He couldn't see, feel, smell, or hear the person in front of him whom he was fighting. He closed his eyes and used what Power Master himself was sensing. It was very hard to defend an attack that looked and sounded like he was making.

Ricky jumped a leg swing and hit an unseen arm. He was rewarded with a momentary lapse of his foe's power and a curse. He backed up and gave Ricky the feeling as if he had been hit in the back with a broadsword. He knew that that wasn't real because Power Master was three feet in front of him, not behind him. It still hurt like a real sword.

Red gave him an idea, and he decided to use it. It had baffled him the first time, so it should've worked on Power Master. He ran at Power Master with his sword ready to swing. He swung and was blocked, but his momentum flipped him over Power

Master's head. He used a little flap of his wings to turn around and was effectively behind him. Red didn't have wings, and he had been unable to figure out how she had done it.

She smiled, glad that her tip had worked.

Before Ricky could hit him, Power Master made Ricky disoriented and dizzy. Power Master turned with a kick that sent Ricky wheeling toward the edge of the ring. He almost toppled out of it, but he reoriented himself in the nick of time. Ricky had the weirdest feeling of directions switching themselves. Normally, he would've tried to move forward, but, understanding that fighting Power Master was not normal, this time he ran backward. He ran right at Power Master and swung at him. With Ricky still trying to make sense of what was happening, Power Master easily blocked it and hit at Ricky's leg. The attack only glanced off Ricky's leg, but Power Master made it seem like it was an incredibly deep wound.

Power Master wasn't showing his fabrications to the audience, so when Ricky started limping from an attack that could only bruise him, they thought he was weak. Red closed her eyes so that she didn't add to Ricky's disorientation. She wasn't needed for anything except prayer and an occasional fighting tip right then.

Ricky decided that it was time to end this. He ran backward and ducked—but actually jumped—under Power Master, but this time, he went straight up and hit Power Master's shoulder. The impact force splintered Power Master's scales and made the sword go all the way to Power Master's collarbone. Ricky's disorientation immediately vanished as he landed behind Power Master with his back to him. They turned at the exact same time, and their swords clashed, entering a power struggle, which Power Master had to do one handed since his left arm was useless.

Ricky didn't dare open his eyes to find himself pushing on air. Power Master couldn't dare let Ricky get further away or push him back. There was a temporary stalemate. Both minds raced for an advantage. Ricky found one first. He pushed Power

Master and spun, hitting him with his tale. This made Ricky overly dizzy. Ricky opened his eyes to find that he could trust them. Knowing that this could change, Ricky kept his contact with Power Master's mind.

A true-blue sword skirmish followed where Ricky had a strong advantage. He was ten times better than Power Master, so he had knocked Power Master's sword out of his hand in a little more than a minute. Power Master felt one of his neck scales being pushed up and a strange prickling sensation of Ricky's sword on his neck. He stepped back, and Ricky matched his step. He knew that there was no point in going all the way to the edge of the ring. He stopped and wondered why the V-scale didn't just kill him. He took advantage of that supposed weakness.

He rid Ricky of all his senses, thinking that Ricky would just stay completely still, like many of Power Master's opponents in the past. He didn't realize that Ricky was trained to kill and that it was his second nature.

Ricky felt all of his senses disappear. The only things he could actually sense were his and Red's thoughts. He couldn't see, hear, smell, taste, or feel, so he didn't feel his arm muscles plunge forward and chop off Power Master's head. All he knew was that one second, he couldn't feel anything, and the next he saw Power Master's body and head in front of him. He regretted sending him to the place no one wants to go.

He jumped when Power Master's body suddenly caught fire. He didn't know that it happened to every Rept's body after they die. Ricky sighed; only one-fifth of his job was done.

The four had sat idly on the floor of the underground chamber. Some were hoping that Power Master would win by himself, but the other two wanted Ricky to win for various reasons. They jumped when stairs grew out of the ground to join with a new hole in the ceiling. They cautiously climbed the stairs to find themselves where they had started. Once they were all out, Ricky closed the hole.

"Where is Power Master?" asked Commander.

Ricky looked at him steadily with his sword tip on the ground. "Dead."

Commander cussed under his breath and told the other councilmen to huddle. He put himself in a position where he could see Ricky.

"We can do this," said Craft Master. "We outnumber him four to one."

"But Power Master was the best dueler in the council," said Fighting Master.

"Because he relied heavily on his power," explained General. "Maybe the V-scale found a way to counter it."

"My name is Ricky," he said from across the ring.

Commander told them how to attack. "I'll fight him head on. Fighting Master, you take his right. Craft Master, the left. And, General, take the air as backup. We'll force him out of the ring."

Red was laughing quietly. She guessed that not all Rept had Ricky's capacity for hearing. He sheathed his sword and silently joined her laughing.

The remaining council turned to find Ricky looking amused. Without further ado, they went to their separate tasks. While they advanced, Ricky took off into the air. General was right on his tail, the worst place to be. Ricky back flapped, causing himself to stop in midair; General ran right into him and dropped to the ground. Those on the ground had foreseen this possibility, so they were not there to cushion his fall. The collision sent Ricky spinning out of control toward the wall with his wings collapsed onto his back. He struggled to open them and succeeded right before hitting the wall. He controlled himself enough to hit the wall with his feet and pushed off into a back spiral flip, making him face the other direction.

He ran right into Craft Master. He grabbed Ricky and closed his wings, acting as a dead weight. Ricky couldn't keep them both in the air, so they dropped like sacks of flower. If Ricky hit the ground, Craft Master would keep his position, even if he hit the ground as well, so he was willing to go out without style. Ricky's right hand was pinned to the burly Craft Master, but his left hand was free. He sucker punched Craft Master and kicked him between the legs. The pain was too much for Craft Master, so he let go eight feet from the ground. He was facing up, so he was unable to regain flight. He landed on an unfortunate yellow-green spectator.

Everyone in the vicinity dropped to the ground as Ricky snapped his wings open, three feet from the ground. He put his hands on his head to make sure that he didn't accidentally touch the ground. He gained four feet and skimmed over spectators' heads to the ring. He landed there and drew his sword. His mind was back to the calculating.

There were two of them and one of him, and he was not in his best shape. He had no idea how good these two opponents were. He smiled at the fact that a few years ago, he probably would have fought for the other side.

Commander and Fighting Master landed behind Ricky. They hadn't been fast enough to engage Ricky in the air, so they crept up behind him with swords raised. Ricky twirled as soon as they were in his range. He sliced at both of their swords, causing Commander's to hit Fighting Master on the arm. They backed away, and Fighting Master circled around Ricky so that he and Commander were on opposite sides of him.

Ricky had to divide his attention to two opponents, and he had no idea how good they were.

You are doing great! Red told Ricky.

Please try not to distract me.

Remind me to tell you something later.

Shhhhhhhh!

Right then Commander and Fighting Master charged at Ricky, Commander swinging at his head, Fighting Master at his feet. They were not in perfect sync, but he was not Red and was unable to do her block-turn-slash-block-turn tactic. He had to throw himself parallel to the ground. He also opened his wings and hit both of his opponents in the gut. They staggered back a little, and Ricky used a Red move and flipped to the other side of Commander.

Commander recovered and ran at Ricky with his sword ready. Ricky parried his attack, leaving his chest momentarily open, so Ricky took that opportunity to kick him there. That sent him reeling backward. Luckily for him, he hit Fighting Master; otherwise, he would've gone out of the ring instead of Fighting Master. They were a sword's length away, circling each other, trying to find weaknesses.

"Good, one on one. Much better," Ricky said.

"I'd prefer to have the upper hand," Commander muttered.

"Then I'll let you attack first."

Commander wondered how the V-scale knew he had said that.

"Let's make this a fight to the death, now."

"Why?"

"Because I don't want to live with a figurative loser on my head."

"Well, I do not make it a habit to kill anymore, so I will try my hardest *not* to kill you."

"You will regret that decision, V-scale."

"I told you, my name is Ricky!"

As if this had been choreographed days before, they stepped forward together, and Commander attacked first. Ricky attacked after that, but neither could get an advantage. They were evenly matched. Overhead slashes were blocked, deadly fakes were knocked aside, and kicks were given as frequently as they could muster. Still, neither could gain an advantage. Major wounds were nonexistent; minor wounds were numerous. To change tactics, Commander started taking long, powerful, hacking swings and advancing forward. Ricky's only options were to give ground or be hacked into several pieces. Soon, he was at the edge of the ring. He thought about flipping over but saw that Commander's wings were slightly unfurled, a sign that he was ready for air combat.

Ricky blocked a hard swing lightly, intending to retaliate when Commander recovered from the momentum of the attack; however, the sword flipped out of his hand, spinning in the air above the crowd.

"Well, that's not good," Ricky said out loud. He came up with a plan while Commander ripped the left side of his shirt. Commander put his sword tip between two of Ricky's chest scales.

Commander asked this with a self-satisfied smile, "Don't you wish that it was a fight to the death now?"

"Nope, not really. You only think you've won."

Commander's smile wavered. "But I have."

"I'm not out of the ring, and I will never quit."

Commander pushed the sword in, and Ricky didn't move. It went in an inch before Commander realized that it wasn't helping anything. Ricky didn't even flinch.

Can you even do that? Red asked.

It'll work, Ricky reassured her.

Ricky started reading Commander's mind right then. He had to time this perfectly. If he didn't, then he was either dead or back where he started. He also had to goad him into doing it.

"Even if you win, all you'll gain is another Rept slave."

"You don't know, do you? Can anyone believe this? The V-scale doesn't know who he is!"

"I have a name, so please use it. I know I've told you what it is."

"If you don't step back right now, *V-scale*, then I will kill you."

"Have fun with that."

"Fine," Commander said as he pulled back the sword.

Ricky had to time it just right.

Commander lunged. Ricky dodged to the side right before it hit. He shuffled to the side, trying not to get out of the circle. He lost his balance, and there were a few intense seconds of getting it back. He ran to the middle of the circle and turned to see the angry, swordless Commander.

As Ricky had moved to the side, he shot a pillar of gypsum out of the ground, and the sword plunged easily into it. Before Commander could take it out, Ricky had turned it into diamond. It proved impossible to get out. They faced each other, weaponless.

Commander's nostrils were smoking. Ricky had just recently relearned how to breathe fire, and he recognized that Commander was planning to do so. He hoped that he could do hand-to-hand combat with someone of his own race. He normally beat people of other races.

Commander ran at Ricky and tripped on a ledge. He knew that it had not been there before, so he watched his footing as he walked to Ricky. Once he was within Ricky's tale length, Ricky spun and hit him with it. That started the Rept hand-to-hand combat, which was composed of fire breathing, scratching, tail whacking, and not nearly as fluid as human hand-to-hand combat. Commander was more used to fighting his own race, so he had grabbed Ricky's wrists in less than two minutes.

He kicked Ricky in the chest, and they both fell to the ground, Commander on top. Ricky strained to get up, but Commander put all of his weight on Ricky's wrists and dug his feet into his knees. Commander let go of Ricky's left wrist and reached for the back of his belt. Ricky used those fast few seconds to get on top of Commander, but he used the momentum to get back on top and plunge the dagger that he had gotten from his belt into Ricky's chest.

Ricky grunted. Commander expected him to be dead in a matter of seconds; thus, he was stunned when Ricky grinned.

"My heart is on the other side," he growled.

Ricky pushed Commander's chest with his feet, and he flew in the air to land on his back to Ricky's right. Ricky didn't flinch as he took the dagger out of his chest. He threw it barely outside the circle, saying, "It is illegal to use this thing."

Ricky walked to the pillar of diamond holding the sword. The pillar dissolved for him, and the sword came out in his hands.

He threw the sword handle as hard as he could at Commander's head, but he managed to duck it. The sword hit the wall because the audience was paying attention to make sure that they didn't get hit.

Blood was flowing freely from Ricky's chest, and half of his shirt was stained with it. Some of the crowd wondered how he was still standing with that much blood loss. He coughed into his hand and stained his golden scales with blood.

Ricky ran at a spot three yards away to Commander's right, and he thought that his opponent's blood loss was making his vision funky. Ricky jumped into the air and hit a wall that shot out of the ground. The angle made him go straight at Commander's side. Commander catapulted out of the ring, and Ricky had to back flap so that he did not go out of the ring too.

As soon as he landed in the ring, he won, but he was barely aware of the fact. He felt like he was floating, but in reality, he was lying on the ground as a hundred thousand Rept stared at him. One of them rushed forward and started to bandage his chest. Ricky felt something pass from Red to him, but he was unsure what it was. He never remembered that afterward, but Red did.

He noticed Red next to him right before he fell asleep.

⟿⟐⟞

Ricky awoke to find himself in a dark room on a bed. It was so dark that he could only see the outlines of everything in it. Red came in with a torch and put it in a holder.

"What happened?" Ricky asked.

"You fell asleep because our link let a little of my fast healing go to you. It just exhausted you more than it does me. You're not completely healed, but it is *way* better."

Ricky blinked at her. "How long was I out?"

"Two hours. I haven't left your side, so I don't know what's going on, but apparently it's important. Justin and a lady wanted to come see you, but I wouldn't let them. They're still out there, so do you want them to come in?"

"Sure."

Red turned and walked out. Ricky stood up and wondered how he had gotten there, so Red told him in their heads. He noticed that the only clothing on his torso was a bandage, so he put on a shirt. He coughed up a little blood, but he was sure that it was only a little residue from before. He felt perfectly fine now except for a flesh wound above his lungs.

Red came in with Justin and a lavender, female Rept. Red then turned back and went into the room next door that had been assigned to her.

"Hello," Ricky said and bowed to the lady.

The lady looked Ricky up and down and said, "Aren't you going to hug your mom, young man?"

I forgot a crazy amount, Ricky realized.

You think? At least you have a mom.

Your biological one might be alive.

Who knows, Red thought with a sigh.

"Uh, Mom?"

"Yah, me," said the lady.

Ricky looked at Justin and back at the lady. He did not know what to say.

Justin sighed and rubbed his head. "How much do you remember?"

"Only anything about you, but nothing else before fifteen."

Right after he said that, he recognized his mother.

"Okay, scratch that. It just hit me, and I remember you, Mom, but vaguely."

That was unexpected, Red commented. *Can I go back to Alexa now?*

I might still need you.

I thought as much. I'm going to try to sleep.

Okay.

"Well, I guess that's good. Do you remember your father?"

Ricky shook his head.

"Then you must come meet him," she said.

She grabbed his arm and put hers in it. She walked purposefully, and Ricky had no choice but to follow. He heard Justin chuckle a little. As she led him farther in the caves, he started to remember backward from his fifteenth birthday.

He stopped and faced her in the middle of a hall. Her eyes were a question.

"I'm sorry about how I treated you…back when I was a stupid kid."

She smiled. "That's good. I forgive you."

She kept on walking, and he followed still. A minute later, they were in the dungeon. She led them to the back of it, and they found the only closed door. Justin looked around for someone with a key, but there was no one around.

"How are we going to get in?" he asked no one in particular.

He flinched as the door seemed to melt into the ground. He looked at Ricky for a fraction of a second, but said nothing. They walked into the cell. Ricky saw a rust-scaled Rept with no feet lying on a stone bed.

"That was not how I expected you to come back in, Dee." He looked at Justin and smiled. "You finally got the guts to resist eh, boy? Good job."

Justin scratched the back of his neck. "It wasn't just me."

The footless Rept looked at Ricky. "Of course, I knew that, but you started it."

Ricky felt like he wasn't considered in the room.

"And you are back," he said while looking at Ricky, "but whether to haunt me or not, I don't know."

Ricky was slightly confused at that. "Haunt you?"

"If you are no different, then we will have to exile you, and I will have it haunting my conscience that I raised a bad son."

"Exile. What?"

You're turning into me, Red told Ricky.

He looked at Justin. "You haven't told him yet?"

"I wanted you to tell him, after he remembers who you are."

The rust Rept looked at Ricky again. "Who am I?"

Ricky tilted his head. He knew that Justin and his mom had said that they were going to see his dad, but this may not be him. He had to look at him for a minute before any memories came back. The others were patient.

"You are my dad, and your profession was…tradition keeper."

He guessed that 3 was the magic number, because after he recognized three people from his past, all of his memories came rushing back. He sat down heavily against the wall. He was *not* a good kid.

"I'm sorry, I was a terrible kid. Please forgive all that *junk.*"

That seemed to surprise his dad.

"You're sorry? You want *forgiveness!* Whose son are you?"

"Yours."

Ricky's dad blinked. "I forgive you. I never thought I'd get to say those words. Come give me a hug, son."

Ricky stood and gleefully hugged his dad, whose name was Greg. Greg let go and held his youngest son at arm's length.

"I think that you'll make a good king."

Ricky stopped cold in his tracks. "What did you just say?"

"You are going to be king."

Ricky stared at his dad, dumbfounded.

"We were supposed to tell you on your fifteenth birthday, but you were not ready for it, so we decided to wait it out. Then when Justin came home and told us that you were dead, we kind of rejoiced. A month later when the council caught up to us, we told them you were dead. They looked high and low for a V-scale baby, but there was none to be found.

"Since you had been stabbed in the heart, we *knew* you were dead. The only other explanation besides you surviving, which was said to be impossible, was that God didn't want us to have another ruler. That is how we have lived for eighteen years, thinking that the council was right to treat us like trash because God had abandoned us."

"God did not and will never abandon his people," Ricky said.

"How are you so sure?" Dee asked. "It is common knowledge that he abandoned us after we first sinned."

Ricky faced his mom. "Then I must tell you that common knowledge is wrong. God had a plan that he put into motion to save all people. He poured himself out and became a person, a human if you want to know. His name was Jesus. He lived a normal life among his people, but when he turned thirty, he started to teach as his people had never heard. He traveled through the land healing people, but some people hated him for being him. They had him shamed and crucified on a cross, which was the death of a common thief.

"Three days later, he rose from the dead. He died to forgive your sins and rose from the grave to defeat death. He did this as a free gift to all people, including the Rept. All anyone has to do is accept his gift."

Greg looked at his son. He wondered where his rebellious, drunk son had gone to be replaced by this confident, caring son.

"Was this what changed you?" he asked.

"Yes. Christ changes those who accept his gift. He gave me a new life and forgave and forgot my sins. Now I live to serve him."

"If God can forgive you, then he can forgive me. How do I accept his gift?"

"I want to as well," said Dee.

Ricky smiled happily. "It says in his written word that he gave us that if we confess with our mouth that Jesus is Lord and believe in our heart that God raised him from the dead, then we will be saved. Repeat after me. Dear Heavenly Father, I admit that I am a sinner. I confess that Jesus is Lord, and I believe that you raised him from the grave so that I may be forgiven. Please come into my heart. I promise to serve you as long as I live. In the name of Jesus Christ I pray. Amen."

There was silence for a moment.

Greg asked, "You said that God has a written word?"

"Yah, the Bible. Red is bringing mine right now."

"Red?"

"My meld."

"Oh."

There was a moment of silence while they thought about different thoughts.

"Is the king thing because of what I did or what?"

"No, it has nothing to do with what you have done, really. What did you do anyway?" Greg asked.

Justin answered, "He challenged the whole council and won."

"You did that? What were you thinking! They could've killed you and gotten a baby to control!"

"There is a baby, though," Dee pointed out.

"There is a V-scale baby?"

"Yes, but you wouldn't believe how," Justin said.

Ricky remained silent.

"Oh, and there is one more thing that you need to know, Ricky," Greg began. "Before you become king, you have to tell our whole race your whole life story."

"Everything?"

"And then we will decide whether you'd make a good monarch or not. If the majority says that you are unworthy, then you will be exiled."

Ricky's eyes got big. "Then I might as well save everyone the trouble and exile myself now!"

"Why would you want to do that?" Dee asked.

"I was a good kid compared to how bad I was as an adult six years ago."

That was when Red came in with the Bible. "Yep, he was *bad*."

Greg basically stared at Red. "What are you?"

"A Raggy."

"But I have seen Raggies before. They all had white skin."

Red shrugged. "And I've never seen a footless Rept before."

That was rude, Ricky told her.

He was rude first. He implied that I lied and that I am not a Raggy.

"I have no feet because I resisted capture, and that was my punishment so that I can't leave. Why is your skin red?"

Red just looked at him. "I'm sorry that I was rude."

"Well, I guess that we will all learn when you have to tell your life story too."

Red's face turned a little less red in what would have been turning pale. She handed Ricky the Bible, turned, and left.

"She is nicer when you get to know her," Ricky said as if that would explain her behavior. He didn't add that it was his fault she was that way.

There was silence for a few minutes.

"Did they set a coronation date yet?" Greg asked no one in particular.

Justin shook his head. "Most people are still arguing about whether or not we want a ruler or if we want to be individual families again. I need to go back to put my vote in."

He turned and left. Dee followed for the same reason. Then, only Ricky and his dad were in the cell.

Greg put out a hand and said, "Help me up."

Ricky took his dad's hand and put his left shoulder under his arm. He maneuvered him to a sitting position. Ricky backed up after he was done and asked, "I still don't get it. Why am I to be king?"

"You are the V-scale, if you haven't noticed. Everyone else has round scales, but yours are pointed. V-scales are the only ones in our race who are able to speak in large crowds without some sort of backup; thus, they are the only ones able to lead by themselves. That is why tradition makes you king. Besides, if you are bad, then you will be exiled; the problem with that is that we would have to pick a new council to rule us. I doubt anyone wants to go back to that."

"Do I have any choice in the matter?"

"No. Either you are king, or you are exiled from our entire race. If you came within sight of any of our race after being exiled, then they would have an excuse to kill you. One time there was a really bad V-scale that was denied the throne. That was before we knew of places outside of this forest. It became a sport to try to kill him. Eventually an arrow pierced his heart. I think that would've been a sorry existence."

Ricky sighed. "At least I'll be able to go to other countries."

"Don't give up before you try."

"Right."

"So are you going to tell me about that thing in your hands?"

Ricky started to explain the Bible to his dad. When Justin came back, they moved their dad to a room with a comfortable bed.

⸺◈◈◈⸺

Red found that she was figuratively invisible. No one seemed to notice her presence, even though she was only a foot shorter than all of them. Most of the Rept were in the huge chamber, talking in groups about the best course of action for the future. Red could walk up behind a group of them and listen to their conversation without anyone commenting on her presence. Using this method, she learned the many different opinions of what needed to be done.

One popular opinion was driven by the same attitude that Ricky had: we might as well try and see what happens. Another thought was that he was a ghost because he was dead before that day; thus, he would disappear, and someone would have to raise the baby to be queen. Some people who had been loyal to the council said that if he was real, then they should not even listen to him because he obviously was a killer; they also said that it would be best to elect a new council right away. The last opinion was split into two separate parts: the ones who didn't want to listen to Ricky and wanted to go straight to family clans separated from all the others and the people who wanted to listen to Ricky but then go into clans if he was exiled.

None of the groups wanted to reelect the old council. Those who were loyal had been told to kill their disloyal loved ones. Even though the order had been stopped, they still held a grudge against the old council. The disloyal Rept were about to be executed for doing nothing wrong, so of course they didn't want anyone of the old council to be in control.

The old council themselves had been put in separate cells where they had imprisoned several of their own race. Once it was decided what direction the race wanted to go, then the issue they presented would be discussed.

Red also learned about the We Investigate Simply Everything (WISE), the elders who represented different crafts and occupations. They were supposed to be the backup plan that would ensure a ruler did not oppose the people's wishes. They were any ruler's advisory board, no matter what type of ruler there was. Since they were established by the first generations of the Rept race, any ruler who tried to remove them got his or her head removed from his or her shoulders. The old council had not removed the WISE for that very reason, but they had had absolutely no effect on what the council did. The debate was about whether to replace the WISE since the council had replaced them to whom they wanted years ago.

The one thing that all of the Rept agreed upon was that the fake-name real-name law had to go. Everyone was telling people their real name and not liking it when someone called them by the fake name that the council had given them.

After learning all of this, Red found out why she seemed invisible. She ran into an adolescent Rept who was her height and had the same color scales as her new skin was. They stared at each other for a while before one of them said something.

"What are you?" asked the teenage female Rept.

"I am a Raggy, and no, we normally don't look like this. What is your name?"

"I don't exactly have one yet because when the council ruled, they didn't name kids until they turned twenty. I am only fifteen. Do you have a name?"

"Yah, Red."

"That is your name, Red, or was it what you were calling me?"

"That's my name."

"Does it feel odd not to have scales?"

"I've never had scales, so I wouldn't know."

"Does all of your kind have no scales?"

"Yes, but everyone else's skin is white. Can you please stop asking me questions?"

The kid smiled. "Okay, but just one more. Are you the V-scale's meld?"

Red rolled her eyes. "His name is Ricky."

"Then you are. Do you mind if I follow you?"

"I thought you said that you had one more question, not two."

The teenage Rept smiled and shrugged in an "I'm totally innocent" gesture. Red sighed and said that she could follow her but that she was just going back to her room. The girl answered that it was perfectly fine with her. Red turned and went to her room. The girl followed, talking to Red, who said all of one sentence for the whole way back. The Rept said at least fifty.

You are being tolerant, Ricky noted.

She reminds me of how much my mom talked when I was a kid.

Oh. Your adopted mom? Missing her?

Yeah to both.

Once they got to the door of Red's room, she asked the girl, "Do you mind if I go in alone for a second? I have to change."

She laughed. "We are both girls. What are you afraid of?"

That confused Red enough that she didn't object to the girl going into her room. She noticed Red's sword and bow leaning on the wall right away. Red had only been carrying a dagger around because she didn't want the cumbersome sword or the quiver. She would have to get used to them again; she hadn't had them because Ricky kept them while she was with Alexa.

"You have weapons! You can't be any older than me, and we aren't allowed to touch weapons until we are, like, seventeen."

"I am almost eighteen," Red said from her bed. She was looking under it for her clothes, which Ricky had brought in his pack. She had taken it while he was sleeping. "And I have been handling weapons since I was nine. Was that a council rule?"

"Yes, so can I touch your sword?"

Red shrugged. "Why not?"

She took out a green shirt that she had only worn once, when she had invaded the fort of Alebu right after Ricky had broken her ankle. This time she was wearing it because she didn't want to be *completely* red. She changed quickly as the other girl fondled her sword. The girl turned and frowned at Red.

"Do you not always wear the same color as your skin?"

Red shook her head. "Before my skin turned red, I always wore red, but I keep thinking that I look like one huge drop of blood."

"So you are wearing green?"

"Anything wrong with that?"

The girl did her "I'm innocent" gesture. Red flopped on her bed. She was still recovering from dying, so she was tired. Plus, she had stayed awake the whole time Ricky was asleep. She needed rest.

"Do you need to sleep?" the girl asked.

Red nodded at the ceiling.

"Then I will come back tomorrow to hang out."

She left and Red sighed. She was so tired that she barely noticed her arms start to itch.

When the girl entered Red's room the next morning, she awoke Red. Red unsheathed her dagger and had it ready to throw in two seconds. That scared the girl, who yelped a little.

"Oh, sorry," Red said, sheathing the dagger. "You startled me awake."

"*I* startled *you*! It was the other way around."

Red shrugged. "Reflex."

Then the girl noticed something. "What did you do to your shirt?"

Red stopped absentmindedly scratching her belly. She looked down at her shirt and saw that the top half of it was the same color as her skin, and the bottom was green. As she watched, the red seemed to leak onto the green. Red also noticed that her skin itched where the shirt was green but didn't where it was red. It seemed to speed up as she woke up more.

"Well, that is weird," Red said.

It is probably part of the thing that the devil did to you, Ricky said.

That would make sense. Where are you?

Trying to figure out what the rest of my race has decided.

Do you need me at all?

Nope.

Crum.

"So you didn't do anything to it?"

"Nope."

"You are right that is weird. Guess what!"

The only reason Red didn't like hanging with this Rept was that she reminded her too much of her adopted mom. "What?"

"I found my mom and asked her if I could have a name, and she said that I could pick my own name!"

"Good. I think."

"So I want to ask you what you think I should name myself."

Red stood and started making her bed. "I am bad with names."

"Well, now is as good a time as any to practice for when you have kids."

Red laughed at that. "It is custom among my race to wait until a baby has opened his or her eyes and then to name them whatever first comes to mind."

"Well, what came to your mind when you first saw me?"

Red shrugged. "Oh."

"You're right; you are not good with names."

"I told you so."

"How did you end up with a coherent name with that method?"

"I was raised by humans."

"Humans?"

"Like every other race, you have to see one to know what they look like."

"Okay."

Red went over to her quiver and shouldered it. "Do you want to join me hunting?"

"Sure. I'll shoot ideas at you as you shoot game!"

Red didn't let the girl see her roll her eyes. The only thing that happened the rest of the day was that the girl decided that she would name herself Lucy.

※ ※ ※

Ricky had been bothered all night about a memory from his teen years. That morning he decided that he had to do something about it. He went to ask his dad something.

"How long will it take everyone to agree if I am wanted?"

Greg answered, "It could take an hour, and it could take a week. Why?"

"I have something that I need to do, somewhere else."

"What something?"

"I need to find Saze and Pave."

His dad was appalled. "What do you need with those two?"

"I want them to know what God did for them."

Greg thought for a minute. It was true that those two needed it.

"If you leave, you need to leave your meld here. Is she okay with that idea?"

Ricky asked her and nodded his head. Red's only problem with staying was that Alexa's birthday was in a week.

"How long after they agree do you think they would want the coronation?"

"At least two days."

"Then I better leave now."

"Good luck."

"Luck isn't real. Will you pray for me?"

Greg nodded, and Ricky left. He went outside and flew to his destination.

The three days that Ricky was gone were enough for the whole race to agree on a plan. An hour after he got back, they agreed that the best course of action was to listen to Ricky, and if he wouldn't make a good king, then they would go into family clans. They set the day that they would decide and the day that Ricky and Red would tell their life stories, to be three days later. The day after that was either the coronation or the banishment.

Red realized that the day that Ricky was crowned, or banished, would be the same day as Alexa's birthday. That meant that Red wouldn't be there for Alexa! God told her to help Ricky do what he needed to do, so she guessed that Alexa didn't need her then. Obviously, Kim would not give up the throne, because Red wouldn't have been born if she would. Red had to trust God that he knew what was important, so this adventure with Ricky must have been important.

In those three days, Greg told Ricky as much as he could and as much as he needed to know about the coronation.

Red didn't really do much besides hang out with Lucy in those days of waiting.

—◦◦◦—

On the morning of the day before Alexa's birthday, everyone in the Rept race gathered into the grand hall. Ricky stood next to the platform that used to hold a semicircle table. Now it was empty, waiting for him. Some of the crowd chatted quietly. Everyone looked for a comfortable position. This would take awhile. It would start at eight, but it was now seven thirty.

Greg was giving Ricky last-minute advice. Red was listening to the rain outside, away from all of the people whom she would have to face. Commander was not five feet from Ricky, with his back to him. Ricky wasn't exactly sure what to think about him. There had to be someone to question him, because it ensured that only the whole truth about his life was told. The people had chosen Commander because he was the most likely to hold a grudge against Ricky; thus, he was the most likely person to try and make it hard on Ricky.

Thirty minutes later, Commander jumped onto the platform.

"Hello, again. As you know, I am the interrogator. Now we must listen to"— Commander had to think about what the V-scale's name was—"Ricky."

He hopped down, and Ricky jumped up. He clasped his hands behind his back and started, "It may take awhile to get to the good part, so please don't tune me out while it is bad."

He then told about random childhood memories, swinging, first flying lesson, first fire breath (he forgot about how to do that with his amnesia), and other normal memories. You could tell by the nodding in the crowd that these were normal childhood stuff. He got to the interesting things after his fourteenth birthday.

"After that birthday, it seemed as if my parents were becoming stricter. I started to rebel by…" He told of small things like not cleaning his room. "One day while I was exploring the woods when I was supposed to be studying, I happened upon this shed. Outside of it were barrels of some weird liquid. I tasted it, and it had this frothy, rotten taste. I heard a sound behind me, so I looked to see who it was. I saw two crazy, thin humans with huge eyes looking at me.

"I asked them who they were, and they said that their names were Saze and Pave. They invited me to join them in enjoying life. I said sure, and they gave me a cupful of the liquid. They were looking at me as if it would be fun, so I drank it all. They got some cups, and we all drank more than we should have. My parents came looking for me, and when they found me, they freaked out. Dad dragged me home by a wing and told me never to go there again. I disobeyed him."

He gave multiple examples of the many times he had not followed that order.

"Eventually, I avoided my dad completely. The only time I was home was to eat and bug my parents. They'd lecture me about bad addictions and bad friends, but I'd roll my eyes and tune them out. When they were done, I'd leave and not come back for a long time."

No matter how embarrassing it got, Ricky looked different people in the crowd in the eye. He didn't shy away when telling any part. He talked in detail about quite a few incidents that his parents had tried to get some sense into him.

"All of that came to a head when I came home about half a year after I met my new friends. I came home late for dinner, and my mom started lecturing me about how hard it was to make dinner and that I should be grateful. In the middle of it, I interrupted her and called her a name that I do not want to repeat."

For the first time, Commander asked a question for clarification. "What exactly did you say?"

"Okay, but if you have kids, you might want to cover his or her ears." Then Ricky repeated what he said all those years ago. The crowd gasped in unison. That was *not* something to be repeated.

Ricky continued. "My dad was in the next room, and he heard what I said. He stormed in there and raised his voice at me for the first time. He yelled at me to show better respect to my mother, but I called him a different name."

"What name?" Commander asked.

Ricky waited a second for parents to cover kids' ears, again, and then told what he called his dad. Their reaction was the same as before.

"He told me to leave and never come back. I said that I would be glad to. I flew to a clearing five miles away to plan what to do next. Would I stay with my friends, or would I leave to make my own concoctions somewhere else? While I was thinking, my brother Justin flew in with the two swords that our family owned. He threw one at me and suggested that we fight to death.

"I was *mad,* so I accepted the offer without much thought. Before I had become rebellious, my dad had started to teach me how to read minds, so I used it. I was not that experienced, but I knew how to push hard. He had five more years of experience in sword fighting, but I was sure that I would win with my mind reading. He ran at me and did a face-leg fake, which I blocked."

He then described in as much detail as possible the fight that followed. Justin was listening and nodding. He remembered as much about it as Ricky did.

"He tried and succeeded to make me angrier. I pushed my mind as hard as I could into his, and suddenly all my strength disappeared. I have no idea how he did that, not even now. I fell to my knees because I couldn't stand. He told me that I was a disgrace to our family and our race, and then he plunged his sword in right here."

Ricky tapped the exact place that Commander had plunged his dagger in some days before.

"The next thing I remember, I was lying on a hospital bed. I asked the doctor looking over me what happened. He told me that two crazies had dragged me to his doorstep and disappeared. He asked me what race I was and how I didn't die of blood loss. I had no idea of the answer to either question. He diagnosed me with amnesia and told me to stay in bed for a week."

"I did as I was told. After he let me go, I became a beggar on the streets. That was all that I knew how to do, sit. I didn't remember my name, my race, anything. When a huge Orv with multiple weapons asked me about those things, I just looked at him. For those of you who do not know what an Orv is, they are a race twice as big as ours with no scales and coal-black skin."

That was hard for most of them to visualize.

"He told me to stand up and come with him if I wanted to do anything. He turned and left, and I followed."

Ricky then told of how he learned that he was an assassin and that he wanted him to be his apprentice. He also told of how one night he woke up with two names on his mind: Ricky and Rept. He asked the assassin, Chafgee, what that might mean, and he said that Ricky was a name, so Rept must be his race.

"I accepted Chafgee's offer of apprenticeship."

He told how Queen Ruth was killed by a mob of Raggies on the day he started his apprenticeship. For thirty minutes, he explained how he was trained. It was much different from how he trained Red, for he had been a willing apprentice, and he was not naturally good at every fighting thing like her. He was trained for eight years before Chafgee declared that there was nothing more he could teach him. In the middle of those eight years, Chafgee had become a servant to Queen Kim and only served her.

"When he told me that I was no longer his apprentice, I walked away three steps. That was all it took to respark the anger in me. He was not a kind master. I turned and threw a dagger between his eyes. He was dead before he hit the ground. I stood over my first kill, and I loved it. I took all of his weapons, most of which I don't have any more, and burned his body.

"The next day I presented myself to Kim as her new assassin. She wasn't too happy about having an assassin of another race, but I was the only one available at the time, and she needed one."

He told of the various nobles that he had killed for her, then of what he did at Fort Alebu when he was not on a mission. Commander asked him to describe some of those "games," and Ricky obliged. Red already knew all of this because he had often bragged about it when she was his apprentice, but she was reacting how she had every time. She had to restrain herself from jumping up and running so that she couldn't think or hear his thoughts. She wanted to fight someone. If she was in the chamber with everyone else, she might have hurt people. She hated to hear how he had tortured and killed her race, almost as much as she hated watching it.

He then told of how he found Red in the arena at Alebu and chose her as his apprentice. Several of his listeners couldn't equate this pathetic Raggy he described with the Red they had seen briefly in the halls. When he told of how she ran away and then came back and pledged herself to him, they all wondered—along with the Ricky—of the past. What in the world could change her? And then he told them of his conversion to Christianity. They were amazed at how he changed after accepting Jesus into his heart.

"After Red became Alexa's slave, I went Raggy hunting, but for a different reason. I wanted to help as many as possible, and I wanted to ask forgiveness from those that I had hurt. One Raggy that I had tortured had escaped afterward, and while I was 'playing,' he had told me that when I would meet the Raggy liberator, I'd be sorry that I had ever touched a Raggy.

"We both met in the Fort when he ran into me. As soon as he noticed whom he had run into, he turned tail and ran. I yelled after him that he was right. He stopped and looked at me. He asked me what I meant by that, and I said that I was sorry for how I had treated him and others of his race. I apologized and turned to leave. He ran up to me and asked me to follow him. He led me to the mainly Raggy-populated area of the Fort. About one of every four recognized me or knew of me. I apologized to them all, and most of them forgave me. I must confess that I couldn't stop the waterworks that day."

He told about how he went through all of Syn-Cynthia and asked for forgiveness of every living Raggy he hurt. He also studied the Bible as much as possible and amassed knowledge from the many libraries that he visited. This part of his life was not exciting but was essential for his spiritual growth. Over the three years that Red spent as Alexa's slave, Ricky studied as much as possible on many various subjects. He only exercised for one hour a day, so he did not keep his ability to plain defeat *anybody*, just most people.

"The day after Red let me meld with her, I tried to find my power. I decided that it probably wouldn't be what anyone I knew had, so I had to search. I tried many things; eventually I gave up. Then a few weeks later, there was an earthquake. I was near a volcano, and it was dormant. It decided to choose that day to change. The earthquake opened the crater, and there was a massive lava flow going toward the small town where I was. Normally, the inhabitants would try to call Sunny or Tess, both of whom control fire and would have been able to redirect the lava flow, but there was not enough time to get either one because the lava was going too fast, and usually if such an event was to occur one of them would have been there before it started. It would be at the town in an hour, so they started to evacuate, wondering why neither their queen nor the Prophetess were there to help.

"I had this crazy idea, supernaturally inspired, to stop it. I told the earthquake to stop, and it did. That made the lava travel a little slower. I went to right in front of the lava flow. It would reach where I was standing any second. I had no idea how to stop it, but I stood there. I thought that if the earthquake listened to me, then so would the ground itself. I told it to go up, and it did. I did not have enough time to tell it to do all that I wanted, so I thought to it, like with people. It did as I told, and I found my power.

"After that, I tried to look for you all. The only things I knew were my race, my name, and the fact that someone had tried to kill me, so I didn't have much to go on. I found every scrap of paper that mentions anything near the doctor's house that I woke up in. I searched whole libraries for the word *Rept*, and I never found it. All of the weird things around that area I can sum up in one sentence: no one wants to go farther than ten feet into these woods. I had just decided to try to explore this forest when Justin brought Red here."

"I was reading a geology book, *The Diverse Strength and Types of the Rocks of Tanlindia*, in order to better understand what I control, when Red noticed…"

He told about the last few chapters in detail. When he told of what Power Master had done to his senses, the crowd finally understood why he had acted the way he did during that part of the fight. They also understood why he had stopped the council right then and not earlier. If he had stopped it earlier, the majority of the population would not have known about the council's plan.

Shortly after that, he explained that he had left to find Saze and Pave. "It was taking you forever to decide what course of action to take, so I had time to find my old drink mates. I went to their last known location and found not them, but their son and his girlfriend. They had become sober and moved back into their old town, only to marry and have their son repeat their mistake. I shared God's love with them, and they accepted him. When I left, they were going back to find his parents, apologize, and share what I had told them."

When he was finished and had told of his feelings right before getting on the stage, it was question time.

The first question that Commander asked was, "Is that salvation thing for everyone?"

"'If you confess with your mouth that Jesus is Lord and believe in your heart that God raised him from the dead, you will be saved.' That is true for anyone who asks for it. I mean, look at me. I was the lowliest of sinners, but he forgave me, and I am a totally different person now."

"How do you do it?" Commander asked.

"Anyone who wants to have Jesus's gift, repeat after me. Dear Heavenly Father, I confess that I am a sinner. I have done many things that have brought shame upon me. I believe that you sent your Son to earth to die on the cross for my sins. I believe that you raised him from the dead. I say that Jesus is my Lord. Come into my heart and change me. In Jesus's name, I pray. Amen."

As he said that, the rest of his race repeated it. If he could change *that much*, then every one of them should accept Jesus and change themselves. Ricky thought that even if he was banished, this trip would've been worth it. He noticed Red sneak in while they all prayed, and she was now sitting in the corner between the stage and the wall. She was freaking out.

The people were ecstatic about this new belief, but they were here for a specific purpose. They quieted down and listened as Commander asked another question.

"What was it like to die?"

"It was beyond simple description. I met Jesus, and he told me some very personal things. That is all that I can hope to describe, but know that it was awesome."

Commander asked some other questions for clarification on many different aspects of Ricky's life. After he had asked all that he could, he turned the questions over to the crowd. Once everybody had asked whatever question they had, they left for lunch. It was one o'clock in the afternoon. Red had all of the rest of the day to tell about her life.

She was going through a miniature crisis. Luckily, Ricky had kicked Commander out of their minds so that she could have some peace for a while. She was sitting, staring blankly at a wall, but her mind was in a tornado.

How am I going to do this?

The same way I did it.

But you are you! *You are meant to be up there, leading. I can do the grunt work. I'll leave the talking to you and Alexa.*

You only have to do it once.

For, like, an hour! Probably more!

You could distract yourself with something.

That works for a total of one minute.

Make it work for an hour or more.

Do you know how long that seems to me?

Just remember what you were told by God. You should eat something.

I don't feel like eating.

Come with me to get food from Justin.

Red sighed and complied. Justin happily gave them both ham-and-cheese sandwiches. Red just nibbled on hers until

Ricky specifically told her to eat. In ten minutes, it was time for everyone to go back to listen to Red. She fiddled with the dagger handle sticking out of her belt. It was the only weapon besides her teeth knives that she and Ricky had with them. She didn't look at the gathering crowd.

If Alexa were here, she'd be laughing her head off.

Be quiet, Ricky.

Right then, Ricky let Commander back into their mind.

Red said out loud, "I can do all things through Christ who strengthens me."

Soon, everyone was back and settled down. Commander jumped back on to the stage.

"Okay now that we have heard the, err...Ricky's tale, it is time to hear his meld's. May I present Red."

He jumped down, and she hesitated before jumping up.

"I can do all things through Christ who strengthens me." She jumped up and said, "Please excuse the pacing, dagger fiddling, or the fact that I won't look up, for I am extremely nervous."

Commander snorted, and Red started to pace.

"I'm pretty sure all of you have been told by your parents what happened when you were a baby. Well, that is where I start, with a prophecy uttered years before I was born—"

"Please tell us the exact prophecy." Commander interrupted.

"'When the war drums beat against all the Raggies, a liberator will be born from the womb of a widowed mother.' It is widely held among the Raggies that a liberator has red eyes."

Commander then had her explain the importance of eye color to Raggies. She did to the best of her knowledge and then told about her birth and of her mom putting her up for adoption. He pushed her into telling as much as she knew about the full-scale Raggy persecution. She complied. About that time, she took out her dagger; she had the fidgets, so she twirled it in her hands as she paced and looked at the ground.

She started to tell about her important tenth birthday, but Commander wanted her to go through everything that she could remember. As she talked, her pacing got faster, and so did her talking. Ricky had to admonish her so that she would slow down and relax.

Commander was only satisfied after she had told everything that she could remember up to her tenth birthday. She continued with much interruption from him as she moved on. And so it went: Red talking, Commander asking for clarification, Red clarifying and continuing. When she got to when she met Ricky, Commander wanted full detail about *every* little thing she thought and he said. Red was annoyed at this, but she endured.

To Red, this whole process lasted forever, but she kept herself in check and didn't talk fast again. Commander, on the other hand, wanted her to go *slower*. No one knew why she suddenly threw the dagger she had been fiddling with at Ricky. He easily caught it, expecting it.

"What was that about?" Commander asked.

Red shrugged. "I thought I might have thrown it at you if I had kept it."

That got more than a few murmurs from the crowd. Red had to find something new to do with her hands; she found that something in wringing a piece of her shirt. Commander was glad that the shirt wasn't his neck. He was doing his job as well as he could.

She told about everything afterward with more and more interruptions.

She recollected all of her adventures, including those with Tess, the Raggies, and with Alexa and Zera. She was forced to explain her every thought and feeling and her reasonings behind melding with Ricky. She happened to glance up at the sea of faces looking at her, and she almost had a panic attack. She froze, but composed herself enough to look back at her hands and start talking again. Luckily for her, she was close to the end.

When she got to her visit from Satan, many a person wondered at how strong she was, when she wasn't in front of a crowd. They heard how much it hurt for her skin to change color and the agony of watching herself taking Ricky's life. She recounted the joy of seeing her Savior, as well as the everlasting love she felt from him. She told them her feelings about her new skin color.

"I figured out why he left my skin red. It makes me a living, breathing, reminder of the blood he shed for my sins."

"Would you go back to white skin if you could?"

"Nope."

She then got to the events of the past few weeks. When she told of what she did when Ricky was telling his life, she was relieved. She was almost done! It was time for questions.

"Have you ever regretted letting Ricky meld with you?" Commander asked.

Red had to think for an answer for a minute. "Yes, when I lay dying. I didn't want him to die, and he was prolonging the process for me. It took twice as long because I started to feed off his strength."

"Did you ever regret making him your master?"

Red scowled at the ground. "I have never liked that word; for to me, it implies slavery, and I am *not* a slave! No, I have never regretted submitting to him, or God for that matter."

"Why are you pacing and fiddling with your shirt?"

"Because I threw my dagger at Ricky."

"I am asking *why* you need to."

"Because if I look up, I think that I will freak out."

"I have no more questions," Commander said. "They are now open to the public."

A voice came from the crowd that Red recognized as Lucy's, "What is your full name?"

Red answered, "Redache."

A different voice asked, "Have you ever felt girly?"

"Nope, never."

There were a few more random questions and one important one: "If you could change anything in your life, what would it be?"

"Nothing. It is not my place to take away important moments; that is God's job."

When everyone was satisfied, Red and Ricky were ceremoniously kicked out of the chamber.

That was embarrassing, Red thought.

I knew that you'd say that.

You think that I can leave soon?

You need to stay until they decide, then you should ask my dad if you are needed.

Red went to her room and picked up her weapons.

I'll be outside.

Okay, but there is a practice room with targets.

Where?

Straight left to the intersection, hang a right, and you're there.

Thanks.

Ricky felt sorry for the targets.

ONLY GOD KNOWS

Shrrrk. Phhhhht. Thud.
Shrrrk. Phhhhht. Thud.
Shrrrk. Phhhhht. Thud.

On and on it went, not stopping until Red ran out of arrows. Then she would walk to the targets at different levels and yank them out. The cycle repeated, and repeated. And repeated.

Red tried not to think about the gathering crowd behind her that was watching her hit bull's-eye after bull's-eye. She didn't acknowledge them until someone tapped her shoulder. She shot the arrow that was in the bow and turned to see that it was General who was holding a bow.

"Hello," he said.

Red's eyebrows met in a puzzled expression. "Hi."

"Are you going to let someone else shoot?"

Red shrugged and went to dislodge the arrows in the targets. She stepped aside and let him shoot a round, then someone else stepped up to practice. She thought that she had no need for target practice, so she decided to go outside and just shoot at random things. Besides, there was bound to be less people outside. How wrong she was!

As she went through the halls, the people who were behind her followed, and others joined the crowd. By the time she got outside, she had close to three hundred people following her. She didn't turn around because she didn't want to see them.

I'm not going to run away, Red told herself. *What's with the people?*

I have a few following me as well, Ricky commented.

Annoying!

Keep cool. It's not forever.

That is going to be hard.

You can do it.

Red found a glade and started shooting random targets: a tree knot, the odd leaf, a nut, etc. He followers stayed far enough away not to be shot, but soon, these faraway onlookers surrounded her.

Shrrrrk. Phhhht. Thud.

This was going to be a long last few hours of the day.

—◆◆◆—

Ricky took out his geology book and started to read it. He was in his room, so the people who had been following him were outside. After a few minutes, he decided that he wouldn't leave Red by herself to take the brunt of the attention. He wasn't exactly sure what he would do, but he had to do something publicly.

He walked out of his room and stood there thinking for a few minutes. He didn't seem to notice the crowd in front of him. His dad had told him what was expected of both him and Red during this period of time. Neither were supposed to talk to anyone unless spoken to, because they wanted to see what the future king and his meld would do when isolated and under pressure.

Ricky decided what he would do, so he went to the huge chamber. He jumped and flew to the roof that was made of black volcanic glass. Using his power, he made it slightly thicker; then he made a bar that could hold his weight hanging from that slightly thicker spot. He sat on it and took out his book.

A few minutes later, someone on the ground asked him what he was doing.

He yelled back down, "I'm trying to find what type of rock this is."

The voice came back up to him, "I might be of some help with that. Can I come up?"

"Yah, just give me a minute."

He jumped off and snapped open his wings. He circled the seat and turned it and its support bigger. He sat back on it and a smoky-white–scaled lady came up and sat next to him.

"I'm Susan," she said, holding out her hand for him to shake.

He shook it, saying, "Ricky."

"I am the geology expert. What does your book say about this rock?"

"I know it is igneous, so I looked under that heading, but I am not entirely sure where to go beyond that. I believe it is extrusive."

"Yes, it is called obsidian. This type of obsidian is rare. Normally it appears black and does not let light pass through, but this formed in a way that light can pass through."

"Huh. So it is transparent obsidian."

"Yep."

"Do you think that you could show me some other types of rock around here?"

"Why are you so interested in rocks? I mean, they fascinate me, but why do you like them?"

"I want to better understand my power."

"Oh. Follow me."

She used her wings to glide down. He dropped and circled the bar he had made. He was about to put it back how it was, but a voice from below asked him not to so that it could be used as a perch. He glided down and followed Susan. She showed him the many types of intrusive and extrusive igneous rocks that were around the caves that the Rept called home.

Red got bored with just shooting things, so she started to twirl her sword. She didn't scratch herself once. She spun it in front of her and tossed it into the air. It sailed up, still spinning, ten feet into the air. It came back down with a few branches. She caught the handle and did figure eights around her body. She smiled and closed her eyes.

Now, this is life, she thought to herself.

Suddenly, with a very loud clang, her sword stopped right in front of her. She opened her eyes and saw that a different sword had blocked her own. Teal hands supported it. She sheathed her sword, crossed her arms, and looked at him with eyebrows raised.

He sheathed his sword and said, "My name is not Commander. It's Gillford."

Red cocked her head at him and said nothing.

"I just wanted to tell you because, uh"—he glanced around and cleared his throat—"I wanted you and Ricky to know."

Red finally spoke, "And it helps that there are a bunch of people around."

He looked at her. "I also wanted to thank you, because if you hadn't helped Ricky see Jesus, then the rest of us would never have either."

Red shrugged. "God would've called him anyway."

"Right. Anyway, so, thanks."

He turned and walked into the crowd. Red wondered how he had changed so fast. She checked the sun's progress and noted that she had an hour or two before sunset. She took out her sword and started to spin it again. She was just content to spin her sword. She didn't care that she had over four hundred people watching her do it. She closed her eyes and flowed with her sword.

After sunset, she and Ricky arrived at the doors to their rooms at the same time. Both had a crowd behind them, but they had become more used to them by then.

"Time to retire until called upon," Ricky said.

"That is why I stopped by a fallen tree on the way here. These are weird bugs, but they taste good."

"I actually got *food* at the *kitchen*."

Red stuck her tongue out at him as she opened her door. Ricky laughed and entered his room. He had several books that he had brought with him to entertain himself the next morning. Red only had her weapons and a Bible. She could find something to do.

—⁓—

The next morning, Red got up as late as possible. It was seven o'clock. She had never been good at sleeping in. She knew that the earliest that they would come get Ricky and her was noon. Five hours, great. She blindly felt her way to the door and knocked on it. A Rept came in with a torch and put it in the holder. She smiled at Red and left without talking. Red took out her Bible and went to the Old Testament. She loved to read about the battles in there. After she had gone through the whole book of Judges, it was eight o'clock.

She decided to do a New Testament book. After 1 John, she got bored with reading. She picked up the torch and wrote her name in the air. She then proceeded into a fake battle in her head, with the torch as her only weapon. She got so wrapped up in this that she almost hit someone coming through her door. She pulled back just in time to not hit Justin.

"Whoa!" he said as he ducked. "Watch what you are doing!"

Red placed the torch back in its holder. "Sorry, I didn't expect you. What time is it?"

"Ten o'clock."

Ricky agreed with that mentally.

"Then why are you here?"

"Because you are wanted in the chamber."

"For what?"

"One more question."

Red frowned, but followed him out. He led her to the chamber, where the whole race had gathered again. He asked her to get on the stage, so she did.

Immediately, a question was thrown at her, "If Ricky were allowed to be king, would you stay by his side?"

"I have no clue as to what you mean by that."

"Would you stay near him, or would you leave to do your own thing?"

"I would have to leave. Alexa's birthday is today."

"Thank you."

Then she was led back to her room. That confused Red.

What do you think that was about? she asked Ricky.

I have no idea. This either means that they want me to be king, or they are trying to make us be overconfident that I am going to be king. I guess we will learn in two hours.

Right. Want to play tic-tac-toe?

On the wall?

Yep.

Sounds like a good idea.

So, Ricky made a tic-tac-toe board on the wall between their rooms. He was granite o and she was silver x. By twelve, the wall was riddled with fifty cats' eyes. They knew each other way too well for either of them to win, and it was nearly impossible to hide their intent, what with being able to read each other's thoughts.

At 12:05 noon, by Ricky's count, a knock came at both of their doors. Red opened hers to find Dee, Ricky's mom, standing with a handkerchief in her hands.

"Hi," Red said.

"Hello. Do you mind if I blindfold you?"

"No, ma'am."

Red turned and let her tie the handkerchief around her eyes. Dee led her right next to Justin, who was leading Ricky. Normally, it would have been Greg leading Ricky, but he was unable to walk; thus, Justin was doing it.

Red asked Ricky, *Did you memorize the routes?*

Yah. If we turn left next, then we are going to the chamber.

And it is a coronation.

But if we turn right...

Then we shall be banished.

Yep. Interesting, isn't it?

Yep.

They continued to converse as they were led straight for a while. Then they turned right. Ricky mentally sighed.

I guess that my past wrongs were too much for them to accept.

I don't think that God would tell us to do this venture at this particular time if it wasn't going to bring some type of fruit.

We shared his sacrifice with all of them, and I think that everyone accepted. That's fruit.

Right. May God's good and perfect will be done.

Amen.

Red felt the breeze right before Ricky did.

With dignity?

Of course.

Dee untied the blindfold, and it took Red a minute to observe everything that was happening. She was in front of a platform at the cave entrance with Ricky right beside her. Many tables scattered among the trees all loaded with an incredible feast, but they weren't just among the trees: they were *in* the trees— hanging from them to be more exact. Sitting on the branches of those trees were all of the Rept. On the wooden platform was a throne. Because they were in the trees, Red did not see too many Rept at one time, so she did not get nervous.

It also confused Red that it was quiet. The stillness made it look like a painting.

Red raised her hand. "Is anyone else confused?"

She got a few laughs from somewhere. Greg was sitting at the front of the platform.

"Ricky, by stepping up to this platform, you will put the responsibility of your entire race on your shoulders. It will be your job to lead, guide, and sometimes discipline the 11,111 separate colors that make up our race. On you will be the burden of war, and on you we wish to place the Rept mantle.

"Do you accept?"

Ricky said, "I do."

"Do you swear to abide by and enforce the laws that our forefathers established?"

"I do."

"Do you swear that you will never lie to, steal from, cheat, or deal unfairly to any of us under your command?"

"I swear it."

"Do you promise to be a fair judge, even if the guilty is someone that you hold dear?"

"I do."

"Then by my right as your father, I declare you king of our race."

As Ricky jumped onto the platform and sat on the throne, his people yelled, "Long live the king! Long live Ricky! *Long live King Ricky!*"

Red was sure that everyone within a hundred miles could hear that the new king was Ricky; it was so loud. She turned to ask Dee why it was held outside, but she was gone. She turned and saw Ricky and his dad fly into a tree to join the enormous feast. He asked him that question, and the explanation was that it was just too good of a day outside to waste it by having everything indoors.

Red was feeling shy, so she sat at the base of a tree and started looking for worms. She didn't feel like socializing. She decided that as soon as he came down, she would ask Greg if it would be okay to leave. New rules.

All throughout the day, the Rept gathered in the trees. They would fly between them to change who they were talking to or maybe to taste some other culinary dish in a different tree. The only people who were working were cooks and moms, and they had breaks to join the festivities. Ricky tried to meet as many people as possible to better know his charge. Red stayed at the bottom of the tree, occasionally looking for and finding an unlucky insect. After a while, she took out her sword and twirled it, careful not to disturb any of the tables.

At about sunset, Rept started dropping from the trees. Most would just drop without opening his or her wings, but one from the tree where Red was sitting back down under tried to glide down. She assumed that this one was Greg. She stood and realized that she was right. He started to actually fall when his legs were five feet from the ground. She caught him by doing this: as soon as his shoulders were at the same height as her, she inserted her right arm under his arms. He jerked to a stop, and she slowly lowered him to the ground.

"Thanks." he grunted.

"I'm sorry it was so sudden. I didn't know that you were dropping so fast."

"It's no problem. That is better than landing on random ground as hard as I could on my buttocks."

Red laughed. "Would you like help getting to your room or something?"

"If you can manage it."

Red put her arm under his shoulders and raised him up. She walked, and he leaned on her.

When they were about halfway there, Red asked the question, "Am I needed for anything else?"

Greg was silent for a minute. "Do you remember the question we asked this morning?"

"Yes."

"We asked that because in the past, all of the V-scales melds, if they needed one, were Rept, and being Rept, they stayed close to the V-scale. As you can tell, this means that your relationship is unique. We decided that it would be okay for you to leave, but you will have to have a Rept escort with you at all times."

"I can't just go by myself?"

"No. Remember, you are melded to the *king* now. If you die, he dies, and if he dies, then we have to go back to square one. We need to make sure that you don't die."

"So if I don't find someone to go with me, then I have to stay here?" Red asked as she led him into his room.

"Yes."

Red sighed. "Okay then." She set him down on his bed.

"Thank you very much for helping me get here. I hope you find someone willing to leave."

"Me too."

She started back to her own room.

I'd go with you, but—

You're needed here, cheese brain.

Where'd you get that name?

Your scales are a similar color to cheese, thus, cheese brain.

You are a little annoyed.

Yah. I just wish I knew what was happening to Alexa.

———

Alexa was sitting in the corner of her tent, feeling a little dejected. All of the people whom she had gathered started calling her Queen Alexandra that morning, but it seemed hopeless without Red. Alexa sighed and got out her Bible. It always helped to read Psalms.

She had read only a chapter when Zera came in.

"What in the world are you doing sitting on the floor, Queen Alexandra?"

"Zera—"

"I'm going to call you that no matter what you say, so don't even think about protesting." Zera walked over to Alexa, grabbed her hand, and tugged at her. "There is someone here to see you, so you need to look like a queen, not an orphan on the streets."

Zera pulled Alexa until she stood up, and she placed her on her bed. Zera then went about grooming Alexa, straightening wrinkles on her shirt, fixing her hair, and making her sit up straight.

When Zera was satisfied, she said, "Good. Now don't mess it up while I go get her."

Alexa rolled her eyes at Zera's back. She loved that girl; she was just a little bossy at times. She started to wonder where Red was again.

Zera had been gone for thirty seconds when a different girl came in. The girl was a fair-skinned human with strawberry-blonde hair, but that was not what stood out about her. Her eyes changed color.

"Hello, Queen Alexandra. I am Tess, one of the powers from Syn-Cynthia, and I have come to tell you what happened to Red."

Alexa stood up. "Um, hi. You are *the* Tess? The one that Red talks about so much?"

"The one and only. I am needed back home, so I'll make this quick. Red found someone spying on you, so she confronted him. He turned out to be Ricky's brother, and he had a power to freeze whatever he looks at. In the Uncivilized Woods, where he brought her, Ricky contested against the leaders of his race. Then Red was confronted by a demon who turned her skin red. Ricky was told that the V-scale is always the king of his race; thus, he had to go through a series of tests about whether or not he was eligible, where Red was required to do them as well. He is being crowned king right now, and Red will be here tomorrow morning."

Tess had stopped talking and was waiting for the inevitable question.

"How do you know all of this?"

Tess smiled her "if only you knew" smile. "Let's just say, I have a weird insight. Any other questions?"

Alexa shook her head in bewilderment.

"Then I must go. *Ta-ta!*"

The girl stepped out of the tent and put herself on fire. She was gone within five seconds, not that Alexa noticed the exact time.

"That was peculiar," Alexa told herself. "I wonder if she is right."

There was no knowing. Alexa spent the rest of her birthday wondering if Red would be there the next morning.

———

Red was about halfway to her room when she heard someone behind her asking her to stop. She turned and saw Commander coming toward her. Red sighed inwardly and wondered if there was any possible way to avoid him. She couldn't think of any. He stopped right in front of her.

"Hi," he said.

"Hello."

"Uh, I just wanted to ask if you, um, would be okay if I was your escort."

Do you know if he accepted Jesus? Red asked Ricky.

He did, and he was sincere about it. He was the one who asked the question that led to it.

Right.

"Why?"

"Because I am not very popular around here, and I am pretty sure that you don't like me either. I just want a second chance."

"Okay, that seems to be what I am good at. Are you okay with leaving now?"

"Sure."

"Then get whatever you need to travel; I'll get my supplies."

Red turned to go to her room.

"What do you normally need to travel?"

Red turned and raised an eyebrow at him. "Clothes and weapons. If you want to, you can bring food, but I don't like carrying that."

He nodded and went to get those things from his cell.

He can't be any worse of a traveling companion than you were, she told Ricky.

What is that supposed to mean! he asked in mock horror.

They laughed as Red packed her stuff up. Her bow and arrows were in her quiver and over her shoulders; her swords and three daggers were in her belt in less than a minute.

She didn't know exactly where his cell was, so she waited at her door. Lucy came up.

"Hi, Redache! How are you tonight?"

"Please don't call me that."

"Why? It's your full name."

"Because the only people I've ever wanted to call me that were my parents."

"Oh. Where are you going?"

"To find Alexa."

"How do you know she isn't still at her castle?"

"I just know that she is either fugitive or in prison, or she might be dead. In any case, I need to find her."

"Dead!"

"I doubt it."

"Who is your escort?"

"Him."

Red pointed behind Lucy. She turned and gasped at the teal Rept walking toward them.

She pivoted to face Red, "*Him*! You are going to trust *him*? He's *Commander*."

Red shrugged. "If he decides to betray me—I don't know how he would—then I can protect myself. Besides, everyone deserves a second chance."

"I still don't understand, but you can protect yourself. Especially if you are right and you can beat King Ricky."

"Are you two done talking yet?" he asked.

Red raised an eyebrow at Lucy.

"Yah, we're done. Promise that next time you're in the woods, you'll try to see me?"

Red shrugged. Lucy hugged her farewell, shot Commander a look, and left. There was silence for a few minutes as Red inspected Commander.

"Well, it's not getting any lighter," she said.

She walked past him and to the entrance. He followed. They disappeared into the woods past the feast trees with quite a few confused looks directed at them. They all wanted to know why the king's meld decided to trust *him*.

It was dark, but Red kept going.

"Can you see anything?" Commander asked.

"Not really, but it's not like either of us are going to be hurt by a thornbush."

"Right, but we could be going away from Rov, not to it."

"I am just going keeping the North Star slightly to my right. We'll eventually get out of these woods by going northeast."

"You know which star is which?"

"Yah, Ricky studied astronomy among other things. We kind of share skills."

"What skills do you share?"

"When you stabbed the wrong side of his chest, he would've taken about a year to recover on his own. Some of my healing went to him, enough to close the wound and lightly knit the muscles together."

"I said skills, not power. As in knowledge."

Red had to think for a moment as she went through the underbrush.

"I help him remember people and faces."

He laughed a little at that.

"So he is definitely the smart one in your relationship."

"I didn't ask you to inspect my relationship with Ricky. What do you want me to call you?"

"What do you mean?"

"Commander or Gillford?"

"Gillford."

"Then can I call you Gill?"

"Sure."

Red smiled. He did look like a huge fish, but she wouldn't tell him that.

They didn't talk much more for a little bit, until Red suddenly said, "Stop."

She had seen a flash of fire in the distance. As she looked, it became more distinct. It was a torch.

"What?" Gill asked.

"A torch, at twelve o'clock. Get in a tree, please."

"Okay."

They got on trees on opposite sides of the game trail that they had been following for a few minutes. They waited there for the torch to come nearer. Soon, Red started to hear talking in the distance.

"So what exactly are we looking for again?"

"Any sign of someone else in this forest. We don't want to be surprised at camp when a native comes into it or something."

Red heard Gill hiss out the word *native*.

"Do you think that Queen Alexandra has some other reason?"

"No, but if she did, it wouldn't be our worry."

"Well, I hope we don't run into those natives."

At about that time, they got on the game trail.

"Do you think that this is some secret path or something?" said one of the Orvs who had been speaking as he bent to the ground to see it.

"It looks more like a game trail, but we'll follow it and see. You go left, and I'll go right."

Red inspected the Orv heading toward her. His only weapon was a quiver with a bow and arrows in it, and his clothes were that of a forester. When he was two feet away from her, she hung upside down from her branch.

The Orv stopped. All of the sudden, there was a red person hanging right in front of him! He dropped his torch and screamed. Red smiled, amused.

"Natives!"

His buddy came running, and they stared at Red together.

"Is it dead?"

Finally Red said something, "Do I look dead to you?"

That startled them.

"Who and what are you?" one of them said.

"Red and a Raggy."

One of them squinted at her. "You don't look like a Raggy to me."

"I don't? Oh yah, the skin, but I can promise that I am a Raggy. Can you take me to Alexa?"

"Wait a second, you are not the right color to be a Raggy."

Red dropped to the ground. "I promise you that that is the only thing that is non-Raggy about me."

"You have weapons."

"Like I said, I am Red, the fighting Raggy."

The one on her right reached for his bow. She didn't do anything as he took it out and put an arrow on the already-strung bow.

"Prove it."

"Okay then."

Red didn't even need a weapon. Before he could pull the string back and shoot, she jumped and kicked the bow out of his hands. She rotated while still at that height and kicked him in the head. Because she had already hit something, her momentum was not great enough to knock him out, only knock him to the ground. She landed with one leg bent and the other straight out to her side. She landed about at the same time as the Orv that she had knocked down.

"That enough?" she asked as she stood up.

The one still standing shook his head.

"Then what will prove that I am who I say I am?"

He had to think about that. "I am going to shoot at you. If you are Red, then you will be able to catch it, behind your back."

"And if I am not, then you will kill me."

"So why take the risk if you are not Red?"

"Good thing I am." She turned around and walked ten more feet away and said, "Do it."

He took his time taking out, stringing, and putting an arrow in his bow. She closed her eyes so that she could hear it better. She heard the twang of the bow and reached behind her. She knew that if he served Alexa, then he would not want to kill her, so she grabbed at height of the middle of her back, where she guessed he would try to hit her.

Right as she grabbed, she felt an arrow. She grabbed hard and closed around the arrow. She knew that the momentum was not gone, so she yanked her arm up before it would hit her back. It yanked her arm forward, but she just let go of it. It dropped five feet in front of her. She turned to see the one who had been standing shooting another arrow at her face, and the one who was on the ground reaching for his bow.

She deftly caught the arrow and twirled it in her hand to let its momentum go. She then threw it at his bow. It shattered the bow in his grip before he could get another arrow.

"I thought you said one arrow."

The Orv who had been on the ground said, "Yep, she is Red."

"I agree. Will you come with us to Queen Alexandra's camp?"

Red rolled her eyes. "Really? You mean it?"

"Yes."

"Good. Come on, Gill."

Gill dropped out of the tree and scared the two Orvs.

"Who's he?"

"I don't know. Who are you, Gill?"

"A friend?"

"Yah. A friend."

One of the Orvs scratched his chin and said, "If he is with you—"

"Yes, he is."

"Then let's go."

The two Orvs led the way to the middle of the trail and beyond. Red followed them and Gill followed her.

———❦———

Alexa woke up and stayed in bed for a minute. She didn't need to do anything while she was asleep. She sighed and got up. She changed quickly and went out of her tent. She had moved it to the edge of the little camp and a bit farther away for privacy when they first set it up, and the day before three of her men started guarding her tent.

She had set up the sentry shifts, six four-hour shifts throughout the day, when they first set up camp, but she suspected that her sentry captain, who assigned the men and made sure they did it, assigned her the guards. She had no way to prove that Opo did it, though. Oh well.

The three guards who were on duty saluted as she came out of her tent. She had found that the only way they wouldn't do that was if they bowed, so she didn't complain. It was just a little too formal for her. She went to find Opo but stopped when she heard something coming from the woods. She saw two scouts coming through the underbrush. Once they moved aside, she saw why they were coming back when they weren't expected until noon.

Red rushed forward and hugged Alexa. She hesitated a second and hugged her back.

"So Tess was right."

Red separated and smiled lopsidedly at Alexa.

"Don't you know that Tess is never wrong? What was she right about?"

"That you'd be back this morning and that you have red skin. You are going to have to give a full account of yourself, Redache."

"Okay, but haven't I insisted that you not call me that?"

"Yes." Alexa noticed Gill and groaned, "Oh no! Another Rept!"

"Should I take offense at that?"

"Alexa, this is Gillford. Gillford, this is Queen Alexandra."

Alexa held out her hand, and he shook it.

"I only say that because the only other Rept that I have known stirred up a bunch of trouble."

"Right, Ricky is definitely a troublemaker."

Red shot him a glance, but said nothing.

She went with Alexa to find Opo, Gill followed, and the two scouts went to their own tents. After Alexa told Opo what she wanted him to know, she had breakfast while Red gave her an account of what happened. Alexa would have to ask questions for clarification, of course.

When Red was done, Alexa shared her own problems.

"Kim lied about me and now permanently has the throne unless I overthrow her, but I do not have enough people. One hundred people, twenty of which are kids, is not enough no matter how brave they are."

"I can help with the numbers."

"How?"

"Remember how Raggies seemed to flock to me when I wasn't trying?"

"Yah."

"What if I try?"

Alexa had to think about that for a second. "So you want to go gather troops for me?"

"I can try, it won't hurt anything."

"True."

"But I want to teach the Raggies here how to shoot a bow and arrow before I do it."

"Then I will think about it while you teach them. Ask me about it again in a week."

"Okay then. Where are the Raggies in this camp?"

"There are only nine, including the seven from the castle. They are on the west side of the camp."

"Right. I'll get to work."

Red smiled and saluted at her.

"Oh yah, that reminds me, if you ever call me Queen Alexandra again, then I will always call you Redache. I have the same threat for you saluting to me or bowing. Is that clear?"

Red rolled her eyes. "As a trumpet."

Alexa swung a playful punch at Red's head, but she was gone before it reached its mark. Alexa smiled.

GATHERING

By the time that the week was up, all nine of Red's pupils could hit the target once every two tries, which was better than any other nonliberating Raggy in the past. She told this and repeated her request to Alexa, and she consented.

Red told Gill where they were going, and he asked if she would like to ride on his back.

"Do you know how to do that?"

"There's a first time for everything."

Red nodded. They decided that the best way was to have Red in a bag, but that had never been her favorite mode of travel. She did it only because she knew that they were going to need to move fast.

They got to the Fort the night after they left Alexa's camp in the Uncivilized Woods. It was past midnight, so they set up separate tents and went to sleep.

The next morning, Red awoke to find a black-haired and blue-eyed Raggy with a tiny nose looking down at her.

"She's awake!" the Raggy squealed.

Red sat up. She saw several other Raggies in her tent. Luckily, she had slept in her clothes, so she didn't have to hurriedly put on a shirt or anything like that. She stared at her visitors.

"We've been waiting for *ages*, but Goldie told us not to wake you up, but now you are awake!" said the one above her.

One of the other Raggies said, "I think we are crowding her. Let's go outside, where it isn't as crowded."

They hesitated.

The same voice said, "Come on, Gold Squad. She needs a little more space than the rest of us."

They all left, and Red decided that it would be best to get out there sooner rather than later. Once she had put on a fresh red shirt and red shorts, she went outside. There, she was surrounded by many of her own race. She couldn't hear anything past all the gabber. She was about an inch taller than the tallest of the Raggies, but she could not see much over the bouncing dreadlocks. She stuck two fingers in her mouth and whistled loudly. They quieted.

"I can't hear anybody talking past everyone else!" she said.

Apparently that was funny. Red didn't see it; still, the others found it hilarious enough for three full minutes of laughter.

"I think that you have spent more time among other races than among your own," one of them said.

Red shrugged, which made them laugh harder. They just didn't want to stop. She was unfazed by the laughing; she just thought it had gone on long enough. They started dropping to the ground and rolling; they found it so funny. Red saw beyond them then. There was a group of Orvs talking among themselves about twenty yards away. As she watched, one of them noticed her predicament. He said something to the others, and they all headed over.

Just the Orvs' presence was enough to calm the Raggies down. They stopped laughing and sat down instead of rolling on the ground. Now, they sat on the ground, picking at the grass. Red nodded at the Orvs in thanks; they smiled and sat behind the Raggies. Red was now in front of *another* crowd, but this one was much smaller.

"So I heard something about a Gold Squad?"

A Raggy with yellow hair, yet so dark it was almost gold, and the same eye color stood up.

"That's us, all the Raggies and Orvs of the Fort. I am the captain of the Raggies, and Chud"—he pointed at the first Orv to notice Red—"is the Orv captain."

"And what is your name?"

"Goldie."

"Why'd you name your group a squad?"

"To get ready for the war!"

"What war?"

"The war that you are going to start to bring Rov back to God."

"Who said I was starting a war?"

"Tess."

"Oh, that makes sense, but she is right. I came to recruit an army for a war. Alexandra is creating a fighting force just inside of the Uncivilized Woods. I'm trying to find as many willing former citizens of Rov as possible to back her up. Can you help?"

"Would this happen to be the same Alexandra who tried to assassinate her aunt in order to gain the throne earlier?"

"That was a lie that Kim staged. In fact, I had to thwart several attempts on Alexandra's life made by Kim."

The Gold Squad talked about this among themselves. This meant that Kim was a liar, which they all knew that she was already.

"I believe you," said Goldie. "What do you want us to do?"

"Everyone feel this way?" Red asked. When she got several nods, she elaborated on her plan.

"I am going throughout Syn-Cynthia to find former Rovian citizens as I said. I would like you to travel in pairs and gather as many as you know of. I would like you to meet me on this side of the Rov to Syn-Cynthia trading post in two weeks. Between now and then, I need you to get as many as possible. Any questions?"

"What should we bring?"

"As much as you can without slowing yourself down. Definitely bring whatever you need for your craft if you have one."

"Can we bring non-Rovian citizens?"

"Please don't. This is a Rovian thing, and we don't need to get all the nice people here pulled into it."

"Where will you be?"

"I'll be going around other places as well."

After that, there were no more questions, so Red made sure that they understood the two-week time period. She wanted them there in two weeks, not on their way in two weeks. Once she was sure that they all understood, Goldie and Chud started to assign the pairs. They put a Raggy and an Orv together and pointed them in a direction to take. Red left with a satisfied feeling to go find Gill. She found him taking down her tent; he had already taken his down.

"What are you doing?" she asked.

"Getting ready to leave. We are going to other places, right?"

"Yah, I just didn't know that you knew that was my plan."

"How could I not? Could you take your stuff out of the tent please?"

"Sure."

They headed out for Last Water Lake. Red was protesting the bag silently.

At least you are not listening to a lecture about the best types of crops to plant on the Sile Plain.

Yah, but I kind of have to listen to it now.

But you get to fall asleep.

Sounds like a good idea.

You silly Raggy.

You crazy Rept.

They laughed together and started paying attention to the lecture. Red was asleep in five minutes.

Red awoke when Gill landed. She stayed awake as he slept through the night. He woke up shortly after dawn, and they traveled the rest of the way to Last Water Lake. Once Red had attracted the local Orv and Raggy population, she gave them pretty much the same speech that she had given those at the Fort. The main difference was that she told them to meet her in one and a half weeks. Then they went to the trading post between the three countries in the habitable plain where Red told them to meet her in six weeks.

Red's plan was simple enough. She gave the Fort two weeks; then she traveled a week's walking distance away and gave them one and a half weeks to meet her. The two-week people could spread the word while the one-week people did so while traveling there. Then she went to the other side of Syn-Cynthia and told those people to meet her in six weeks, which was enough time for her to have escorted the other group to Alexa's camp.

The six-week people would tell new people as they traveled southeast for three weeks to get there; this gave them time to stop and explain. Red also visited two other border towns that she told to meet her in five weeks and four and a half weeks. These people would get there at the same time as the six-week people, and they would provide more mouths covering more area about the news through Syn-Cynthia.

Red made sure to stress that Alexa only wanted former Rovian citizens. She didn't want to rid Syn-Cynthia of its entire population. At the end of her own two-week deadline, she had set into motion a massive exodus of former Rovian citizens.

She met the first group at her predescribed meeting point at noon of the assigned day. She led them around Rov and into the Uncivilized Woods. They ran into surprisingly little opposition. Red expected Kim to hear of the mass movement; however, there were no troops sent to intercept her party. That was fine with everybody else, but Red was itching for a fight. She secretly hoped that the next movement would be exciting. No such luck. It seemed as if Kim was ignoring what could end up in a major rebellion, or God was concealing it so that none of her people died. Whatever the case, there was no action.

Alexa was overjoyed at the amount of troops that Red had brought. All of them were Christians! She gave Red's suspicions about Kim a whole minute of thought because she was sure that God was protecting them. Red agreed with that soon after.

She stayed at the camp just long enough to teach all the new Raggies to shoot a loaded bow. After she taught a Raggy how to shoot a bow, he or she could usually practice and better themselves without her help, so she was free to do what she wished with occasional visits to check on their form. No one understood why they were unable to learn without her.

After she was confident in all of the Raggies' abilities, she asked Alexa if she could try to do something similar in Rov. She said yes because she thought that Red just couldn't go wrong. Everyone makes mistakes sometimes. Gill wasn't so sure that going to Rov was a good idea, but Red convinced him.

They walked to the closest Rovian town that was north of the camp and just in the fringe of the Uncivilized Woods. They arrived at the outskirts of that town at five o'clock the next day.

Red and Gill hid behind some bushes and watched the townsfolk go about finishing the day's work. Gill was curious about what Red was going to do. He was expecting some practical plan, so he didn't start worrying until she told him to stay where he was. She then walked straight down the main road of the town. Gill thought that might be hazardous, but that could be her idea.

As Red walked through the town, everyone stopped what they were doing. The carpenter and the smith stopped their hammering, and all the kids stopped their playing to gape openly at the bright-red Raggy walking through their town as if she had nothing to fear. Maybe she didn't.

The burly Orvian blacksmith stepped in front of her with a glowing iron rod in his hands. Red stopped and looked up at him.

"Hello!" she said cheerily. "How are you this fine evening?"

All he did was grunt at her. She looked around and saw other male Orvs surrounding her. She kept a bright smile on her face, even though this reminded her of her own town's invasion. Good thing she wasn't planning on doing that.

"What is it?" she heard a small Orv ask his dad.

An adult told the kid to go home, and all the moms took their kids into their houses.

"What's the matter? Do you treat all travelers like this?" Red was still acting like she had no cares in the world.

"What and who are you?" asked the smith who had first stopped her.

"Well, my name is Red, and I am traveling to Rovto."

"The man asked what you are!" said someone else.

"I am a Christian. Do any of you believe in God?"

The smith growled deep in his throat, and Red almost laughed. It sounded incredibly weak compared to Ricky's growl.

"It is illegal to believe in God."

"I just figured that there are some people who do anyway."

"Then you figured wrong."

Red just shrugged and said, "Okay then."

She continued walking right where she had left off. The smith grabbed her shoulder to stop her but let go cussing when both of his wrists started bleeding. No one saw what happened except her. But after that, no one else tried to deter her. When she had passed every one of them, she turned.

"If anyone has held on to his or her faith in God, they can follow me; I will protect you."

No one moved. Red turned and continued walking through the last few yards of the town. She could feel a bunch of eyes watching her, eyes that she couldn't see. As soon as she knew that she was out of sight of the town's occupants, she dragged her foot across the dirt road, creating a line. She took out her bow and put an arrow in it and waited.

Gill relocated himself to a tree near the road, but not close enough to be seen. He wanted to ask Red what her plan was, but she had signaled for quiet.

About seven minutes after Red had made the line, a female Orv with a little kid and a teenager came into sight. She was running slightly and looking over her shoulder frantically. She noticed the line and Red right before she crossed it. She stopped there. Red had her bow at her side, and her grin had disappeared.

She said, "Only cross this line if you believe in God and want to learn more about him. If you don't, then it would be better for you if you went back."

The lady led her kids firmly over the line.

"Hello," she said. "I am Riley. God told me that he would make a way for us to leave this country."

Red smiled. "So that is why he told me to come here. Anybody else we might need to wait for?"

"Yes, the Floo family. They were packing."

There was a shout from around the corner, "There she is!"

A group of men came running but stopped at the line. Red gave them the same command that she had given Riley. They didn't cross the line.

One of them called Riley a bad name and said, "Get your butt over here!"

"No. I divorce you, Fret."

"You can't do that!"

"I have three witnesses, the legal number for a divorce."

As he started calling her names, Red noticed a family of Orvs and a Raggy trying to sneak around the three men standing at the line. One of the men who was not cussing noticed where she was looking and went to intercept them. Red shot an arrow that landed right in front of him. He hesitated.

Red returned her attention to the scene in front of her.

"Gill, could you take Riley and the kids out of range of fire?"

To the Orvs, Gill appeared out of thin air. Riley happily followed him away from her now ex-husband. The Orv who had headed toward the group coming toward Red had regained his nerve over the arrow. He was heading toward them again, but this time Red shot him in the foot. She then ducked a saber that was lunged at her. She dropped the bow, drew her sword, and blocked a crushing blow from an axe. She kicked, and her opponent bent over in pain. Now that he was at her eye level, she grabbed his ear and slammed his face into the ground. She hit the back of his head with her sword hilt as she jumped onto his back.

The saber wielder tried to chop off her head, but she blocked it and did that weird twirling of her sword around his saber and sent it flying out of his grasp. Before he fully realized that he was weaponless, she had him knocked out.

She jumped off the Orv whom she had been standing on and grabbed her bow. She notched an arrow and pointed it at the Orv who had been trying to get to the newcomers. He was pulling her other arrow out of his foot, but when he looked up, he noticed the arrow pointed at his head ten feet away. He froze. There were very few people who could miss at such a short range.

The Orv family and the Raggy got to the line right then. Red told them her line rule, and they stepped over.

"Don't you dare even think of following us," she told the Orv whom she was pointing an arrow at.

He nodded, and she turned, saying, "Follow me."

She found Gill, Riley, and her kids past where the road ended.

"Let's get as far away from here as we can before dark," Red said.

The others agreed, and they set off. They stopped and made camp at dark. The next day, they awoke at dawn and walked to Alexa's camp.

On the trip back to Alexa's camp, Red told them of God's sacrifice, and they accepted his love joyfully. They were glad to be rid of the burden of not letting anyone hear their praises to God that they had to carry while under the atheist rule of Kim. When they got to Alexa's camp, she greeted them warmly. Once Red had checked on the Raggies' progress, she left with Gill in tow.

They walked because Red had told Gill that she needed to request something from him, but she didn't say anything until they had been traveling for a few hours. Then she turned around and said, "What I am going to ask you to do will be tricky, but I think that you can do it."

"It can't be too hard. Did you ask both Alexa and King Ricky about it?"

"Both but I don't want you to agree until I tell you what it is. I want you to betray me."

"What! You *want* me to do that?"

"In an organized fashion, yes. I would like you to turn me into the Rovian authorities and then follow my captors and me around, keeping an eye out for me."

"How could I assure them that you won't escape?"

"I'll only tell you that if you promise to keep an eye on me."

"I'm already doing that, aren't I?"

"But I need a *promise.*"

Gill shrugged, probably something that he caught from Red.

"Okay then, I promise that I will keep both eyes on you until I die from it."

Red crossed her arms. "You didn't have to go that far."

"But I will. No one else has ever trusted me as much as you have, let alone let me 'betray' them."

"Well, this is a way to prove to me, Ricky, and yourself that you've changed. If you leave me, then you might as well have betrayed me by yourself."

"Anyway, how could I assure them that you can't escape?"

Red hesitated. This was something that had only been an idea floating between Ricky and herself, but she was sure that if anyone were to tie her up in a certain way, then it would be really hard for her to get away from those who did it. It would take a very, very, very, careless person or four to mess it up for her to get away. She doubted that a careless person would be allowed anywhere near her anyway. She told Gill what it was.

"Are you sure that would work?"

Red ducked under a random branch that protruded from a tree that was almost parallel to the ground. Gill had to jump over it because he was too tall to crouch under it.

"Oh yah, especially if Orvs were to hold it."

"So when do you want me to do this?"

"I—"

Red stopped as she heard the very faint *phhht* of an arrow in flight. She had time to duck it but in the end decided that it was a good idea not to. She prayed as it hit the back of her head. She blacked out.

Gill saw her fall; thus, he turned to see why. There was a knockout arrow by Red's head, and an Orvian archer was standing on the tree that was almost parallel to the ground. Gill drew his sword and thought that this guy was dumb to attack the fighting Raggy. A group of Orvs stepped out of hiding places from his right. They each had some type of deadly weapon.

Their leader said, "We have no quarrel with you, dragon. Step away from the Raggy, and you'll have no trouble."

"Why would I do that? It'd make it too easy for you."

"She did tell you to betray her."

"You heard that conversation?"

"Walk away slowly, and we won't capture and enslave you for affiliating yourself with her."

Gill hoped that Ricky wasn't freaking out because Red was knocked out.

"Good luck with that."

The Orvs charging at Gill made the conclusion of that conversation clear. He would've tried to fight from the air, but he needed to protect Red. He couldn't allow the giant Orvs, who were at least four feet taller than him, to push him three steps back onto Red.

The first Orv to attack him would've lost his right leg had he not been wearing armor. That Orv swung his axe at his own chest level, barely missing the ducking Gill. He tried to duck back without moving his feet, and that move put him off balance enough to topple him backward. Another Orv plunged his sword at the fallen dragon's stomach. Gill rolled, and as soon as he was facing upward again, a sword tip appeared at his throat but not under a scale.

The Orv with his sword at Gill's throat told him to stand up. Gill did so, faking a submissive attitude. The Orv told him to drop his sword, but Gill used it to hack aside the weapon at his neck. He turned to see another Orv picking up Red. He ran to rescue her, but he got a sudden headache, and the world went black.

———

Gill woke up two hours later. He found himself tied with a rope hands and feet to a pole that was being carried by two Orvs. He bent his head back and was rewarded by the grotesque sight of an Orv's buttocks. Instead, he looked at his hands, which were tied with expert rope knots. Rope burns easily. These guys obviously had no experience with dragons. They didn't even tie his wings!

He blew on the ropes holding his hands to the pole, and they easily caught fire and broke as Gill pulled against them. He tried to reach his ankles, but the Orvs dropped the pole when he was only halfway there. His ankles dropped eight feet to the ground. He presumed that he didn't have enough time to get his ankle bonds on fire or to untie them, so he tried to fly.

The pole provided an advantage and a disadvantage. The disadvantage was that it put him off balance forward, but the advantage was that when he swung his feet, he could hit someone. The Orvs learned that once one of them was hit over the head; they gave him room to swing with no obstruction. He flew to the highest branch of a nearby tree that could hold his and the pole's weight. He had to set the rope on fire because he didn't have a sharp object.

He looked down to see all the Orvs but two, deciding whether to recapture him. One of the other two had the unconscious Red slung over his shoulder, and the other had a bow loaded with a knockout arrow in case she woke up. Gill contemplated rescuing her but resisted the idea. For whatever reason, she wanted to be captured. He wasn't going to try to save her unless she asked.

The Orvs decided that it was not worth it to climb a tree. Besides, they reasoned that he would follow them anyway. They could capture him later. They continued to run toward their town. Red awoke an hour later, but she didn't stay awake long, for the Orv with the knockout arrow promptly did his job.

Because they ran instead of walked, it only took them another hour to get back to the town at the outskirts of the Uncivilized Woods. Once they got there, they went straight to the smith and told him what they needed. He stopped all his other work and started on that. He and his son worked hard for the better part of an hour and a half to get it done before Red regained consciousness.

Just as two Orvs started putting an iron neck collar on her, she awoke. In the moment it took her to become oriented, they had it locked around her neck and were speedily getting out of there. She had been lying where an Orv had thrown her, so she stood up to a squat. She stood there balancing on the balls of her feet as she inspected her surroundings. On her neck collar, four six-foot chains were connected, which were each held by a muscular Orv. This was the binding style that she had told Gill about. The Orvs had obviously heard that conversation.

The Orvs holding the chains and others watched her like a pack of coyotes watches an unsuspecting rabbit. No one, not even Red, knew what to expect. She stood to her feet, and the stalemate continued.

I guess we get to see if it works, she told Ricky.

She grabbed a chain and yanked. The Orv holding that chain stumbled forward a bit, but not enough for Red to reach him. She then grabbed the chain to the left of the first one and pulled on that one. That Orv was ready but stumbled forward. Red jumped away from those two Orvs, which put them a little close to her and her a little closer to the other two. She jumped at the first two, which pulled the other two toward her.

Red repeated the process until some others joined their companions to pull the chains tight, leaving her standing on her tiptoes so that it wouldn't choke her. They kept her like that as the ten men of the town, except the smith and the one whose foot Red had shot, said farewell to their families and packed clothes. They were going to take her to Orvinta, the capital, so that they could collect the one-million-dahl ransom. They would do whatever they had to for that money.

Red had been in that uncomfortable position for a few minutes when some airheaded youth started throwing rocks at her. For a while they missed by a long shot. Eventually, they started to throw within Red's area. That's when things got messy. She caught a rock and threw it at the hands of her captors. It hurt, so they swore and dropped the chain. Another rock had come within her range at that time span, which she threw to the right of the first.

Before the second chain could hit the ground, Red had grabbed them both. Since the Orvs had been pulling so tight that the chains had been taut as a bowstring, the Orvs still pulling chains fell over and pulled Red with them. She whipped her captured chains back over her head and was rewarded with several yelps.

Red stood up with no resistance and started spinning her two chains. With those two chains, she could reach the ends of the other two; thus, no one could reach them without fear of getting whacked. Red turned slowly while spinning her chains; she was looking for a way out that wasn't blocked by kids. They had been watching her before she tried to escape again, and more came running when Red hurt her first captors' hands. Now it was impossible to hack through the crowd without hurting a kid.

Red would never hurt anyone under ten, even if one had a dagger to her throat. Call it a weakness if you like, but she wouldn't. Maybe it was because she had been an innocent child until she turned ten, or maybe it was because any other race's kids reminded her of Raggies. For whatever reason, she *refused* to hurt any kid. She deemed them untouchable.

This was a problem, for easily half of the population was younger than ten. Every angle of escape was blocked by an untouchable. The townsfolk didn't understand why she didn't try to escape through them to freedom. They thought that she was trying to find the weakest people to fight; therefore, most told their kids to go home. The only archer in town shot at Red, but she easily knocked it aside with one of her rotating chains.

Once every kid was gone, Red attacked. Red lashed her chain out at a man, and it hit his wrist and wrapped around it. He grunted in pain, but held on to it. Red reached for an inanimate chain only to find it being held by one of the men; the other chain was likewise held. She sighed heavily because she knew that she had been beaten. Though it was against every instinct, she submitted and tossed her one remaining chain at the ground. An Orv picked it up with a puzzled look on his face.

I think that was more brave than if you had tried to escape with that one chain, Ricky told her.

I guess, but it made me seem weak to them.

On the contrary, you seemed more self-controlled. You proved that you can accept defeat.

Red crossed her arms and thought back, *To you maybe, but not to them.*

We'll see.

The Orv who had caught the chain Red had thrown at him started arguing with someone else. She didn't really pay attention to them; however, like everyone else, she paid attention when he said a few disgusting words and, "I don't care if it's broken; I'm going!"

The other Orv put her hands in the air out of frustration and told him to let her cast it at least. He agreed, and she led him away. Five minutes later, he was back, and the group headed out with Red in the middle. She didn't struggle much at all, which was surprising to the Orvs. They only traveled two hours before the light started fading, so they set up six tents and set four guards on Red. They camped at a watering hole in the plains of Liebochney.

The guy with the cast on his wrist went away and returned with some plants. These he passed among his companions, and he threw some at Red. When he ordered her to eat it, she refused, and he asked why. She explained the various diseases each could cause and the one that could kill in five minutes.

All the Orvs had been listening to her, so most of them started spitting them out. One person didn't believe her and kept on eating.

When asked why, his excuse was, "She's a fighting Raggy, not a scientific one."

He died about seven minutes later. Red watched in horror as his companions laughed at his foolishness, looted the body, and threw it in the open for the buzzards. Someone went hunting and brought back two brace of rabbits. Those rabbits quickly became a stew, and the Orvs brought out celebratory beer. Pretty soon only the four guards on duty around Red were the sober ones. Red watched with fascination.

How could any sane being want *to humiliate themselves and drink that stuff that smells so horrible?* she thought to herself.

Ricky answered with a mental blush, *Some of it is social status, and also because the feeling it causes is addicting.*

Then why start?

Like I said, social status. I really don't expect you to understand.

Okay then.

From the men's comments, Red learned their names: the guy with the cast was Talron, the leader; everyone else's were Fret, Ly, Dur, Mitch, Motch, who were brothers; Evo; and Petra. She sat watching that crowd, and she didn't even try to escape because they had wound and locked her chains around four trees that were all wider than her. The chains were loose, so she was free to sit or lay down as she wished. The four guards were between the trees with weapons close.

Normal guards face out toward the wilderness, but they were not normal guards, but guards who were guarding Red; so they faced her to be sure she didn't try to get away. That's why they didn't see Gill in a tree just outside the camp. Gill had retrieved Red's bow and arrows from the town; consequently, he decided to shoot one at her. It landed near her right hand.

The guards jumped, and one went to get it. Of course, Red got it first. It had a note wrapped around it, asking if she wanted Gill to rescue her or if she wanted him to get caught as well. She found a rock and some dirt and smeared the dirt into a big *no*.

Red threw it back, and it hit the trunk next to Gill's head, and then she lay down to fall asleep. Someone asked her what was on that, and she deigned it unimportant to answer. They thought that she was asleep, so they started to discuss what they thought was in the note. She fell asleep while they bickered, not overly caring what they would decide it said.

Red awoke when an arrow pierced her upper thigh. She grunted and reached to yank the arrow out, but her arms were tied behind her back. She guessed that they had done that when she was asleep. Her muscles knit themselves together around the arrow as she inspected how she was tied.

Normally, when a Raggy's hands were tied behind his or her back, there are two knots, one on the wrist behind the head and another that was connected to that one on the elbow, but for her, the Orvs went to an extreme measure of tying. Not only did they tie those knots *incredibly* tight, but they also tied knots on her midforearm joint and three other knots between those three, and all of that was connected to her collar so that her arms stayed behind her back.

Talron yelled at Dur, the archer, "Since you're the dumb one who shot her, you go get the arrow!"

Red was standing by the time he got there, and she said, "Next time could you just shake me? I promise that I won't hurt you."

He just glared at her as he yanked the arrow out. She ground her teeth in pain. He had the audacity to wave it under her nose, so she took advantage of it. She bent forward and bit the arrow, breaking it close to the tip. It fell at her feet. While he was bending over to retrieve it, Red grabbed it with her toes and tossed it behind her to her hands.

They hadn't thought to tie her feet now, had they?

That day passed with a bunch of walking and a few rest stops. Red had all of her bonds except her collar undone by two o'clock that afternoon, and she hid the arrowhead after she was done. They had just stopped for the night when Red asked one of her captors, Petra, to do her a favor.

His answer was, "Why would I do anything for you?"

"Because if you do, you can get the arrowhead back, and I won't attack you with it either."

"Then it depends on the favor."

"Well, I put the arrowhead up my tiny sleeve, and while we ran, it dug into my shoulder. Could you please get it out for me? It kind of hurts."

"You can't reach it?"

"I can, but it's under my skin, and I can't get it."

"I'll do it but not as a favor. I want you to promise me that you won't let me die between now and when we hand you over to the queen."

"But that means that I have to go to the queen."

"Yep."

Red sighed and said, "Fine."

He came up to her, and she pulled her sleeve up. He immediately noticed the bump on her shoulder and why she couldn't take it out. Her skin had healed around the arrowhead; therefore, he had to cut the skin under the bump. As soon as he did, her body rejected the foreign object and shot it into the ground. Red bent, grabbed it, and held it out to Petra with her hand flat. He took it from her and looked her in the eye.

"You keep that promise, you hear?"

Red nodded, and he returned to his post. She fell asleep before anyone else because she was tired from healing herself.

The next day, they came into a city named Rovto. As they led Red through the straight road that ran through the city, the usual hustle and bustle of the streets seemed to freeze. Every noble, beggar, soldier, and street brat alike stared at Red and her captors. No one looked up; thus, no one saw Gill, watching from the sky.

The quiet was almost palpable. Instead of her captors having to push through the crowd, the crowd separated and formed a lane for them.

A voice said in awe, "They caught the fighting Raggy!"

Then it seemed like the whole city erupted in a celebration. There was dancing, drinking, and all-out craziness. Some teens started throwing whatever came to hand at Red to prove their valor. She caught everything that came within her range and threw the missile back at whoever had it. She didn't want to escape partly because of the crowds and partly because of her promise. She didn't want to have to keep Petra alive for the rest of her life! Within a few minutes, all of those valor seekers had new bruises to rub, but they persisted on doing it.

Every Orv was throwing insults at her. She was offended by only one, the person who called her a demon. She didn't know who did it, but that was a good thing for that person. One missile hit its mark as well, the back of her lower calf. She stopped and picked it up, and her guards were unable to make her go forward.

The crowd quieted.

Red tossed the rock between her hands as she said, "You are brave enough to insult me from afar, but do any of you think that you can stand in front of me and do so?"

It was quiet. No one seemed to want to do it. Then she heard a rustle behind her. She turned to find the crowd parting to reveal a thirteen-year-old only a few inches taller than her. By the looks of his clothes, he was a street brat, and he had a dagger clenched in his right hand.

Mitch, one of those who caught Red, said this to the kid before he crossed the invisible boundary, "That is a bad idea, boy."

He seemed offended as he said, "I can handle myself!"

He walked all the way to within the range of Red's fists.

So quietly that only Red could hear, he said, "Back left pocket." Then he said the following so that even the guys a couple hundred yards away could hear, "You, Raggy, are an abomination upon Rov! You are a filthy, greedy, stubborn, *Christian!* Your kind should disappear forever and become the first extinct race!"

At that, the crowd went into a frenzy. They started hurling insults at Red again, and some even goaded the kid into attacking her. Seeming to take energy from the crowd, the kid attacked with his dagger held high. Red's captors kept the chains taut because they thought it would be easier for her to get hurt that way.

The kid lunged at her left side, and she shifted out of the way. His dagger hit right in the center of a chain link on one of Red's chains. No one saw her hand go into his back left pocket with her right hand because she hit his head with the rock in her left hand. Before he landed, she barely kicked his chest, sending him into the crowd, but she didn't break anything in him.

"Anybody else?" Red asked.

There was silence, and no one else taunted her. Her captors got her out of there as fast as possible. After that episode, they traveled through the countryside and avoided towns and cities alike.

The next morning, Red read the note as her captors recovered from another night of beer. It read,

Miss Red,

I don't know your real name, so please don't be offended by me calling you by your most prominent color. If you are reading this, then my young cohort has succeeded. On the back of this paper are the locations and names of all the Christians in Rovto and the names of towns that I believe have Christians in them. I wrote all of that in a code I taught Alexa as a kid. Make good use of this information, for I do not part with it lightly.

Sincerely,
Qitryo

On the other side of that paper were more of those same weird words. She folded the paper and stuck it in a secret place. She wondered at how fast that person could write if he wrote all that when she was in Rovto.

A few days later, they came upon the capital. The trip through the main part of the city was very much like the trip through Rovto. The only difference was that Red didn't lose her cool, and she didn't challenge them. All she did was catch the missiles thrown at her and throw them back harder than they threw them at her. Once they got to the gate of the castle within the city, the crowd had thinned considerably. No one wanted to be anywhere near the castle when the queen got angry, because when Kim was angry, she ordered her castle guards to shoot randomly into the peasants below. She and her guards loved to watch people suffer, and it generally lifted her spirits.

When they got to the barred gate, the watchman asked what was their business in the castle.

Talron yelled back, "An audience with Her Majesty Queen Kim! Tell her to get that reward ready!"

The watchman just then noticed Red. She thought that he must have been the worst watchman in the world to overlook her red hair or eyes that were upturned to him or her red skin that anyone could see from a mile away. With his eyes widened, he said that he would be right back. In record time, the gate was open, and then it was shut even faster. A page told them to follow him.

As they were taken to the throne room, Red's captors stared at all the finery in the castle. There were tapestries that depicted scenes of valor from past centuries and many articles of solid gold, silver, and other precious metal. These trinkets did not awe Red because she had seen them before; instead, she was inspecting the route. She would eventually need to escape, and she needed to know the least-populated and guarded areas.

Finally, they approached a door twice as tall as the Orvs guarding it. One banged on the door, and it opened slowly. As

Red and her captors entered, the nobles sitting along the walls fell quiet. Red's gaze fell on Kim and stayed there. Kim was the only one in the room bold enough to look her in the eye, but even she turned her head aside after a minute or two.

"And just how did you country bumpkins succeed in a feat that my men have found impossible?" she asked Red's captors.

Talron patted his chest in pride as he said, "We got the information out of her ourselves."

"Uh-huh. And how did you do that?"

"We tortured it out of her!"

Red laughed at that. As a way of explanation, she said, "They overheard me tell a friend about how I thought someone could tie me up and did it themselves."

"And where is this 'friend'?" Kim asked.

Red didn't answer but made the mistake of looking up at the skylight. She saw a small patch of teal against the blue. Kim noticed it too, so she ordered some of her men to check the roof.

Kim congratulated Red's captors and asked them to hand her over to some of her men. They refused to do so until they got their reward.

To that, Kim said in an almost-too-sweet voice, "Of course, how could I have forgotten? Guards!"

Her guards were familiar with her wishes, so they knew exactly what she wanted. Red saw the bows a fraction of a second before her captors. She remembered her promise and yanked Petra, who was holding one of the chains, to the ground. He fell flat, as his companions became arrow pincushions. The arrows aimed at Petra had to go somewhere, and most went into his thrice-dead companions, but the rest went into the nobles.

The general came up to those who had aimed at Petra and told them to dispose of the bodies for missing their target. Red noticed that Petra had been hit on his left shoulder but was fine otherwise. No one else noticed that he was alive, for he tried to act dead.

Kim dismissed all the nonmilitary nobles, and the bodies, including Petra, were hauled away in a timely fashion, as if it had been done many times before. Red could only hope that Petra would survive; she did her best. Four muscular guards quickly grabbed her four chains, and they held them tight.

The general walked up to her and said, "So, Raggy, you were dumb enough to tell villagers how to tie you up; now tell me something I want to know."

"I don't have paste on my skin. You wanted to know about that, right?"

Kim told her general, "You are not going to get her to answer anything of importance with that tactic. It would be better to try to ask her specific questions like Alexandra's location and how many people she has gathered in force."

Red answered those indirect questions with, "I am not giving a location away, but she gathered one hundred people."

"Only a hundred!" said one of the captains that had stayed. "We could wipe them out in five minutes!"

"There's something she's leaving out, or she wouldn't have said that," Kim told the lowlife.

"We could possibly make her come to our side," the general said.

Red snorted, "I'd like to see you try!"

"General I, you couldn't do that with a year's worth of torture," Kim said. "You will interrogate her tomorrow, and then we will hold a public execution the day after. You four holding her chains, take her to the cell in the middle of the prison."

They saluted and marched away with Red in tow. They must've thought that Red had given up awhile back, because they held the chains loosely and didn't even look at her as they talked to one another. Red thought this was the best time to take out a tooth knife and unlock her collar. She held it so that it looked like it was locked as they approached the prison entrance on the back wall of the castle.

The entrance was a gate that many Orvs would have to duck into so that they wouldn't hit their heads. There was a guard in full battle gear guarding the gate from this side. It was made of five-feet-thick oak wood and was supported by iron bars. Red noticed that the big bar that opened the gate was on this side of it, even though it opened to the other side. It was easy to get in, but nearly impossible to get out from.

Once the prison guard saw Red's guards, he started lifting the bar on the gate. He opened the gate right before they got there. As Red passed by him, she gave him a look that said, "You're going to see me again." She heard armor clanking behind her, and she knew that he either shivered or shifted position.

For ten feet beyond the gate, they were in the castle wall, but as soon as the brickwork changed, so did the corridor. It dropped into a deep chasm. On one side of this deep chasm was a retractable ladder that reached all the way to the bottom; this was the side that Red's new escort led her down. The other side of the chasm had several holes leading to rooms where at least a hundred archers were watching her. It was hard for Red to keep the unlocked collar on as she climbed down with two guards below her, one with the chain taught, the other slackened. The top chains were the same. She had to keep it on because she didn't want to get shot down by the archers on the other side.

At the top of the ladder, there was a precarious ledge that led to those archer rooms. The holes mentioned were one foot-by-one-foot windows at Orvian head height that were used like a castle's parapets to provide a way to attack and a way to duck out of fire. The only way in was the ledge at the top, and the lowest window was thirty feet off the ground.

It was an intimidating entrance that most prisoners looked upon and immediately assumed could not be breached. Red was the only prisoner to go down that ladder who had hope of getting out.

Many torches lit that chasm, but the corridors and cells were pitch-black except near where a sentry patrolled or guards escorted a prisoner. Each of Red's guards grabbed a torch from a pile of them and set them on fire before they entered the actual prison. Red kept the collar on for a few minutes before she took advantage of the poor lighting.

She loosened the collar enough to slip her head under it, and then she jumped on a chain and ran up to the guard on that chain. That only took her a few seconds, so he was unprepared for her attack. She jumped and hit his forehead with both of her knees, then flipped over his head, turned, and landed facing the others. She grabbed the downed Orv's sword from his belt as the others dropped their torches. She felt sorry for the other three.

To their credit, they ran at her. True, normally the odds would be in their favor in a three on one fight, as long as that one hadn't been Red. She wondered how many times Orvs had charged at her, and Ricky thought that it was too many to count. Red agreed as she blocked a foot swipe and jumped between that sword and its bearer, and as she jumped, she kicked his chest. Before the sword he was holding cut her in half from his fall, she flipped over it and landed where she had begun. She pivoted and sliced the fingers off the Orv who had gotten behind her. It would've been easier to kill them both, but she didn't want to yet; instead, she flipped over the Orv on the floor and drove her borrowed sword's handle into his skull, enough to knock him out but not kill him.

At the same time, the Orv whose fingers she had sliced off watched them fly five feet away, and his sword fell to his feet. He turned and ran as if his life depended upon it, which, in his mind, it did. The last Orv didn't attack Red but bent over and checked his comrade's pulse.

He stood and said to Red, "You are a wimp."

Red raised her eyebrows. "Why do you say that?"

"You didn't kill Hale, and you didn't kill me as I checked his pulse. You won't kill, so it makes you a wimp."

"And you are trying to stall so that your friend can go get help."

She jumped in an arc that put her right in front of him. She swung at his side, expecting him to block it. He didn't or couldn't fulfill her expectations. Blood sprayed as she cut him in half through his gut. He was dead before his first half hit the ground.

Red fell to her knees and dropped the sword. She stared at the body. That was where Fingerless and the help he had gotten found her. He had found other guards escorting Gill down. The soldiers that Kim had sent to the roof had surprised him enough to be able to knock him out. They had hit him until he awoke after they had cuffed his hands behind his back, tied ropes around his snout, and run chains around his wings and tail, pinning them to his back. They were taking him to a cell near Red's so that General I could use him the next day, when they ran into Fingerless. They convinced him that they had no need of any additional reinforcements.

Once they found Red, she stood up. It had been a minute since she killed the Orv, which was only really long enough for Ricky to get Red to stop hyperventilating. Red assessed the situation. There were three Orvs, one of which was fingerless. She had just killed somebody. Gill was tied up. She had just killed somebody. Red looked at the fallen sword. Since she didn't move, an Orv walked slowly up to her. He pushed her slightly, and all she did was sway, so he grabbed her arms and tied them together. She stared off into space. Her fiery spirit had left.

They were taken to separate cells across from each other; Gill struggled the whole way, and Red went where prodded. Gill knew that Ricky was probably trying his best to get Red back to her senses, but there was no outward sign of it.

As Gill was thrown into a normal tiny cell, he started to find a way of escape. The cell was a seven-foot cube of wall and a door. The door was iron, and it had a tiny opening on the bottom for food and a small barred window for prisoner ID. He started to work his mouth up and down to loosen the rope. That could take awhile.

—⁓—

Red was still in shock. It wasn't her first kill, but last time she had not known Christ. Things were different now. Now, she knew him and she knew where those who didn't know him went. Ricky tried his best to comfort her.

Maybe he was a Christian.

And working for Kim? As if! Have you not heard of the pledge?

Yah, I enforced it. Remember? When a new recruit joins the queen's service, he has to vow that he is not a Christian, and he will kill anyone who tries to convert him.

And if he became a Christian, he would seem odd to his comrades, and they would report him, and pretty much a day after he accepted Christ, he would be executed!

Ricky tried a new tactic.

If you didn't kill him, then he might be torturing or killing some innocent right now.

Or that innocent might've brought him to Christ.

And he would've died.

And gone to heaven.

Fine, you did what you did, and there is no taking it back. You can respond by accepting that you did it and that you will need to do it again. This will either make you not care about life, or it will make you only do it to protect the innocent.

I'm lost.

Ricky's mental sigh was almost audible. *Do you need to figure this out by yourself?*

I think so.

Okay, then tell me when you have won the battle in your head.

Ricky returned to listening to the We Investigate Simply Everything (WISE) debate about his idea. Red didn't want to think about her predicament; therefore, she searched her pitch-black cell, after cutting her bonds. She found that the ceiling was beyond her reach standing, so she guessed that it could be tall enough for an Orv. She found two chairs, one that was big enough for an Orv and one that would barely fit a Raggy comfortably. Both were made of stone, so Red could not lift them. The only other thing of interest was the door made of solid iron with no doorknob and no, well, anything.

Red couldn't find anything else to do; thus, she curled up on the big chair and thought about the Orv she had killed.

One of the Ten Commandments is not to murder, but was that murder? Murder is the killing of another person with thought beforehand.

Ricky was mildly paying attention as he thought an affirmative. Red was slightly annoyed at that, but it was impossible to get rid of him, so she didn't act on the annoyance.

It was not murder; it was an accident caused while trying to escape, but Ricky is right. I will have to do it again. He is also right about it is a way to protect the innocent, even with all the ifs.

Red fell asleep slightly less downhearted.

Gill finally had the rope loose enough to slide off his snout hours after he had started. His jaw was sore, and his mouth had a stale taste in it, so he blew fire to get rid of the taste. He still had chains on his wrists, wings, and tail; but it felt much better not to have a rope around his mouth. He regretted the many times he had done that to another of his race; thus, he resolved to ask forgiveness of them.

He then tried to slip his tail out of his chains. It didn't work. He sighed and sat down, resigned to the situation he had put others in countless times.

Alexa was starting to wonder where Red was. It was almost time to make her presence known to her aunt, but she couldn't do that without Red; she was the key to everything. Without her, the Raggies wouldn't follow Alexa, and any war would probably be lost if Red was not in it. The clock was ticking; Kim would sooner or later find Alexa's camp. Everyone was preparing for battle.

Where was Red, and why was she stalling?

———◦◦◦———

Red awoke when her door scraped open. While she was still dazzled by the light of the torches and trying to get out of dreamland, two Orvs grabbed her wrists and chained her to manacles she hadn't noticed on the wall by the Raggy chair. By the time she had adjusted, they had retreated to the corners with their torches. Then the general came in.

He sat in the Orv chair and said, "Hello, Raggy."

"Did I sleep a whole day, or what?"

"I don't know or care. You know why I came."

"For tea and biscuits? Sorry, but I forgot to make them."

"No. The queen needs to know where Alexandra is and how much force she has behind her."

"Well, I think that she could dent a breastplate with her fist, but I'm not sure."

"I'm not in the mood for jokes, Raggy."

"Why is it that *everyone* who is trying to degrade me calls me Raggy? It gets annoying."

"Because Raggies are the lowest of races and the most annoying of them as well."

Red became more than cranky at that statement.

"Do you want to say that to my face, where I can reach you, or are you going to be a coward and stay over there?"

General I just looked at her. He didn't answer her but called in his two other guards they had Gill between them, and he was trying his best to get out of their grips but failing. He was trying to burn their hands but failing in that venture because he couldn't lean over far enough.

"If you don't give me some useful information, I'll have them kill him. And when he dies, I have plenty of other prisoners to threaten you with."

Red looked from the general to Gill and back to the general.

"And if I tell you, then you'll just have me killed."

"We are not barbarians, Red. If you join Kim, then life would be much easier. We'd squish Alexa, and you'd be pampered for the rest of your life."

Red laughed at that. "Last time I was tempted, this happened." She gestured at her whole self.

"What happened?"

"My skin, and let me tell you, that hurt."

The general looked annoyed. "Tell me what I want to know, or he will die."

One of the Orvs holding Gill took out a dagger and held it to his throat; he didn't move. He had to trust Red to make sure he didn't die. He also made a mental note to apologize to anyone he had put in this situation as well. He thought that might be *everyone* in his race.

Red quickly asked Ricky a question and then said, "She is in Deathsand."

Gill understood, but the general did not.

"Deathsand! Where in the world is that?"

"Check a map sometime; it might help," Gill said.

While the general was looking at Gill and trying to decide how to respond to that, Red took out a tooth knife. Before he looked back, she had one manacle undone, but before he could say anything, she had the other one undone. God must have messed with those locks for Red to do it so fast.

A soldier had been coming to stop her, but he stopped himself before he ran into the wall. Red had moved to the left, and she cut the strap holding the quiver on the soldier's back with her tooth knife. As it fell, she grabbed it. Both the bow and the arrows were in it, and the bow was strung.

"Guards!" barked the general.

The two holding Gill tightened their grip and the one with the dagger pushed harder on one of Gill's neck scales. He just then realized that Gill had scales, so he put it under one of them.

Red was only holding the quiver, but she knew that she could have the bow out, and an arrow notched on it in three seconds.

Gill had seen her shoot the day before the coronation, so he knew that she wouldn't hit him unless she wanted to.

Red said to the general, "If you have them kill him, then I'll kill you."

"You threaten me when I hold all the cards?"

"I have a bow and arrows; that is all the cards I need."

The Orv she had taken the quiver from lunged at it, but Red switched hands and kicked him, sending him across the huge cell.

"So we are at a stalemate, wimp. If you get out the bow, I will tell them to kill him; you'll save him and knock me out. You don't have the guts to kill me."

"I don't make threats or promises that I don't intend to keep."

Red reached into the quiver and took out an arrow. She didn't need a bow at such close quarters.

"I'd advise you to tell your men to unlock him."

"And give you the upper hand? I don't think so."

"I really wish this wouldn't take too long," Gill said.

Red thought for a second. "Ricky can use his power through me."

None of the Orvs understood that, but Gill did. He nodded, and the chains holding him seemed to melt and condense into a ball in front of him. As the ball dropped, Gill grabbed the dagger Orv's hand and wrenched the dagger away.

As they both backed out of the cell, the general said to Red while looking into her eyes, "The next time I see those nightmarish red eyes, I'll take them."

Gill closed the door, and it automatically locked. They hadn't gotten a torch, so it was pitch-black.

<hr />

Ricky went back to his surroundings to find WISE taking a vote whether to accept his idea. Not one person voted against it. His idea was to seek an alliance with Alexa for trade purposes. Some of WISE had not wanted their presence made known to the other races, but Ricky convinced them that they would prosper from allying themselves with a more industrialized country, which Rov was. Then he had to convince them to sign a treaty *before* Alexa went to war against her aunt, not after. She would trust them better if they helped her win.

They had debated among themselves about their new king's idea. Ricky was not allowed to participate after he sat down, so all he could do was listen to them argue about the advantages and disadvantages of allying themselves with someone who needed to regain her country.

Finally, a full day later, there was a unanimous vote that it was a good idea. Ricky used that time to help Red, but then he needed to fly to Alexa's camp with WISE's chosen envoys.

———⁓———

"He means that when he says that," said a voice that neither Red nor Gill knew.

Red pulled out the bow and put her arrow in it as she said, "Means what?"

"Next time he sees you, he will take your eyes out."

Gill breathed out a spurt of fire, and they both saw who had addressed Red. He was considerably large, even for an Orv, so large in fact that he had to stoop a little so that he wouldn't hit his head on the ceiling. His clothes were ragged, and he had no weapons or armor, but his build and muscles suggested that he would be a considerable opponent in a duel.

"Why are you so sure? I can protect myself."

"That is exactly what I thought when he said something similar to me."

Red thought for a second and then said, "Can you do that again, Gill?"

He did, and this time Red looked at his face. He had a kind of square jaw and ears like most of his race. His nose and mouth were a bit small, but none of those drew a gasp from Red. His eye sockets were still there, but he had no eyeballs; they were gone.

After Red could find words, she said, "I'd really love to hear your story right now, but we have prisoners to free and a prison to get out of."

"I'll help; I know this place better than the people who dug it out."

"You're not a guard? Are you loyal to Kim?"

"No to both."

"How do I know that we can trust you?"

The big dude sighed. "General I took out my eyes, and then I was exiled down here where one of the prisoners brought my heart to Christ. I've tried four times to get keys from a sentry, and each time I was beaten almost to the point of death. Kim and her pet general have ordered some whole branches of the prison forgotten, and I was the only thing that stood between those prisoners and starvation. You can't find your way to the entrance, let alone all the cells. Face it, you need me."

Red had to think about that for a second. "Fine, but if I sense any foul play, you'll regret it."

"Understood. There is someone coming."

Red didn't hear anything, and then a faint thump came from somewhere. Then Red saw a faint glimmer in the distance. As it got closer, she could make out three Orvs, not just one.

"It's not a sentry; it's a prisoner escort," Gill said.

The Orv led them to a side tunnel, and there they stayed. When they were close enough for Red to make out their faces, Red recognized Petra as the prisoner. Red made a quick decision and pivoted into their line of sight. She killed both guards in quick succession by shooting their necks, the only unarmored part of them.

As Red walked to those she had shot, she said mostly to herself, "If anyone dies by my hand, it is because his decisions led to that outcome. It still doesn't feel right, but I hope it never will."

Petra said as she walked up, "I think I owe you now."

Red retrieved her arrows and said nothing.

She found keys on one of the bodies and unlocked his chains. As she unlocked him, Gill asked, "Why did you not kill him? Wasn't he one of your captors?"

"Because I owed him."

Red saw Petra's shoulder where the arrow had been yanked out, and she ripped a piece of her sweats. She gave it to Petra to wrap the wound, and he did so without a word.

Red jingled the keys and said, "We're going to free the prisoners; you can join us if you wish Petra. Lead the way, um…"

"Echo," said the big dude. He walked off, and Red followed. Gill and Petra stopped to get the escort's torches. Gill made another note to self about asking forgiveness for putting people in damp, dark cells.

———

Alexa just finished writing the challenge when one of her self-assigned guards said, "Who are you, and what is your business with the queen of Rov?"

She had moved her tent a little away from the others because she wanted a little more quiet. The guards had taken that to heart, even though she insisted that she had no need of protection, and would challenge anyone who came near. Alexa hadn't really given them power to do so, but they wanted to protect her. She usually told them to let the caller in, so it was nothing special that she did so this time. Freg, her self-appointed head of the guard, gave his "you got lucky, punk" speech, and in walked Ricky and three of the WISE.

Ricky wondered if he should slightly bow or what; he had no idea. This whole king business was harder than he had originally thought. He mentally asked his dad, one of the three, what he should do, and he answered that it was best to slightly incline his head, befitting one of equal rank. The three WISE bowed because they weren't royalty.

Alexa stood and inclined her head back. "To what do I owe this unexpected visit?"

"We are here to propose an alliance between our two countries."

"So your race is willing to mingle with the other races now?"

"I have convinced them that it would be to our advantage."

"Would you please introduce me to your entourage?"

Ricky introduced his rusty father as their expert on etiquette. Benny, who was slate gray, was the war expert, and the purple Megan was the trade expert. Benny's post was established by the council before Ricky, when they planned to take over the other countries, but he was not the original holder. Megan's post was brand-new. Technically, Ricky was the expert, but she was the only person besides him that had contact with all the other races.

"What would you bring to such an alliance?" Alexa asked after Ricky introduced the WISE.

"We will help you to regain your country."

"And what would you want in return?"

"Just to establish trade."

"Well, I would greatly appreciate help with overthrowing my aunt, but trade discussions will have to wait until I have full control of the country."

"I understand."

"I have one last personal question. Do you know how long Red will take to return?"

Ricky answered, "She is thinking a month or so."

"That will put my plans off, but if it has to be done—"

"And what exactly are those plans?"

Alexa leaned on the table and pointed at the note she had just finished.

"First..."

———

Red unlocked the cell that Echo had said was the last one.

"You're not forgetting anybody?" she asked.

"Nope."

The Raggy in that cell reacted like all the other Raggies that they had freed; she automatically hugged everyone in sight while crying and generally just enjoying being with people. Loneliness was the main killer of Raggies in a prison. They either died or survived as a shell of their former selves if left alone for more than two weeks. That Raggy had only been in there for three days, but she was hysterical. She hugged Red and didn't let go, all the while crying as if she hadn't shed tears for a whole week.

Red smiled to herself as she said, "Don't thank me too much; I still need to get us out of here."

Red and Echo led that Raggy to where Gill was with all the other prisoners. They all looked underfed and wiry, even the Orvs. A member of all the races except Ricky's were held prisoner, some with cellmates, most alone. There weren't that many Raggies, because most were taken to Alebu, but there were some that Kim just wanted forgotten. All of the prisoners were gathered near the cell that Red had started in but now held I, his men, and three sentries that had been knocked out and their weapons taken.

Now that all of the prisoners were gathered within earshot, Red could address them all. There was no need to quiet them, for she had asked each as they went there to stay quiet. Since she could only see two humans, an Orv, and a Raggy in the torchlight, she had no problem with stage fright.

"I know that some of you have been in here for years, but I need all of you to be patient with me and wait a few minutes longer. After you hear three whistles in a row, then you can go to the entrance. I'll need anyone who feels capable of fighting to grab a weapon from the weapons pile and to be the first to the chasm entrance. If you are injured, I need you to grab a helper and to be last to the entrance. I also need someone with a loud voice to help me get past the entrance. If you are interested, come see me immediately after I stop speaking."

"Like I said before, please sit tight and be quiet. Remember, after the entrance we still need to get through the castle and the capital. I don't plan on losing any one of you."

Red heard a few excuse me's that she supposed meant that someone was taking up her offer to help take the entrance. As soon as she saw the volunteer, she knew he was loud. It looked like God had put most of this Orv's talent in his chest and very little anywhere else. He looked like a human wearing a barrel but twice that big.

She beckoned for him, and Gill to follow her as she said, "Echo, lead the way to just below the entrance."

No one questioned her authority in this situation. As they walked, she explained her plan to the Orv who introduced himself as Pastor Xair. As soon as they got within sight of the light in the chasm, Xair yelled, "The prisoners have—"

Then he fell on purpose to make the entrance guards think he had been shot. His voice was so loud that even the people at the top of the chasm heard him clearly. They automatically went into lockdown as they had practiced many times before. The guards on the ladder side cranked it up until it was all rolled into a ball at the top. The archers put arrows on their newly strung bows and pointed them at the ground. Those who were there to make sure no one got past the archers loosened their swords in their sheaths. They all knew that the fighting Raggy was being held prisoner and that it was most likely her. There was silence as they anxiously watched the tunnel leading to the cells.

Those with Red didn't understand why she wanted it to be known that they were escaping, but they knew that she had a plan, even if it was slightly crazy. They watched her raise the bow and shoot an arrow.

The guards jumped as an arrow went straight into the wall. It was easily a foot deep into the sandstone. Another arrow plunged into the wall forty-five degrees to the right and four feet away. Seven arrows in all plunged into the wall, each forty-five degrees and four or five feet away from each other, forming a diagonal line on the wall up to thirty feet in the air, the height of the lowest window.

Before Red did anything else, she knelt on her knees, bowed her head, and closed her eyes. She prayed, "Father God, thank you for giving me this awesome talent. Thank you that I am alive. Please help me to stay that way and to get your people out of this place. If anyone here is not your child, please help them to see your light within us. In the name of my savior, your son, Jesus Christ, I pray. Amen."

The archers saw a red flash as Red ran to the first arrow that was five feet off the ground, just a few inches shorter than her own height. She jumped onto it and that was when the archers first got a good shot at her. The lower half of the archers shot at her, but she was too quick. She was gone by the time the arrows hit. Then a dance that very few people could have done happened. She hopped from arrow to arrow, staying just long enough to draw fire from the archers. As soon as the arrows were on their way, she would jump to the next wall arrow. At the top arrow, she did something that only she could have done.

She seemed to have moved gravity to the wall as she flexed her legs and jumped from one wall to the other. She had aimed that last arrow directly below one of the lowest windows on the opposite wall so that she could jump off of one wall into another. The part that would make it impossible for anyone else to do was that she aimed and shot with her bow and arrow at the archer in the window she was jumping into. As he fell, she landed with another arrow in the bow.

Red shot in a random direction and mortally wounded an archer in front of her. She pivoted and shot someone who was behind her. She kept pivoting until she ran out of arrows. Every arrow had hit its mark and killed an archer. She ducked and jumped a volley of arrows, which put her parallel to the ground in the one and only place that had no arrows, some of which came from behind her. She landed next to the first archer and noticed in the one second that she had that he had a dagger, and in her last three seconds of peace, she grabbed and unsheathed it. She rolled and arrows sprouted where she had been.

There were at least one hundred Orvian archers, and not just regular archers either. These were handpicked by General I just for making sure Red couldn't get away. It took them twice as long as Red to get an arrow and shoot it, but it only took her two seconds. Really, their only flaw was that they were too efficient; they shot as a group and not as individuals. This made their shots easy to anticipate—well, for Red.

She had three more seconds to do something after she stood up. Every second was a minute to her because time had slowed down considerably. She figured the best course of action was to get a fresh supply of arrows.

She waited until the last second to make her move. She pushed off the ground like she had the wall but fifteen seconds ago. Or was it fifteen minutes? She twisted and hit the ceiling of the archer room and flipped onto the second archer she had shot. In the three seconds she had before she had to move again, she had cut the strap holding his quiver to his body and picked it up. She jumped and pushed her whole body against the ceiling. She watched arrows fly under her in slow motion, a really cool and death-defying show.

To the archers, it seemed as if she just disappeared when the arrows came within a foot of her. Or maybe she was made of smoke, and they went through her. Whatever she did, it was creeping them out. Red descended out of nowhere and landed right next to a group of those archers. Some of them had wounds from their comrades on the other side of the room shooting at and missing Red.

Red mainly used her captured dagger to break bows for four seconds; then she jumped as arrows from other groups of archers plowed into those whose bows she had broken. She then proceeded to shoot in her faster than most style, one into each group of archers, while jumping and dodging arrows. Once she ran out of arrows, the cycle of retrieving arrows and avoiding oncoming missiles repeated.

The room was in the middle of the bottommost row of archer rooms, so a continuous stream of opponents came from both sides, keeping Red very busy. That room soon became full of bodies, so as Red retrieved arrows, she moved the battle to the right. The cycle of shoot, dodge, shoot, dodge, retrieve, dodge, shoot seemed endless to Red. She had all her moves planned in four-second increments, and she could only think in those four-second increments as well. She was greatly surprised when she pivoted and jumped to find no one behind her. She turned again, and there was no one anywhere.

Red didn't feel like counting the bodies to make sure she had killed all one hundred. In fact, she felt as if she was about to throw up. She got some arrows to fill up her current quiver and went right through the rooms. She encountered no opposition until the winding stairs. As she was climbing up the stairs, located at the very end of the row of rooms, an arrow sailed past her head. The torch was behind her and cast her shadow toward the attacker, so she moved back so that when he moved, she would see his shadow.

The archer above her didn't move, and no shadow was visible. Red heard enough of a *swoosh* of an arrow in flight to realize her mistake. Pain raced up her body to her brain. As soon as she had noted the pain and its location, she reached down and yanked an arrow out of her ankle. She then saw the archer's shadow from in front of her. She thought of her own shadow behind her and moved to right in front of the torch closest to her. She noticed two shadows coming from both sides.

The two archers came in her view at the same time. They both had their bows aimed at Red's heart, one down and the other up. Red was sure that when they shot, they would hit each other in their chests if she avoided it. She knew that if she made the first move and shot one of them, then the other could shoot her in the time it took her to draw and shoot again. She had to wait for them.

They aimed at her but didn't shoot. Maybe they were trying to make her make the first move. The one above her said, "We don't want to die, Red."

Red sighed. "Then get out of my way. I'm going to get out of here, whether I need to get by you or not."

The one at the top lowered his bow, and the one below followed suit.

"We'll help you if you promise to let us go with you."

"Go with me? Why?"

"My sister," the top one started and gestured to the bottom one, "is a mute and is not overly blessed with femininity. She joined me in the army as a man, but some people have noticed her and wanted to hurt her. Obviously, I can't let this happen. We are going with you."

Red shrugged. "Fine with me, but if you cross me or I *think* that you are crossing me, you'll regret it."

The one at the top nodded and said, "Follow me."

He led Red and his sister through the maze of fifty rooms. There were a few other survivors, but Red had no need to take care of them because the brother and sister did for her. They got to the top and in sight of the ledge. None of the guards on the other side were archers, so they waited and glared at Red. She carefully stepped on the ledge and said, "Watch my back."

She stepped one foot in front of the other while firing at the footmen at the other side of the chasm. She did one shot per step and ran out of arrows halfway to the other side. She killed twenty with those arrows. She noticed a footman with a spear get ready to throw it at her, only to fall with two arrows in his chest.

Things got fun once Red finally got to the other side. A footman lunged at her with his sword as his comrade swung above her head with his axe. That forced Red to duck into a low swipe with someone else's sword or jump. She took the second option and jumped into the chasm. She didn't know what she expected, but she reached up her hand, and an arrow slammed into the stone. She grabbed it and flipped over it back onto the floor at the top of the chasm that led to the doorway.

She flipped onto the axe wielder's back and covered his eyes. He swung at his back, but Red moved to in front of him. He killed himself and fell forward. Red was already gone. She jumped and landed on the head of a sword bearer. He did not make the mistake of trying to kill himself, but he actually lunged backward at Red. He normally wouldn't have been at risk of killing himself, if Red hadn't been on his head. She jumped and landed on the flat of his sword. Using her feet, she maneuvered it into the back of his neck. As he fell to the ground, dead, she grabbed the sword with her hands and flipped off of him. She avoided several weapons that hit the body that she had rolled off. Now that she had a weapon, she stood and started attacking.

She noted the arrows plowing into the attackers behind her as she attacked those in front of her. The footmen noticed this and started to only attack her from the front. That was like lambs going to the sheerer of their own accord, stupidity in its simplest form. They were all dead in less than two minutes. Red looked back at the carnage she had caused and tasted bile in her mouth. She had to look away and calm herself before she could do the next part of her job.

Red whistled loudly, three times. She heard her call repeated below her as she started cranking the ladder down. She also yelled at the archers across the chasm, "Go get yourselves more arrows and please get me some too."

They nodded and went to do that. After the ladder was all the way down, Red started to inspect the gate that barred her from the capital.

—◦◦◦—

Two guards stood in front of the impenetrable gate to the dungeon that no one had ever escaped from. They were confident that it would be impossible for anyone to defeat the one hundred and fifty men in there after getting out of a cell and then knock down this five-foot-thick gate. It was impossible, and they had the easiest job in the prison guard.

The guards talked lazily, until one of them noticed that the general had not come back yet.

"Do you think we should get backup?" he asked his comrade.

"No, he's probably—ouch!"

The guards turned and saw that the door that they were guarding was on fire. Before they could run for reinforcements, the door fell on them.

"Thank you very much, Echo. I definitely couldn't have done that," said Red as she stepped through the flames. Echo followed, almost bent completely over, along with Petra and the two archers, then everyone else. Red had already explained the archers to those who wondered, but Gill was the only one who didn't look at them as if they would betray them all in a minute. She had told all of the prisoners that felt like fighting to get whatever weapons they could, and there was a sword and a one-sided axe left after they did so; thus, they were her weapons, besides the bow. Red led the way through the castle to the back entrance with her bow drawn and ready to shoot. They ran into practically nobody but a page and a maid, both of whom Red knocked out.

The action started when they ran into the guards at the back door. There were only four, Red took one out, and so did the two archers, but the last one managed to avoid being shot by ducking behind a barrel. He got all the way to a place where a sentry on the wall could see him before he was shot down. Immediately, the alarm was sounded.

Not only did Red now need to get close to a thousand prisoners out of the capital, but she also had to get them out without anyone dying and with the whole capital ready for her. This was going to be fun!

She led the column of prisoners. She had arranged for the wounded or really weak to be in the middle, just outside of them were the weak and not able to fight, and on the outside were those who could fight. Red herself was wherever she deemed appropriate.

Red shot a footman who was cranking the gate down, and the two archers took down some sentries. Gill had also gotten a bow and quiver full of arrows, so he also shot people. Red ran to the gate crank and got the gate all the way up. Her three archers shot all of the enemy archers before they could shoot at the prisoners. Normal archers took five to ten seconds to load, draw, aim, and shoot their arrows, so Gill and the brother and sister were at least two seconds faster than the archers that they shot. That gave them an overall six-second advantage in the worst-case scenario.

Red saw a bunch of soldiers running to the gate that she was using, so she took out her sword in her right hand and her axe in her left hand. Echo came up beside her with a regulation-sized sword that looked like a dagger in his hands.

"You can fight?" Red asked as she threw her axe at a soldier five feet away.

"Yep," he said as he cleaved the head off of a soldier through his body armor.

Red blocked, stabbed, and smashed her way through the soldiers to the axe that she had thrown. She wrenched it out of the breastplate of that soldier's body. Red, Echo, Gill, and the siblings created a path through the soldiers for the prisoners to follow and defend. Once they were outside of the inner gate, they were besieged from all sides. To Kim's soldiers, it looked as if they would only need to fight for a few minutes before they overwhelmed the prisoners.

What they didn't know was that there was something about Red that inspired those on her side to go beyond their own fighting ability and into the ability of the spiritually gifted. They all defended themselves almost as well as Gill could, which was odd because they were undernourished and he was not. Not one of the prisoners died, but a hundred soldiers did before they realized this.

The soldiers backed up and looked at the prisoners. The prisoners were completely surrounded and underfed, but the only bodies on the ground were soldiers.

Red was now so used to confusing people that she expected the stalemate.

"If you let us pass, then no more of you shall die today."

She heard talking among the soldiers, and the ones in front of her parted in a lane wide enough for all of the prisoners to get by. Red told Gill to lead the way to the back entrance, and she went to the back of the prisoners. She watched the soldiers that they had fought stay where they were for a moment, then disperse to do whatever they were doing before the small battle. The alarm stopped going, and there was no more opposition to the prisoners as they went through the capital and the outer gate.

Red and the prisoners walked into the countryside, and they camped that night in full view of a small town near the capital. The Christian ex-prisoners got together to thank God for their miraculous escape.

Kim's head was resting on one of her hands as she listened to a captain telling her what happened in the battle. He had watched from the top of the wall as the soldiers below had moved out of the way of the prisoner's path. He had watched the prisoners go through the outer gate with no opposition at all, and he was now loyally telling his queen.

When he was done, she said, "So you found it to be your job to *watch* and report to me your comrades' failure. You did nothing to stop the prisoners?"

The captain nodded as if he was proud of the fact.

"Guards!" Kim called. They came in, and she told them to take him to prison.

He was baffled. "What did I do?"

"I had almost a thousand prisoners, which is a record from the past. I now have to start all over with you."

Once the guards had dragged him away and were gone, she sighed. She was thinking about what she would do to that Raggy next time she saw her when there was a knock on the servant door.

"Who is it?" she yelled.

"General I," came the answer.

"Come in."

The door opened, and her general stepped in. His eyes were bloodshot, and his hair was messed up. This was the first time Kim had seen him not looking very professional.

"What happened to you?" she asked.

"That *Raggy!*" he almost yelled.

"Why are *you* mad?"

"She outmaneuvered me and locked me in her cell. I imprisoned the guards who failed to keep her in the room after we were let free by some soldiers. That *Raggy* killed all the archers and footmen in the prison and the guards in front of the door. We need to stop her."

Kim grinned wickedly. "What do you suggest?"

———

Red can you look at that note again? Ricky asked her.

It was the middle of the night, but Red was on a sentry shift, and Ricky was thinking too much to sleep.

Why?

It mentioned Alexa, and I was thinking that if I copied it down, then I could show it to her tomorrow.

Okay, I'll look at it after my shift.

Her shift ended in thirty minutes.

The next morning, Alexa had only been awake for ten minutes when Ricky came to see her. He inclined his head as he came in.

"Hello, Queen Alexandra."

Alexa inclined her head back. "Hello, King Ricky. You know if Red were here, she would laugh her head off from hearing us say that to each other."

"She actually is chuckling right now, but that is not why I came. I was wondering if you recognize this code."

He handed her as exact a copy as he could make in candlelight of the note Red had been given in Rovto. In full daylight, he noticed a few minor flaws, but he thought it wasn't that bad. Alexa read the note and then the encoded name at the bottom. She gasped.

"What?" Ricky asked.

"He is supposed to be dead, and I am sure that no one else knew this code."

"Who is he?"

"My dad. My aunt had sent him on a diplomatic mission to a town of ours in the Tusk Mountains. One of his traveling companions came back with a report that he was the only survivor of a caravan raid, implying that my dad was dead."

"How long ago did he teach you this code?"

"He died when I was seven and taught me the code a month before he left. I never understood why, but I kept up with the code until I was ten and the whole assassination episode. I still remember it though."

She hadn't just kept up with it, but she had also written several letters to the father she had believed to be dead.

"What is on the back?"

"First, I want to know how you got this."

Ricky explained what happened to Red and how he had copied it. Alexa agreed that it would be best to use this information before starting the plan. She wrote down the names of towns and cities and families for Red and Ricky.

———

Red went to Gill to ask him something. He was talking with the sibling archers when she found him. She pulled him aside and posed her question.

"King Ricky wants me to tell you that he convinced the WISE to allow me to go alone for a month. Would you lead these former prisoners to Queen Alexa's camp as I do some gathering?"

Gill thought about that for a moment.

"Why can't I go with you?"

"Because you and I are the only people who know where Alexa's camp is right now. One of us needs to guide them there, and I have some gathering to do."

"Gathering?"

Red explained.

Gill sighed. "Okay, fine. But you better be within earshot in a month, got it?"

Red nodded and turned. They were already moving along, so she already had all of her possessions with her. She turned back to return to the town that they had camped by the night before. When she was well away from the former prisoners, she stopped and enjoyed her momentary aloneness. She still had Ricky in her head, but she considered him part of her by then.

Red heard a footstep behind her. For some reason she had expected him to follow her.

"Come out, Echo."

She also didn't understand how he had managed to hide, since he was blind and huge. He stepped up from the slope of the hill that had concealed him.

"Your ears are getting better," he said.

Red shrugged and realized that he couldn't see the movement.

"Why are you following me?"

"You attract trouble, and I'm bored of no action. If General I—"

"I can protect myself."

"I'm not saying you can't. I just want to be there when you face each other."

"So you are going to follow me around until we do."

"Yes."

"Come on then. We have a long day ahead of us."

Red wondered how she seemed to attract defenders and enemies.

—⌘—

By the time Gill and the prisoners had gotten back to Alexa's camp, all of the non-Christians, including the archers, had seen Christ in his followers and decided to accept him into his or her heart. Gill was one of those examples. He and the rest of his race had received Bibles when Ricky had sent five messengers to Syn-Cynthia to buy as many as the money they had allowed. Tess and Jasmine had given the messengers as many as they could carry for free. Ricky had then sent a messenger with a Bible to hunt Gill down and give it to him. He had read it diligently as often as he could.

Gill was definitely no longer Commander.

Alexa was delighted to receive a thousand more people, and it had only taken Gill two weeks to get them there. He immediately went looking for King Ricky and tried to get Red's location out of him. Ricky didn't let him know because Red was not in a place where a conspicuous Rept would be wanted. Gill tried to argue that Red herself was conspicuous, but to no avail.

Red led her ten new recruits to the others that she had gathered. So far, she had found 793 Christians willing to help Alexa and escape persecution. She had a week until her deadline to be back with Gill, her Rept escort. Still, she had yet to visit Rovto, and she was the only one who knew where to find Alexa's camp.

I can do this in a week, Red argued with Ricky.

If you only spend an hour or two in Rovto, and you all run back to camp.

I don't know how, but I'm doing it.

You aren't going to break your promise.

No, I'm not.

Ricky did the mental equal of rolling his eyes. *Be here in a week. If you aren't, I'll tell Gill where you are, and he'll drop in on you, telling everyone where you are.*

Understood.

A few minutes after that conversation, Ricky stood in front of his whole race in the grand hall, again. This time it was different.

"Thank you all for coming. I know that some of you oppose this new alliance with Queen Alexandra. I also know that some of you are uncomfortable around other races. I know that you all know that I have no problem with other races.

"So, I propose that if ten of you want to end this new alliance, then we will break it. Does anyone want to be of those ten?"

Ricky was silent for a few minutes as he scanned the faces of the crowd. Very few of them shared the feelings that Ricky had described, but those who did knew that there were not ten of their people, so they didn't want to publicly share that. Ricky nodded at those he knew opposed the alliance.

"I also want to ask that we go to war for our new allies. If you find Queen Alexandra's cause a lost one, you may stay here. Even if we decide that they are no longer to be our allies or that none of you want to fight for them, I will got to battle with my meld and her friend. Only join me in this endeavor if you want to."

Ricky stepped down from the rock. His people knew that when they allowed him to be king that they were accepting that he would fight with Red. They just needed to decide if they would go with him or not. He left, and they all decided.

Red found all the families on the list and a few others attending their own little church. She convinced them to follow her to Alexa's camp. Among them was Alexa's dad. When they got to where Red had left the people from the other cities and towns, they were already ready to go. They ran as if demon dogs were chasing them.

In a sense, they were.

General I watched the small army of Christians run as if they were being chased. He had been found out!

He yelled at his men, "Break cover and catch those traitors! Don't let even one escape!"

———*◦/◦/◦*———

Red heard more feet than she knew her people had hitting the ground. She turned and saw as many soldiers as she had people running to catch up with them. She stopped and yelled at those around her to run to the Uncivilized Woods. They spread the word, and everyone knew in less than five minutes.

Red had to stop the pursuers. General I was in the back of his men when he saw the ones in the front tripping over bodies. He knew that it was the *Raggy*. He yelled at his men to stop and fall back. He had a thousand men, but he didn't want to confront that *Raggy* with any less than ten thousand. Even then, all he hoped to do was knock her out.

He wasn't overestimating her at all.

———*◦/◦/◦*———

Red saw them retreat after she had fought for ten minutes. She stopped fighting, and the lucky soldiers who had been facing her ran away like puppies with their tails between their legs. Red ran after those she had gathered. Hopefully, they had kept running, and she wouldn't catch up to them until they didn't know where to go in the Uncivilized Woods.

———*◦/◦/◦*———

Alexa had sent the letter about the same time as Gill had come back with the prisoners. She got the reply two weeks later, a day before Red was expected back.

Alexa had sent a volunteer to deliver this letter to her aunt:

Kim,

You have lied to and about me all of my life. You have taken my throne and abused it; thus, I challenge you for it. It can be one of three challenges; we can fight it out, just you and I, or we can pick champions for ourselves. The last option is to combat each other with those under our command. I will assemble my forces, and you can assemble yours, and we will have an all-out war as our duel. You pick the place and time of any one of these choices.

Queen Alexandra

Alexa's volunteer survived this trip and got this letter as a response.

My dear, crazy niece,

I do not know why you think of me with such malice, but if it is a fight you want, then I will oblige. I take your third option on May 1 at Devil's Stream. I feel sorry for your tiny forces. Please tell them that I will accept any personal surrenders and that I will give any captive the best my dungeon has to offer. In fact, I have a cell especially for you and your Raggy.

The Real Queen,
Kim

May 1 was a month and a half away. Alexa had to start moving her people there, but she needed Red.

———ɷɷɷ———

Red finally caught up with the refugees at the edge of the Uncivilized Woods. She was glad that they didn't wait for her. She led them to Alexa's camp.

———ɷɷɷ———

Gill was watching the Rept portion of the camp. All six Rept who opposed the alliance had stayed at the caves to watch the kids, along with the kids' mothers. One of those kids was Victoria, the silver V-scale baby. Gill was embarrassed for a second for thinking about her. He was ashamed of what his plans for her had been just a few months ago. Now he was just glad that God forgives and forgets.

He spoke to himself, "Red said that she would be within earshot in a month a month ago."

He was surprised to hear her say, "Well, I've been within, like, ten feet of you for about five minutes. Do you think that that is in earshot?"

He turned and saw her red form. "When did you get so quiet?"

"I didn't, you weren't listening."

He turned his whole body around, and she smiled in mischief.

"Maybe your ears are turning to metal, then Ricky could control them."

He rolled his eyes.

"Where do you need to go? I'll follow."

"We go to tell Alexa that I'm back."

Red walked to Alexa's tent as Gill tried to hide his astonishment that Red had come to him first, then to Alexa. Once Alexa saw Red, she gave the order to break camp and head to Devil's Stream. Zera was in charge of the weaker Orvs and Raggies in the Uncivilized Woods; they stayed with the Rept.

They arrived at Devil's Stream on March 30. They had one and two-thirds days of rest and preparation until the battle. It was called Devil's Stream because it was a canyon with a dry riverbed at the bottom. It was wide enough for whatever formation a monarch wanted to operate, yet it had natural fortifications on both sides for base camps.

Alexa had to admit that her aunt had chosen a great battlefield. She just wondered if there was some type of trick to it, like it flooded badly whenever it rained.

Ricky sent a patrol into the air to check for a different type of trick, like an ambush or a dam that held a river that would kill all of Alexa's cohorts. The only thing this patrol noted was that there was a considerable army on the other side of the canyon. It was easily twice the size of Alexa's and her allies', and it was growing.

He went into the air to check for himself, and he didn't notice anything unusual.

Red spent the traveling days and the rest days teaching Raggies to shoot and to shoot better. During that time, Gill told her of how hard it had been for him to fight Orvs, so she, Alexa, and Ricky arranged a time for the Rept to spar with Orvs so that they weren't slaughtered by total inexperience.

The night before the scheduled battle, Red had an idea. She told it to Alexa.

"You want to do what?"

"I want to talk to everyone."

"Are you sure that you can?"

Red nodded. Alexa shrugged and told her captains to gather all of their troops for a speech. Her army was arranged just like Kim's. She had a general who was directly under her, and below him were colonels who were in charge of captains that each had a thousand troops under his or her command. Red was the colonel who was in charge of the Raggy division of troops. Her captains were Orvs, but that was because they were more organizational than Raggies. Alexa had wanted Red as her general, but Red didn't want that much responsibility. She was a colonel in charge of three captains, which was enough for her.

Once all of the about thirty thousand of Alexa's army and the exactly ten thousand Rept army were gathered, Red climbed on to a natural pillar the ancient river had carved. She was only a little above the heads of the Orvs. Red looked into some of her audience's eyes and didn't freeze. The Rept and the Raggies understood how hard that was.

She started speaking, and her voice did not betray the fact that she was terrified.

"In the morning we will fight, and some of us will die. Others will live to tell the tale to our grandchildren, but we all need to know *why* we are fighting. Is it for glory and the spoils of war? Or is it so that when the history of Rov is told around the campfire in future generations, our names are among those of Andrew and Tor?

"I tell you that neither those nor any other reason matters compared to the real reason we are here: to put a Christ-following, God-fearing ruler on the throne of Rov!"

There was some applause at that, but not enough to drown out her voice.

"If that is not your intent for the battle tomorrow, then the most help that you can give is to leave. If your reasoning is not righteous, and you go out there and kill, you will be committing murder.

"If you are here for the right reason, then I need you to pray tonight for your leaders. Pray for the loved ones of those who will die tomorrow, and pray for yourselves. Pray that God will do everything in his power to help us do what needs to be done with as little death as possible.

"This is my charge to you."

Red jumped down from the pillar and went straight to her tent. There were a few people who tried to catch her for a moment, but she waved them off. She had something that she needed to do.

Gill didn't have to be around her 24-7 anymore because she was around thousands of Rept, and near Ricky to boot, but he still liked to keep an eye on her. He was following her when she got to her tent. As soon as the flap closed behind her, he heard a retching sound.

A few minutes later, Red scooped dirt onto the remains of her dinner. She had barfed because she had talked in front of so many people, *looking at them*. She had known some faces—pretty much all of the Raggies and more than a few Rept—but that didn't help much.

Red lay on her small cot and almost immediately started drifting off to sleep. Before she was fully asleep, a scenario jolted through her body; it was so sudden she was sure that it was from God. She thought about Gideon and about how the opposing army was in a canyon. She got up and redressed. Ricky took up the suspicion that had aroused Red and took off to look.

Sure enough, in the highlands, there were soldiers stationed. From reading the mind of the colonel in charge, Ricky found that they were instructed to ambush Alexandra's army at noon the next day.

Red told Alexa, and Alexa asked her to lead the Raggies in stopping that force in the morning. Of course, Red agreed. She went to her tent and slept until Alexa sent someone to wake her the next morning—time for the battle.

THE FUN PART

Red's only armor was her normal clothes. She insisted that all of the Raggies wear some sort of armor for defensive reasons, but she didn't want to be encumbered by it herself. Truth be told, she cared more about the other Raggies' well-being than her own. Ricky and all the other Rept needed no armor because of their scales, and he knew how good Red was at fighting. He was sure that she had no need of armor.

So Red stood next to Alexa, looking like herself. They stood at the edge of the camp, watching the sunrise. Neither girl said anything. No one was moving, even though the camp was gone and replaced by an army. There were still tents; they were just hard to see for the number of people around them.

Every Orv had on enough armor for his or her needs, and everyone had their chosen weapon or weapons. Red had two regular swords, five small daggers, a bow, and arrows. Ricky had his whole array of weapons that marked him as a former assassin, and none of them were in a bag. Alexa just had her sword, which is about as much as most of the rest of the army.

Together, the army of 31,000 faced the rising sun. On the other side of the canyon, Kim's army was just as still. Kim had her men paint their armor black, and Alexa had copied that idea by making her army paint their armor red, after the color of their champion. Red's cheeks had turned a deeper red when she was told about that. Ricky's forces were to the right of Alexa's.

Both armies were waiting for some sort of signal to start the battle.

Time had become slower for Red, even though she was not in a battle; she was expecting one. The wait seemed to last hours to her, but it only took a few minutes.

There was a trumpet call from the other side of the canyon and a trumpet on Alexa's side echoed it.

Alexa yelled, "For truth!"

Her whole army echoed her and started running to the middle. At the other side of the canyon, Kim's army was doing the same. While they ran, Red got quite a ways back from her original position beside Alexa. That was okay, because she had to lead her troops to the edge of the canyon, where they started to climb the walls. There, the yellow-eyed athletic Raggies passed Red, and all of the others stayed about even with her. They waited at the top for further instructions from Red.

Kim watched as a division of Alexa's army peeled off and climbed the side of the canyon. She slammed her fist into her thigh. She wasn't part of the army because—though she wouldn't admit this—she would have been a liability to her men. She was the only female in her own army, and she expected the men to do all the fighting, and dying, for her.

General I was at her side watching the side of Alexa's army climb the canyon wall.

"How did she find out?" he asked.

"I don't know. However she did, at least we tried."

"Should I go out there now?"

She knew what he was asking, and it wasn't about wanting to fight.

"Not yet. The force that climbed the wall was mainly composed of Raggies. I think *the* Raggy would lead them."

"Yes, that would make sense."

"When we see Raggies among those fighting in the middle, then you may go."

General I nodded.

His time for revenge would come soon.

———◈◈◈———

Red found the ambush men still sleeping. They were not needed until noon, so why get up early? She had the Raggies surround the ambushers and start firing arrows into the midst of them. When they awoke, all was confusion, and the soldiers started to kill each other. The Raggies stopped shooting and stared as the soldiers killed themselves to the last man. Not one of her troops died.

Well, my idea about Gideon was right, Red commented to Ricky.

He gave no reply as he threw a dagger of deadly venom at a colonel in the battle below.

Red yelled, "Raggies are people too!"

Her troops laughed and echoed her. They ran down the path hidden from below toward the battle.

———◈◈◈———

General I could hear Kim's teeth grinding. They watched in silence as a group of Raggies came running out of the hidden path and plunged into the side of Kim's troops.

They both glared at the battlefield.

"Is it a good time now, My Queen?" General I asked.

"Yes," Kim answered.

His revenge would benefit Kim more than it would him.

———◈◈◈———

Red fought her way to where Alexa and her guards were fighting. Red heard Alexa's swings of death before she saw her. Her friend was almost cutting in half anyone who stood in front of her. Red saw several of Kim's soldiers flying in the air; thus, she concluded that that was where Echo was with the huge sword two smiths had spent a week making for him. She didn't have to look to know where Ricky was; she just knew.

Red was the only person who had time to see what other people were doing between what she was doing because no one wanted to attack her. She could've just sat on the ground, and no one would mess with her, if she wanted to. But Red wasn't that type of person. She would charge at a clump of Kim's soldiers that were attacking someone on her side, and soon the only person standing was the soldier with red armor.

She seemed like two totally separate people with her two swords because each would fight a person as if Red was giving her whole attention to that one person, not two. She rushed at a group surrounding Alexa and scattered them.

"Stay at my back?" Alexa panted.

Red nodded, and more enemies surrounded them during the time it would've taken her to say yes.

Time wore on, and what seemed like hours of fighting lasted ten minutes. She somehow got separated from Alexa and was being attacked from all sides. This was quite different than how they were treating her earlier. She had a hard time defending herself, which meant that she was being attacked *heavily*.

Suddenly, something flashed in front of her eyes. It was a dream from the past.

Red sidestepped a downward head swipe and thrust her right blade into the attacker's chest. She jumped as a pike came sailing for her feet. It was utter chaos on that battlefield. Red had been fighting with her friends, but the tide of the battle separated her from the others. She fought her way back to her best friend, but it was too late. She lay dead with a dagger in her heart breathing her last breath.

Red then sidestepped a downward head swipe and thrust her right blade into the attacker's chest. Then the meaning hit her. She needed to get to Alexa!

Red front-flipped into the air and landed on one of her enemies' head. She hopped from one head to another, toward where she had last seen Alexa. In her slow-motion time sight, she saw a dagger going straight to Alexa's back. It was five feet away, and she was ten feet away. Red dropped her swords and sprinted as fast as she could. She got there right as the dagger did. Even with her fast reflexes, Red couldn't catch the dagger. It was an inch from her friend's back and above Red's head. She couldn't get there in less time than the dagger.

Red jumped without thinking about what would happen. It hit her outstretched arm, hit the bone, and broke it. She fell, rolled, and pulled the dagger out of her arm. She watched the bone put itself together. Then the muscles knit themselves together, and lastly the skin did. Red fought to stay awake. That kind of healing usually made her tired. She stood up and looked for her swords.

Her swords were five feet away, but she was unable to traverse those five feet due to the crazy number of Kim's soldiers between her and those swords. All of those soldiers had weapons out and pointed at her. Alexa was not to be seen, and Ricky was all the way on the other side of the battlefield. Red had just reached up for her bow when she heard something about to hit her. She would have been able to duck it, but her reflexes had slowed considerably.

Not again! she managed to think before whatever it was hit her.

———※———

Ricky fought his way to where Red had been. He did not find her, so he looked for Alexa. To do that, he jumped into the air. He looked down at the battlefield and stared in awe. At the beginning, Kim's army outnumbered Alexa's and the Rept' three to one. Now, they only outnumbered them two to one. He saw a skirmish surrounding one of his men and Alexa, so he dived to help.

A few minutes after he got there, all of their opponents were dead. He knew that it would be pointless to talk to Alexa, so he thought to her.

Red was knocked out, and I don't know where she is.

Alexa was shocked. She chopped off a rival soldier's head.

The last I saw her, she was protecting my back. She somehow left.

Ricky threw a small dagger into the face of an Orv wreaking havoc with his mace. *She had gotten farther away but came back right before you were almost killed by a flying dagger. She deflected it.*

Alexa blocked a leg swipe, reached up with her free hand, and punched that soldier in the face. She beheaded him while he lay on the ground. She turned and saw Ricky, covered in blood that was not his own, ripping the head off an enemy soldier, armor and all, with his bare hands. She was glad that he was on her side.

So should we call a lunch break? Alexa asked.

I don't think I brought myself food, but sounds good.

Ricky launched into the air by jumping on his newest opponent's head and pushing off him. Once he was in the air, he yelled loud enough for the whole battlefield to hear that his men should fall back. In less than two minutes, all of the surviving Rept were in the air with him. As he turned to go back to the camp at the head of his race, he heard the call for Alexa's troops to fall back.

Back at camp, Ricky helped the wounded of any race. Alexa looked for and found him wrapping a Raggy's broken shoulder. After he was done, he stood up as if he was a puppet on string. He jerked his head in a nod at her.

"How many?"

"Three hundred and twenty-two."

"Is Red awake?"

He shook his head and went to a Rept with gray scales and a large cut on his left leg.

"Hey, Phil," Ricky said as he bent down to examine his wound.

"No. You have more important things to do," said Phil. "Give me the wrap, I'll do it myself; then I'll help others."

Ricky sighed. "You are right." He handed Phil the wrap, stood, and addressed Alexa. "I'm still not used to being a king. What do I do?"

"Strategize so that less of our charges die."

"Right."

They returned to Alexa's tent and talked about the best places to put each type of troop. They had been discussing for thirty minutes when Ricky stiffened. He wasn't looking at or listening to Alexa. That lasted about a minute before he did what she didn't expect at all.

Ricky jumped in the air with every ounce of his strength. By the time he got to the top of her fifteen-foot-tall tent, he was going fast enough to rip the canvas.

Something was wrong.

BREAKING POINT

Red awoke to pain. She didn't locate its position until she noticed that she hadn't opened her eyes, but she was seeing out of the left one. Before she opened the other one, pain bloomed on her right eyelid.

There right in front of her was General I holding two slabs of red skin. Red tried to blink, but she couldn't. He was holding her eyelids. She tried to reach up and punch him, but she was strapped down with an iron ring around each of her joints and one between each of them, and her head was encased in an iron shackle as well. She was on some type of bed, and General I was leaning over her head.

"Nice of you to wake up, *Raggy*."

Red strained against her bonds.

"I've been relishing this moment since you left me in that cell."

He had put her eyelids down and now held a sharp spoon-looking tool in his hand. By then, her eyelids had healed, but they did not replace the missing parts.

General I held the spoon and dug into the right side of her left eye with it. With an expert hand, as if he had done this many times before, he scooped her eyeball out and used his other hand to cut the nerves and tendons that connected her eyeball to her brain. Red gritted her teeth to keep from screaming. She would not give him that pleasure. It didn't hurt nearly as bad as when the devil tried to kill her, but it *hurt*. She struggled to get up but was unable.

Red's eye healed fast, and he watched in fascination. The nerves and tendons coiled back in the socket, and skin grew over the pink tissue.

"I must admit that I have never seen that before."

Red tried to break her bonds, move her head, anything! She couldn't move at all.

General I then proceeded to take out her other eye. The process only took a minute, but it was an hour of pain to Red. That eye healed quickly, and she was unable to see.

Red was blind.

———⟋⟋⟋———

Ricky was right above Red at that point. As General I had taken Red's eyes, Ricky had flown as fast as possible to help Red. In his rage, he forgot that he could use his power through Red.

Ricky dived into the tent and ripped a hole in the ceiling. He roared, something no one knew a Rept was capable of doing.

———⟋⟋⟋———

General I said, "Good-bye, nuisance." He held his dagger in the air.

It was a foot from Red's chest and descending fast when he heard something *really loud* and a rip. He was tackled to the ground.

———⟋⟋⟋———

Ricky grabbed the dagger from General I's hand as he tackled him to the ground. He plunged that dagger into Kim's general's chest. He jumped up and turned the bonds holding Red into a ball above her. He flung that ball at no one in particular and hit another of the tents occupants. The rest ran off in fright.

Ricky hurried to Red, picked her up in his arms, and flew off. *Don't fall asleep until we get to Alexa's camp*, he told Red.

She mentally nodded. She was *so* tired. So tired!

Ricky managed to fly with her in his arms, but it was a difficult task. He flew to her tent and put her on her bed.

He stormed out of the tent and yelled, "No one is to go in there until Queen Alexa or I say they can!"

Pretty much everyone in the camp heard him. He jumped and flew up as high as he could stand. There, he circled until he calmed down. He started to breathe deeply because of the thin air. He asked God for tolerance and grace before he went back down to Alexa's tents. He landed outside of the tent and walked in the door flap.

Alexa raised her eyebrows at him. "What happened?"

Ricky suppressed a growl. "General I had Red strapped onto some type of bed, and she couldn't get out. While she was helpless, he took out her eyes."

"What!"

"She is now asleep in her tent, and I"—Ricky cleared his throat—"I yelled at everyone not to disturb her."

She nodded. "I heard that. You know being a monarch means that you have to control your emotions."

Ricky nodded. "We were talking about where to place the Raggy archers."

Alexa nodded back; she understood the topic change. They started talking troop placement again when a trumpet sounded from the other side of the canyon. They both rushed to the front of the army, where they had been only hours before to start the war. Kim was at the front of her army, holding up the green flag of negotiations.

Ricky was having serious issues with imagining ripping out her throat. He thanked God for his peace that passes understanding, and his anger slowed and stopped. Kim walked to the middle of the canyon with two guards. She didn't seem to mind the bodies littering the ground.

Alexa asked Ricky to join her in this; he gladly accepted. They walked to the middle of the canyon, careful to avoid their comrades' remains. Ricky was a little disoriented by Red's dreams.

Once they came close to her, Kim walked forward, leaving her guards behind. Alexa and Ricky met her side by side. The three just looked at each other for several minutes, sizing each other up.

Finally, Kim said, "I see that you employed my former assassin. Is it his job to kill me?"

Ricky glared at her, his arms crossed. "I can talk, you know. I haven't been an assassin in years."

Kim looked away from him and only talked to Alexa from then on.

"I have decided to change the challenge. I want it to now be a battle of champions. We shall each get one champion for every ten thousand, not including the overgrown lizards in the count or the champions. They may use whatever weapons they wish, and it will start in thirty minutes."

At the insult to his race, Ricky let smoke boil out of his nostrils.

"What made you want to change?"

"I started with three times as many people as you, and now I have only double your numbers. This way, I have more people in case you go back on your word."

Alexa was surprised. She had lost two thousand in all, including Ricky's forces. That meant that her aunt had lost *thirty-five thousand!* No wonder she was willing to change the rules.

"Is that one champion for every solid ten thousand?"

"Yes."

"I wish to move the time of it to three hours."

"In forty-five minutes."

Ricky understood that Alexa was trying to give Red time to heal and rest. She was obviously going to be one of those champions.

"Two hours."

"One hour or thirty minutes. Nothing more, nothing less."

"One hour."

Kim held out her hand, and Alexa shook it. They let go and turned. Alexa walked as straight as possible back to the camp and asked Ricky if it would be okay for Red to fight; he said that it was not his decision to make.

When she and Ricky got back, they ordered several people to pick up the bodies on the battlefield and put them in a place where they may be claimed by loved ones. She thought for a while about who else she could use as a champion but came up with no names. Then Alexa went to Red's tent. She hated to ask her this, but it was necessary. She shook her until she woke up.

Red groaned and rolled over. She definitely didn't look like a champion at that moment. Alexa shook her again and managed to get a "Go away" out of her. Alexa remained persistent until Red sat up.

"Okay, okay, I'm up. What do you want?" Red was thinking that she was just keeping her eyes closed for some reason.

"I want to ask you something," Alexa said.

Once Red heard her voice, she sat up straighter. She stated the obvious.

"I'm blind."

"Yes."

"It just hit me. My eyes aren't closed. I don't even have eyes."

Red said that so plainly that Alexa was thinking that she was handling this well.

"Red, I need you to do me a favor. Kim changed the rules, and now it is a fight of champions, one per ten thousand troops. We have twenty-nine thousand, so I want you to be one of them. If you are too tired, or you have no idea how to fight blind, then just say no and—"

Red interrupted her, "I will not have it be said that I am a coward to back down from a fight. I accept. Do you know where Echo is? And who is the other champion?"

"Echo is the captain over the freed prisoners, so he would be close to the Raggies. I haven't decided who the other is to be yet."

"How long do we have?"

"Thirty minutes."

Red shook her head. "You should've woke me up earlier."

To Ricky she said, *Is what you are doing right now important? Not really, why?*

I need you to help me find Echo. He fought that whole battle blind; I need him to teach me how.

Sure, I'll lead you. I'm coming.

"I'll leave to find who will join you. Good luck."

"No such thing as luck."

"Right."

Alexa left, and Ricky came in a moment later. Red stood; that wasn't a problem. When she stepped forward, her sense of balance moved. She held out her hands as if she were walking on a tight rope.

Red no longer had the main guides of movement called eyes, so she had to rely on Ricky to get her where she wanted to go. They found Echo sharpening his sword outside his tent. As they came, he touched it, and it cut his finger. He grunted and put the sword in his sheath. He cocked his head to listen to his surroundings.

Ricky put Red's hand on a tent pole and left to do something that he just remembered might be important.

"A Rept is leaving," Echo said.

"Yah, and I stayed," Red answered the unspoken question.

Echo smiled, "Why, hello, Red! Am I right to assume that this is not just a simple visit?"

"No, I need your help."

"Whatever help I can give, I shall."

"Can you teach me to fight blind?"

Echo was silent for a moment. "So he got you?"

Red nodded and realized that that motion was meaningless. "Yah."

Echo sighed. "It took me years to figure that out for myself; I have no idea how to teach it."

"How do you tell the difference between friend and foe?"

"Friends usually don't try to attack me, and I only attack when I know that my only friends are behind me."

"How do you block anything?"

"I normally listen for the sounds that a weapon usually makes as it tries to hit me, and then I estimate where that noise is coming from, and I respond accordingly."

"How in the world do you practice that?"

"I never do. Like I said, it was a skill that I gained over time."

Red had to think for a few minutes. "Then will you help me pray that God will guide me?"

"Yah."

"Thanks." Red sat on the ground next to the pole and started praying out loud. Echo prayed after her. They were in agreement.

———

Ricky asked the WISE leader, his dad, if it would be okay if Red was in a duel, by herself, without a Rept.

"We knew that this type of thing would happen eventually. A week after you became king, we came to the conclusion that if the meld of a V-scale ruler has their own agenda that would put their life and our monarch's in danger, then it would be best if the ruler could join. Since none of us can, then it will be fine for her to do it by herself, as long as she doesn't die."

"Does that mean yes?"

Greg nodded. "But we also decided that if our monarch dies because their meld dies, then we have to banish the meld."

"So you'll banish a dead person?"

"It sounds funny, but it is the only way to circumnavigate the protection rule."

"That's good, I guess."

"So don't get your meld banished, King Ricky."

"I'll try my best, Dad."

Ricky returned to Red. He led her to her tent for her weapons and a handkerchief that she tied around her eyeholes. Then he brought her to Alexa's tent. They waited outside the tent and heard the following conversation:

"Do you know how much you are gambling? You could leave Kim on the throne for good by putting a blind Raggy in this!"

Alexa answered the exasperated voice of her general with, "Do you have a problem with Raggies?"

"No. Especially not her, but she's *blind*! If she dies, then so do the rest of us. Do you have that much faith in your friend?"

"Yes."

"And there is no way to change your mind?"

"No."

"Then will you at least let me go with her?"

There was silence for a few seconds. "Why do you want to do it?"

"Because I want to make sure that you are on the throne, not that atheist Kim."

"Okay then, you may if that is what you wish."

"I do!"

That was when Ricky decided to walk in.

"Are you getting married or something?" he asked.

Red was holding on to the crook of his arm. She let go and walked to the place where Ricky saw a seat.

"I thought that you didn't want to marry until you turned twenty, Alexa."

Alexa scowled at them playfully. "He was just accepting the challenge of being the other champion. And I did say that."

"Good. It would be very awkward to barge into a marriage ceremony," Ricky said.

Alexa rolled her eyes. Red took out her sword and felt along the edge.

"How tall are you, exactly?" Red asked Opo.

"Ten five. Why?"

"How long do we have until the fight, Alexa?"

"Twenty minutes. I too am confused."

"I would like to spar with you Opo, if you don't mind."

"Why?" he asked.

"So that I can get used to you and learn what an Orv's swings sound like. Do you need either of us for ten minutes, Alexa?"

Alexa shook her head. Red didn't see it, but Ricky did, so she stood up and went outside. Opo took that as that he was supposed to follow her. He looked at Alexa, and she made a shooing motion with her hands. He went out of the tent and found Red in a small, unused clearing between tents.

As he stepped over a tent rope, he asked, "How in the world did you get in here?"

"I felt ahead of myself with my sword, and I kept a hand on Queen Alexa's tent."

"You didn't cut anything?"

"Yes, I didn't cut anything."

"So what do you want me to do for you?"

"First, I want you to slice at the air without hitting me."

He complied, and she listened to the sound. She swung her sword at the direction where his swing sounded and was rewarded with the clang of him blocking her from hitting him.

"Don't cripple me before we have to fight Kim's men!"

Red smiled. "Okay, I think that I will be fine. I'm going to need you to tell me as much as you can about our opponents, preferably before we start attacking."

"Okay. Would you like help getting back into Queen Alexandra's tent?"

"Yes, please."

She sheathed her sword, and he grabbed her hand. He led her back into the tent. Ricky wasn't there anymore; he was in a different area trying to make gold. He hadn't done that before and was wondering if it was possible.

When Red and Opo came in, Alexa said, "That was not ten minutes."

"We were afraid that I might accidentally hurt him before the battle," Red said as Opo let go of her hand.

Red heard mirth in Alexa's voice as she asked Opo, "Is that true?"

Red heard leather creak. "Did he just nod?"

Then there was a small sound of leather creaking from Alexa's direction.

"Okay, it is not nice to keep nodding. The only way I can tell is because you both are wearing armor."

No one said anything for a moment. Then Alexa did. "Yes, we were nodding. We probably need to go to the front of the army. I have no clue if Kim is ready or not."

"We have about fourteen minutes, right?" Opo asked.

Alexa answered, "Yes. Would you take my hand, Red?"

Red sighed. "If I knew *where* your hand is."

Red felt Alexa's huge hand grab hers. Alexa tugged her out the flap, and Red followed in her wake. She had to jog a little to keep up with her friend's long strides. She had to trust that Alexa wouldn't let her run into anything. Red heard several people ask their neighbor why the fighting Raggy had a blindfold on. She didn't have time to stop and explain to anybody because she had enough trouble trying to keep up with Alexa as it was.

When Alexa stopped, Red almost ran into her. She moved beside her and let go of her hand. Red heard all the camp noise behind them, so she knew that they were at the front of the camp. Ricky was coming by air. He landed between her and Alexa.

Ricky handed a ball as big as his fist and the same color as it to Alexa.

"What's this?" Alexa asked.

Ricky smiled. "Gold. It is a mineral, so I can make it."

He was very pleased with himself.

"That is a good thing, I think," Alexa said.

Ricky finally looked across the empty space between the two armies. The people he and Alexa had sent out had done their job, and there were only a few more bodies that needed to be moved. On the other side, he could see Kim with four of her men standing a few feet from her army. Alexa walked forward to the middle with her champions, and Kim did as well. Ricky stayed back but kept an eye on Red's progress for her.

—◦/◦/◦—

Kim had a card that made her victory sure. She had fifty-eight thousand men, so she had five champions. One of them was hiding behind another. He was her back up, just in case that blind Raggy could beat her best fighters. She had known that Alexa was going to put that Raggy in the fight. She noticed the blindfold and told her men while they were still out of earshot, "Look, she is so arrogant that she will win; she is taunting us by fighting blindfolded."

One of her champions cursed the Raggy, which made Kim smile. She stopped ten feet from her niece.

"These are my men. Since we are betting the throne on this, we should also bet a little more. What do you say, girly?"

"I say that the throne is the most important thing to bet. We need no more. I just hope that you will keep your end of the deal."

"I will go beyond that. You and I should go to each other's camp so that when you lose, you can't lead your people to attack mine."

"But how do I know that your men won't kill me?"

"Because I told them not to when I left, and if they kill you, then your people will kill me, and we go back to square one. They don't want me dead."

"That sounds like a good idea then. They will fight after we both get to each other's side?"

"My men have instructions to blow the horn after you get to my camp."

"Good. If I find that you have cheated in any way, then we will go back to square two, the battle."

"Same here."

Alexa bent over and whispered in Red's ear, "Red, please ask Ricky to watch from the sky."

Kim was immediately suspicious. "What did you just tell her?"

"It is none of your business."

Kim said something very inappropriate to her niece then added, "Shall we?"

They walked past each other and walked at pretty much the same pace to their opponent's camp. Five feet from her aunt's camp Alexa turned and watched her walk into the red armor camp. Alexa turned back to the camp of black armor.

———

Ricky jumped into the air and circled above the two armies and their champions. He tried to watch both Alexa and Red but found that quite hard.

Do you need my help? he asked Red.

I'd prefer to do this myself. I have to learn how to operate without eyes, so I have to start with what I know best.

Okay, but if you need help, tell me. Don't get killed.

Be quiet!

As the two queens had walked away, Opo was trying his best to describe their opponents to Red.

"Two wield an axe and two have swords. They all have chest plates, chain mail on their necks—"

One commanded, "Stop telling her what she could see for herself if she took that blindfold off. The demon Raggy is trying to taunt us."

Red reached back and untied the blindfold. It would just get in her way, anyway. It fell, and she heard gasps from her opponents. As it hit the ground, a trumpet sounded. Ricky kept an eye on Alexa, and she had not been so much as touched yet.

Red felt more than heard the two Orvs running at her. Of course, they had a battle cry, but their footsteps seemed to shake the ground into an earthquake. She knew that wasn't true. She had time to think about that stuff because time had slowed again. They were running in sync, so there was an even second between each ground pound. She estimated that it would take them two strides to reach her; therefore, right after the second "thump," she jumped and flipped over their heads.

She used their breathing to estimate where one of their heads was, but the one she hit had a helmet on. Her sword badly dented it; it was way too deep of a dent for it to be any more use to him who had it. He threw it to his left, and Red pivoted at that sound. She heard a *swoosh* that started from the soldier who had not thrown his helmet. All Red could do was duck the head swipe, because she wasn't sure where it was coming from. She heard another *swoosh* right after that but lower to the ground. She jumped over the leg slash.

For ten more minutes, all she could manage to do was avoid being hurt. Opo was doing much better. He had received very little injuries but had given one of his opponents a deep cut in his leg, and the other didn't have a left arm, just a bleeding stub. Since that guy was left-handed, Opo easily killed him after blocking his other opponent's lunge. Now that Opo only faced one soldier, that one was dead in two minutes. He walked over to help Red.

The problem was that Kim had fifty-eight thousand. Where was the fifth champion? Opo would never learn. While he was going to help Red, a dagger hit his chest. He was dead before he hit the ground.

———⟨⟨⟨⟩⟩⟩———

Kim smiled. Everyone around her stared in horror. There was a white Raggy on the field!

———⟨⟨⟨⟩⟩⟩———

Red knew none of this. She was still getting the rhythm of fighting blind. She was weaving around the two soldiers and was avoiding every hit. She decided it was about time to employ her offensive. She blocked a foot-head fake and catapulted her foot into that soldier's jaw. She heard a snap and realized that she had broken it. He fell, and she plunged one of her swords into his chest. She drew the other sword and blocked the other soldiers attempt to behead her.

Now that she had both swords out and had the hang of her new rhythm, he was destined to last only a minute, at most. She parried a lunge and jumped into the air. She was sure that just hitting the area she thought his head was at would be enough, but she spun in the air to add greater momentum behind her sword. With the spin, she cut off his head through the chain mail. She landed and rolled away from those two bodies.

Red stood and listened.

Alexa stared at the Raggies on the field. The white one had white hair. He was facing the other way, but she knew what color his eyes were, red. He was old.

Remember when it was said that Raggies were teenagers throughout their adult life? Well, around seventy-five a Raggy turns old. They totally skip the adult stage that a human goes through.

There was only one old, red-eyed Raggy: Tor. He and his Orvian companion, Andrew, had established Rov seventy years ago. Andrew had died thirty years into the new country. His daughter, Ruth, had inherited the throne and ruled another twenty years until she had Alexandra. Kim had ruled eighteen years. That made him ninety, for he had been twenty when Rov was established.

What was he doing fighting for Kim?

Red stayed still and listened. It was too quiet. If Opo had won against his two, then he would've helped her. If he had lost, then she would have had to kill more than two. If he was still fighting, then she would be able to hear him. All she heard was the wind. Maybe he and his two had killed each other.

Still, she didn't hear anything. She figured that if she had won, she would be able to hear some rejoicing or groaning or *something*. She tuned out Ricky's thoughts as best as she could to better hear what was happening. There was only wind.

Red finally heard something besides wind, something in the wind. It had a whistle, so she assumed that it was a sharp object coming at her. She located the sound and raised her swords to block her head and chest. The projectile was coming from behind her, so she had to wrap her arms around herself to do that. The throwing dagger hit her left sword guarding the back of her chest. She turned before it hit the ground and hit the handle with her heel. That sent it into the air next to her right sword, and she hit it with that sword, right back at the person who had thrown it at her.

She had assumed that he was an Orv, and she didn't know how far away he was; thus, the dagger went over his head. Red heard it hit the dirt. She listened for footsteps, breathing, or any other sound of her attacker. What she didn't expect was talking.

"You've been through more than I have, kid."

Red straightened. That was a Raggy voice. "Who are you?"

"Tor."

"Wait a second. *The* Tor?"

"I'm definitely not Lib or Era, for they are both dead. I am fighting for Kim because she told me that if I didn't, then she would kill my kids and grandkids and even my great-grandkids. If I lose, she will have them killed as well."

"Where are they?" Red asked.

"Why do you want to know?"

"Because we can help them. I just need to know their exact placement."

"This better not be a false hope. They are at the back of Kim's camp, probably surrounded by soldiers. I don't know more than that."

Red relayed the message to Ricky, who thought toward Justin and a few others under his command.

———❧❧❧———

Alexa watched the two Raggies talking. She looked up to see Ricky joined by some other Rept. They were heading for the back of the camp.

She was expecting it when she heard Ricky think to her, *Tor's family is being held captive, so we are going to save them.*

That's why he's fighting! Don't kill anybody.
Right. I'll tell you when we are done.

—◦◦◦—

"You do realize that I can't give up and that one of us has to die," Tor said.

"Yes, but I don't think I can kill you."

Red heard a dagger being unsheathed. "Too bad this is a fight to the death."

Red sheathed her left sword. "This is going to be interesting."

She heard several whistles, indicating that Tor had attacked. Red had determined how far away he was and his height while they were talking, so if she wanted to, she could have caught them and thrown them back at him. Instead, she caught two of them between the fingers of her left hand and deflected the other two with her sword. Those she deflected hit the ground at the same time, and the two she was holding she threw at the ground by her feet.

Red heard him walking to the side. She turned and faced him. Since he was a Raggy, he was much harder to hear than a Rept or an Orv. His footsteps were barely audible past the wind because of his bare feet. From what she remembered, he always carried six throwing knives and a sword. She tried to get him talking.

"Where did you go during the Act of No Toleration?"

"Right before Kim issued that decree, she offered my family and I a room in her castle. She kept us there as long as you have been alive."

He was circling her, and she was following his voice.

"Why didn't you shun her and leave?"

"She had us under room arrest and didn't let us have any news of the outside world. Then suddenly one week ago, she decided that I would be of some use."

Tor looked the young Raggy up and down. He felt sorry for her because she had been through so much, but the dangers came with being a liberator. She was blind, and her skin was red. His conscience was plaguing him. If he killed Red, then Kim would kill all of the Raggies who helped Alexa. If he didn't, then his family would die. He was getting too old for this.

Red heard him take out his last dagger. She checked Ricky's progress. He was just getting in the tent where the Raggies were being held. She heard the last little whistle that signaled his last dagger. She moved her left hand to the place where he had aimed it, her heart. She caught it and threw it right between her feet. Five of them were near her feet, and the other one was nowhere near him, so he was unable to reach them.

Red listened to Tor, checking how close he was and listening in case he had more daggers for some reason, but most of her mind was not there. She was watching Ricky and his three people try to fit six Raggies on their backs and carry two each. They got them situated and were in the air before Tor started to attack.

"Wait," Red said.

She heard him stop a foot away.

"You see those dragons flying from Kim's camp?"

Tor looked up and wondered how in the world Red knew about them.

"They have your family and are taking them to Alexa's camp, where they will be safe."

"How do you know?"

"One of those dragons can mind speak."

There was silence for a moment as Tor thought about that.

"You know that this means that you have to kill me," he stated.

Red's eyebrows met. "No. You can forfeit."

Red didn't see it, but he shook his head "If I forfeit or kill myself, then Kim will have an excuse to start the battle again. You need to kill me, Red."

"I have never, and I don't plan to kill a Raggy."

"There is a first time for everything. You *have* to. If you don't, the only other options are for me to kill you, which is not good under any light, or for one of us to forfeit, making the battle start again and many more lives will be lost."

"But I can't kill you."

"You have to."

I can't kill him!

I agree with him, Ricky said.

"It is my choice, not yours," Tor said.

Do I have to tell you to do it?

That wouldn't work anyway. Remember?

"Then at least help me. Just swordfight for a few minutes, and I might be able to."

"Right."

With that, he swung at Red's arm. She blocked it with the only sword she had out and unsheathed her other sword. She used one to swipe at his feet and the other to block his next move; he jumped the leg swipe and swung at her arm.

They entered a place that they had both been in before, just never together. After a few minutes, Red was in the groove, and all of her strokes were deadly. Tor noticed this and also noticed that she was concentrating. He knew that she knew that he could put aside his sword, and she would hack him in half. She was concentrating on making sure that she would keep swinging if she didn't hear the clang of his block.

Tor saw a lunge coming straight at his chest. He dropped his sword and accepted the inevitable. Red was going too fast to stop. Her sword went straight into his heart. She drew it back and sheathed it. He fell dead.

He's dead.

I killed him.

You had to.

Can I run?

Go ahead.

Red used what Ricky was seeing to run into the caves in the side of the canyon. Obviously, he wasn't in the caves, so she had to go through them herself. She sheathed her left sword and used the other as a guide. She wanted to get far away.

Tor was dead.

———⟨∾∽⟩———

Kim watched in disbelief. She had thought that it would be impossible for the Raggy to kill Tor, but she did. She walked to the middle, dreading what that meant.

———⟨∾∽⟩———

Alexa walked to the middle. It was possible to think that she would be happy, but no one on that battlefield was happy. Kim's men were mad at her for putting Tor in that battle. Alexa's soldiers were angry with Kim for making his sacrifice necessary in the first place. Alexa was eerily void of emotion.

Tor was a person that they all respected. Without him, there would be no Rov. They would all be under the rule of Slythia if he and Andrew had not worked together to form their country.

When they met in the middle, Alexa said, "If you dare even suggest that we go back to battle, I will cut your throat right now."

Ricky landed next to her. "I wouldn't mind helping her with that."

Kim looked from one to the other. "I really don't understand why you let him confer with you."

"Because I am the Rept king."

That took Kim aback.

"Are you going to submit? Or do you insist on killing every single person to surrender the throne?" Alexa asked.

Kim looked at her niece. "I submit."

That moment, Alexa became queen.

———⟨∾∽⟩———

Red sat down on a small ledge. She hung her head. Her emotions were conflicting. She was happy that Kim submitted without further bloodshed, yet she was sad that she was the last to shed blood. She slowly took off her quiver and sword belt. She laid her sword on top of them and walked farther into the caves. She no longer had her sword to tell her if she was about to run into anything, so she had her arms stretched out to make sure she didn't.

She left her weapons behind. She was trying to separate herself from who she was and represented. She was the fighting Raggy. She represented blood. Blood represented death. She sat against a wall and tried to cry.

She couldn't cry; General I had taken her tear ducts; thus, all she could do was sob, without tears.

Ricky understood that if he tried to comfort her, it would be like her trying to comfort herself. It wouldn't work, so he left her alone. She was sobbing so loudly that she didn't hear someone approaching. All she knew was that there was a sudden clang right in front of her. She jumped and instinctively reached for her sword that wasn't there.

"You need these," said a male Raggy voice.

Red tried to look up, but couldn't. "Who are you?"

"That doesn't matter. What I want to know is, *who are you?*"

"Red."

"Yes, that is your name, but who are you?"

Red put her head in her hands again. "The fighting Raggy."

"And what do you do?"

"Kill."

"No! That is not what you do! *What is your purpose?*"

"To...to...free the Raggies. To make sure that we are not killed."

"And?"

"To put a Christ-like leader on the throne of Rov."

"Very good. Now, what was Tor's purpose?"

"The same as mine, to free the Raggies."

"And how old was he?"

"I don't know."

"I'll answer that for you. Ninety. Did he accomplish his goal?"

"Yes, but years ago."

"Not just years ago. Did he help save the Raggies by dying?"

"Yes."

"And I can tell you that he was a firm believer in Jesus Christ. Does it give you any consolation that he is with Jesus?"

Red thought about her own experience. "He ought to love it."

"Then why are you crying, and why were you trying to separate yourself from who you are?"

Red answered with a shrug.

"That is not a good-enough answer."

Red sighed. "Because there are at least a thousand deaths on my head, one of which I know was innocent."

"It was his choice. Jesus's death was on your head too, but that was his choice as well. Just think of Tor as an image of Christ."

Red sighed and stood up. "Thank you very much. Who are you?"

"Tor's grandson, Gi."

"I'm sorry—"

"There is nothing that you need to be sorry about. You did what you needed to do. Now pick up your weapons at your feet, and let's go celebrate Dad's sacrifice."

Red squatted and picked up the sword belt, with both swords in it. She stood and buckled it onto her waist. Then she bent over and shouldered her quiver. She proudly stood up straight.

"Thank you so much, Gi."

"No problem. I have one more thing for you. Stretch out your hand."

Red did so and felt a cloth being put on it. She felt it and realized that it was a handkerchief.

"I retrieved it from the ground. I wasn't sure if you would want it back."

"Thank you."

Red tied it around her eyeholes. She silently thanked God for Gi.

"Do you know which way is out?"

"Yah, we are at the back of the entrance cave. That route you wandered in led you right back to where you began."

Red shrugged, but this time she had a playful smile on her lips.

"What can I say? I am so good at getting lost that I accidentally find my way home."

Gi laughed and led her out of the cave. Red smiled. It was good to be alive.

———*๑๑๑*———

Trumpets blared over the immense crowd. Every man, woman, and child in Rov had gathered for the coronation of their new queen. At the battlefield, none of Kim's soldiers had resisted, and they all had declared Alexa as their new queen.

Now, two months later, everyone was ready for the coronation. There was a throne sitting at ground level at the top of a hill on one side of a valley. Alexandra stood next to that throne. In front of her, her whole country stood in the valley. The trumpets blared again.

There had been some debate about who would crown her. If it had been the normal gain-the-crown-when-you-turn-eighteen scenario, then the person who had held the throne before her would've crowned her. The problem was that Alexandra didn't want Kim to crown her. Besides, she was under room arrest with two guards for the rest of the foreseeable future. Alexandra asked Red to do it, but she flatly refused.

That was when her dad decided to stop by and say hi. He had tried to avoid her throughout the battle and prebattle, but he wanted to see her before she became queen. He thought that she might be mad about him leaving her when she was seven, for that was what the "caravan raid" was, him trying to get away from politics.

When she saw him, she didn't listen to his explanation; she just hugged him. She convinced him to crown her at the coronation as the start of a new relationship.

So he was on the other side of the throne holding a pillow that had the crown that Kim had not been allowed to wear until she got rid of her niece. It was the official crown of the ruler of Rov.

If there was a king and queen, then there were two. Right then the other was in the treasury.

Red was sitting behind the throne, where no one but Alexa and her dad could see her. She was unable to see the crowning, anyway, so she just sat where she couldn't be seen by anyone else. There was not a Rept present, the only five in the country right then were Ricky and his four WISE representatives, but they were in the castle waiting to construct a trade agreement after Alexandra became the official ruler. This was not something that they were needed or wanted in.

On the third trumpet blast, everyone quieted. The only sound was that of the wind in the grass and some birds.

Alexandra amplified her voice so that everyone could hear it. "I, Alexandra, vow this day that Rov will not fall to ruin under my rule. I will uphold the traditions that our ancestors decreed, and I will follow in the footsteps of my mother, Ruth, in ruling fair and justly. I promise that I will treat you all as my equals, and I will respect your opinions. If anyone objects to me becoming queen, please speak now."

There was silence everywhere. Everyone wanted her to be queen. The only other alternative was Kim. She had all of three supporters, one of which was dead.

"Then if no one opposes..." Alexa stepped in front of the throne and paused. No one said anything. Then she gracefully sat upon the throne. Her dad placed the crown on her head and stepped back. The whole country gathered in the valley erupted in shouts and dancing. All 110,000 people wanted to talk to or give a gift to their new monarch, so a line formed leading to the throne. It was a pleasant early summer day, and they got in line by people they liked, so only the Raggies had any trouble with the waiting in line. Even most of them only had problems with the waiting, but nothing else. After someone congratulated or gave a present to Queen Alexandra, they would join some friends and sit down in the grassy valley.

Alexa found it very similar to her homecoming party, except on a much larger scale. Red fell asleep in the shadow of the throne. If she was needed, Alexa knew where to find her. She awoke, stood, and stretched, but she was still hidden behind the throne as the last Rovians talked to Alexa. It was dark and had been for a while.

She smiled and thought, *Now that the fun part of my life is over, I get to relax.*

⟨∘∕∘∕∘⟩

The day after the coronation, while most of the country was still in the capital, Alexa publicly humiliated Red. At least, that was the way Red saw the ceremony where Alexa gave her the title champion of Rov. She was glad to receive the title that had remained empty since Andrew had died, and Tor had given it up, but she just hated the whole ceremony. She had to wear a dress; she had to stand in front of thousands of people, and she had to stand still the whole time. She survived with quite a bit of complaining that only Ricky heard.

Afterward, she went to her new room right next to the queen's suite and changed out of the itchy dress and into nice and comfortable red shorts, shirt, and her sword belt with both swords in it. Not that she had seen the colors, but they didn't itch, so they must have been red. She sighed and thought about all of the people who wanted to congratulate her.

I'd rather be in combat.

That's what you're always going to say.

Yah... but it's now a thing of the past.

That's a good thing.

Red didn't respond to that as she walked out of her room.

The title *champion of Rov* basically meant "queen's bodyguard," but no one seemed to realize this as they congratulated Red for being honored with it. Since it was an honorary position, it came with a seat in the royal court of Rov, and the fact that it was a bodyguard position meant that Red could sit wherever she wanted to; thus, Red decided to sit behind the throne.

However, when she told Alexa this, she was adamant that Red should be where people could see her.

Red's response was, "If I can't see them, why should they be able to see me?"

Alexa couldn't argue with that.

———⟨v⟩⟨v⟩———

A few weeks into Alexa's reign as queen, Red was listening to Alexa reorganize the pay for the mayors and sheriffs for the west portion of Liebochney. It was altogether unexciting because most of it was paperwork and Alexa consulting with various bureaucrats who had held their positions since her mother ruled. Ricky was even less exciting, because he was educating some of his people who wanted to be merchants on the agriculture in the plains of Liebochney.

Red was extremely bored until she heard a few muffled thumps coming from above her head; she listened intently and realized that they were footsteps on the roof. The WISE had gotten rid of the Rept guard since it seemed stupid for a bodyguard to have a bodyguard; besides, they all knew that Red could handle herself; thus, she knew it was not Gill.

When she heard a rush of wind, the thought that someone was on the roof was confirmed. Alexa was sitting in the throne with a table pulled up to it, and Count Lont was sitting on the other side. They were talking, so Red assumed that they hadn't noticed the person opening the sky light. As Red was trying to discern if the rooftop person was a threat, she heard the barely audible whistle of a dart in flight.

"Duck!" she yelled as she jumped to the precise height she remembered the top of the throne to be at. As soon as she felt it under her left foot, she pushed off toward the whistling sound. She couldn't pinpoint its exact trajectory, but she had an idea, so she threw herself in that general area. It hit her left shoulder; she hit the ground and rolled.

Red stood up and yanked it out of her shoulder as she listened for any other incoming missiles. She didn't just hear a missile, but she heard a whole body coming down. He hit the ground and rolled as she took a step forward, but the movement seemed slow and sluggish, and her body was entirely unresponsive. She reached for her right-handed sword, but it took her easily five times as long as usual to touch it.

She heard the intruder running at her, and he was there before she could get her sword more than an eighth of an inch out of its scabbard. She heard the head chop coming, so she relied on gravity and let it pull her entire body to the ground.

When Red yelled "duck!" Alexa immediately got under the table; Count Lont was just leaving and was at the door. Alexa saw Red hit the ground and stand up, and then another body hit the ground. She recognized Jontosh before he stood up, so she rolled out from under the table. It wasn't going to protect her from him.

He ran at Red, but Alexa was too far away to stop him from trying to chop her head off. Luckily, Red fell to the ground in one piece. Jontosh turned to face Alexa, keeping Red in his peripheral vision.

Alexa usually didn't wear her sword to court due to its cumbersomeness, and she immediately noticed the foolishness of practicing with it but not having it with her as the assassin lunged at her. She sidestepped it, but he redirected the momentum and sliced at her chest. Alexa jerked her arm in the way of the sword, for she realized that it would be better to lose her arm than her life. The sword cut through her flesh and hit bone right above her elbow. The assassin tried to yank the sword out but failed. Alexa balled her unencumbered hand into a fist and punched him in the head.

He was knocked out cold. The pain in Alexa's arm was worse than any other she had ever experienced. She had gained a few wounds in battle, but none had been this deep or painful. She set her jaw and yanked the sword out of her arm. Blood squirted two feet out, and a steady flow ran down her arm.

Upon Red getting hit by a dart, Count Lont had run to get help. He came back right after Alexa yanked the sword out; he had with him five soldiers and a medic. The medic immediately went to help Alexa. She swayed and he persuaded her to sit down, where he started to stitch and disinfect her wound. Two of the five soldiers dragged Jontosh to the dungeon, and the other three guarded Alexa like a mother eagle guards her chicks.

It took Red's body ten minutes and an emptying of her stomach to get over the drug entered into her body by the dart. After she cleaned up her mess and checked on Alexa, she retired to her room, confident that the five soldiers weren't going to let anything happen to Alexa. She crashed in her bed without changing and was asleep within a few seconds.

—◦∂∕∂◦—

Red awoke, and the only reason she knew it was morning was because Ricky was already awake. She sighed and felt where her eyes were supposed to be.

If only I could see, I would've been able to stop him!

Yes, but you taught Alexa how to protect herself.

Don't sugarcoat it; I failed. It seems as if everything *I do ends up in some type of disaster. I'm a failure.*

You, a failure? That is a complete lie! You single-handedly stopped the Rovian civil war.

By killing my predecessor!

Red sat up and threw the covers off herself.

But you saved countless lives!

I still failed to save him!

She went to her closet and put on fresh clothes that did not itch. She heard a small gust of wind but thought nothing of it. As she put on her sword belt a voice interrupted her and Ricky's mental conversation.

"You're not a failure, Red."

She unsheathed her sword and spun to face the speaker.

"Who are you, and why are you in my room?"

"Tess, and because you need me."

Red sheathed her sword but kept her hand on the handle. From the direction her voice was coming from, Red deduced that Tess was standing in front of the door.

"Why do I need you?"

"Because you think that you're a failure."

"I thought that you don't read minds."

"I don't, but I know the general direction of your emotions."

Red's grip on her sword handle tightened. "Then what do I feel?"

"You feel that you were a failure for not saving your parents, for not saving the Raggies at Alebu the first time, for letting Ricky beat you, for not being with Alexa at her birthday, for killing Tor, and for not saving Alexa from the assassination yesterday."

"That's not general."

"Nope, but it is six ways that you think that you have failed. I could explain how each of them wasn't your fault, but you already know that."

"Then tell me something I don't know. I've heard stories about you, you know."

Tess smiled, even though Red couldn't see it. "If not for you, all Raggies would be dead; Alexa would be dead; Ricky, as an assassin, would have joined the council and killed hundreds of thousands; and Kim would be invading other countries, causing much more death than you have caused in this Rovian civil war. And I'd eventually have had to stop them both, so I'm really indebted to you for not causing me to do that."

"That's only four."

"You want more?"

Red nodded.

"Without you as an apprentice, Ricky would've chosen an Orv, who would've tried to kill him and them would become

Kim's newest assassin. He would've killed Alexa and several of Kim's court that now helps Alexa. No one would have saved the Raggies from Alebu, and Jach has saved near a thousand Raggies from torment since you rescued him. If you hadn't given Gill a second chance, he would've committed suicide, thinking no one could forgive him. I could go on and on, but I'll stop there. What I'm trying to say is that even the things you see as failures, God has used for good."

Red thought about that for a few minutes.

"And my eyes, how's that good?"

"If you could see, do you think that you could've killed Tor?"

"I don't know."

"Anyway, besides trying to boost your confidence, I have one other way to help you. Do you want your eyes back?"

"Can you do that?"

"No, but God can, and he's already told me he will if you do not doubt that he can."

Red breathed in deeply.

"What's healing my eyes compared to bringing people back to life? He's the creator; he can do anything."

"Then take off your blindfold and open your eyes."

Red did so without question and without a shadow of a doubt that it would be done. As soon as she saw Tess's face, tears started to flow out of her eyes. She fell to her knees and prayed. Tess closed her eyes and bowed her head in agreement.

"Thank you, Father God, thank you so much for healing me! Thank you for this incredible life you have given me so far, and thank you that the violent part of my life is over. Please help me to use all of these gifts and talents you have given me for your kingdom and your glory. I shall never be silent about you. I love you, I love you, I love you! In the name of Jesus Christ, my Lord and Savior, I pray. Amen."

EPILOGUE

Red looked up from the Bible in her lap when a knock sounded from the doors of her quarters. The last person to occupy these quarters had been Tor, before he married and started raising a family. She had just started to clean them the day before, so they were looking a little better, but not by much.

Though her rooms were Raggy sized, the doors and halls were Orv sized, so it took a bit of work for her to open the large door on old hinges. Once it was open enough, she smiled politely at her Raggy visitor.

"Hello. How may I help you?"

The petite, black-haired, green-eyed Raggy stared at her and stood there, blushing. Red was used to it by then.

"You do realize that staring is rude?"

The visitor nodded. "Um, yeah. Sorry. I'm here on behalf of the medical society to inquire how your skin turned red."

Red suppressed the urge to sigh. She gestured into her quarters. "Please come in; it's a long story. Are you hungry? I have soup."

The visitor stepped in and Red shut the door. She hurried to the pot she had over the fire, and in her haste to serve her guest, she spilled some of the scalding fluid on her wrist. Her hand jerked, spilling some on the floor. She slightly growled and handed her visitor the unspilled bowl before she used a rag to mop up the spills. She rubbed the cool skin on her wrist as she sat down across from her visitor with her bowl.

"Are you burned?" her visitor asked, seemingly worried.

Red shook her head, "Not anymore, thanks."

The other Raggy stared at her but snapped back to the real reason she was there. "My name is Matty, by the way."

There was no recognition in Red's eyes, but Matty expected none. After all, the last time they had seen each other, Red had been a newborn. She listened patiently as Red described what happened to her, and tears came to her eyes. She tried to hide them with her bowl, but Red noticed and chalked it up to normal Raggy sentiment.

Finally, after Red was finished, Matty allowed herself to cry freely. She blurted out, "I'm so sorry!"

Red joked, "It's not your fault. If it's anyone's it's mine for refusing."

Matty shook her head. "But if I had never let you go then maybe you wouldn't have gone through so much pain and hardship."

Red froze in mid-stride, going to pick up Matty's bowl and clean both of them. She connected the dots, but still asked, "Let me go?"

Matty nodded and hesitated. "Red, I'm your mom. Your real mom."

Red didn't move for a good two minutes before she continued what she was doing. She picked up Matty's bowl and brought them to her wash bucket, where she cleaned both bowls with vigor.

Matty asked, "Red?"

She shook her head, "No."

"No, what?"

Red closed her eyes and leaned on the bucket. The memory of her adopted parents' deaths replayed in her head, looping over and over, clear as a bell, rung right next to her ear. She stood and opened her eyes to dry the dishes and put them up.

Finally, she opened her mouth to say something, but no words came. She went back to her seat and flopped into it.

Matty said, "I know it's kind of a bit much—"

Red interrupted her, "A bit much? My parents were killed right in front of me on my tenth birthday! You can't just come in and say that you're my real mom and expect me to be okay!"

Tears freely flowed down Matty's cheeks. "And you think I'm okay? Giving you up was like ripping my heart out."

Red took a deep breath and silently thanked God for his peace that passes understanding. She unsheathed a dagger and started to fiddle with it.

She continued, less emotional, "I thought you were dead, and that's why I was raised by humans."

Matty shook her head. "I had to make sure that as you grew up, no one could have any suspicion that you were the fighting Raggy. If I had kept you, I was sure whoever you were destined to fight would find you and use you."

"Use me? Like train me to hate Raggies and turn me into an assassin?"

Matty was glad she understood. "Exactly."

"Well, it happened anyway."

Matty's face fell. "It did?"

Red nodded, and Matty hung her head.

"Then I failed you, Red. I didn't take care of you as I should have, and I am sorry."

Red shrugged, "It's all okay now. I forgive you."

There was silence for a while, only broken by Matty's sniffling as she calmed down her crying.

Once she was composed, she asked, "Since I am here now, do you want to get to know each other?"

Really, that was something Red deeply wanted, a family. The problem was, she had been parentless for almost half of her life. She had gone through adolescence as an assassin's apprentice, and had made most of her important decisions without a parent around to help. She didn't really know how to act around one.

She tilted her head, hesitant. "How?"

"By just hanging out whenever we are both free. Does next Friday night sound good?"

Again, Red was unsure. "We'll try it."

"Good! My house is next to the carpenter on the south side. Will you come over?"

Red nodded and yawned. Matty stood.

"I should get going."

Red nodded and got the door for her.

As she left, she said, "Goodnight, Red. See you Friday."

Red answered back, "See you, Matty."

The door shut behind Matty. She had tried, and she would keep trying. She had heard stories about her daughter and how standoffish she usually was. She prayed that one day she'd be able to penetrate that shell. She also prayed that one day Red would call her mom, but she knew there was still a bunch of work to do.